OF MONSTERS AND MEN

OF MONSTERS AND

MEN

K.H. KOEHLER

"I can still tend the rabbits, George? I didn't mean no harm, George."
— John Steinbeck, Of Mice and Men

"I've definitely evolved into a monster."
— Kemp Muhl

Of Monsters and Men (A Clockwork Vampire #5) Copyright © 2024 K.H. Koehler

All rights reserved. The characters and events portrayed in this book are fictitious. Any similarity to real persons, living, dead, or undead is coincidental and not intended by the author.

No part of this book may be reproduced, or stored in a retrieval system, or transmitted in any form or by any means, electronic, mechanical, photocopying, recording, or otherwise, without express written permission of the publisher.

No part of this book was created with Artificial Intelligence.

Paperback ISBN: 9798330551163
Ebook ISBN: 9798330551170

Cover design by: KH Koehler Design
https://khkoehler.net

Prologue

He had returned to the mountain, and not for the first time. But they were gone. All of them.

Tommy, Leo, Foxley—gone. Eliza—gone.

Edwin, standing knee-deep in the ice and snow beside the crevasse where he buried his friends, lifted his face into the swirl of freezing cold whiteness and bared his teeth in a savage grimace. The sky above was both dim and glaring, a cobalt cold sky, no sun. He had to take a deep breath to center himself. Otherwise, he might split apart. He might become something more monster than man.

He could barely see through the storm roaring around him. It blew the tails of his coat back and raked its freezing claws through his hair. Thankfully, he was as dead and as cold as these ancient frozen mountains, and he could barely feel the chill biting into every part of him with its sharp little vampiric teeth.

The pain inside was so much worse.

The pain. The darkness. The Nothing. It seemed to laugh at him, inside and out.

Is this all you have for me, little Prince? Anger and loss and bitter years? Soon, you'll be the last of your kind. The last vampire.

It was too much. Life had given him too much to carry. Death hadn't been any kinder to him. Edwin, helpless and beaten down, dropped to his knees and screamed. He screamed out his loss and his despair, the noise riding up and up into the seething white night full of thunder snow and loss.

| i |

Somewhere in the mountain range that would eventually become Afghanistan

The Late Pleistocene Epoch, about 15,000 years BP

Ainslee bent to observe the spider spinning its web between the low-hanging branches of a shrub, one of the few in this mostly frozen hell of a landscape. The spider was beautifully shiny black like a polished river stone, with a speckled white back and spines in two rows along its abdomen. The gigantic web it was weaving glistened wetly in the early morning light it had rainbows in the fine thread.

"Boy, what are you doing?" Ainslee's father asked in their language, giving him a muted kick to the side with his heavily booted foot before moving past along the well-traversed path.

The blow was substantial. Ainslee dropped to the frozen ground. But he and his kind were of durable stock and he quickly recovered. As one of the People of the Earth, he was strong. Not, perhaps, as strong as the stocky, apish men he had seen in the low country, fighting amongst themselves over bones, and he certainly didn't have the invulnerability of the wolves-who-were-men, but neither were the Fae as fragile or as vulnerable as some seemed to believe.

He had witnessed one of the apes attacking his father when he was only a child, and though his father had made short work of the creature, it left its teeth and claw marks on his father's body. His parents often mentioned their concerns that the apes were growing smarter and faster. Some had even begun using weapons they fashioned of stone and bone. He feared they would take over the world someday.

But such musings did not concern Ainslee at the moment. He was a Fae boy of fourteen summers, and the world was beautiful and white. He was looking forward to joining their clan in their new camp. His father, despite his display just now, was protective of his family. His concerns caused these darker moods of late. The scarcity of food in the lowland forests had driven Ainslee's clan to higher altitudes, and though much of that was due to the large predators that prowled the plains—the cave bears and the cats with their saber teeth—Ainslee's father blamed the apes the most.

There will be enmity between their species and ours. Something his father often said to his mother and Ainslee's siblings late at night when he was deep in his cup of drink.

Ainslee stood back up, clutching his injured side with his stump of an arm. When Ainslee was only an infant, he was left unattended in their mud cottage. His older sister was assigned to watch him while his father and mother went off to hunt the great beasts on the plains, but Lara had been lured away by the cry of a young animal in the forest. In the interim, one of the great bears attacked Ainslee's cottage, severely mauling Ainslee in his cradle before Lara, alerted by her baby brother's shrieks, returned to beat off the hungry predator.

As for Ainslee, his wounds were severe and his clan elder was forced to amputate his mangled limb all the way to the elbow. Ainslee also bore scars over his face and a bite in his shoulder that never fully healed and hurt him greatly when it grew too cold. One of Ainslee's wings had been ripped away by the creature as it thrashed him. Thus, he could not fly like others of his Fae clan. It meant his family had to trek many miles with him on foot—because the Fae never left their own behind.

Ainslee often wondered if that was the source of his father's frustration with him.

The family continued up the mountain steppes, reaching the plateau just as the sun set and the great cold began to settle in. Here they set up a temporary camp and lean-to shelter, unrolled their fur-lines bedrolls, and Ainslee's mother began preparing their evening meal. It was made up of scarcely edible foliage they had foraged during their long journey and a rabbit his father had snared.

But it wasn't enough, and as the family sat around their pitiful fire, Ainslee felt his stomach clenching even after eating his share. "Here," he said, giving his little sister Betta a portion of meat off his plate.

His mother and father spoke at length about their hardships, but only after they thought everyone was asleep. But Ainslee slept little, too worried about everything happening to his changing world. The Fae camp was still many leagues away, and there was no guarantee it even existed now. They had heard rumors of it several winters ago.

As a family, they were seven in total, always hungry, and growing weaker. Ainslee's father was a hunter-gatherer, so they could not afford to lose him. Ainslee was good at making snares even with his disability, so they would not turn on him. But his mother had begun postulating that she and the older children should return to the lowlands and eke out a living so his father could take the younger children with him onto the camp.

"We will not make it back," his father reasoned to his mother that night. "We need sustenance whichever way we go."

His mother thought long and hard but could come up with no solution.

"We may need to cull the children," his father suggested.

"No!" his mother cried in horror, almost waking her youngest, cradled to her breast. "I would rather you take me."

"You cannot offer yourself up," his father said. "You still have a suckling. It will be the death of you both."

Ainslee's mother began to weep silently, but his father ignored her, going on in his plan by saying, "Betta is slow in the head. She may be the best first one to cull."

Ainslee lay in the dark, shuddering. Sacrifice was also their way, and it was how they had survived for millennia when times were lean. But Betta was special to him. Though she brought little value to their family, she was Ainslee's best friend in the world. And she was not slow! She simply communicated differently.

The next day, at suppertime, Ainslee gave Betta some of his wild greens, and the little girl bunched them up in her fist and shoved them into her mouth, though she only sucked on the juices. He loved his little sister with her huge green, silent eyes, always looking up to him like he was a hero in a tale, someone who would protect her. He couldn't bear the idea of the family turning on Betta—especially if it was he who was slowing them down.

Were it not for him, his family could at least fly some of the time to relieve their fatigue.

Ainslee gave it some thought. Not long after full dark settled in, he moved to where his older sister Lara was tending the fire with a stick and sat beside her. "I've made a decision, sister."

Lara turned to him, her gaunt face shining pale in the moonlight. Her eyes told him she expected this. "Ainslee...no..."

"I want to do this. I want to be the sacrifice."

"Why tell me?" Tears spotted Lara's pale azure eyes—the same color as his own.

"Because I don't want Mother or any of the family to pursue me. I would like you to stop them, speak to them. Reason with them." He shrugged. "I want you to explain that this is my decision and they are not to come seeking me."

Lara, who always felt responsible for what had happened to him, put a gentle hand on Ainslee's shoulder. "I don't want to lose you, brother. Besides, you will be a fine hunter one day. It will be a loss for us."

He glanced around, finally settling on the shivery little form of Betta under her furs. "We cannot lose our sister, Lara. She is not the burden; I am."

"You are not a burden!" Lara cried in a hushed whisper.

He turned back to his big sister. "You must learn to forgive yourself, Lara. If you wish for me to truly forgive you this..." He held up his stump. "...then I would ask that you put Betta's wellbeing ahead of my own. Do you understand?"

Lara cried into her hands for several moments before removing them. Ainslee was proud to say her eyes were red-rimmed but dry. "Yes. I understand."

Nodding once, Ainslee rose from the rock he was resting on, but Lara grabbed his good hand, and before he could pull it back, she took the small iron ring with a white stone in it that was on her finger, a gift from their Mother, and put it on Ainslee's ring finger. "Please take it, brother. That way, a part of us goes with you wherever your travels take you."

* * *

Ainslee left the camp well before dawn. He took only his clothes, a few of his snares, and Lara's ring. He also took the mental pictures of his family with him, especially Lara and Betta, with whom he'd always been close.

His family was taking the northern trails beyond the mountains. Ainslee, in an attempt to dissuade any of them from following him, took the southern one that wound around the great rock formations and down into the vast golden plains beyond with their tall grasses and short trees.

There was little cover here, and it was a risky move on his part. The plains were home to some of the largest and most dangerous beasts, the ones with horns on their heads and armored shells on their backs, but he knew that for that reason alone, his family—Lara especially—would not follow. It was too great a risk even for his father.

Ainslee was hungry and thirsty even before he reached the plains. But despite his various discomforts, he pushed on. Unfortunately, once he arrived at the grasslands, he found there was not only little game but also few watering holes along the way. It would be a thirsty hike to...somewhere.

In truth, he had no destination. Nowhere to go. Most of his people had migrated to the higher grounds. The ones who had chosen to remain in the glens and forests had begun speaking of hibernation beneath the ground the last time he had seen them. Life was hard for them all.

He traveled for three days, finally coming upon a watering hole, but upon close inspection, it bore a sheen of black oil and had several large hoofed animals on their last legs entrapped in it, along with several saber-toothed cats who had gotten themselves trapped atop their preys' sinking bodies. Ainslee shuddered at the macabre sight and the pitiful sounds of the dying animals. He was glad the big cats could not reach him.

Several large sloths charged him, but they were only protecting their young. Ainslee was able to duck their attacks. But none of this helped his hunger or his thirst, and by the thirteenth day, he was weak and barely able to set up camp for himself in a cave at the foot of the mountain. Along his travels, he caught only one small fish in a stream that he ate raw and with great relish, yet it hardly filled him. Sometimes, he came upon centipedes or beetles, and these he ate as well, though they hardly filled the yawning hunger inside him.

Looking around the cave, Ainslee wondered if he shouldn't make it his destination, settle in, and just let the hunger have him. He considered tying his ankles together and sealing himself inside his fur-lined bag so he could drift in and out of sleep until Elder Death came for him—whether that was in the form of starvation or a passing cave bear.

That night, he lay tossing and turning, besieged by hunger pangs and loneliness and hopelessness. He hated being Fae; it meant he was a durable creature and that his death would be prolonged and painful.

What a cursed existence...

A sudden bright light caught his attention and made him sit up. After a wary second, he picked up his furs and moved cautiously to the opening of the cave. He watched in awe as a great, burning star fell from the sky. It blazed across the night sky, lighting up the whole region, its tail bright, flaring red like fire as it slammed into the not-too-distant mountains.

Ainslee felt the impact under his feet and watched the great spray of earth and rock as it erupted from the impact point. It seemed to go on forever.

It was beautiful. Magical.

He had witnessed such impacts in the past, but never one so close. It was almost like a sign. Something to follow.

Ainslee sat down on the rocky ground and watched the spot in the mountains for a long time, trying to decide if it was something worth pursuing. A part of him wanted very badly to see what a fallen star looked like—maybe examine one up close before Elder Death came for him—but he wasn't sure he had the strength to complete the journey.

Why not try? What else had he to look forward to?

In the morning, Ainslee packed his rucksack and started across the plains on a trajectory for the mountains.

***

The ground was still steaming hot where Ainslee stood teetering at the edge of the crater. He carefully leaned over the burned edges and looked down into what was the largest hole in the ground he had ever seen. It was at least the size of his whole village where he had grown up, and the sides were rough and pocked with small holes and long ridges that slopped down to the center where something metallic flickered in the bright sunshine of the noonday sky.

The surrounding earth was arid and cracked, and the sun sat amidst the clouds, looking red from the impact dust. Ainslee couldn't fly down into the crater, of course, but he could slide down on his backside and kick his booted feet to control his descent. It was a long, steep slide to the bottom.

When he finally reached level ground, he got to his feet and started cautiously toward the fallen star. Or what he believed was a star. He wasn't sure what it was. The closer he got to it, the less convinced he was that it was a star. His people believed that stars were bits of burning rock in the heavens, but this resembled some kind of dark metal ball, fairly large, and badly scratched and dented, wispy steam rising from it.

He stopped about ten feet away from it and observed it from what he hoped was a safe distance. Waves of pressure emulated from it like the pulse of a heartbeat. It gave him a slight headache. Ainslee tilted his head and used his stump of a hand to brush away the insects in his face while he watched the star for signs of danger. After some time, he sat down cross-legged on the rocky ground and waited for something interesting to happen.

Nothing did until nightfall. The ball of metal pulsed with faint red light in the dark. The headache in his head had gotten worse, but it felt more like a tapping at his skull now, like something trying to get his attention. On impulse, Ainslee said, "Yes. I'm listening."

Come closer.

Maybe he had made the voice up in his head—the results of his starving, dying mind. But he was now so weak from hunger and thirst that he no longer cared if what he was hearing was real or his own madness rattling around his skull. He no longer had the strength to get to his feet, but he did crawl closer to the black fallen star glowing in the rocky earth.

It seemed to pulse faster and faster with light the closer he grew to it. Finally, the glow went out of it and the star fell silent before him.

No!

"Hello?" Ainslee leaned forward, frantic to find life in the silent black rock, something to tell him he wasn't completely alone. "Hello, is anyone there? Can anyone hear me?"

The black stone cracked open like the egg of one of the big birds down on the plains. Ainslee started and shrank back, but he didn't immediately retreat. He was too interested in seeing what was inside the egg-like rock. Inching closer, the vibration beating at every corner of his body, he eyed the inside of the star.

Darkness swirled within the stone egg, but it didn't stay there long. Within seconds, it shot out of the broken black shell and moved in a swirl of shadows around Ainslee, who was sitting back on his knees. It encircled his shoulders, flying in a spiral that grew ever tighter until it was face to face with him. He gaped at it. Something in the darkness, something primal and basic, made him suddenly afraid. The darkness in the rock felt viral...it felt malevolent. He had already opened his mouth to emit a small cry, and when he did, the darkness took the opportunity to slide like a wet kiss past his lips.

The Darkness took Ainslee and filled him and made him one with It.

***

When next Ainslee woke, it was still dark out. He was lying on his back and staring up at the billions of stars strewn across the heavens. He felt...strong. He felt a powerful need to move, to climb up and out of the crater.

He was at the top and over the ridge before he even realized he had used both of his hands to escape the crater. Falling back onto the still-warm rocky ground on his back, Ainslee rested a long moment before lifting his arms and holding up his hands to look at them...both.

He had two hands!

Surging with excitement, he flexed the fingers of his new hand, admiring it. Both of his hands were very pale and thin, almost like bird claws, with long, sharp, dark nails, but they were whole and very beautiful to his way of thinking. His sister's ring still glinted on his finger, though it felt warm now, almost hot.

Then it started to burn just as if it had come fresh out of a forge...so much so that he was forced to rip it off and throw it away from it. It didn't matter, though. He couldn't stop staring at his good arm and hand and his lovely fingers where he had had an almost useless stump for most of his life. He clenched his hand into a fist, his long nails clicking against one another.

Leaping to his feet, he felt as light as air, as if nothing could stop him. Almost immediately, he felt his wings unfurl—much larger than they ever were and different from the long, fragile, insect-like wings of his people. These were more like a butterfly's wings, but more ragged and much sharper. Like his healed limb, he had two wings. He was no longer a cripple.

Ainslee bleated out a cry of excitement and turned in a circle, admiring the way the wind caught in his great big, beautiful, otherworldly wings. They were much darker and full of colored specks, reminding him of the way the sun had caught in the threads of the great spider's web.

And he wondered...could he fly?

It took him a while to gather his courage to answer that question, but in time, and when he felt the wind ruffle over him, he unfurled those beautiful wings and felt them cup the wind, eagerly lifting him a few feet off the ground. He did a few practice lifts, but too soon, the fatigue of his body began filtering in once more and caused him to glide back down to the earth.

Out on the plains, one of the big predators growled. It did not sound like it was alone. Though Ainslee felt much stronger than he had previously, he knew he didn't yet have the strength to fight off one of the saber-toothed creatures. Worried suddenly, Ainslee gathered himself and started down from the mountains and back to the relative safety of the caves.

* * *

Maybe it was a dream? The fallen burning star? The wings?

But no, on awaking the following night—Ainslee had slept straight through the entire day—he found he still had his two clawed hands and the magnificent wings, which he was forced to fold carefully against his back before gathering his rucksack and leaving the cave.

Traveling at night was forbidden among his people. It was much too dangerous. But in the darkness, he felt invigorated and alive, and he did not want to sleep through the night and miss its beauty. Besides, it wasn't very dark to him any longer, everything glowing in contrasting shades of grey.

As he started across the plains, Ainslee continued to admire his arm and hand and the fact that the terrible bite mark in his shoulder, and the scars on his face had disappeared, leaving his cheek smooth and cool. When he came upon a watering hole, he spied a pride of the large cats drinking.

Normally, he would have retreated and hid among the rocks, but he was feeling thirsty and aggressive in a way he had never before experienced. He boldly stalked up to the lions. When a huge male growled at him, its great, hinged jaws yawning open to reveal foot-long incisors, Ainslee growled back at it, spreading his wings threateningly.

The cave lion quickly backed down, lying flat like a little kitten.

Ainslee brushed past it and knelt by the water. Finally, he could see his reflection.

No wonder the lions were slinking away. He was bone-pale like a corpse and his eyes burned bright and black like river stones in his lean, hungry face. The teeth of the Fae were small but sharp, good for chewing coarse vegetation, but though that remained, his incisors were long like the cave lions', glistening and faintly curved. His wings blanketed him on both sides like a cloak, stirring slightly in the night winds. They looked more than large enough to lift him into the air.

Ainslee, not a born flyer for obvious reasons, practiced takeoff a few times. He fell at first but finally caught an updraft that lifted him higher than the stubby conifer trees around him. It was terrifying…exhilarating. And even though he had no experience or real practice, he managed to find his balance in flying. Soon, very soon, he was moving at tremendous speeds through the air. He laughed, the ground and its life forms flashing away far below him—many of them scattering in terror at his approach.

For the first time in his life, Ainslee felt truly safe. Alive. And perhaps a little bit invincible.

* * *

Life changed for Ainslee.

He slept in caves during the day, the weight and brightness of the sun too much for his light-sensitive eyes to endure, but the nights belonged to him. He learned to fly faster and faster, so much so that, soon, he was moving even faster than the wind, covering hundreds of miles in one flight. He flew over a minor inlet ocean in one night.

It was in this way that he reached new lands he had never before seen or even heard about among his people. It was exhilarating to see new lands, and he never felt so alive as he did now. But there were drawbacks, too. Aside from the sun, he quickly learned that despite his incredibly powerful body, he hadn't ceased to require nourishment. If anything, it was worse.

He hungered in a way he had never experienced before.

Less than a week after his transformation, he woke up one night with hunger pangs unlike anything he had ever felt, even when he and his clan were at their hungriest and eyeing the skinny rats running through their village's trash. He got to his feet, went to the mouth of the cave he was sheltering in, and ripped at his face and hair with his long nails. He screamed at the gravid moon hanging far overhead—not a human sound. He sounded like one of the cave lions dying on the plains.

The hunger tore at him. It felt like his body was being ripped in half. Driven entirely by instinct, Ainslee picked a long, bloody gash in his arm and sucked at the blood that spilled past the grievous edges of his injury. He even ate a little of own flesh, but it hardly satisfied him. It was how he learned he had to feed on the creatures that lived on the plains.

His first victim was a saber-toothed lion that he fell upon from the sky. The blood was warm and thick, but it hardly slaked his hunger. He needed more. Or he needed something else. The great plant-eaters did little more than stave off the madness creeping through the darkened byways of his head. Their blood was enough to keep him from turning on his own body, but he decided the composition of animal blood wasn't quite right.

When he spotted the tribe of seafaring Fae living on the coast he was flying over, he slowed his flight and spiraled downward, landing in the tree line outside the village. It was good to see one of his own kind even if they were not of his tribe. He approached them cheerfully, but the men and women bringing in nets of fish were wary of his appearance. Still, he asked if he might accompany them back to their village.

"Who are you? What is your name?" the village elder asked, a large, dark-skinned Fae man with a white beard.

Their language was different from the one used by his clan, so Ainslee had to pick over it in his mind to understand it. When he finally deciphered it, he started to say the name his mother had given him at birth but hesitated. He realized he was not that young, helpless Fae man any longer. But since he did not know who or what he was at this point, he answered using the word for "nothing" in his own language.

"Mkgor."

The village elder eyed him carefully and not without deep suspicion. "We are a simple people and have little here to offer you, friend Mkgor. I fear you would be rather disappointed by our people and our simple ways."

In a subtle way, the elder was saying he did not wish for Ainslee—no, no, he was Mkgor now—to accompany his people. He did not trust Mkgor, which was both wise and understandable. Still, he could smell the fish cooking in the village and even the sweat and blood of the Fae surrounding him, and that sealed his fate—and theirs. He wanted very much to stay. He reached out and put his long, thin hand on the elder's shoulder.

"Surely, my friend," he said, looking deep into the man's eyes, "we can work out some sort of deal. I wish to spend time with your people."

The elder squirmed uncomfortably but ultimately gave in. It was not their way to turn away a fellow Fae in need. They returned to the fishing village, and the elder allowed Mkgor to take a bed in one of his people's round, thatched-roofed huts.

Mkgor, being a creature of the night, did not sleep. As soon as his hosts had bedded down, he was up, uncomfortably awake, roaming the little house and then the village streets beyond. It didn't take long for him to realize he was looking for something to stave off the agony of his hunger. When he stumbled upon the drunk who had fallen asleep in the space between two of the village huts, he understood he had been drawn to this place. By morning, what the man's people found of their fellow villager was little that could be said to be recognizable.

ii

4,000 years later

"The people are angry—restless," Rark, the son of the village Elder, told his father that morning following the slaughter of several of their people. "Make no mistake: they want satisfaction for this unforgivable breach of contract."

His father was sitting cross-legged in his hut, meditating, seeking their goddess's council, but he had been doing that for hours now. His father was known to meditate for days without food or water to find answers for his people. He looked gaunt and almost lifeless. So far, the Morrigan, the goddess of the Fae, had sent none of them any signs.

Rark, a headstrong young Fae brave, stepped forward, raising his fist. "Father, we have to do something! I will not stand by and feed more children into the maw of that...creature."

"I know," his father responded at last, his voice low and almost lifeless. "I understand."

"Do you?" Bristling, Rark cried, "If you understood, you would create a hunting party to destroy the thing before it returns. And you know it will. It hasn't finished with us."

The village Elder squirmed uncomfortably under his son's accusation. It was true that the Nothing, sometimes called the Darkness, was a persistent and never-ending threat in these lands. His own grandfather had faced Mkgor in conflict and fallen, as had everyone in their clan who had raised their fist against it.

No one knew what the Nothing was, nor where it had come from. It had simply always been here, feeding upon them like a lion preys on elk. He sometimes wondered if he shouldn't take his people away from these lands, except that the hunting was good here. Besides, there was no guarantee the Nothing would not follow them. It was the reason his people had created the Lottery.

Opening his eyes, the Elder focused on his son's distressed face. There were many dangers in the mountains, the glens, and on the open grasslands. The apes, for instance, had evolved into violent men. The great beasts, who were not so great any longer, had mostly died out or been replaced by smaller, more manageable creatures. The wolves-who-were-men were another threat. But all of them paled in comparison to Mkgor.

The Elder suspected the Nothing was some kind of tainted Fae, condemned to be bound to the land and survive on the blood of its own kind forever. And that was almost acceptable. After all, the world was full of predators. They, the Fae, were formidable hunters in their own right, and they preyed on weaker animals.

The problem came in that the Nothing could not be filled. And nothing seemed able to stop it. It could wipe out a whole village of strong Fae in one night—and it had done so not too long ago when another village of hunters tried to take it down. It was unstoppable, a slave to its unending hunger for Fae blood and flesh. Ancient tales told of it weeping as it fed on its victims' flesh and blood. Pitiful. Unstoppable.

Centuries earlier, the Elder's grandfather drew up a contract between his people and the creature. He delivered it strong young men and women to feed upon in exchange for leaving most of them in peace. It was, at least until recently, the only way they could hold the Darkness at bay. The yearly Lottery sent those beautiful children to the mountains where it dwelled. None ever returned.

It was a terrible but necessary thing they did. After all, self-sacrifices were their way.

But now it wasn't enough. The Nothing wanted more. It wanted all of them. And last night, it had taken some of them who were not on the Lottery tickets.

Angling his head up, the Elder sucked in a sharp breadth of the sight of his towering son with his long white hair and piqued face. His body was hard and lean, a hunter's body, and his hands were clenched into rock-like fists around the spear he carried. His face was full of righteous fury.

The village Elder feared the Nothing, yes, but Rark was right. The Nothing had broken their contract, and even though many of them might die in the process, they now had a responsibility to respond appropriately.

* * *

Grandfather was a fool—that much Rark knew was true.

They should have ended the Lotteries generations ago and gone hunting the Nothing—or died trying. He hadn't wanted to challenge his grandfather's position even though he was more than ready to take control of their clan. He had complained about the Lotteries since he was a child, and now, to take the leadership role meant he had to see good on his complaint and challenge the Nothing. It was what his people expected.

And what Rark needed and feared.

Now, here they were, he and his soldiers, trekking up the mountain to face their enemy. Rark wondered if he should have said anything at all.

Part of his bitterness was rooted in personal loss. When he was still a suckling child, his own mother had been chosen by the Lottery. She had taken on the responsibility bravely and ensured that Rark would be cared for by her sister. Still, even as a toddler, Rark felt the loss. At the time, he couldn't understand it. As an adult, he could not accept it.

When a cave bear became a nuisance, or when one of the plain's lions invaded their village, they were dealt with appropriately. A father—and that was what Rark was—was expected to protect his mate and provide for his children, not hand them over to the enemy for the sake of convenience. You didn't make deals with devils.

The Fae were dwindling in numbers despite the accord that was supposed to protect their future. Fae women could not bear enough children to replenish their losses and satisfy the hunger of the Nothing. But then, they should not be expected to.

Something had to be done. Something needed to give.

As his braves marched up the mountain pass that so many Fae children had taken before them, all of them armed with spears, bows and arrows, and some bearing short iron swords, they chanted the names of the lost, the ones who had gone before them, been sacrificed to the Darkness. Their collective voices grew louder and fiercer as they approached the honeycomb of caves pocked into the mountain—the place where it rested during the day.

It was not invincible, Rark told his people. It had weaknesses, many of which they knew of and could exploit. For instance, it could not endure the light of the sun. It crumpled at the touch of cold iron. It could be starved. It could be forced into hibernation. And, he believed, it could be killed.

Rark was deathly afraid of the Nothing, yes, but he felt it was well worth their sacrifice to try and save his people. His children.

The cave system, carved out by wind and water over millions of years, loomed ahead, each of the holes punched into the black mountain looking as welcome as an abyss into darkness. Wind soughed through the caverns, sounding like the collective weeping of the lost. As a result, his warriors began to flag in their conviction.

"I thought there would be one entrance," his second, a Fae warrior named Morla said. Her eyes shifted uncertainly over the perforated mountain. "How will we ever get the Nothing out where we can kill it if we don't even know where it sleeps?"

Rark, like the others, had never seen the Black Mountain up close before. He too was taken aback by the wild array of entrances to choose from. Still, he would not be dissuaded.

"Come close, we must speak," he told his people, motioning them to gather.

As one, they sat in a tight circle, two guards watching them front and back, while Rark worked out the details of a plan.

It was dangerous and would require a Sacrifice, but the soldiers were as determined to end this suffering as he was, and several raised their hands to volunteer…including Rark's firstborn son, Niall, who had come along purely for the experience. He'd told the boy he could observe but not fight. And now…?

One of the female braves whose child had been taken by the Nothing commented, "It should be Niall. So far, you, Rark, have remained relatively unscathed by the Lottery. Unlike the rest of us."

"That isn't true," Rark insisted. "The Nothing took my mother."

"When you were but an infant. You have never felt the agony of outliving a child," the female warrior stated, her eyes boring into Rark's in challenge.

Her words were damning and sealed Niall's fate. Rark could not possibly excuse his son now. To do so would raise dissent among his people. They would rebel and probably overthrow him and his father the Elder.

Rark looked at his son, his heart squeezing with horror.

Niall only lifted his cleft chin. "I am not afraid, Father. I know you will not fail me."

* * *

The hunger. It was what drove him. What he lived for. What rode him like a cruel horsemaster.

Mkgor lay crumpled at the bottom of the Black Mountain. Over the millennia, he had grown larger but become less substantial. He still had form, it was true, but he was malleable like water and had lost most of his defining characteristics. Perhaps it was because he had become more like the star creature that had taken him long ago. Or maybe this was always how he was? Maybe he was born this way? After so long—so many nights feeding on the blood and flesh of the living—he found it hard to differentiate what was real from what was a dream or a nightmare told by those who feared him.

He only knew he hungered, constantly and completely. He could strip the blood and flesh from a dozen men in seconds and it would only soften the edges of his incessant need. The contracts he made with the Fae were not enough. The Lotteries were not enough. He feared the world would not be enough, and he would one day wipe it of all life.

If only there was some way…to stop it. To end himself. But he did not know how to die or even sleep. Most of the time, he could barely rest.

The moment he scented the Fae nearing the mouth of his cavern, his whole body twisted and warped, pushing him to fly into action. He shimmered into the form of a large, winged creature, snake-like and legless, able to flow like a shadow. It took him but seconds to slide like an oily substance through the tunnels and chimneys of his mountain home and into the cave where the Fae boy waited, the latest in an endless procession of Sacrifices.

He loved the Fae. Loved that they gave him this. That they were generous. It helped him to stay in control. Otherwise, he might fly right out into the night and attack the first village he came upon. He might wipe it—all of them—from the Earth. These days, he had little to no control over himself or the hunger. He had lost nearly all sense of self and self-control centuries ago.

Crawling awkwardly and almost bat-like on his gigantic black wings, Mkgor edged toward the boy—a young Fae man of perhaps fifteen summers standing nervously at the mouth of one of the many cave entrances. Mkgor's mouth was full to brimming with saliva. He drooled over his saber teeth and from the corners of his mouth in anticipation of the hot blood and flesh that his warped and monstrous body sorely needed.

The unarmed boy stood tall, fists clenched, though he shivered with fear. Mkgor could smell the terror on him. They were always so afraid at the very end, which is why he took them as quickly as he could. He tried to make it as painless as he could. But as he approached the boy, grunting in anticipation, the boy edged back and out of the cave and into the moonlight. Mkgor followed, so attuned to the delicious sight and smells of the boy that he could see or feel nothing else.

Over the centuries, Mkgor had grown much larger than the Fae he fed upon—as large as the huge, shaggy elephants his people once hunted down on the plains. He loomed over the boy, who suddenly stumbled back and then fell on the rock-strewn ground. He released his fists, lost control of his bladder at the site of Mkgor, and threw his arms up in defense.

Mkgor moved faster now, his head just clearing the roof of the cave. He opened his massive, toothy mouth and unfurled his long, heavily barged tongue, which moved like a snake all its own to entwine the boy, who had begun to scream in fear and fight. In one slick motion, Mkgor ungloved the boy's entire body, drinking in his skin and blood while his shiny red skeleton stiffened and trembled on the ground. The boy was not quite dead but his nerves were shutting down.

Mkgor watched the boy suffer with a heart full of anguish. He never sensed the trap until it was too late.

There were other Fae perched atop the cave entrance, and several of them, giving a collective shout, levered a larger boulder over the edge with their swords and staffs. It slammed into Mkgor's neck, driving him to the earth where the boy lay dying—though, Mkgor noted regretfully, not fast enough. Normally, he sucked the remainder of his victim into his mouth and crunched their bones in his big teeth, ending their pain quickly.

With the boulder on his neck and shoulders, Mkgor couldn't move.

The Fae warriors, perhaps twenty in all, quickly rappelled down off the edge of the cave entrance. They shouted in terror and war lust. The sudden terror of his dire situation sent Mkgor into a frenzy. Even though he did not want to live like this, he was too frightened to die, too afraid to face Mother Morrigan after all of the deaths he had incurred.

Still, the Fae warriors, all of them shouting battle anthems, fell upon him, stabbing him with their small weapons. Some of those weapons hurt in ways they never had before. His skin burned and scorched at the touch of their swords—new weapons forged in iron, he noted.

At the same time, one of the warriors, a large brave with long white hair, moved to care for the flayed body of the boy lying shuddering on the ground a few feet away. "Niall!" he cried, almost grabbing him before stopping and making the sudden decision to separate his head from his shoulders with his sword and end his suffering.

Mkgor felt a great swell of relief open inside of him despite the agony lacing his body from the Faes' many prolonged attacks. He was glad the boy was dead and at peace.

The Fae warrior, their leader, turned to him, tears in his eyes and rage contorting his face into a monstrous visage. He resembled a fierce beast as he made a great bellowing noise before plunging his sword into one of Mkgor's eyes. Mkgor was not displeased by this turn of events.

He was happy and even proud that the brave, clever Fae had found a way to end his miserable life.

He melted into darkness and nothing, truly, a smile on his face.

* * *

Millennia passed.

The plates of the earth shifted and changed the entire surface of the planet. Seasons of wet heat and dry, freezing cold passed over and over again like shadows of day and night over the earth. Dry land was turned to seas, and flatlands were thrust into mountains. The opposite happened as well.

The place where Mkgor once dwelled, the Black Mountains, was eventually flattened by centuries of earthquakes and erosions into a huge, sprawling canyon. That canyon, in turn, was flooded and filled with life that, over time, dried up and turned into basins. The ground heaved and changed constantly. Grasslands took over, followed by fecund wetlands that turned into thriving forests. So much time passed that the land became unrecognizable.

But the Darkness, like so many fossils that had sunk deep into its bedrock and become one with it, remained.

* * *

The Sumerian city-state of Uruk, southern Mesopotamia, 2350 BC

Lilit stood up from weeding her little square of a garden and stretched her back. The sun baked down brutally upon her, making her clothes stick to her aching shoulders. The heat and the lack of rain were sucking the little life out of the struggling vegetation at her feet.

The root vegetables were small and bitter, barely enough to feed her, her husband, and their six children. She sighed in exhaustion but immediately perked up when she spotted her husband Maacah and eldest son Chrysanthos trudging down the road toward their thatched-roofed little cottage at the edge of the deep woods. They were tall men, wiry but strong, and they were carrying a long pole between them. Upon that pole hung the answer to her prayers: a large, field-dressed elk.

She felt her mouth water at the prospect of meat in their bowls that night.

Gathering up her pitiful basket of herbs and greens, she raced back to the cottage as quickly as her sore feet would allow and poured water and some root vegetables into the large cauldron hung on a hook over the open fire of the hearth. Forever stew, all manner of foodstuffs were cooked continuously. She was feeding the fire with their store of chopped wood when Maacah burst in with the meat, a victorious look on his handsome face.

"Your son is a fine hunter!" he said, giving Chrysanthos all of the glory as, together, they set the elk down on the butcher block.

Maacah then rushed to his wife to squeeze and kiss her. In his joy, he even twirled her around so she cried out.

After setting her down, Lilit kissed him one last time before racing up to her tall, handsome, dark-haired son and patting him on the cheek. Chrysanthos only grunted. A shy, introverted boy, he often squirmed in the face of any kind of physical affection.

"I'm going to go wake the children," she announced.

Because they were experiencing a starving time, she encouraged the children to sleep as much as they could. But she knew they would be as overjoyed about the stag as she was when they saw it. They would even help her prepare the meal.

Some hours later, husband, wife, and their children sat down to a grand feast. They had been through great hardship this past winter, but it seemed the gods Innana and Marduk were smiling down upon them at last. The room was soon filled with the aroma of broiling meat and the sound of happy chatter.

The family had not even finished their meal when a peal of thunder rolled across the sky overhead, and, not long after, the first hard rain of the season began to tap upon the roof of their small, thatched home, playing a merry tune of fertility and abundance. All of the members of the house stopped feasting to send their prayers of thanks up to the gods of generosity.

***

The following day, Maacah left the cottage to visit the town a few ticks away to sell the parts of the stag that might net them enough coin for the root vegetables and fruit that did not grow on their little farm. While he was gone, Lilit and her two eldest children went out to tend to the garden.

The rain had refreshed everything, and the little vegetables were standing at attention at last. Tears filled Lilit's eyes at the sight.

"Mother!" Her eldest daughter Shada was waving her forward.

When Lilit joined her, Shada asked if she might go deeper into the woods and hunt for berries.

"If you are careful," her mother warned her. "And do not approach any mushrooms, especially those growing in a circle. Otherwise, the Fae might take you."

Shada promised her mother that she would watch for the Fae, even though no one had seen a Fae in a thousand years at least. Most people believed they had retreated to the forests and mountains long ago or that they were hibernating or had died out completely. In the meantime, Lilit and Chrysanthos went out to attend to the newly rain-swollen field.

Near dusk, Shada returned with a multitude of wild berries and one very strange fruit. It was round and narrow and so deep purple it was nearly black. Lilit held it up in the dying light of the sun, wondering aloud about it. "Where did you find it?"

"Deep in the woods. It's very sweet." Shada smiled to show the red juice that decorated her teeth.

Tasting it, Lilit found Shada to be correct. The fruit was so sweet it gave her heart a sharp but not unpleasant jolt. And as soon as she had tasted the blood-red flesh, she wanted more. "Can you show me where you found it?"

"Yes, but the tree is very large. This one had fallen on the ground."

Lilit and Shada journeyed deep into the woods to find the big tree growing at the edge of a sharp ravine that fell away into a distant, ancient canyon. The sight of the tree gave Lilit pause. Not only was the fruit black but so was the tree which grew crookedly up and out of the ground at an odd angle, its branches twisted.

It bore no leaves, only the fruit that Shada had brought her, and most of that was located in the upper branches. But Shada, who was nimble, easily shimmied up the tree and, with a long branch, knock the large, dark fruits to the ground, which Lilit gathered into a basket.

While they were finishing up, they both thought they heard a distant rumble, not above as in a storm, but from under their feet like the earth was talking. Suddenly wary, they scampered home, their hands and mouths bright red with the juices of the deliciously sweet fruit.

Maacah, who had returned with a purse full of coins, was dubious of the mysterious fruit. He turned one over and over in his hands, commenting that he had never seen anything like it before.

"But it's so sweet." Lilit broke the fruit open and gave her husband a piece to eat. "Not bitter at all."

Maacah tasted it, his eyes suddenly watering. "Yes, it's very sweet." Maacah, she knew, wasn't fond of very sweet things.

Before the night was through, Lilit and their children had consumed all of the strange black fruit.

* * *

Sometime in the night, Lilit jolted awake from a half-forgotten dream. She sat up on her cot, gnashing her teeth together. In her mind's eyes, she saw a tall warrior with white hair beheading his son—his son who was in terrible pain. The dreadful image made her cry out. But then, just as quickly, the dream broke up, leaving her lying back on her cot, drenched in a horrible sweat.

Feeling sick and full of a dull, throbbing pain, she tried to get up, but she found to her dismay that she was too weak and instead fell to the floor. She lay there stunned in the dark, groaning and twisting with the pain flooding her thin body.

When she finally managed to turn to her side, she slowly became aware of the changes in her body. The back of her simple nightshift was torn to shreds from the two great wings that had sprouted there. They were fluttering in distress to the rhythm of her panicked heartbeat. Likewise, her mouth was sore and her teeth long and sharp like broken bone. She groaned in horror.

Other changes were taking place in her body. While she lay on the floor by her cot, she noticed the pitch darkness around her was softening, turning to delicate shades of grey. Not as bright as noontime, but it was enough to see well by. Her hearing was suddenly much sharper. She could hear the gentle crunching, lapping noises coming from a corner of the cottage where the children slept.

Lilit dragged herself forward, her eyes growing wider as she gradually took in the horrific sight before her.

What was left of Maacah lay on the floor. Her husband had been torn open like one of the purple fruits, and her six children were huddled together about him, heads bent forward in a way that reminded her of a pride of lions surrounding a fallen elk. They were licking the insides of their father clean and even chewing some of the bright red flesh.

Shada turned to glare at her, her eyes fully black like the fruit but full of a simmering white fire. "Mother, join us," she said, holding out a hand cloaked in her father's red-black blood. "All through our tribulations, we are family."

For one moment, Lilit was appalled by the sight of her children consuming her mate. But then the smell of the kill drifted to her, and, after that, it didn't seem so strange or terrible after all.

* * *

Deep in the earth beneath the tree of blood fruit, Mkgor stirred, but only once.

He had eyes in the world once more, and he could feel what his children, the hybrids—the Children of the Nothing, the Dark Fae, what the localized humans called the ekimmu and others farther to the East called the upyr—could feel. And that satisfied him.

For now.

| iii |

Aboard the gyro Asclepius

Now

"Throughout the ages and all through our tribulations, we are family."

It was how the Seven—the most powerful Vampire Lords in the world—traditionally concluded each of their sessions. They spoke the sacred words in Upyrese, the ancient language of vampirekind.

The Council of High Courts stood leaning in, their fingertips touching at the center of the round table they occupied as they recited the oath. Edwin said the words as well, for he was part of them now. One of the Seven, sometimes called the Sacred Seven. Seven members to rule over all of the other Courts, all members lawfully elected to their positions. It was a development he would not have been able to guess was in his future even a few years ago—but here he was.

We are family.

What a joke.

The Seven existed in a pact of sorts to honor the seven founding members of the vampire race: Lilit and her six children. The six others beside him—Lord Trasch, Lord Endicott, Lady Aiyana,

Lady Danesti, Lord Adrastas, and Lady Kai, all hated each other to varying degrees depending on the day and their particular moods. In just the three years he had served on the council, he had seen alliances forged and broken repeatedly—some at an alarming speed. Still, there was etiquette, and the Council of the High Courts had a duty to show a united front. They had too many cutthroat constituents waiting in the shadows to end them.

Everything about the Vampire Court system was about how one played the long game. The Seven, the most powerful vamps in the world, were responsible for the whole structure of the vampires' political world. But their power reached even beyond the Courts because the most powerful Supes in the world looked to them for guidance, including the Fae, the werewolves, and even the otherwise insular Striga.

That concerned Edwin. Because, with few exceptions, the Council was made up of a bunch of greedy idiots he wouldn't have put in charge of taking care of a goldfish.

Lord Trasch, the Speaker for the High Courts, stepped forward, crooked but resplendent in his draping red robes, to wish them well until next month's session.

"A reminder that tomorrow night I will be hosting a fete. Bring your Brides and Heirs to the event. It's important the Seconds mingle." Lord Trasch made a point of glancing at Edwin.

Always there was rank and order for these chaps. Not that Edwin was going to listen. There was no way he was exposing Eliza or any member of his Congress to these monsters—a point of ongoing contention between him and the other Council members who were just salivating to try and get their crooked claws into his people.

Lady Kai, the only member he could tolerate, walked with him back to the changing rooms. "You were unusually quiet during session, Eddie."

Edwin sighed as they entered the chambers and staff rushed forward to take their session robes. The changing room was a large open space with a spa and massage hall, and public nudity was both acceptable and encouraged. Lady Kai enjoyed getting as naked as possible in front of him, the meaning not lost on him. She had been subtlety pushing for an alliance with his Congress for a while now.

"These sessions are inconvenient," Edwin grumbled as his assigned valet slid his favorite dark green tailcoat back over his shoulders. "We could do them virtually instead of here and it would still get done."

"But that wouldn't be nearly as much fun," Lady Kai beamed as her favorite valet, a muscle-y young palomino Poppet, dressed her in her black and white floral yukata and obi belt. He even fixed her hair for her. When she was done, she cooed him a thank you and then unfurled her fan and pointed it at Edwin. "And I wouldn't get to talk to your beautiful face, Eddie."

He smiled noncommittally. An alliance might be useful in the future, but he didn't trust her any more than the others. Still, Edwin took her hand and kissed it, a formal gesture that made Lady Kai blush profusely. "You do make it worth my while, my Lady."

It paid to be diplomatic. Plus, Lady Kai, like him, was on the younger side for a Council member and had shown herself to be one of his biggest supporters. The fact that she was going through all of this work to get into his pants amused him, though he was hardly fooled by her motives. After all, he might be young, but he controlled one of the most powerful Vampire Courts in the world.

Eight years ago, Edwin's master Lord Foxley disappeared without a trace. A descendant of the Chrysanthos bloodline, he'd held his position as one of the Seven for centuries. His place on the Council was frozen for five years—until he was officially declared dead—at which time his seat came up for election by the vampires all over the world.

A dozen high-ranking Vampire Lords and Ladies campaigned for the spot. As Foxley's only surviving Heir, Edwin was encouraged to campaign. He was reluctant, but Eliza suggested he might better protect his Congress—and their son, Oliver—from a position of power. He had pretty low expectations on the night of the election results, which went surprisingly in his favor.

Or perhaps it was no surprise at all since Trasch had likely manipulated the vote. Edwin was fully aware the old bugger considered him a major threat, and one of Trasch's more popular tactics was to keep his friends close but his enemies in his front pocket.

"Will I see you at the fete tonight, Eddie?" Lady Kai asked politely.

"I'm afraid I can't attend, my Lady. I'm expected back on the *Queen's Gambit*. But I will see you in a month." Edwin bowed to the vampiress before gathering his things and exiting the changing room.

Once out in a corridor of the vast *Asclepius*, the older-model gyro owned by Trasch—he picked up his pace, eager to reach the lifts that would take him down to the docking station. He couldn't wait to get back home.

But as he was about to step into the lift, Trasch, whom some called the Mind Eater, appeared beside him. He was still dressed in his scarlet Council robes, which he favored. Edwin had come to detest many of his own kind over the past two and a half centuries of his existence, but he loathed Trasch—the vampire that had murdered his ex-wife Yrsa for no other reason than to test Edwin's mettle.

Edwin considered taking another lift, but he knew that would make him look weak. Instead, he lifted his chin and boarded. "Were you waiting for me?" he asked to be wry.

Trasch looked him over, practically licking his withered lips in anticipation. "I know it may be hard for you to believe, Lord Edwin, but I do not run the course of my life around you. I simply need to be somewhere."

Edwin grunted and looked away as they began to descend.

Trasch leaned on the staff he always carried with him, a long, blackened thing that half-resembled a twisted tree branch. "I am curious to know if you will be bringing your family to tonight's fete."

"My family is too busy to attend your little party," Edwin said dismissively, now wishing he had taken another lift. The man—creature?—was over seven feet tall, gaunt-faced, and as crooked as his staff, his dark red robes seemingly burning like fire in the dimness of the lift. He looked like a blackened skeleton in robes, except for his rheumy yellow eyes.

The creature tilted its head at him, something Edwin always felt should be accompanied by the creak of bones and a puff of dust, but, alas, never was. Long ago, a deceased friend of his called Trasch "Lord Skeksis." He thought about that now.

Edwin took a tentative step sideways.

"I disturb you," he said.

"You disturb everyone, Trasch."

Trasch laughed at that, which nearly sounded like a low, breathy scream. "Still. Consider my request. It would be delicious to meet the infamous Lady Eliza. And, of course, your lovely son."

Edwin clenched his fist against his side. He wanted to take Trasch by the throat and wreck him against the wall of the lift. Stomp on his bones until nothing remained. But he didn't. It wouldn't be diplomatic.

Raising his eyes until they met Trasch's own, he saw the ancient monster grin in response, reveling in the emotional turmoil he was invoking in Edwin. It was an old game, one they had played many times during Edwin's service on the Council.

Trasch's smile grew, showing off a hint of broken brown teeth. "There is a fire in you, my Lord, that the others do not possess. I enjoy seeing little glimpses of it."

"Is this the place where you proclaim I am so very human? The very best of us?"

"I never said that, though if I inferred it, I apologize."

"So you don't believe I'm more human than the others."

"Indubitably. The devil has a pretty face." Lord Trasch turned, grinning like a skull, and added, "You will soon find your teeth. I sense that."

The lift settled and the doors opened. Edwin slipped out much faster than he should have but turned to face his enemy, unwilling to give Trasch his back.

"You said I have a fire," Edwin reminded him, feeling clever. "If you believe that's true, then it's best you not play with me, Trasch."

The moment he said it, he realized how stupid it sounded and cringed inwardly.

Trasch, unperturbed, gave him a courtly nod even as the doors closed off his terrible, crooked image from sight.

"Wanker," Edwin breathed out to no one in particular.

***

Oliver McGillicuddy sat in a seat at the back of the lecture hall, head down, attention on the doodles in his notebook. His professor was droning on about the near-impossible physics of bumble bee flight, but Oliver was familiar with all of this already. He'd taken the time to peruse the course materials in the days leading up to his first semester at MIT. He was sure he knew it better than his stodgy old professor.

He had an eidetic memory, and he only needed to attend classes and pass all the tests to graduate. An easy "A" across the board, he'd thought at the time. And it had been for a while.

Then, about three weeks ago, he'd started having persistent headaches and dizzy spells. He didn't tell Mum, not even during their weekly meetups in the virtual café. She worried far too much about him as it were. If she thought he was ill, she'd drop all of her duties aboard the *Queen's Gambit* to fly to his side, and he didn't want to be a burden.

He graduated early from high school at the age of sixteen. She insisted that was too young to start college. He knew she wasn't ready to say goodbye to him, so he had taken a gap year. But as much as he loved his mum, he couldn't just ossify aboard his parent's gyro. He had dreams of being a flesh mechanic. He knew how important the work was for the survival of his Uncle Tommy, who was all prosthetics except for his brain and nervous system.

Eventually, Mum let him go, and here he was, attending his first semester at MIT. It was all going well, too, except for the headaches. He saw the doctor on campus, a tall, slender young woman who smiled and wouldn't stop making eyes at him. "You have low hemoglobin, Oliver. Anemia," she announced. "Are you fatigued some of the time?"

"Sometimes," he admitted. "I have a tight schedule."

"You're in the Gifted Program?"

He didn't like to talk about that. It made people uncomfortable. He asked about the anemia, and she gave him a list of iron-rich foods and the name of a nutritionist on the campus. But three weeks later, he wasn't feeling any better.

Lately, he felt worse. He was starting to oversleep and had missed several of his classes. When he did show up, his thoughts were foggy and his notes indecipherable. He couldn't remember what he'd read in the textbooks. After failing two tests, he decided he had to get his life back on track.

A fellow student and kinda friend of his, Pierce, suggested study drugs. He said they could help him focus if taken in moderation. He even showed Oliver the little pink pills he kept in his back jeans pocket. "Concerta," he explained. "It won't hurt you or anything. Try one."

Oliver was desperate. He wanted to do well. Neither of his parents had had a formal education, and he was the first in his family to go to college. He wanted to make his mum proud, show her that all of the hell that his coming along had put her through had been worth it. As for his dad, Lord Edwin...well, he didn't care what Edwin thought of him. Edwin was a wanker.

The pills helped at first. Pierce hooked him up with his dealer, a guy who lived off-campus. Lately, though, the fatigue had returned and the little pink pills weren't helping much. Oliver had since doubled his dose, but he wasn't sure how long it was going to last before he built up a tolerance.

After class, Pierce loped up beside him. "Want to get some burgers?"

Oliver nodded, his mouth watering at the suggestion. He was almost always hungry. Together, they jumped on one of the electric steamcoaches that circumvented the campus, the speedy trolley-like transport reminding him of his childhood among the clouds and the Hummingbirds that one had to take to get on or off a gyro. During his gap year, he'd learned to pilot, and he still enjoyed doing it when he could fit it into his schedule.

Sometimes, he experienced nostalgia for his childhood. But more often than not, the future occupied him these days.

There was a shady little diner built from a railroad car off-campus that all of the kids hung out at after classes. It had stainless steel piping around its edges and windows, a mirrored ceiling, and little jukeboxes in all of the booths. He knew kids got hookups there and it was where Pierce met his dealer.

When they arrived, Oliver and Pierce met up with Pierce's friends, who were mostly basketball jocks. Oliver didn't know them well. They were loud and boisterous, although he liked to watch them from a distance when he attended the games. Some of the boys were really sexy in their jerseys.

But if he was being honest with himself—and he made a point of doing that—he was too shy to talk to anyone. He liked Jonah. He was so cool, with icy blond hair and beautiful, sky-blue eyes. Toned and fit, he filled out his uniform nicely. Everyone laughed at Jonah's jokes and seemed to like him, but Oliver had never gotten up the courage to talk to him.

What if someone found out that Oliver was a freak? What if Jonah did?

Oliver: The monstrous and improbable offspring of a Vampire Lord and his Poppet. He wasn't human. He understood that. He didn't have a race or a people. He didn't even know if there was a word that described what he was.

Jonah was among the boys waiting for Pierce. Oliver hung back, nervous butterflies started up in his belly at the sight of his crush. Jonah knew exactly what to say in every situation, and everyone paid attention to him.

Oliver didn't normally like such intense people. People with the Bright, as he thought of him. Oliver thought of himself as especially Dim—maybe not intellectually so, but certainly socially.

Jonah was bouncing a soccer ball on his ankles for the entertainment of his teammates. As soon as Pierce joined him, he and the rest of his friends started pushing him around and laughing with him. It made Oliver feel lonely.

The soccer ball bounced past Oliver and hit a wall. One of the diners told the boys to cut it out.

Jonah, smiling wryly, raced up to collect it and said, "You're Ollie, right?"

"Oliver."

"Sorry."

"You can sit with me."

"All right." It took Oliver a moment to move. He wasn't sure he wanted to sit so close to a Bright like Jonah. Still, he followed Jonah to where several boys had pushed two tables together to create a longer one to accommodate everyone. Oliver sat near a corner.

The boys ordered sodas and burgers.

Jonah leaned close and asked Oliver what classes he was taking.

Oliver rattled them off, unsure why Jonah was asking.

Pierce grinned at that. "Whoa, you got Silent Ollie to respond with more than a monosyllable!"

Oliver felt his cheeks flush. He didn't know that Pierce called him that.

But when Jonah laughed and responded with, "Tall, dark, and silent. I like it!" Oliver felt the tension in his shoulders relax. He offered everyone an uncertain, close-lipped smile.

Their burgers arrived, with Oliver's extra rare, the way he liked it. One of the other boys, the team's forward, said to him, "You look like someone who would eat that. You're not a grottie, are you, pretty boy?"

Oliver flinched internally at the derogatory remark, unsure of what to say. He knew his skin was very pale and his hair very dark, but he couldn't help those things. After all, his mum was Black and his dad was a vampire.

Jonah hissed between his teeth at his friend. "Ollie's gorgeous, like one of those magazine models. Shut your stupid pie hole, Reg!" He then turned to Oliver. "Forgive my boneheaded friend. He got hit in the head with the ball a few too many times."

Everyone at the table laughed at Reg. That made Oliver shrug.

Before they left the café, Reg sauntered up to Oliver, and by way of an apology, he asked him if he would be at the game tonight. Ollie had planned an early night, but feeling invigorated by having talked to Jonah, he said instead, "Aye. All right."

"Cool, man. And if you come around the back of the bleachers, we hang out some and have drinks. We're not supposed to, but...you know. You're welcome to join us."

"Thank you."

Reg chuckled. "Sorry about earlier, Ollie. Can I call you Ollie?"

Oliver shrugged.

After Reg left, Jonah slipped up alongside him. "Reg can be a dickhead. Sorry about that." He smiled widely. "And for the record, I don't care if you're a Supe. That's cool."

Oliver nodded.

Jonah gave him a sympathetic look. "My little sister was like you. She was autistic, but I enjoyed looking after her." Jonah winked at him. "It's okay to be different. I hang with way too many loud, dumb hosers anyway. See ya tonight, beautiful!"

Oliver felt an odd quiver at Jonah's words. He was suddenly excited for the night and the game.

Home won the game. By then, Oliver was practically walking on cloud nine and couldn't wait to hang with Jonah's friends. In the public bathroom, he checked to make certain he looked nice. His face was pale and his eyes a little uncertain and, yeah, he supposed he did resemble a grottie in some ways, but he had worn a nice suit and his long hair was neatly plaited. Jonah seemed to like him.

It was full dark when Oliver stepped out to join the boys. He was nervously rubbing the strap of his backpack as he turned the bend behind the bleachers. He'd begun practicing what questions to ask Jonah.

No one was there. Maybe he was early?

He sensed a presence behind him. He turned, but not fast enough. Something heavy clunked into the back of his head—a bottle, he thought. The impact caused him to bend at the waist and sent a spike of dull pain down his spine. He saw bright stars for a microsecond, but the blow didn't knock him out or anything. Like his dad, he was wiry and tough. Whoever hit him seemed disappointed by his reaction because he swore and tried to back away, which was not going to happen.

He dropped his pack and whipped around, his lips drawn back over his teeth like a wolf. He saw as well in the dark as if it was high noon, and when he spotted Reg standing there, a wine bottle in his hand, his friends behind him, he wasn't unduly surprised by this sudden turn of events, though he was deeply disappointed.

Deeply hurt.

Reg swore and swung the bottle at him again. Oliver caught it before it could connect with his face. With a low growl that made Reg's eyes widen, Oliver ripped the bottle away and crushed it by applying pressure. The ragged shards crumbled, lacerating his hand, but he didn't feel the pain. The pain inside of him was so much worse.

"What the...?" Reg glared at him. "I knew you were a fucking grottie!"

Oliver didn't think; he grabbed Reg by the throat, moving fast now. He turned and forced the boy back against the bleachers so hard the entire structure vibrated from the impact. The world grew brighter still around him and his mouth hurt something fierce. Blood dripped down his throat from where he'd been chewing his tongue. He knew his eyes had gone all black; it happened when he was upset.

Reggie's eyes bulged and his mouth gaped as he struggled to breathe, but no sound came out.

He knew he should stop, that it wasn't right. But neither was it right for Reg to hit him. So instead of releasing the boy, Oliver jerked his arm upward, lifting Reg right off his feet. Reg's feet banged against the bleacher wall in distress.

Oliver could see right through Reg's flesh to the massive network of red veins, arteries, and capillaries running tree-like beneath his skin. Some went up to his eyes and nose and some down to his heart. At the front of his throat, just above his Adam's apple, was a bright red spot that beat like a little moth...

"Ollie!" someone was crying just inches away. "Ollie, put Reg down. He didn't mean it. He's an idiot!"

Oliver, shaking with rage, finally realized what he was doing. It was wrong. Grotesque.

Grotesque...which is where the term grottie came from.

Oliver, disgusted, threw Reg down on the ground at his feet. Gasping and holding his throat, he looked up, a horrified expression on his face. He tried to say something out of his bruised throat, then changed his mind and scrambled up instead, darting off into the darkness and leaving Oliver to contemplate his wounded hand. It was bleeding profusely from the broken glass.

Oliver turned to look at Jonah, the darkness clearing from his eyes. The other boys had long since scrambled off, leaving the two of them alone. But Jonah, despite what he had just witnessed, didn't flinch.

Instead of running as he should, Jonah took a step forward. "Are you okay?" He looked concerned about Oliver's hand. A ragged slit like an open mouth dripped blood down his arm. It glistened in the darkness like tar.

Oliver never responded because his shoulders lurched against the bleacher wall as a wave of weakness overwhelmed him, knocking the strength out of his body.

Jonah caught him as he fell. "Let's go back to my dorm. We need to see to that hand."

iv

As was her habit, Eliza rose at five-thirty in the morning, wound her husband up (six turns of the scarab key), kissed Edwin off to his day of running a gyro as the Lord of one of the most powerful Courts in the world, and then prepared herself for the day.

She dressed in one of her red tailcoats—red the official color of the Vampire Bride—and, while munching on her breakfast, her Mechi-maid released her hair from her bonnet into a fury of black coils and went about the job of shaping it into something sensible. After that, she usually took a lift to the bridge of the *Queen's Gambit*.

Comfortable routine. Sometimes she spoke with Captain Violet for a few minutes to get a feel for how the ship was running. Their Mechi-captain always greeted her fondly and took the time to go over possible upgrades. Even though Eliza was a layperson with no formal mechanical training, Violet still valued her input. Eliza, after all, could communicate with the ship simply by laying hands on it. That meant she could discover the source of an issue faster than any diagnostic program.

The process made her feel useful. An integral part of the crew.

Captain Violet looked quite polished today. She wore a sleek, recently upgraded suit of white armor containing the same "tree of life" that the woman had had as a human. Gone were the days of awkward metal-alloy armor; the new breed of Mechi wore Polyamideimide plastic, which boasted the highest strength of any unreinforced thermoplastic. Wear- and radiation-resistant, it had inherently low flammability, plus high thermal stability.

"Good morning, Captain," Eliza said with a wave.

Violet, stationed at a large radar scanner, perked up the moment Eliza stepped onto the deck and waved back. "Good morning, my Lady!"

After Edwin liberated the Mechis from their masters at Core-Civic, they began to reset to their original personalities, but most, even Violet, were still remembering what it was like to be a real person. Eliza often noticed Violet studying and mimicking her gestures.

"Come, come! We have something interesting today."

"Do we?"

As Eliza joined her, Violet switched on a virtual model of their time-space coordinates on the readout, which sprang up as a 3D map of the ionosphere in a two-mile radius around their gyro. The *Queen's Gambit* was hovering 400 miles above the surface of the Earth, and even though she was fully aware of that fact, it still managed to blow her mind.

Five years ago, JAXA, the Japanese Aerospace Exploration Agency, contacted Edwin about upgrading and lifting their ship even higher into the atmosphere than gyros currently occupied. They wanted to take the *Queen's Gambit* right to the edge of space, turning it into a low-altitude space station. JAXA assured Edwin that they had a solid panel of engineers on tap and that would take care of all of the upgrade expenses. Edwin's gyro, in return for the makeover, would act as a launch point for deep space exploration.

After discussing it at length, she and Edwin agreed it would elevate their position physically but also metaphorically among the Courts. There were some risks involved, of course, but she and

Edwin decided they were worth it. This experiment would bring humans—and Supes—one step closer to deep space travel. The data the experiment would generate would also make the *Queen's Gambit* invaluable to science. That fact, more than anything else, appealed to Eliza. If they were valuable, they were also safe from the other Courts.

The upgrade took one year, and during that time, Eliza, Edwin, their son Ollie, and some of their close friends and crewmembers relocated to Earth. Edwin's old friend Baldy, the Lord of Whitby Hall, invited them to stay with him during the renovations, and for Eliza, it was a pleasant change of scenery. She had forgotten how beautiful Earth's seasons could be. It also allowed her to catch up with some of their friends on Earth, including Robbie and Juliana.

But there were bittersweet developments as well. While they were enjoying the golden, sunset-touched Cornish countryside, Eliza noticed how much more alive Malcolm, Edwin's Dog of War, was. Since his separation from his mate Anjou, he'd been seeing increasingly less of his children, and Eliza recognized the toll it had taken on him. He'd gone from a passionate warrior to a man who barely spoke. He'd grown thin and drawn, and his drinking was becoming a problem. Being back on Earth made him smile a time or two, and he seemed to be getting his big werewolf-y appetite back.

One day, Eliza asked him to go motoring with her across the moors.

"Remember when we did this all those years ago?" she asked, the wind tangling her curly hair into a huge mess because she'd chosen to drive with the top down and no scarf despite the very British constant of rain.

"Aye, I remember," Malcolm admitted. "You told me all about automobiles." He played with the radio, ultimately deciding to shut it off. Lifting his face to the sun, he said, "It is always so beautiful out here in the evenings."

"Stand up and howl."

Malcolm gave her a surprised look. "What?"

"You heard me." She grinned mischievously. "Stand up and howl while I gun the engine. Your queen insists on it."

Malcolm, always eager to impress her, stood up and did so while Eliza roared down the windy dirt road. Malcolm's soulful and lonely voice echoed over the moorland. And to both of their delight, it was soon answered by other lone werewolves.

They both laughed about it afterward.

"You could stay, you know," she told him later when they stopped for tea and biscuits in one of the familiar little teahouses that dotted the village. She had discussed it previously with Edwin, who'd had no real objections. "Stay here and rebuild the Bloodthorne Pack. This is your home, after all."

"But Lord Edwin relies on my input where the politics of the ship are concerned."

She knew he would say that and had come armed, so to speak. "I don't mean that you wouldn't be part of the Congress any longer, Malc, or that we wouldn't include you in important decisions. I'm suggesting a long holiday—a chance to get your perspective back. If we need you, we can summon you."

She knew he wanted to stay, and, in the end (and with a little prodding from her), he did.

Months later, with the gyro successfully lifted to the very edge of Earth's atmosphere, Eliza and her little family prepared to board her using a specially designed Hummingbird that could withstand the increased pressure of space. A Phoenix, the Japanese engineers called it. It was essentially a simplified space shuttle, just with its own propellant.

Eliza felt a pang of sadness when they had to say goodbye to the Earth once more—and to Malcolm!—but, at the end of the day, the Queen's Gambit was their home, and "the stars were their destiny"—something Edwin was wont to say these days.

Now, Captain Violet pointed out what seemed to be a radiating signal about ten thousand miles from their current position. All data her bosses at JAXA found fascinating.

"What is that, Captain?"

"Hawking radiation being emitting from an incredibly light-dense pocket of deep space."

Eliza, ever curious, had paid close attention to the renovations on their ship—and how it had changed it. She had some idea what that meant. She just wasn't sure about the small details.

"Are you saying there's an event horizon out there?"

"Yes, and only a short distance from us—relatively speaking."

Eliza felt a chill crawl spiderlike down her back, and her hands clenched into involuntary fists in the flowing long fabric of her tailcoat. "A...black hole? That's a black hole, isn't it?"

The Captain considered the radar. "I am not sure what it is, my Lady, but a black hole is certainly not off the table." She turned her head slightly, her servos making the common sliding noises that all Mechi-people's joints did, and looked directly at her. Eliza could almost feel the anticipatory smile that the captain could not properly form on her nearly featureless humanoid face. "Rather exciting, yes?"

"More like exciting no," Eliza insisted. "Black holes emit gravity. If it damaged the Queen's Gambit, you and your Mechi might survive a cataclysm that bad, but the rest of us would be flattened like pancakes."

She knew enough to know the event horizon could suck the Queen's Gambit into it, and that its gravity could crush their gyro like a wad of paper. All organic matter would be rendered cosmic dust.

"I would never allow that to happen," Captain Violet insisted. "If it becomes an issue, I will move the ship immediately."

Eliza let out her breath in a relieved sigh. "In the meantime, I think it would be best if I informed Edwin about this development."

"I agree that would be prudent."

***

She considered writing Edwin a mind text about the black hole, but some matters she didn't want crossing the neural network. On the lift ride back to their private quarters, Eliza wondered how he had gotten on at the session aboard Lord Trasch's ship and which of the vamps was trying to get into his shorts this time. She never questioned his fidelity, and they often had a laugh about it later, but lord, was it tiring.

"Edwin?"

The runner lights in their private quarters were turned down low as they often were when a space wasn't being occupied. Shadows slanted across the space, picking out the artifacts of their lives together—the poster that Hollywood made of one of Edwin's crime novels, his beloved typewriter snugged away in the writing nook he never had the time to visit anymore, the refrigerator art that Ollie had made her as a child that she refused to part with—some huge vase of sunflowers on the kitchen table that Edwin gave her four days ago.

She wondered if he had gotten hung up. She hoped not. They needed to talk about this recent development.

When someone grabbed her unexpectedly from behind, Eliza yelped and whipped around. Her body tensed and her vision turned bright for a moment—something that had been happening of late when she was surprised.

Edwin had her fast in his grip, having crept up behind her without her hearing him. Typical stalky vampire jerk!

"Edwin!" She smacked him in the chest with her fist. "You scared the hell out of me!"

He gave her a devilish cartoon villain laugh. "I've got you now, my lovely!"

So she smacked him again, which shut him up. Honestly, though, Eliza found it virtually impossible to stay mad at him. He looked so natty in his suit, slim and foxy, though his curling dark auburn hair looked a mess like he'd been running his fingers through it.

He held up his hands in surrender. "Sorry, lovey. That played out funnier in my head."

She gave him a cross look. "You think scaring me is funny?"

"Erm...no. But remember when I got you on the stairs at Whitby Hall?"

She tapped his chest with her finger. "It wasn't good then and it's not good now, you big horny vampire."

He gave her a sassy smile and wandered to the wet bar to pour himself a drink from the collection of decanters there. "I don't recall you complaining much afterward. I believe your exact words were, 'There's nothing like a good shag after a scare.'"

Eliza rolled her eyes. "You said that, not me."

"Did I?" Edwin thought about that. "So, you're not back here for a snogging then?"

"I am not. We have an issue with the ship."

While she clued him in, he refreshed his drink and seemed to think it through. "I like it when you talk science. It's sexy."

"It's a black hole, Edwin."

"And that's bad."

"Not if you don't mind being vaporized."

"Right then. We should move the ship." He checked one of the clocks on the walls. "How much time before we all die?"

"Violet says we have a week."

"Excellent. More than enough time."

"For?"

He went to her and swept her up, pushing her back against the nearest wall. One look into his eyes seemed to have the power to hypnotize her. "This is unexpected. Do you find black holes sexy, husband?"

Edwin grinned a little goofily. "Not black holes."

His aftershave made her head swim and her thoughts tangle. The familiar angles of his body made her jumpy inside. She hated that—that just his presence could turn her into a giddy, melty schoolgirl. It wasn't fair. They'd been married for nearly two decades, but every time with him was like their honeymoon, all nervous, anticipatory energy.

With that mischievous smile still on his face, he said in a low, whispery voice, "I can hear your heart beating and your blood pulsing."

"Yes, husband...that happens when you scare the hell out of me."

"Are you sure that's it?" He looked at her demandingly with those wolf-yellow eyes. No one had ever looked at her like that, with such insatiable hunger. He impaled her with his look.

She trembled ridiculously in his arms. She couldn't seem to find the words...

"Well now, I don't think you're frightened at all." He leaned in to kiss her, a deep, rough kiss that left her mouth numb and tingling. His fingers dug into her hips. "Are you?"

"No." She swallowed hard.

A look of profound satisfaction overcame his face. Making a decision, he lifted her easily into his arms so that she squeaked in surprise. Turning, he deposited her on her back on the glassy edge of his home office desk, which was a windstorm of papers.

"Edwin!"

"Aye, wife?" He had the absolute worst accent she had ever heard on an Englishman, harsh and nasally because of his eternally broken nose, but, even so, he more than made up for it with his wit, humor, and sexual prowess. He was beyond doubt one of the sexiest and sweetest cockney vampire jerks who ever lived, and the disparity of it made her snortle.

He looked her over as if he were taking in the sight of a great feast. "Bloody hell, you're beautiful. You're everything," he said as if all of his prayers had been answered—as if he had gotten the happy ending he always wanted. He moved his hands up her body to her face to brush her cheek and then tangled a finger in her curls. "What would I do without you, eh?"

"Well, you wouldn't be able to find anything in this mess," she said, indicating his desk.

He laughed at that as he went about the slow process of unbuttoning her jack and the blouse beneath, his fingers moving silkily and with great practice over her exposed skin.

"My god, you are always so horny when you come back from session," she said. "What do you guys do at those things?"

"Things that make me wish I was here with you...things that make me want only you."

His words made her heart beat faster. Surprised tears sprang to her eyes. He could be so charming, so funny, but it was a rare thing to see him this sentimental. She wondered what had happened at session. Probably nothing good.

He bent to her and kissed her again, this time more gently, breathing into her. His fingers curled in the fabric of her blouse, nearly ripping it. He kissed her so fiercely that she groaned. Turning her head, she tapped his mark on her neck, a little sore spot under her ear that ached whenever he was near.

He nuzzled the spot, licked it, and while he snaked one hand under her long jacket, gently teasing her in ways that should be illegal, he finally bit down on the mark. The whole shebang sent her off like a rocket. He drank and she writhed. In the course of their little dance, a picture of the three of them—her, Edwin, and an eight-year-old Ollie—was knocked to the floor and cracked.

That made her sad. She tried to reach for it, but he wouldn't let her go. He grasped her face in his big hand and turned it, kissing her like he meant to consume her body and soul. At the same time, his hands continued to work at her blouse, tugging at the many buttons.

"Christ, I hate this shirt. It's beyond frustrating!"

"You're 250 years old, and during most of that time, women wore everything but the kitchen sink. You'd think you'd be an expert at undoing buttons by now."

He growled as he worked.

The room was suddenly cool against her legs where he'd yanked down her flare trousers. He had given up on the blouse and now just pushed it up. When he licked and nibbled across her midriff, she let out a small cry of surprise. At the same time, a delicious tingling sensation moved through her body and was concentrated at her fingertips, which snapped with ambient electricity. She had to work hard to contain it and not accidentally set the back of Edwin's jacket on fire.

She writhed upon the desk for him, wanting him in a way she had never wanted anyone. He seemed to be equally starved, and things might have gotten very interesting at that point, but a polite knock on Edwin's door stopped them dead in their tracks and made her groan.

Captain Violet's voice drifted to them both. "Lady Eliza? Lord Edwin? We appear to have a very serious problem."

* * *

Up on the navdeck, Eliza, Edwin, and Captain Violet huddled around the scanner while the captain pointed out how the anomaly had changed in just the last hour.

"We thought the event horizon was putting out Hawking Radiation, and we weren't wrong about that," Captain Violet explained. "But...and here it gets interesting...someone or something is using the radiation to boost the signal on a coded message. The message is embedded in the radiation."

Eliza blinked up at the images on the screen that showed a series of blips and coordinates, not all of which she understood. "Is that possible? To use radiation to send a message?"

"In theory," one of the JAXA Mechis, Haruki, explained as he joined them. "There are theoretical models. But we don't have the tech to do that right now. But whoever sent the message apparently does."

"What does the message say?" Edwin asked. He looked around the whole console, his eyes clocking about. Eliza knew he was struggling to keep up with what everyone here was discussing and how it might impact his Congress. Tech was never his strong suit—but protecting his people was.

"It took us over an hour to untangle it from the radio signals, and then we had to pass it through some very sensitive equipment, so—"

"The message. Captain," he said, interrupting her. "Please."

Captain Violet turned to him, inclining her head respectfully. "It's very curious, my Lord, because it reads...'The stars are our destiny.'" The captain paused and her large synthetic head shifted up and down as she considered the many blips. "It is nicely poetic but makes no sense to me or my crew."

Eliza, meanwhile, felt the color drain from her face. She turned to Edwin, who gave her an equally worried look. They stared at each other for a long, dark moment. "How...why would someone send that message to us?"

"Or who," Edwin said. He looked suddenly very concerned.

Before Eliza could make any further inquiries about the strange phenomenon, there was a commotion behind them as a figure stepped onto the deck. "Captain? A word?"

The three of them turned to find Navigational Officer Ari of the Unseely Court standing there, clutching the doorway and leaning down, which he had to because he was nearly eight feet tall, including his long, curling horns.

Eight years ago, during the ice vamp outbreak on the ship, they lost Narissa, their former navigational officer and official representative of the Fae part of Edwin's Congress. It was a painful blow to them both emotionally and politically. Not only was Narissa an integral part of their crew and their friend, but she was also their link to their Fae allies. After her passing, they went a whole year with temps filling in for Narissa. Then they learned that Ari, formerly a Captain of the Guard in the Unseely Court, had put in a request to join the Queen's Gambit.

Curious as to his motivations, Edwin set up an interview with the young Fae, during which he learned that Ari was Narissa's cousin on his mother's side. "She was dealt a hard hand in life—one no Fae should have to bear." Ari's eyes glinted, hard and steely but with an underlying tenderness. "I was not the kin to her that I should be. After I learned of Cousin's passage to the Summerlands, I took my year of mourning and then set myself on a different path. I know that Cousin would want me here now, continuing her work and representing our Tribe."

Edwin nodded at that, but he wasn't convinced the young warrior wasn't just playing out whatever personal regrets he had. "A loss can cause us to act rashly," he suggested, but Ari shook his head.

"I asked Narissa if this was the path she wanted me to walk and she said is it so."

Eliza, who was there at the interview, asked him how he knew.

He lifted his head, pinning them both with a sharp look. "I spoke to her in visions." Which was all the explanation he offered. "I was a navigator before I became Captain of She Who is Three's guards. And I wish to return to that path aboard your ship. If my Lord will have me."

Ari rose from his seat and went to one knee, bowing his head in humility, his great, curling horns glinting under the harsh lighting just as his eyes had. "I will serve you with all of my blood and soul if you will have me, my Lord." He even kissed one of Edwin's rings.

After that rousing speech, Edwin could not find it in himself to deny Captain Ari the chance to fill his cousin's shoes. He told Eliza later that he had no idea if Ari actually could speak to his deceased cousin or if he was making that bit up, but he knew never to cross Narissa's wishes, dead or alive. She had been a firebrand.

"My Lord, I bring news from the navdeck," he announced now. "My officers have picked up a foreign body moving toward us. A transport of some kind."

Captain Violet interrupted by saying, "Can you not see we are dealing with a volatile situation here, Chief Navigator?"

"That's just it, Captain. The transport appeared suddenly. My people have confirmed it has passed through the event horizon and is on a trajectory to intercept us. What's more..." He looked particularly aggrieved. "The transport has requested docking permission. Shall I tell the gunners to send a warning and then to open fire if it draws too close?"

Edwin scowled, the thought line between his eyes deepening. It had gotten much deeper during the last sixteen years of being the Sitting Lord of the Queen's Gambit. Everyone in the room looked to him for direction. He glanced at her and then back to Ari. It took him a moment to respond. "No..." he finally said. "Let it dock."

Ari shook his head. "My Lord...?"

"Just so," Eliza said, lending support. She had a feeling about this. "Let the transport dock."

"As you say, my Lord...my Lady." Ari bent his head.

V

The stars are our destiny.

What an extraordinary message for the unknown space transport to send. But one that had saved the unknown craft from certain annihilation as it docked. Sleekly streamlined, it fit smoothly and with room to spare in one of the narrow bays of the receiving bay. Edwin reflected on how he would have had the gunners at the ready were it now for that message. But he and Eliza knew that phrase. It was their code.

The problem was...only he and Eliza knew that code. They had never shared it with anyone, not even their son.

He turned to glance at her. She was standing next to him, grasping her hands together fretfully. Despite the unusual circumstances, he took a moment to appreciate how fetching she looked in her long red tailcoat, her enormously thick black hair curling haphazardly around her head, her white streak sagging through it like a bolt of lightning. Her jacket was buttoned down tightly over her generous cleavage, which was snugged down into her frilly white poplin shirt. He'd almost had the chance to free her lovely curves from her clothes before Captain Violet interrupted them, a frustration he was trying not to take out on whoever was piloting the ship.

The transport intrigued him. It was bullet-shaped with a thick shell built to sustain the incredible pressure of deep space travel.

When he asked one of the hangar engineers, he said the ship was made of Graphite-epoxy composite materials, along with polymer, practically indestructible short of an atomic blast. The ship looked less like any Hummingbird he had ever seen—or even the upgraded Phoenixes his gyro now used—and more like the Sky Sharks the Jotnar piloted on and off their little floating world of hodge-podge ships.

Captain Violet stood on his other side, her posture soldier straight, yet he sensed her concern as she considered the foreign transport. The ship was pretty obviously not a product of JAXA or any other company any of them were familiar with.

After the transport had successfully docked, Captain Violet had several of her Mechi airmen engineers go over it with wands to check for radiation. They also did an infra-scan for different body temperatures.

In time, their leader, an older male Mechi named Gus, moseyed up to the captain and nodded. "The transport is clear, Captain. It appears to have its own radiation sieve. The pilot is registering as a Mechi, only..."

"What is it?"

"No biological elements."

That was odd.

"Passengers?"

"One signature—cold. Thirty-seven Celsius."

"A vampire," Captain Violet intoned. She glanced at Edwin for instruction.

"Clear it."

Gus inclined his big synthetic head before turning and stomping back toward his people. The small group of Mechis folded up their wands and nodded to one of their fellows waiting in the wings. That Mechi drove an EV out with the airstair and parked it at the door of the *Demeter*. This ship was built much taller, and its carriage sat higher than a normal transport. Airstairs would be necessary.

Unless one has wings, Edwin added.

Violet, an astute and experienced leader, motioned her guards forward. They were twelve of her best Mechi warriors, their huge bodies imposing and their giant hands clenching massive boomer rifles. They made two lines of six on both sides of the airstair, rifles at the ready should there be any issues. Violet then turned to Edwin, who nodded her on.

"Newton," she told their ship-wide AI, "give the passengers the clearance to deplane."

"Yes, Captain," Newton intoned over the neural network.

Moments later, the door of the transport slid open and two figures stepped out.

Edwin as much sensed as heard Eliza gasp in shock.

* * *

The transport's pilot deplaned first, a gangly tall Mechi-creature covered in black armor. Eliza couldn't gauge its gender, assuming it even had one. It had six long, spindly arms and clusters of red-eyed sensors encircling its narrow head so it could see in all directions at once. It more resembled an upright walking spider than a human. She had never seen such a design before.

It powered down the airstairs but moved with an almost liquidly grace. Its design was surprising all on its own, but the vampire walking behind it stopped her dead in her tracks.

It was none other than Edwin himself—but not the stately man she knew with his shining auburn hair, devilish goatee, and wolf-yellow eyes. This one was drawn and painfully thin in a tattered green frock goat rubbed raw in places, his greying hair fastened at the back of his neck with a band. His pale, greyish face bore a terrible scar that had rendered one of his eyes blind. It sat lazily in its socket and looked like a boiled egg. The rest of him didn't look much better: battered, starved, and exhausted, a mere shade of the man she knew.

Eliza immediately turned away before she was sick.

| vi |

"You have a cool accent," Jonah told Oliver as he let him into his dorm room. "Did you grow up in London or something?"

Oliver, clutching his hand and the makeshift bandage about it that Jonah had made for him with a handkerchief, mumbled nervously, "I wasn't born on Earth."

Jonah lifted his brows at that. His dorm was dim and not very large. It sported a narrow bed, a large desk pushed against the one wall with a window, and a small kitchenette to the side. The window faced a large courtyard where he could hear a distant soccer game going on and a ball bouncing off the walls and windows. On the wall opposite, Oliver spied a bank of cages, about ten in total, with maybe five rabbits occupying them. All of the rabbits were munching on grain and sweet timothy.

"They're my pets," Jonah said by way of an explanation, a blush tingeing his cheeks. It made him so cute that Oliver wanted to sit down and drink in his embraced expression forever.

It was a private dorm with no roommate, from what Oliver could see. That filled him with relief. He generally stayed away from the campus when he wasn't attending class; he didn't like the crush of people and the loudness of crowds.

He had rented his own small apartment in the city, private and quiet, one he paid for himself with a combination of a swing shift job at a local coffee shop and some online tutoring he did. His parents had offered to pay for everything but Oliver hated the idea of his dad supporting him. His mum insisted he was too stubborn for his own good.

Oliver hovered uncertainly.

"It's okay," Jonah assured him, undoubtedly reading his anxiety. "I'm not going to jump your bones or anything. I didn't lure you up here for sex."

"I never thought that."

"You looked worried," Jonah laughed. "Like maybe I brought you here to seduce you."

"Oh."

Jonah gave him a saucy look. "Is that a oh, you didn't think that, or an oh, please don't seduce me, Jonah?"

Now it was Oliver's turn to blush. "The first."

Jonah touched some light fixtures, adjusting the brightness so they weren't so glaring, which Oliver appreciated. "So...what you're saying is...you wouldn't mind being seduced?"

Oliver opened his mouth, then closed it, unsure of what to say.

"I'm just joshing you," Jonah told him. "I would never do anything you didn't approve of, Oliver."

Oliver smiled nervously.

"Wait here. I'll get the first aid kit. There's some stuff in the kitchen if you're thirsty."

Oliver did not visit the kitchenette. Instead, he went to look at the rabbits. He'd always liked animals, though he'd never had a pet growing up. Gyros weren't the best environments to keep pets. The rabbits lifted their heads to stare at him through the bars of their cages, their small bodies shivering.

When Jonah returned with the first aid kit, he indicated a stool at the coffee bar. "You can sit if you like."

"Right."

Jonah took the second (and only) stool beside him and opened the first aid kit. "You don't say much, but that's okay. Talking too much is overrated. Don't you agree?"

Oliver shrugged.

"I talk enough for both of us." He gently took Oliver's hand and undid the scrap of cloth. Even though the handkerchief was soaked through, the jagged wound in his palm had mostly healed already. Jonah disinfected it anyway. "But I wouldn't mind you talking a bit more. Like I said, it's a cool accent. You don't run into too many Brits here. Plenty of Germans, though."

"I'm not British"

Jonah gave him an interested look as he worked. "You mentioned you were born off-world. Aboard a gyro?"

Oliver thought about how much he wanted Jonah to know, then decided to take a chance. "Aye. My father is British."

"Ah. Your parents are floaters."

Oliver looked at him questioningly.

"They work off-world. On a gyro," he clarified.

"Aye."

"See, there's that cool accent again. Your dad must be quite the Brit for you to have picked it up."

"My dad is a prick."

Jonah opened his mouth in an "Ahhh" gesture. After he finished cleaning the wound, he started binding it with clean gauze even though Oliver didn't think the wound needed attention. "Does it hurt?" Jonah asked with genuine concern. "I have pills. Just aspirin, I mean."

"It's fine."

"Tell me about your prick of a father and I might tell you about mine."

Oliver squirmed. He didn't want to talk about Lord Edwin. No one understood the nuances of his and Lord Edwin's relationship—not even his mum.

It wasn't that Lord Edwin was abusive. When he was younger, they even had fun together, but when it came down to it, his father was a Vampire Lord with a vast Congress and all that entailed. The vampire world called him the Prince of Hell, and for good reason. He was once a blood-hungry Enforcer who would do anything for his master.

Oliver was more familiar with the stories than most believed. He'd seen the portrait before it was taken down and replaced by a more suitable painting of Lord Edwin and his Bride. The old one was a picture of Lord Edwin on fire as the Devil.

But that was only part of the issue. It bothered Oliver more that Edwin had lied to him. That he hadn't told him he was Oliver's father until he could no longer keep it from him.

Oliver didn't like liars.

And, if he was being honest, he also didn't like Lord Edwin. He never discussed it with his mum because she wouldn't believe him, but Oliver knew Edwin in a way that she never would. Oliver knew that in Edwin's heart of mechanical hearts (if he could be said to have one) that he secretly loathed his son. He hated that Oliver had been born, that he'd upset Edwin's otherwise perfect little paradise with his mum.

He saw Jonah looking at him with concern and shared, "My dad and I don't get on."

Nodding, Jonah said, "I get it. My dad is gone but he was super abusive. I have a step-dad now and he's way better. We still have our differences, though."

Olive smiled at that. He found it hard to believe anyone could be cruel to someone as sweet as Jonah. Feeling a little less guarded, Oliver added, "My dad lied about something important."

Jonah nodded. "That's hard. Are you close to your mother?"

"I love my mum," Oliver blurted out and then regretted it. Even though it was true, he sounded like a child. "My mom is cool," he amended. "I'm meeting with her tomorrow for breakfast at the virtual café."

He was happy that Jonah didn't make fun of the way he talked. Some people did. Instead, Jonah brightened and said, "That's great. It's important you have at least one parent in your corner."

"You can come and meet her tomorrow if you like."

Jonah laughed at that but not in a mean way. "I'm not sure I'm ready to meet your mother yet. We've hardly gotten to know one another."

Oliver realized his mistake and looked at the floor. "Oh."

"Don't worry—I get you. You're upfront and honest. You don't play games." Jonah moved closer. "For instance, if you liked me, you'd let me know. You would show it. You wouldn't play with me."

Oliver relaxed. He really did like Jonah, and the more he looked at his new friend, the more he wanted...something. Something more. Something that made him feel desperately lonely.

He wanted to touch Jonah. Kiss him. He wanted Jonah to kiss him back.

It was an odd thought to have since he rarely liked anyone touching him.

Growing uncomfortable, Oliver slowly got to his feet. "Thank you for this," he said, indicating his bandaged hand. "You aren't...afraid?"

"Of you?" Jonah asked. He was still seated but shook his head. "No. Why? Should I be?"

Oliver made a decision then. If he was going to see Jonah again, he needed the boy to know the truth. "Reg wasn't wrong. I'm not all human."

"I figured." Jonah stood up too but kept his eyes fixed on Oliver. The intensity coming off the boy made Oliver squirm inside.

"I don't want you to be afraid."

"I'm not."

Oliver nodded and, not knowing what else to say, started for the door. Jonah followed him, which was not what he expected. When Oliver reached the door and tried to take the handle in hand, Jonah put his hand on Oliver's shoulder and turned him around.

Jonah pressed into him. Oliver felt himself melt a little when Jonah applied pressure, pressing him against the wall by the door. His kiss was gentle at first, barely more than a touch to the corner of Oliver's mouth, but the more pressure he applied, the more Oliver wanted it. He made a low groaning noise in his throat, afraid to move, to even react.

Jonah kissed him fully, a hand on Oliver's shoulder while his other slid down over Oliver's chest. Oliver jumped at the pressure and almost bit the tip of Jonah's tongue, which was currently flicking in and out of his mouth.

Jonah didn't seem to mind. He nuzzled into the side of Oliver's neck, sending little sparkles of pleasure zipping down Oliver's back. Oh, Oliver thought. Oh!

For a moment or two, Oliver reveled in the masterful way Jonah was touching and kissing him. He closed his eyes and groaned in delight.

Letting him go, Jonah leaned back.

Oliver immediately missed the touch and pressure of Jonah's kiss. He just hung against the door, staring into Jonah's handsome face. "S...sorry," he eventually said. "I'm not good at this."

"You're very good at this." Jonah ran a hand up Oliver's arm, making him quiver in a way he had never experienced before. He leaned in again, and Oliver raised his hand, instinctively setting it on the nape of Jonah's neck and rubbing at a little spot there.

"Good Christ." Nearly purring with pleasure, Jonah turned his head and kissed him one last time. This time, Oliver's entire body lit up. Jonah's mouth was hot and sweet. When his tongue scraped Oliver's teeth, Oliver was suddenly afraid they might spring downward into sharpened canines, but they stayed small and harmless. After he was sure nothing was going to happen, he clutched Jonah's face and kissed him back, hard...harder. He even licked his lips a little.

"Wow," Jonah said as he drew back. "Are you sure you've never done this before?"

"Aye."

"Well, you're a hell of a kisser. And, if I might add, quite the looker, too." Jonah brushed his fingers through Oliver's braids.

Oliver felt his cheeks flush at the compliment. He wriggled against his new friend, hoping for more, but Jonah said, "I think that's enough for now. Let's save something for Date Number Two, eh?"

"Aye. Right."

Jonah laughed at him and playfully tossed a braid off his shoulder. "That accent. You never know who you'll meet in college."

***

Things became heated very quickly.

One of the Mechi guards down in the bay moved toward the newcomers, boomer at the ready, and, within seconds, the Edwin who had stepped off the Sky Shark had her down on the floor. He'd managed to disarm her of her boomer and pushed her down in a heap, his boot in her neck. He'd moved shockingly quickly, with the ease of a Vampire Lord a thousand years steeped in his power. Her nearly impervious armor was crushed in where he'd stepped on her, and he looked ready to rip her head straight off her synthetic body when the Edwin in the bay shouted for him to halt.

The damaged-looking Edwin glanced up at him, his one working eye full of a brimming, red-rimmed darkness. "Aye...I'll stop when you call off your dogs."

Edwin nodded. "Right then." He motioned his other Court Guards back. "No one here wants a fight, mate."

His other self—he didn't know how else to think of him—eyed him like some berserker, his body thrumming with power and possibly a great big helping of PTSD. He saw the near-madness in his face. It was positively surreal to see himself like this, like some machine ready to tear everything apart.

"Keep the Mechis away," the other Edwin instructed, growling through his sharp, extended teeth. They glinted darkly, and it took Edwin a moment to realize they were coated in some kind of metal. His good eye glinted with rage. "And do not touch my Enforcer."

Edwin held up his hands. "Right, right. You got it, mate. Just calm down." After a moment, he added, "No one here wants to harm you or your Enforcer. But I need you to work with me."

After a moment, the other Edwin nodded and stepped away from the damaged Mechi, though he remained guarded, glaring at anyone who dared to move closer to him. While he glanced around the bay, Edwin spotted some sort of medal or medallion pinned to the front of his worn-out frock coat, but it was so old and tarnished that he couldn't make out any details.

"I'm going to need to put you and your Enforcer in the brig as a safety measure, but I promise none of my guards will touch you if you don't fight them," Edwin said diplomatically. "Does that sound about right to you?"

He hoped it was enough. He hoped the other Edwin believed him—trusted him. He should...shouldn't he? After all, the other Edwin was him, right? He should know he meant himself no harm.

The other Edwin thought about that a moment, his hand reaching up in a compulsive way to rub at the medallion on his coat. "Right. Lead the way then."

Edwin instructed his guards to take their two guests down to the brig but not to separate them or to touch them again. No one was to speak to them until he'd had a chance to interview the other Edwin.

The guards escorted the visitors away. Edwin then told Captain Violet to have her people go over every inch of the ship. He quickly returned to Eliza and asked her if she was willing to take control of matters here while he interrogated their "guests."

"I want to come." Her voice was low and throaty. Her hands were clenched in her long skirts and she was shaking slightly. "I need to know what the hell is going on. Who that other Edwin is."

Edwin gave her a pleading look. "I know you want to be a part of it, lovey, but I'm hoping you will give me a bit of time to determine what level of danger they pose first." He touched her arm imploringly.

She swallowed and, to his surprise, nodded.

* * *

Damn Edwin for being so practical. She wanted to fight his request to hang back, but she knew he had a good point. Even being a Poppet, she wasn't nearly as durable as he was. And now that she had seen what the other Edwin could do, she wasn't sure she wanted to get too close.

"I'll see you later, husband."

He kissed her off, and he smiled and told her it would be all right, but she could tell he had been shaken by the encounter with the other Edwin. She turned and looked at the now vacated Sky Shark and the Mechis taking their tools and instruments to it. There was no point in her hanging there and doing nothing constructive.

Thank goodness she had her little lunch date with Ollie—something sane to keep her mind off this terrible business.

She took a lift to the Bazaar, the level of the gyro that offered parks, theaters, taverns, and dozens of teashops and cafes. She dropped in on her favorite teashop and asked the owner Kimberly for an Earl Grey and cucumber sandwiches, her favorite, while she waited for Oliver to join her in the virtual lounge off the shop.

The room, its walls, ceiling, and floor fitted with softly glowing white panels, was empty except for a nondescript black metal table and two chairs. Eliza took a seat and asked their AI Newton to dial them up some calming seaside atmosphere. Newton happily constructed an outside café by the sea, complete with slightly stormy skies and crashing waves on the cliffs below.

Kimberly arrived with delicate sandwiches balanced on a three-tiered sterling silver serving tray and included some chocolate digestive biscuits just for her—her favorite. "Enjoy!" she said, glancing around approvingly at the scene Eliza had chosen for her date with her son.

Eliza stared into her tea and tried to wrap her head around these strange developments. She had so many questions, and none of them would be answered until she'd had a chance to speak to the other Edwin, which she planned to do—whether Edwin approved of that or not.

Oliver arrived promptly at their appointed time. He glanced around the scene she had chosen before taking the other seat, though she knew, intellectually, that he was doing so in the virtual lounge located on the school campus. But the virtual lounge made their little dates feel so real.

He was dressed in the maroon jacket and striped grey trousers that were his university uniform. He had braided his unruly dark hair into small plaits, which had the effect of making his face look narrow and almost predatory. He looked older than seventeen these days. With his high cheekbones and startling steel-blue eyes, he turned the head of everyone, male or female, when he walked into a room.

"Hallo, Mum!"

She immediately got to her feet as she saw him approach. "How are you, sweet pea?" she said. "You look tired!" Maybe it was silly to call him by his pet name, but some habits die hard.

"I am. A little," Ollie told her with a subdued smile. He took the seat opposite her and immediately unfolded his napkin and put it properly in his lap. Ollie was an incredibly sweet and meticulous boy. Maybe overly serious and quiet, and, yes, particular about some things, but there wasn't a mean bone in his entire body.

Hoping she didn't sound like some fretful mum, Eliza said, "Are you sleeping well?"

"Aye. I had a lie-in earlier. I was up half the night studying."

That worried her because he was a young college boy now. He should be up and about. He should be out with friends and having fun and dates. He didn't need to study all of the time!

"I'm fine," she answered when he asked after her. She didn't explain about the strange ship and even stranger crew. There was no purpose in alarming him. "I was thinking about you all day. How are you really?" As a server appeared with tea for Ollie, one from the campus café on Earth, she added, "You aren't ill that you slept in so late?"

"No, Mum. Just a long night out with friends."

That gave her hope. "Did you have fun?"

"I saw a soccer game last night, and then one of the boys asked me over to his place. But afterward, I came right home."

She laughed. "You can go out with friends, you know. You can have a date! It's the weekend. You should be out all night partying and having fun."

"Why would I want to do that?" Oliver asked. He frowned. "College is for studying."

Eliza felt her heart clench inside her. She didn't know how to explain to her shy, introverted son that it was all right to meet people, to fall in love. It was one of the reasons—the main reason—she and Edwin decided to send him to college on Earth. She hoped that if Oliver was away from the ship and between young people he would find his own path. She wanted him to do things with kids his own age. But he was always so serious, so…reserved.

Maybe they had made a mistake. Maybe he wasn't ready to be away from her? He was just a baby, really.

She moved her hand toward his, wanting desperately to touch her son's virtual hand. "Ollie, tell me the truth, sweetie. Are you okay?"

Oliver never lied. Although he was gifted with a genius-level intellect in not one but several fields of study, he didn't have a gift for subterfuge. He wasn't creative that way.

He stared into his cup of tea. "I've been sleeping a lot," he admitted. And then he brightened suddenly and sat up straight in his seat. "But I met a boy. Jonah. We hung out last night at his apartment." Suddenly realizing what he'd said, Oliver blushed and put in, "I didn't…you know. We didn't have sex or anything. I hurt my hand and Jonah gave me a bandage."

Her heart suddenly hurt so much more for her son. In a low, soothing voice, she told him, "You know, Ollie, it's all right if you see someone. You know that your father and I are all right with that."

"I know that, Mum."

"It's…it's not good that you're alone so much."

"I'm not alone. I have friends. And now I have Jonah."

"Are you seeing Jonah tonight?" she asked hopefully.

Ollie chewed on a cucumber sandwich, also his favorite. Then he swallowed it in one bite. She recalled how hungry he was as a baby. Oliver was always so hungry. "He mind-texted me to hang out with him after my shift was over tonight, but I don't know if he was being serious." He sounded sad. "He's probably just being nice."

"He's not just being nice! You're an amazing person to hang out with, Ollie, and anyone would be lucky to spend time with you."

Ollie grumbled in a way that reminded her strongly of Edwin. "Thanks, Mum. But you're a little partial."

"I know a good thing when I see him!" she said, hoping to raise his confidence. "And you are the best thing there is, sweet pea! You're my little prince."

He suddenly giggled at that in a way he used to when he was young and would jump into her bed in the morning. He was so serious most of the time, but Ollie also had his playful side. He would never admit to it, she knew, but he was much more like his father than he thought. She so missed those bygone days aboard the Gambit when she and Ollie were together all the time.

Suddenly, he looked terribly exhausted to her, and his eyes seemed darker than usual. They talked for a short while about school, but soon enough, Ollie yawned. "I think I should go home and sleep so I'm not so tired for work."

"Of course. I won't keep you."

"Thanks, Mum."

"I just wanted to see you—to talk to you."

He laughed at that. "We see each other every week. And we talk almost every day by mind text."

Someone else might think Ollie was being sarcastic, but Eliza knew it wasn't in him. He was just stating facts. He often said exactly what he was thinking without refining it. She was used to it.

They stood to say their goodbyes. "I love you, sweet pea," she said. Her heart ached to hold him and smooth his hair, but this was virtual space.

"I love you too, Mum."

After they parted ways, Eliza returned to her quarters and sat on her bed in her room, just staring at the wall. A feeling of dread was coiled up tightly in her belly, making her feel sick. She was afraid. Afraid for Ollie as much as she was afraid of these recent turn of events. Neither she nor Edwin had any clear idea of what he was or what he might turn into. Once, long ago, a friend of hers called Oliver a krsnik, a kind of super vampire who could only feed on the flesh and blood of other vampires.

Please, god, no, she thought, almost tearing up at the idea. Whatever Powers That Be, please don't let my baby be a monster...

| vii |

JAXA had upgraded every part of the *Queen's Gambit*, including the brig.

There were a dozen cells installed in the incarceration center, and each was made of reinforced iron and space titanium alloy. They could easily contain werewolves and Fae, and they were graded for assault by the most powerful creatures on earth—the vampires. During the overhaul process, Edwin thought they were overkill, but today he was happy he had opted to have the Japanese upgrade the cells along with the rest of the ship.

The "Enforcer" interested him greatly. He had never seen a design like it.

"It's a Class 6 Mechi," the other Edwin explained. "We call them Sentinels. No biological material, so they can theoretically live forever with a little maintenance."

Edwin turned to face his...other. The ravaged sight of him—of himself—startled him all over again. The starved, cadaver-like face and claw-like hands reminded him in some ways of Lord Trasch. "You mean there's...no one in there."

The Edwin in the cage watched him back, burning eyes locked on him. "No. Nothing that was human, anyway."

Swallowing hard, Edwin approached the bars of the cell. Old Edwin—as he had begun to think of him—mirrored the gesture.

Together, the two approached each other until only the bars and a few feet separated them.

Edwin studied the creature. Though he showed no traditional signs of aging, there was endless pain and years in his eyes and the hard set of his thin, angular jaw. There was the silvery hair—due in large part to a large scar that extended diagonally from his hairline on the right side of his face to just about the level of his top lip on his left side. His eye on that side was nearly bisected. His other was pale and barely focused. Edwin wondered if the bloke could see properly at all.

What kind of weapon could do that kind of damage to a vampire's face that it wouldn't heal properly? It made him shudder to imagine.

"Aye, I see ya, child," the other Edwin stated.

"Have a moment to chat, then?"

The other Edwin smirked in response, a smile exactly like his own, though it was slightly cock-eyed due to his grievous wound. "Always a moment for you, wanker." His voice was of a lower, rougher octave, a heavy smoker's voice, and much of his accent was gone, Edwin noted. Worn away by the years.

Old Edwin smiled, but he was so starved looking, his teeth looked feral and the metallic crowns in his mouth glinted.

"Handsome arsehole, ain't ya?" Edwin persisted.

"Pretty boy," Old Edwin countered. "You're fat and soft. You should get your hands dirty sometime, child."

Edwin laughed at their banter.

"I've missed that," Old Edwin stated. "Your humor. Our humor."

"No humor where you come from?"

"Where do you think I come from?"

Edwin considered. "The Wasp Machine?" It was the only logical answer he could come up with. He knew from experience that Foxley's machine could produce facsimiles of people.

Old Edwin slowly shook his head. "The future."

"Bloody hell. Really?"

"Aye."

That was in no way reassuring. Was this the thing he was destined to become? This ghoulish, undead thing? "Fark," he said.

"You should laugh again. I enjoy hearing it."

"Is there no humor in the future, then?"

Old Edwin tilted his head slightly. "Terrible shortage of it, I'm afraid. You wouldn't enjoy it."

Edwin snorted. "I'd ask questions, but you being from the future, I have a feeling you know exactly what I'm wondering."

"Aye," Old Edwin answered. "We're a writer, so naturally we want the whys and wherefores." Clearing his throat, he said, "The event horizon brought us here. In my time, we've learned to harness their energy for 'skipping.' Quick transport, in layman's terms. We call them infinity holes. But we don't use them often because it's difficult to predict when they'll appear and even more difficult to be in the right position to use them. And, sometimes, they flatten a ship like a pancake just for the hell of it."

Edwin shuddered at the news. "Is that how you got all carved up?"

Old Edwin snorted and dragged a finger down his cheek, following the path of the scar. "This is a parting gift from an old and rather disagreeable friend. Least of my concerns."

Edwin closed his eyes and slowly took a deep breath. "How far...how far in the future?"

"Twenty-four-fifty-four."

He sucked in a sharp breath and did some quick math in his head. "That puts me at almost 700 years. Hell!"

"Why are you surprised? You were always a survivor. If anyone should go on forever, it would be you."

"What about Eliza? And Ollie?"

"I'm not here to talk about them."

"But are they all right?" It took him a moment to form the words. "They are alive? Unharmed?"

A darkness passed behind Old Edwin's eyes. "This will sound cruel, aye, but I can't speak of it. I made a promise to someone. Besides, they aren't important…"

Edwin felt a flare of anger. "The hell they are! Wanker, they're my family. They're important to me!"

Old Edwin never flinched. "Then accept that I can't talk about them. If I do, it may upset events, and certain things must come to pass. I can't risk it."

Edwin opened his mouth to take…well, himself to task, but before he could, Old Edwin snapped his jaws in irritation, surprising him. "I am telling you this and asking that you trust me, child. I am asking that you trust yourself. Understand?"

Slowly, very slowly, Edwin nodded.

"Many years in the future, you decided this was the way it must be. This was the path. Trust I have your best interests at heart." Suddenly, Old Edwin looked sympathetic. Softly, he added, "There are things that cannot change. And there are things you must not change."

Edwin sighed and covered his eyes as he considered his approach to this. It was going to be difficult, but he decided to bite his tongue on the matter. If Old Edwin—god, he was a wreck—had decided that this should be the way, there had to be a reason for it. "Can I at least ask if you have done all you can for our family?"

Old Edwin snorted. "What do you think?"

It was a foolish question. "Aye, of course."

Old Edwin sighed. "Child, we can stand here all night getting into a bit of barney, but I think you should trust my words—trust what I have to say."

"Aye, but..."

"There should be no feelings of guilt on your part. You—we—have always done what we can for those under our protection. And now I am trying to ensure the worst of it never comes to pass."

Edwin, utterly confused, nodded.

"Listen," Old Edwin explained, his voice soft but dire, "Me Enforcer and I can only stay for a short time and then you must let us go so we can take our ship back across the skip. I have people—your people—waiting for me over yonder." His one working eye softened as he squinted at his younger self. "Fark. You're so young. So beautiful and...untouched. So full of life. I'd forgotten those things."

"You look old," Edwin blurted out. "Tired."

"Much has come to pass." Old Edwin frowned a long moment before adding, "You will be tested, child. It will not be easy, but if you focus, you will make it through the dark. You have to remember that. This is not the beginning of the end. This is the return to who you are."

"What does that even mean?"

"It means that one day soon you will need to dig deep...to be the Devil, the Prince of Hell, once more."

Edwin shook his head. Not that. He'd left that persona ages ago...

Old Edwin ignored his reaction. He asked for the date, and when Edwin gave it to him, he swore under his breath. "Bloody close, that is." Leaning against the bars, he said, "Listen closely. The Nothing has already begun to awaken." When he saw that Edwin didn't follow, he explained, "The Darkness. The Source from which all of the vampires spring. It has begun to move, to corrupt the vampire race."

Edwin scowled in confusion. Maybe his twelve hundred-year-old brain was blinkered? "I don't understand. The Nothing? The Source?"

"The God of Vampires," Old Edwin said, both voice and face grim. "The Nothing has been dead asleep under the K2 Mountains for millions of years—for all of human and most of Fae history, in fact."

"The K2? How did it get there?"

"They weren't mountains in the time when the Fae warrior Rark and his braves put the creature down. That came later. But, regardless, the thing you need to know is that it was never fully dead and has been waking up for years—perhaps hundreds of them. I don't understand the mechanics all that well. However..." Old Edwin paused to think. "As it comes fully awake, it will find itself insatiable like a vamp rising from a fugue. And the vampires that are its children will respond."

Edwin felt his clockwork heart trip in that way that told him he believed what he was hearing. He believed the old, war-torn Edwin, completely and instinctively. His mind jumped around for a moment before he blurted, "You sent that message. 'The stars are our destiny.'"

Old Edwin nodded and clutched the bars of the birdcage. "I couldn't risk you shooting me out of the sky before I had a chance to tell you what was coming."

"Which is, exactly?"

"The end of this world."

Edwin noted how gaunt Old Edwin's hand was, how long his fingernails were. His hands resembled the claws of some reptile.

"Pay close attention, child. This is important and we are going to move fast now. All of the vampires are ultimately connected through the Seven. You understand this?"

"I had the suspicion, aye. The bloodlines."

Old Edwin nodded. "And the Seven ultimately go back to the Source—the Nothing. The Nothing is activating those bloodlines and turning the vampires all over the world into walking weapons. It's already begun, and you should be hearing reports about incidents soon."

Edwin was about to ask for details, but Old Edwin went on quickly. "Imagine those Sleepwalkers we fought…only a thousand times stronger and more feral. Once the Nothing takes hold, the vampires will wipe every human off the Earth. A worldwide feeding frenzy. A dead world where the vamps will eventually turn on each other until there is no life left at all on this ol' globe."

Edwin blinked at his other self, a dull shock passing through his body. "Shite. Is that the war you've been fighting?" He knew the answer to that, so he went on with, "Right, then…how have you stayed…you? Why aren't you—we—affected?"

"I never learned the answer to that. Perhaps it is because of our specific bloodline. No one of the Chrysanthos line seems affected."

"And you never learned why?"

Old Edwin shook his head. "I only know you need to kill the Nothing before it wakes. And you will need a very specific weapon to do that."

"Ah, so, a MacGuffin."

Old Edwin laughed hoarsely at that. He had to clear his throat. "I'd forgotten. We used to write books. It's been so long." He grinned his metallic grin and seemed to go to some other place briefly. "I miss the simpler days when all we had to worry about was bloody Foxley's latest interference."

Before Edwin could inquire about the weapon, his double cleared his throat and explained, "To defeat the Nothing, you need to wield a weapon as voracious as it is. You will need a krsnik."

Edwin fell silent for a long moment. "A vampire that eats other vampires."

"That's correct."

A peculiar horror began to filter into him, turning his mouth bitter. Growling low, he said, "I won't use Oliver if that's what you're thinking."

"If not him, then another. You should speak to the High Council about that. They have many agents and may have what you need."

"That's a big ask, old man. They aren't my biggest fan, as you probably remember."

"I didn't say it would be easy. But...you need to move quickly. Convince them to give you the weapon you need and then fly to the K2 Mountains to engage the Nothing. If you can neutralize it..." Edwin stopped and gave him a dark look. "Perhaps the future I must return to won't be quite so grim."

* * *

Oliver had only ever had two dates previously. The first had been his high school prom. He'd taken his childhood friend Ariel as his date. Ariel had been stood up by her date and Oliver, who felt bad for her but hadn't planned on even attending prom until he learned of Ariel's situation, asked to be her escort because he knew how much she was hurting over the breakout.

"Not like a real date or anything," he added and then wondered if he had hurt Ariel's feelings by saying that.

But she threw herself at him, hung her arms about his neck, and kissed his cheek. "Thanks, Ollie! You are so sweet. You are my hero!"

He laughed at that. "That's what I do. I rescue you."

They had grown up together on the *Queen's Gambit*. He had protected her when the Jotnar attacked the ship. Ariel hadn't stopped being his number-one fan since.

The prom was incredibly boring, though, and full of people he never liked or understood. After half an hour, he and Ariel took a lift to the Bazaar, winding up at a kid's playground where they used to play when they were younger. They enjoyed the swings and jungle gym and took pics. Oliver took a million pictures of Ariel in her prom dress. She was deploying for boot camp At Fort Drum in just one week, and he wanted to have a bunch of 3D slides to play when he grew lonely at college.

"You should come with me. I think you'd make a great military man—a great pilot," Ariel insisted. She waved her hands around. "You have mad skills."

Oliver laughed at that. Truthfully, he'd considered a military career, but he was too afraid his fellow soldiers would learn what he was and turn on him.

His second date was a few months ago. He'd met a guy online and they decided to get something to eat at a café on campus. The boy was cute and smart, but over the course of their meal, he commented on how many Black students there were and how "those kinds of people always managed to get in."

"My mother is Black," Oliver blurted out, hurt by the comment.

The guy laughed somewhat awkwardly. "Well, I'm not talking about her. Or you. You're not like them."

"What do you mean?"

"Well, for one thing, you don't look Black."

Confused, Oliver couldn't form a witty response for a long moment. "But...I am Black," he finally said. "I'm half Black."

"You're not getting my meaning."

"What meaning?" He stood up suddenly, enraged. "That you're a bigoted asshole?"

Well, that was the end of date number two. After that, Oliver decided it probably wasn't worth his time. People were weird, and a lot of them were also horrible. He didn't understand them at all.

What if Jonah was like that boy? What if Jonah said something really stupid?

He didn't know how people coped with being let down so much of the time.

He dressed nicely for their date—a button-down shirt and slacks, but nothing that made him look too stiff, he hoped. He even left his braids loose instead of tying them back in a ponytail like he did for class. What if Jonah didn't like his Black hair? Well, then, he wasn't worth his time.

The café where they were meeting was the same one where he had met the previous boy. That worried him. But as soon as he got there, Jonah stood up and waved him over.

"I wasn't sure if you would show."

"I said I was coming," Oliver told him.

Jonah nodded. "You always do exactly what you say you will, don't you, Oliver? And you say exactly what you mean."

Jonah's statement annoyed him. He didn't like it when Jonah talked like he was analyzing him and the ways he was different from others. It made him feel like an experiment. Then he remembered that Jonah was in the psychology program, so maybe that was why he acted like that.

Oliver looked over the menu but nothing caught his eye. He wriggled around uncomfortably. Several other students glanced his way. Whenever he walked into a room, people looked. It was incredibly rude.

When he muttered about that, Jonah responded with, "They think you're cute. That's why they look." He added more softly, "You really don't know how beautiful you are, do you?"

"They shouldn't stare."

Jonah gave him a sympathetic look. "Do you want to get out of here?"

"Aye."

Jonah closed his menu. "You can come back to my place and I could cook for you, unless you think that's too forward."

"I like your place."

Jonah's smile grew. "Well, it's settled then!"

Back at Jonah's dorm room, Oliver felt more comfortable in the cozy, private environment. He looked around, spending some time watching the rabbits while Jonah asked him what he wanted for dinner.

"I like hamburgers," Oliver admitted.

Jonah nodded and pulled down a frying pan from a shelf over the stove. "Rare or medium rare?"

"Rare. Two minutes on each side."

Jonah laughed. "You don't fool around, do you? You know exactly what you like."

Oliver smiled a little goofily at that.

From the kitchenette, Jonah said, "So, what kind of a Supe are you?" When Oliver didn't immediately answer, he added, "Are you a werewolf? You have that rangy build of a werewolf. And the appetite of one, too!"

"I'm not a werewolf. My Uncle Malcolm is, though."

"You have an uncle who's a werewolf?"

"He's not really my uncle. He was my dad's Enforcer before he quit."

"Are you a vampire?" Jonah mused as he banged around the kitchenette, but then corrected himself. "No, I've seen you in the daylight off campus where there are no UV shields." After a pause, Jonah said in a hushed voice, "Are you Fae?"

Oliver looked away from the rabbits, wondering how much he could trust Jonah. "I don't know what I am."

"Really?"

As soon as the hamburgers were done, Oliver wolfed his down. Jonah watched him from across the bar, looking amused.

"What happened to your rabbit?" Oliver said suddenly, afraid that Jonah would continue to ask questions about what he was.

"What do you mean?"

"You have a rabbit missing."

"Oh! You noticed." Jonah held up his half-eaten hamburger. "How do you think I made the burgers?"

Oliver stopped eating and stared at him.

Jonah laughed. "I'm joshing, Oliver! I took him to see a doctor. He wasn't eating."

"Oh, aye." Oliver felt the tension drain from his shoulders.

"I can ring you tomorrow and let you know how he is if you're interested."

"I hope your rabbit gets better."

Jonah nodded and watched him closely. "You're sweet."

Oliver felt his cheeks burn at the compliment. He was a little annoyed by his date's well-meaning compliment. He didn't want to seem "sweet." His mum thought he was sweet.

He wanted to be normal. A regular person.

Jonah's eyebrows crashed inward. "Sorry. Didn't mean to embarrass you."

"Right. I don't mind it so much when you say it."

"I may be wrong, though. Maybe you're not entirely sweet?"

Oliver had no idea what he was talking about, so when Jonah got up and came around the bar. Leaning down, Jonah ran a thumb across Oliver's face, wiping away a little dot of ketchup before tilting his head up slightly. He leaned in. Their lips touched and Oliver felt that flutter deep inside of himself again. It made him moan and smile.

"That's what I suspected," Jonah said when he finally came up for air. "You act like a pussycat, but you have a tiger inside of you. I can tell."

Oliver laughed at that—laughed at the visual of a tiger inside his body.

Jonah took Oliver's hand and pulled him up. Pulled him close. Jonah kissed him again, much deeper this time. Jonah's tongue slid into Oliver's mouth. It sent chilling shockwaves through Oliver's body. At the same time, Jonah rubbed the palm of Oliver's hand, which had healed completely at that point. The points of sensation lit Oliver's whole body up.

Reaching out, Oliver slid a cautious hand over Jonah's shoulder before moving upward and grasping his soft blond hair. He liked the softness of it. He kissed Jonah back, hard...harder. Carefully. He kept waiting for his body to react the wrong way. To change. Maybe for that frightening darkness to fill his eyes as it had when he was little and he became afraid.

Oliver wasn't as naïve as most people thought. He'd read about sex. And he knew all kinds of things happened to vamps when they were sexually aroused. They could become incredibly dangerous. Not for the first time, he wondered how his dad didn't hurt his mum. He wished he could talk to Lord Edwin about these things, about being a vampire, but he knew it would be awkward for them both.

What if he hurt Jonah? But his body, though full of delightful shivers, didn't do anything strange. That was a relief.

When Jonah finally drew back, he smiled.

"I'd like to spend the night with you, Oliver."

"Aye. Right."

Jonah laughed at his response. "Is that a yes, Oliver?"

"Ollie. You can call me Ollie."

Jonah, his smile sweet and hungry, tightened his hold on Oliver's hand and led him away to the bedroom. Oliver followed like a happy little puppy.

| viii |

When Edwin stepped out of the brig, Eliza immediately noted his face. He looked paler than usual, with lines drawn deep across his face that she'd never seen before. "What happened?" she asked as she joined her.

He shook his head. "I don't even know where to begin, love. That man...Old Edwin?" He sighed. "I'll explain everything in a briefing. But first, I need to make a call. Will you meet me in my office in an hour?"

She touched his arm. "Of course."

He looked like he might instruct her to not go in there, but in the end, he just gave her a nod and headed for the lifts at the end of the corridor. She waited until he was gone before turning back to the door and knocking politely.

The Warden let her in. She expected the huge Mechi to say she wasn't allowed to see the prisoners, but he merely looked her over, bowed his head, and said, "Milady."

"I'd like to see him please." She tensed herself for the inevitable. Surely, he would tell her no one was allowed in the brig but Lord Edwin—that Edwin had issued that order.

But the Warden surprised her. "If it pleases my Lady. Do you wish for an escort?"

She hesitated, wondering if this was wise. "No, that's all right. I can manage. Thank you, Warden."

Another bow and the Warden stepped aside.

The door to the containment unit irised open and Eliza stepped through. She stopped, glancing around the unfamiliar space. It was dimly lit with runner lights, but she could see well enough. She started down the long corridor to the last cell on the right, the one she'd seen was holding the prisoners on the monitor screens in the control room.

Her heart started banging painfully hard as she approached the bars of the cell. She couldn't seem to tear her eyes off the other Edwin. Old Edwin, as her Edwin called him.

He quickly turned his head when he spied her.

She moved her lips but it took a moment for the words to come. "Edwin? Is it really you?"

She saw the huge Mechi Enforcer shift to follow her movements.

"Edwin...or whoever you are...please," she begged. "Talk to me."

He squared his shoulders and turned to face her.

He was so painfully gaunt that it hurt her to look upon him. Still, the grey hair, damaged eye, and the scars on his face couldn't erase who he was. She recognized the handsome, chaotic Gaelic vampire she had fallen in love with and married. But, Christ, he looked weary beyond words.

"Oh my god, Edwin," she whispered.

He looked past her or above her but wouldn't meet her gaze.

"Edwin, look at me, please."

After a moment, he said in a surprisingly coarse voice, "It's...difficult."

She realized he was mostly blind, and she felt her heart clench like a tight fist inside of her chest. "What happened to you? Who did this to you?"

He tried on a soft smile, and for one moment he almost looked like the Edwin she knew. But something was off. Something had changed in him. He looked so...dark. "Don't worry about me, lovey."

"I can't help but worry."

"I'm fine. Alive, as you can see."

"Barely." She started to cry.

"Eliza, please..." Edwin insisted. "You should go."

Eliza rubbed at her eyes with the back of her hand and said, "Tell me what happened to you and I will. Where do you come from?"

"Not this place. A future place."

She stared in horror. "This...this is your future? Our future? What about Oliver? Edwin, talk to me!"

Pain clouded his one working eye. "I can't, love. No one here must know too much about the future. Knowing certain things could upset the balance of everything. I can't risk it."

"Upset them more than they are?"

He drew back at her outburst.

They eyed each other for several seconds, neither of them speaking. A thought occurred to her and she shook her head, sadder for him than for herself. "I'm not going to make it, am I? I won't see the end of this...whatever this is."

She could see him struggling to talk—to not talk. In the end, his resolve held. He said not a word.

"I'm not worried about that, you know," she told him. "I've had amazing adventures with you and Ollie, so I have no regrets even if it does end. I'm more worried about you. And about our son." She wrenched back on her tears. "Can you tell me about him at least?" He just looked sad, beaten. "I'm sorry, love. No."

Honestly, she'd had all she could of Old Edwin and this whole horrible situation. Edwin should have barred her. He should have forbid her from ever speaking to his other self. Turning, Eliza fled to the door of the brig.

* * *

Edwin had his secretary send a request to the Sacred Seven for an emergency session. There was no time to waste and it would need to be a virtual meeting. He then immediately retreated to his personal quarters to change for the engagement—which, naturally, meant wearing all the horrible red robes for the second time this week.

As Lord, he had assistants who could dress him if he wanted to, but he preferred Eliza's help. It gave them a chance to discuss his strategy before he met with the High Council of Reptiles, as Eliza called them. She always brought an interesting perspective to every situation.

As soon as Eliza arrived to help him, he knew she had been to visit the prisoners. He sighed and turned away, looking up at the ridiculous robes with their long, flowing sleeves hanging from his closet door. Probably he should have forbade her from seeing them. He could have told the Warden to bar her. But he wasn't in the business of telling his Bride what to do. He trusted she knew what she could handle emotionally.

But maybe he should have intervened this one time.

She looked pale and haggard like she'd been through a war. He could tell she'd been crying. To her credit, she had dried her eyes and cooled her face before she arrived. Her eyes were bright and shiny but determined.

"Pretty strange, aye?" he asked her.

"Terrifying." She reached for the robes he would need. They buttoned at the back with two hundred small toggles that required a button hook. It was a completely impractical outfit, but one the council wouldn't update. They were too set in their ways.

"Did you read the summary I sent you?" he asked as she went to work on the buttons. He now wished he hadn't sent it to her.

"The Nothing? And some war the world is fighting?"

He nodded and watched in the full-length mirror as she worked. She was concentrating on the buttons, her face a storm. "Do you think this is for real? Not some illusion or trick of the council's. Something Chimera cooked up?"

"I think it's real. It feels real to me."

She swore under her breath, something Eliza rarely did. Bit by bit, he watched her stand up straighter and grow more determined. The shock was wearing off and she was going into survival mode.

He turned so she could add the Puritan-like ruff to the front of the robe. As she finished preparing him, she said, "You realize you're going to have to go in like a bull in a china shop and request this krsnik you need. It's your privilege to request agents of the High Courts. Even I know that. That's how Foxley was able to hire Chimera to come after you all those years ago." She paused. "They can't deny you the request."

He reached up and touched her cheek. "I'll do my best, lovey."

* * *

Turned out, he was right to be concerned.

During the meeting, which was held in a virtual room wherein the Seven were seated on a circular white sofa, facing each other, a tranquil noontime forest surrounding them—Edwin explained the urgency of the matter, but Lord Trasch was unmoved. "You own a krsnik, Lord Edwin. Why do you need one of ours?"

Edwin bristled. "I don't own Oliver, Trasch. He's my son. And I'm not sending him to fight the Nothing."

Trasch smiled venomously, showing off his long, discolored teeth. "You are asking that I risk one of our agents for your endeavor, but you won't even consider sending your own?"

"It's not my endeavor. This will affect everyone here. My older self said the Nothing will infect all of the vampires. That will wipe out the human race."

Lord Endicott shrugged. "I say we adopt a wait-and-see position. After all, we no longer need the humans as a source of food."

Edwin gave Endicott a sharp look. "Mate, according to Old Edwin, the Nothing will turn us all into raving animals. Sleepwalkers." He narrowed his eyes at the vampire's flippancy. "And if that happens, you can bet the humans will retaliate. They've been waiting for centuries for a reason to wipe us all out."

He saw the others considering that, and a few even nodded. Good. He was getting them where it hurt. They might not care much for humans, but they didn't want the flow of their undead lives upset by humans gunning for vampires.

Trasch waved his hand dismissively. "Send your krsnik. And if he fails, I will send one of mine."

"No, Trasch, Lord Edwin makes a good point," Lady Kai interrupted, and Trasch turned his low-key burning eyes on her. "Little Lord Oliver doesn't have the fighting skills necessary to take on this kind of challenge. Sending him now would be a waste of his potential, whereas your pet krsnik Samara can actually fight."

She noticed him flinch that she should know that.

"She is not my p—" he began, but Kai had already turned to address the others. "I vote we send Samara to face the Nothing, and, failing that, we consider other options."

The other members of the family started discussing it. Meanwhile, Lady Kai tossed Edwin a private wink. Thank God for small favors, busybody vamps who knew everyone's business, and big libidos. He knew if Kai wasn't so hot to get into his pants, she wouldn't be allying herself with him this way. He also knew it would cost him in the future. But Kai supporting his motion meant that at least it could advance to the floor for serious consideration.

A vote was taken, and Samara was chosen. Edwin was surprised by how quickly it all happened. All of the vamps except Trasch and Lord Adrastas—an ancient vampire of Hungarian origins that was thought to have been the inspiration for Abraham Stoker's book—voted that Samara be assigned the job. But Edwin expected opposition from Adrastas. The chap was, at present, in an alliance with Trash. Still, Edwin was pleasantly surprised to encounter no real resistance. Even Endicott, whom he always felt had it out for him, agreed to the motion.

Trasch, a born diplomat, didn't even blink at Edwin's minor victory. "I should probably inform you that Samara is no longer a part of my Court, nor does she take my orders. "

Well, that was news.

"Thus, you will need to formally contract her for the work." He smiled drily. "The last I heard, she was currently doing wetwork for the Red Door resistance down in Poppettown."

Edwin glowered. "Why would she do that?"

Kai tapped the side of her nose. "She has expensive habits."

"Blow?" Edwin wasn't unduly impressed by the news. He owned the *Oublies*, the largest for-profit supermax for Supes in the world. His accumulative wealth was only second to Foxley. Whatever Samara's price—or vice—he knew he could cover it. Buy her services, as it were.

Several of the others developed wry smiles on their faces, but it was Trasch who answered with: "Twilight."

"It's blow made from the powdered marrow of vampires' bones," Kai supplied.

Edwin's eyes widened at that. "She gets off on that?"

Kai shrugged in a What can you do? gesture.

"Keep her in vice and you might get her attention," Trasch said and smiled dubiously. "But the real trick is in whether you can actually control her."

Well, hell!

* * *

Olive, on waking in a dark, unfamiliar place, sat up suddenly. He was momentarily disoriented. He had no idea how he had gotten here, and, for half a second after he'd opened his eyes, he was certain someone was sitting in the chair in the corner of the room—a tall, dark, manlike shadow with faintly glowing white eyes.

The Walking Man...

He focused all his attention on the spot, which gradually came into soft focus. But, after a moment, he realized it was just a used easy chair with a pile of laundry piled on it.

He knew he wasn't back at his apartment because he didn't do things like that. He was meticulous in that everything had its place and he always put things back where they belonged after he used them. There was never any clutter or disarray. It was how he kept from becoming overwhelmed.

This was Jonah's place. He remembered now.

He thought he glimpsed motion from the tail of his eye and jumped up on the bed, landing on his hands and knees in one fluid motion and without even rocking the mattress. His breathing was rapid but nearly silent. He recalled his half-remembered dream. He was a child again, wandering through the eerily quiet, barely lit corridors of the gyro where he grew up. Runner lights flickered or were too dim to discern shadows. Someone—or something—was behind him, keeping pace with him. Something that was silently hunting him.

The Walking Man?

But he hadn't sighted the ghost that haunted his parents' ship since he was very young. He never told anyone about him, thinking no one would believe him. Bracing himself, Oliver turned slowly to glance at the amorphous lump lying under the covers beside him. It shifted slightly, and he recognized Jonah lying on his belly, clutching the pillow and snoring heavily. He let out his breath in relief.

Unbunching his muscles and relaxing his body, Oliver crawled closer to Jonah and looked his sleeping lover over. He looked so sweet and vulnerable lying there. He licked his lips at the memory of their first time.

It had been…amazing. Jonah told Oliver he was gorgeous and amazing and sexy as hell. He couldn't seem to stop pulling him down for kiss after kiss. Oliver groaned at the memory of every touch and taste.

They'd had only one bad moment.

"What are you?" Jonah asked, interrupting their lovemaking, which annoyed Oliver immensely. He wanted to keep kissing and touching Jonah, finding places that made him gasp and his eyes roll up in his head.

When Oliver didn't answer his question, Jonah put a hand on Oliver's chest and gave him a demanding look. "I have a right to know, Ollie, in case it affects me in some way. Werewolf? Fae? You have to give me a clue here, darling."

Jonah was right. Sex meant different things to different species of Supes. After winding up the courage, he said, "I'm half-vampire." He hoped that would be enough.

No such luck. Jonah's pale blue eyes only grew large in his handsome face. "Wow. I've never heard of such a thing. How does that work?"

"My father is a vampire and my mother isn't." But Oliver saw that Jonah wasn't satisfied with his answer. Frustrated he sat back against the pillows and added, "I don't know how it happened. No doctor can explain it."

"So your mother is a human."

"A Poppet."

That fascinated Jonah almost more than anything. "Your mother is your father's Poppet?"

"They're married." Oliver didn't like anyone talking about his mum like she was property. "She's my dad's Bride. Not his Poppet."

Jonah held up his hands. "Sorry, didn't mean to offend. It's just a little odd." He gave Oliver a sympathetic look. "So...you being half a vampire...does that mean you can mark your lovers? Make Brides?"

"I don't know. I never tried."

"Would you mark me if I asked?"

"No. I could hurt you."

"You could only hurt me if your teeth were human. But you have vampire teeth, and sharp teeth won't hurt as much."

Oliver squirmed. "Why do you say that?"

Jonah laughed. "I was literally inside your mouth, silly. And you have some impressive chompers there, let me tell you."

That made Oliver blush. "Why would you want to be my Bride? It's stupid."

Jonah rolled his eyes. "A hot vampire boyfriend? Do I need to spell it out for you?" Pushing himself up, he ran a hand through Oliver's long braids. "You're cute when you blush. And you blush a lot. But you don't need to be embarrassed, Ollie. I want you to mark me. Right here."

He indicated the spot, not on his neck, which would be potentially dangerous, but at the base of his throat a few inches under his Adam's apple. Jonah rubbed the spot. "I'd like your kiss mark here."

The request made Oliver uncomfortable. He could hurt Jonah. But after some encouragement, they experimented with Oliver making a shallow bite wound. "Oh...that is...oh..." Jonah sighed. He was nestled against a large pile of pillows and shuddered from the way Oliver was licking at the first crimson drops.

Jonah's blood hit Oliver's system like a shock of red energy. It lit up his senses and sizzled along his nerve endings. It was similar to how he'd felt when he took the Concerta back before his body grew used to the brief high. Oliver drank only a little of his blood, but the intimacy they shared afterward was the most intense experience that Oliver had ever had. It left him writhing on the bed and dragging tears in Jonah's sheets.

Now, as Oliver looked down upon the sweet boy lying so helplessly on the bed beside him, he thought about jumping on him, tasting him again. Oliver leaned in, drawn to the scene of Jonah's skin, but then stopped. Jonah was sleeping, and it would be wrong to take him like that.

Jumping off the bed, Oliver slipped on his pants and retreated to the bathroom, closing and locking the door behind him—a good, solid barrier between him and temptation.

He didn't turn on the light. He didn't need to. In the mirror over the sink, his eyes looked dark and blasted, his pupils so dilated they filled his whole irises. Dark arteries twined under his skin. And when he licked his teeth, his tongue, incredibly long and fiercely rough, scraped along his teeth.

He stuck it out. It looked far too dark to be normal and little spines stood at attention. He quickly closed his mouth, a distant fear nipping at him. But even so...

Hungry. He was so very hungry...

So very...Dim.

Reaching into the little side pocket in his pants, he withdrew the small packet of crushed-up Concerta he carried at all times. He studied the pink powder inside, gauging its weight. He would need to talk to Pierce's guy tomorrow. He sprinkled some onto the back of his hand and sniffed it up, letting it go to his head and make it swim in soft, gentle colors until he was happy and Bright again.

He stuck his tongue out. It was only a tongue. No spines.

He was no danger to Jonah, he told himself. Only then did he exit the bathroom and return to bed.

| ix |

Over the course of his unnaturally long life, Jonathan Trasch had not been given many opportunities to follow his own path. He was born in 1665 in the City of Boston, the capital of the Massachusetts Bay Colony, the son of the Reverend Richard Trasch. Both of his grandfathers were prominent Protestant ministers who played major roles in the establishment and growth of the colony. All of the men in his family were college educated, and Richard Trasch (also known as "the Reverend") served his whole life as the faithful minister of the Anglican Old North Church of Paul Revere fame.

So Jonathan Trasch was born into one of the most influential and intellectually distinguished families in colonial New England. Naturally, he was expected to follow in his father and grandfather's footsteps and give himself over to the clergy. To not do so would have been unthinkable.

The problem was that Jonathan was not a Believer. In his heart of hearts, he believed in the religion of science, not the dogmatic fables of his forefathers, whom he saw as little better than superstitious primitives. Of course, he couldn't say such things to his family. Such talk would earn him the switch. Thus, he learned early on to keep his own counsel on most matters. He was a bright boy and entered Harvard College at the age of twelve, the youngest up to that point to do so. He also had a stutter and was ruthlessly bullied by the larger boys, but for the sake of making his father proud, he endured it.

He had an intense interest in and a talent for the medicine of his time, a still controversial subject among his peers. He even considered the possibility of pursuing a career as a physician rather than a religious minister. But when his father asked him to switch his course of studies to theology, he did so without complaint. It was important to him that his father be proud.

After completing his education, Jonathan was ordained and joined his father's church as assistant pastor. But his desire to please the Reverend did not end there. There was also Maria. Even though he had never met the girl, when his father arranged his marriage at the age of sixteen to his thirteen-year-old cousin who hailed from the Rhode Island colony, he readily agreed to the contract. He didn't love Maria, of course, but he hoped that love would come as it had for his mother, who had experienced a similar arrangement with his father when she was only twelve.

And finally, when his father demanded he produce male heirs, he did so without objection, impregnating the young girl as often as he could. He hoped these things would make his father truly happy with him.

Maria bore Jonathan five daughters before delivering him a son at the age of 19—a boy that caused her death in childbirth. Not long after, three of his daughters were taken by a smallpox epidemic that culled many of the members of their small village. His son died not long after when an irate bull accidentally broke out of its pen and gored the child, who was playing nearby. Of his two remaining daughters, one died after falling into a creek and was swept downstream. The other asked to be sent away to her cousin's estate in London, a fateful journey that would end in ruin when the ship was dashed to bits on the coastal rocks of Land's End in Cornwall.

After learning of his last child's death, Jonathan returned to the parish house on the outskirts of the colony and engaged in bouts of excessive drinking that went on for days. He cursed his fate and he cursed his God. Richard visited his son, consoling him with words of wisdom and a hand on his shoulder. He told Jonathan that, like Job, it was all God's will and that this, too, would pass. The elder Trasch would even see to it that a new wife was found posthaste. He would scour the other colonies for the strongest stock. She would be just as young as Maria and extremely robust, capable of delivering him many sons.

"All is not lost, my child," the Reverend intoned over him in the voice that had brought him respect and admiration from his parishioners for decades.

Grunting at the news, Jonathan got up from his seat at the kitchen trestle, retrieved a long boning knife from the shed where they slaughtered hogs in season, and used it to carve his father's heart out of his chest, all whilst the elder was still alive. He then threw his father's body into a ditch in a field where the hogs were penned. The next day, a milkmaid found the remains. Richard Trasch, who had to be identified by his clothing, was pronounced dead, his demise listed as "death by misadventure" by the village elders.

This, unfortunately, left Jonathan in a precarious position. With no one to minister to the colony, he was forced to take his father's position prematurely. It was an interesting twist of irony that he found himself forced to comfort the people distraught by his father's untimely death—the villagers he ultimately hated with all of his core being. It was his wish that someone else would step up, or some other clergyman would be sent from another colony, but no one arrived to relieve him. The village wanted Jonathan as their pastor. For whatever reason, they even seemed to like him.

And so, Jonathan Trasch became his own jailor. Several other plagues swept through the village over the years, but, in a series of ironic twists, he survived them all even though he was constantly exposed and didn't care if he lived or died. His dream of being a physician, of writing books on medicine, and of interacting with his peers, slowly died, replaced by the sleepwalking monotony of everyday life as the village Father Confessor.

He never remarried, though he did dally with the village women when he was visited upon by the urge—always older women, and always married. Women with no hope of attaching themselves to him. And if those women became heavy with his child, he simply visited the tribes of Indians that normally kept their distance from the colony and bought herbs for homemade abortifacients that he mixed himself, not unsuccessfully.

He became a well-respected member of the colony. Men sought his counsel. Women seemed to like him even though he was quite often cruel to them. He had learned long ago that it was people's pain, their horror, and their revulsion, that pleased him the most. And it was what they wanted.

During the Salem witch trials, carried out over the brutal winter of 1693, the village elders asked him to sit on the bench of judgment to hear the women's pleas and even to examine the accused witches for the Devil's marks. He sent several of his more relentless lovers to the gallows.

Jonathan frequently cursed his luck. Despite the terrible uproar of the trials and the fallout afterward, he remained infuriatingly untouched. He was cleared of all charges and went on to live an unusually long life, falling ill of pneumonia at the advanced (for his time) age of sixty-six—though of course years of hard living, near-constant starvation, and misery caused him to look much older. That winter, he knew he was dying, and he even welcomed it.

All in all, his had been a miserable life. The New World was a lie, and he had seen little beyond death, disease, and starvation. He had never gotten to do anything he wanted to do with his life. Every step on his personal and professional path had been dictated by the needs and whims of others. He only hoped that after death, there was nothing but a yawning, empty abyss there to consume him. He had no desire to face any god or answer for any part of his many sins.

While he was on the very trembling edge of death, a young clergyman visited him in his bedroom to speak to him and offer comfort. At first, Jonathan thought this must be his replacement, but he immediately recognized the young man as something more than human. He was exceedingly pale and gaunt, and his eyes glowed faintly (and greedily) in the dimness of the closed-up, stuffy room. Jonathan recognized him for what he was, but he never reached for the cross on his bedside table or the Bible in the drawer. He'd never really believed in any of that rubbish anyway, and he knew it had no real effect on vampires, who might as well be from the stars.

"What do you want?" the dying Jonathan Trasch croaked out of his parched and shriveled throat. He wished his dying would hurry itself up but it seemed to be taking forever.

The creature smiled to show off his inhuman set of saber teeth. They looked nearly metallic in the near dark, and they reminded Jonathan of some reptile's grin—soulless and empty.

"I am here at the behest of one of your victims," the vampire told him plainly, turning to close the bedroom door so they were alone—entombed together. The vampire put each of the candles in the room out with a candle snuffer, working slowly to make the room dimmer and dimmer while he explained the reasons for his appearance.

An old woman in the village had begged the vampire to visit Jonathan whilst he was on his deathbed and repay him for the sins Jonathan had committed against her daughter some years prior. "The old crone gave me her own body and her blood as payment that I should 'repay your kindness,' as she put it."

"She hired you."

"Aye."

"Who was she?"

"Do you care, Reverend?"

Jonathan thought about that. "Nay." He coughed and his body rattled like an old sack of loose bones. Did it really matter?

The vampire returned to his bedside. He spread his clawed hand over Jonathan's chest. He ripped the blankets and even Jonathan's night shift away with supernatural speed to reveal his grey, sunken, age-spotted chest. "The old lady asked me to visit upon your broken shell of a body all of the suffering you brought her daughter. As a result, this may take a while."

"I see." After another fit of coughing, Jonathan said, "The sun will come soon, vampire. Let us begin, then."

With a carnivorous grin, the vampire climbed upon Jonathan's weak, prone body, and sat upon him. He looked like some nightmarish incubus. He leaned down to whisper what acts he had planned for Jonathan. In the total darkness, Jonathan tasted its bloody, deathlike breath. Moth wings and grave dirt. "She told me everything you did to her daughter—every offense. And, now, all of the pain you put into her poor, shattered body shall be yours again."

The things the vampire did to him that night were terrible indeed, rough-edged and dehumanizing. It was like the mythological Devil visiting upon him the ultimate judgment. Jonathan bore it all with as much dignity as he could manage. After all, he deserved every act. He had earned it. His body was nearly finished anyway.

But, curiously enough, toward the end, he found himself begging for death.

It was only when the vampire slashed his own wrist and pressed the wound to Jonathan's quivering lips that he truly understood the living hell the creature had chosen for him. He was not to die. He was only not to live.

Not this, he thought deliriously through the waves of pain and fear twining through his failing body. No, no...dear God (or gods) no!

In life, he had committed terrible offenses. He was willing to accept that, to embrace it and whatever hell came afterward, if any. But the one thing he could not bear was to live with those things he had done forever and ever...

"Reverend Trasch," said the vampire, "I make you my Heir. I give you my blood, my body, broken for you. But I also give you my curse. Blood will not be enough," the vampire said as he slathered Jonathan's lips and forced him to swallow again and again. The black ichor filled Jonathan with darkness. It filled him with pain. It healed his broken body. But it also transformed him.

I give you my blood but also my curse. Blood will not be enough.

It filled him, ultimately, with hunger. But not even the sort of hunger that regular vampires suffered, for something was very amiss with the vampire who had chosen him. Years and decades after the curse took full effect, Jonathan only wished he could recall the name or the face of the girl he had wronged that he should bear such a heavy curse.

In life, had been given few choices—his whole life mapped out into a darkness that was perhaps always his. It was why, now, in death, he made certain he was always in control, always one step ahead of his enemies and his allies. Never again would he allow another man to set the course of his existence. And until now, no one had ever challenged his authority or threatened his power.

Then along came Lord Edwin...

"What do you want?" Lord Trasch croaked to the courier standing in the door of his private laboratory aboard his gyro, the *Asclepius*. Trasch was setting samples inside his clinical centrifuge. His goal was to isolate the nucleic acids in the DNA sample he had collected while he searched for a specific sequence. "Why are you bothering me?"

Whereas most Vampire Lords spent their days wallowing in obscene luxury and obsessing over the expansion of their power and influence, he spent most of his free time in his modernized lab, working out the secrets of vampire DNA. Genetic study and sequencing were of particular interest to him. Through it, he had been able to create Samara by remixing vampire and human DNA samples and amplifying or deleting certain genetic factors.

After he had perfected his human-vampire DNA cocktail, he'd inserted his "design embryo" into the womb of one of his Poppets. Unfortunately, gestation went on far too long, and Samara ate her way out of her host's body, though the experiment was hardly a failure. Samara, a human/vampire hybrid, had proven a valuable agent of the High Courts and was quite possibly his greatest achievement.

"Forgive me, Reverend. You asked for the latest report on Lord Edwin."

Trasch grunted as he set the centrifuge to spin. He had indeed asked. In fact, he had ongoing arrangements with a variety of agents to feed him an almost constant flow of intel. He was interested in what they had discovered. It was only that the very mention of Lord Edwin made his teeth ache in his head.

Vampires enjoyed keeping their lives static and unchanged. They were static themselves, trapped in time like an insect in amber. But Lord Edwin and his Congress lived in a permanent state of freefall. A constant evolution. It was a state very dangerous to the status quo that generally worked for Trasch and his kind. Plus, Lord Edwin was far too clever for his own good, and far too young to have control of a Congress and wield such power.

An example: At the end of every monthly meeting, the Seven used to enjoy a feeding orgy, a communal activity that promoted unity among their little family. At the same time, it helped dispose of any garbage in their Courts: aging or infirm Poppets. But when Lord Edwin found out about it, he was appalled. In only a short time, he convinced the other members of the Seven that what they were doing was both immoral and inhumane, and the others, besotted by the young Lord's youth and beauty and words, stopped making the festivities part of their monthly meetings.

Trasch disliked Lord Edwin with every cell of his unnatural being. He was young and beautiful in that way that caused everyone to lose their good sense around him. He was charming and witty, and he deliberately let others underestimate him and then struck when an enemy's back was turned.

Trasch could appreciate his technique. When he tested the little Lord by manipulating his ex-wife and upsetting his whole Congress some years earlier, he skated through the ordeal and even thumbed his nose at them all. It was the primary—and the only—reason Trasch manipulated the vote that put Lord Edwin on the High Court's Council. He wanted Lord Edwin as close to him as possible so he could observe him. Learn from him. Control the growth of his power.

I see you, Trasch often thought to himself whilst in Lord Edwin's presence. *I know you. You and I are the same.*

He stepped away from the centrifuge and motioned with one long, crooked finger to the courtier. "Come here, you."

The courtier looked aghast as if Trasch had asked him to stick his hand in a box full of hornets. He simply hovered at the door undecidedly.

"Come here, boy! I won't ask again."

Shuddering at Trasch's timbre, the young man glanced around briefly as if there might be some excuse not to do so. Failing to find one, he started forward slowly—too slowly.

Trasch moved swiftly. Due to his advanced age when he was made a vampire, his height (almost seven feet), and the long, heavy red robes he wore, onlookers consistently believed he was sluggish, even frail, but he could move as quickly and soundlessly as the wind. Before the courier could even gasp, he grabbed the man by the shoulder and dragged him close.

The courier winced at the way Trasch was gripping his arm, but Trasch didn't let up. "Give it."

The courier held very still while Trasch looked deep into his eyes. Many years ago, he had upgraded his human couriers with permanent contact lenses that copied whatever information they saw or read. He wore similar contacts that could snap a copy of that info and store it in a neural bank, making it available for him to access at his leisure and without producing a paper trail that could be traced.

After a few blinks, the download was complete. Trasch let the courier go, shoving him away so he stumbled back and almost fell. "Tell our assets I want them to continue to shadow Lord Edwin. Reports weekly...no, daily. Do you understand?"

The courier nodded. "Yes, Reverend."

"Be off with you."

Once the courier was gone, Trasch turned back to the centrifuge, but his thoughts were sufficiently scattered, and the scribblings in his notebook unreadable as a result. His head was growing increasingly heavy, and a familiar ache beat at the back of it. It had been some hours since he had last fed the curse. The energy expended for the download hadn't helped.

He pinched his nose. He was no good to his experiments in his current state. And so, leaving the lab behind, he followed the corridor to the lifts. Once inside, he used his custom-made key to take him up to his personal quarters.

The corridors were dim, quiet, and sparsely populated. He kept only a minimal number of servants to address his personal needs and those of his harem of Poppets. He had many of those, not because sex was of much interest to him these days, but because the curse was a hard mistress to satisfy.

His vision was already growing dim by the time he stepped through the Arabian-style archway and into the oda, the room set aside to house his hundreds of Poppets. The room sported Moroccan stonework and greenery that grew around the tall, arched windows. The room was vast, with tiled walls and floors—like an abattoir, easier to clean. A half dozen heated pools gurgled away. There were pillars and ivy on the walls, and even a tall waterfall that plashed down from a place on high. Unseen songbirds flitted away under the painted glass ceiling. Parts of the oda were covered in plush Persian carpets or full of cushions. There was no furniture and no walls, just a huge, open cathedral dedicated to Lord Trasch's needs. And, strewn across the floors were his Poppets, most of them resting.

A few stared up at him emptily. Speaking to any of them was pointless. Few could even feed themselves and needed to be tended to as if they were infants.

Stalking over prone bodies, his red robes dragging, he picked his way through the living carnage until he detected signs of life—a young male who had shifted to his elbows on the floor. He was new, young, not yet too damaged to recognize his master. He took one look at Trasch and tried to scramble back, but Trasch was much quicker than he was.

Liberating his giant, tattered, saw-edged wings from his robes, Trash moved faster than an eye could blink, snatched him up, and effortlessly carried the young Poppet with him to the ceiling, where he attached himself upside down like a spider, arms and wings pinning the Poppet to a painted mural of gods and monsters at war.

The Poppet clawed him but tired quickly. "Shhh..." Trasch said, soothing the creature with his voice and fingertips until he grew submissive.

He wasn't quite in the proper position, so Trasch deftly turned him about, pinning the front of his body against the painted tiles, and sank his long, painless teeth into the spot just under his skull, the place where the Cerebrospinal fluid that surrounds the brain and spinal cord of all vertebrates was the most plentiful. The sweet, colorless fluid flowed freely into his mouth, giving his darkened vision shapes and colors. It sharpened his mind for its future work. It quieted his body and soul and made him feel warm and nearly alive.

Eventually, Trasch released the Poppet, allowing him to smash to the floor far below, but by then he was mostly gone. Still clinging to the ceiling, Trasch rolled over like a great, red-robed bat and lay panting and twitching in the aftereffects of his meal, the spinal fluid jumpstarting his system in a way that was not entirely unpleasant. It reminded him of an extended orgasm. Sometimes, he had his most genius ideas after a good feeding—new concepts, vivid and almost touchable, coming to him in a steady stream.

His mind separated from his body. He reached out and tried to touch the thoughts spiraling out of him and into the shafts of light filtering through the UV-safe windows above. Glitter and dust passed like ghosts through his fingers, which were unusually long and tipped in lengthy black claws. He stared at them a good long moment, eventually formulating a plan to deal with the current crises and with Lord Edwin. He knew exactly what his next move should be.

And the one, important moving piece would involve little Lord Oliver, the krsnik.

He grinned somewhat drunkenly. He would protect the High Courts and his way of life at all costs. Lord Edwin would not win this battle any more than any other foolish creature that had ever crossed paths with Lord Trasch.

| X |

The Queen's Gambit, 17 years earlier

"Edwin, you can come into the nursery," Eliza told him. "He's not going to bite you!"

His wife was standing by the white crib with the blue bunnies pained on it in the brightly lit room she had decorated herself. Besides the crib, the furnishings were comprised of a large white dresser/baby changer, a rocking chair so she could nurse their son, book ledges on the walls so she could read to Oliver, and an antique rocking horse that Edwin had purchased at auction—the only thing he had contributed up to that point. The ceiling was painted dark blue and speckled with stars installed according to their proper constellation. They lit up when the lights were turned low.

The nursery, even now, two weeks after the birth of their son, was rather spare. Oliver came prematurely. Immediately after, he was whisked away to neonatal care in the ship's NICU, leaving Edwin and Eliza anxious and pessimistic about his fate. All evidence pointed toward their little boy living but a few weeks, and, as a result, they had put everything on hold—their lives, their hopes, and their expectations. Eliza was so distraught by the pediatrician's diagnosis that Edwin refused to fill the nursery with all of the gifts and toys he'd planned. What if Eliza's fears were realized and their son passed? If—when—he died, it would shatter her. But then she would be forced to look at what he had bought while cleaning out the room, and that would glass anything that remained.

So, Edwin opted to wait.

But Oliver surprised them both. Certainly, in the beginning, it was touch and go, but after a couple of weeks, Oliver rallied. Now, he was thriving, growing larger every day. Even the legion of doctors and specialists that Edwin hired were stumped.

"Edwin?" Eliza turned to motion to him. "You haven't properly seen him yet in his new crib."

He made himself walk across the room until he was standing by her side. He had faced down gangsters and monsters. But this was by far the most terrifying challenge he had ever endured: Fatherhood.

The last time he had looked on their son, he had lain still and quiet at the bottom of the hospital's NICU incubator, a fish-tank-looking glass unit, with wires and coils attached to his little body and his heart beating slow, too slow, according to the monitors. He looked bluish and, if not dead, then at least not real.

But the infant in the crib looked nothing like that poor little lamb. He was twice as large, ruddy-faced, with a shock of tangly black hair exactly like Eliza's.

Their son's startling blue eyes were fixed on Eliza with an intensity that was disconcerting. They followed the flashing of the scarab-shaped key around her neck, the one she used to wake Edwin every morning. "Aren't you the most handsome boy ever?" Eliza cooed, lifting her son up from his nap.

Oliver immediately reached out a little hand to grab the metal key and put a corner of it in his mouth. He sucked ravenously and Eliza laughed. "I just fed him an hour ago but he's always hungry! Sometimes, I think he would drink me dry if I let him."

Her statement made Edwin queasy. Truthfully, this wasn't the first time he was looking in on their son. Yesterday, while Eliza was resting, he crept into the nursery and reached down to lift his new son into his arms but then hesitated. Oliver was watching him strangely, and when Edwin didn't withdraw his hand, he snapped down on one of Edwin's fingers. Edwin thought it was reflexive, just a baby thing, but Oliver wouldn't let go. Then Edwin felt a deep pinch, and when he pulled his hand away, he saw a bead of black blood on his fingertip. Oliver had bitten him.

Cradling their son close, Eliza turned to Edwin. "I had hoped Ollie would have your nicer, straighter hair. Mine is always such a mess!"

"Your hair is perfect, lovey," Edwin told her, running his hand reassuring over it.

Eliza giggled at that. The gesture drew them close together, Oliver snugged between them the way a family was supposed to be.

But Edwin eyed his son carefully. Oliver, usually a silent infant, seemed to appraise him. His son had old eyes and a strange, intense expression on his face. There wasn't much that seemed very infant-like about Oliver.

He knows, Edwin thought. He knows what I am...

It was a ridiculous notion, but one he couldn't shake.

He knows...and he doesn't like it. He doesn't like me.

The day Edwin learned that Eliza was carrying his child, their lives changed irrevocably. His and Eliza's whole focus in life became the protection of this little creature, and to do that, they would need to play all kinds of games. Edwin couldn't openly acknowledge Oliver. He couldn't even recognize Eliza as his Bride.

Oliver had changed their lives forever. Made everything more difficult. He might even be the death of them. In many ways, Edwin resented the creature. He only wondered if Oliver knew that.

Eliza spoke low to Ollie, telling him what a sweet little baby angel he was. But Ollie's attention stayed focused on Edwin even as he sucked on the key. Turning slightly, Eliza presented Oliver to Edwin. "You really haven't had a proper chance to hold him."

Edwin hesitated. "It's not that I don't want to. I'm just...what if I drop him?"

"You won't drop him."

She showed him how to cradle his son's small form against his body, his hand supporting the boy's head. He was heavier than Edwin expected. He had to really hold onto Oliver because as soon as he was out of Eliza's arms, he began to fuss. It occurred to Edwin that despite Ollie's rough start, genetics would surely have their way with him. He was going to be an exceedingly large, lean, and powerful man not unlike Edwin himself.

After a few seconds, Oliver settled down. His eyes just became just that of a curious infant. He even reached for one of the brassy buttons on Edwin's coat.

"See? He loves you," Eliza said. To Oliver, she cooed, "You love everyone, don't you, sweet pea?"

Edwin wasn't sure what the baby was feeling, but he knew his own heart. He pulled his son close and breathed in his sweet baby scent, and everything changed for him in that moment. Despite his misgivings, Oliver was beautiful and terrifying, and the most amazing thing Edwin had ever laid eyes on. A part of his soul bloomed in that moment. He decided he would do anything to protect Ollie, fight any monster, and destroy any enemy.

"I will always be here for you, mate," he promised.

***

The Queen's Gambit, now

Tommy was slumped on a bench in what the Mechi-people surreptitiously called "the flesh mechanic's garage" getting a tune-up when Dr. Charlotte asked him if he was well. It was unexpected. Did he seem unwell?

"I am fine, thank you. There is no pain."

No pain...anywhere.

He never believed he would miss such a thing. The stubbed toes. The sore throats. But pain was a part of the human experience. And he wasn't human any longer.

Dr. Charlotte, the head of the "garage"— a lab in the lower regions of the ship—was tightening the ball joint in his shoulder with a sonic wrench. It had become loose after an incident involving a sparring match with one of Captain Violet's guards.

"I am glad you are well. I was afraid I might be distressing you in some way."

"Not at all," Tommy answered.

The guard, a Mechi who was considerably smaller and more agile than Tommy, promised to show him how to properly use his mechanical body in close-quarters combat. He had gotten Tommy down on the mat in a submissive hold fairly quickly—a move Tommy had been replaying over and over in his head in an attempt to learn from it. Tommy, a Colossus standing almost eight feet tall, was built for power and brute force, not maneuverability. Neither of the combatants noticed the damage the fall had caused until Tommy relented and noticed his arm wasn't functioning correctly.

"I am so sorry," the guard said, taking Tommy's hand and pulling him to his feet. He tested Tommy's arm, which wasn't hanging right. "This is my fault."

"It's quite all right, mate," Tommy told his sparring partner. "I'll visit the garage and have Dr. Charlotte look at it immediately."

"I am still very sorry," the guard said, sounding contrite.

All of the Mechi were shockingly well-mannered, and not a few were extremely empathic. Not what one would expect of a race of machine people.

That had been Lord Edwin's doing. Once he became the Lord of the Mechi-people, he freed them from the partial mind control the *Oublies'* home office, CoreCivic, had over them. They now made their own decisions, and most had their own opinions on things. From day one, they made Tommy feel welcomed and a part of the race even though his creation had come about unconventionally. The Mechi were their own people, created to be the most powerful warriors in the world. They'd had no obligation to extend the hand of friendship to Tommy, yet they had.

The guard who had injured him reached up to clench Tommy's shoulder companionably. "It was a good match and you are an excellent warrior, Tommy."

"I'm not but thank you."

Dr. Charlotte, after she examined him, said the damage wasn't too bad. "But you must recognize the limitations of your armor," she explained, not in a way meant to belittle him but with genuine concern in her voice.

"Armor" was what the Mechi called their outer shells. Tommy figured it sounded more pleasant than calling oneself a walking garbage pail to contain a bunch of nerve ganglia and the few remaining organs of their former selves. When he glanced at the monitor beside the work table, he could see and even study his own "armor" and what lurked inside of it. It was frankly horrifying and reminded him that little of his organic self remained.

He sometimes studied his synthetic body in a mirror, a constant reminder of how foolish he had been. He had trusted his heart and body to someone who didn't deserve him. A vampire. Someone who had destroyed him in a way he would never recover from.

"I will remember that," he told Dr. Charlotte before rising from the workbench he was seated on. "Thank you for your help, doctor."

She looked on him sympathetically. There was no change to her synthetic face, of course, but it was in her posture. "Perhaps you should consider an upgrade. Most of us have opted to become far more streamlined and agile than we once were. It is within my ability."

Become...more like the others? His chosen people?

"I will seriously consider your offer," Tommy replied. "Again, thank you. Now, I must return to my duties."

Dr. Charlotte nodded. "I will be off-duty in approximately one hour and twenty-six minutes. If you would like to accompany me to the Commons, we could discuss a possible upgrade in more detail."

Was Dr. Charlotte asking him out on a date? Tommy's first reaction was to turn her down, but then he realized that after he saw to his duties as Lord Edwin's Enforcer, he had no other engagements to occupy him and only a long stretch of time to think and, ultimately, regret things. Why not spend some time with the Mechi scientist?

The Mechi-people had their own private community on a separate level of the gyro, and the Commons was an area set aside for their recreation—no different than any other division of the ship. They didn't offer food because food in the practical sense wasn't needed, but there were game halls, dry taverns, and even movie houses and theaters set up for the Mechi-people to enjoy a wide range of entertainment. Tommy once sat through a production of Franz Lehar's The Merry Widow, with the most beautiful singing being performed by a talented soprano Mechi, all of it in German.

Tommy, after completing his assignment for the day, sat across a beautifully set table from Dr. Charlotte. Classical music played overhead and a lovely set of china occupied the space between them, including stemware. They could not consume food, perhaps, but the aesthetic made the ambiance of a date more real—more obvious.

"You truly are amazing, Tommy," she told him, words he'd heard more than once since joining Lord Edwin's crew. "A miracle of mechanical engineering. I have studied your scans extensively." She made a sighing noise. "The fact that Dr. Veronica Vu, alone and unaided, was able to design you as she did continues to astonish me. Truly, she was a great flesh mechanic."

"She was quite talented," Tommy agreed. "A shame what happened."

"Yes, quite. A terrible loss."

During the Jotnar's attack on the gyro, they had lost Dr. Vu, along with many other crew members, some of whom Tommy considered good friends. But, not wanting to darken the mood for their "date," Tommy brought up the day's activities. Their discussion eventually segued into his possible upgrade. He could have new, more streamlined armor and far better maneuverability.

He thought about the possibilities. But before he could inquire further about the details of the operation, he heard a shout from a few tables over.

Glancing aside, he noticed a celebration of sorts going on among several of the Mechi-people. There was laughter and party paraphernalia on the table, and even magic tricks being performed by a Mechi-magician.

"They're having fun."

Dr. Charlotte glanced over. "It is Joshua's Celebration of Life party. They can get rowdy toward the end."

Tommy looked back at his date. "What is that?"

She looked surprised he didn't know. "Ever since Lord Edwin granted us free will, we have been able to make all of our own decisions—true body autonomy. One of the decisions we hold most dear is when we decide it is time for deactivation. Joshua put in a request two days ago, and his friends have decided to throw him a party to celebrate. It's very sweet."

"Deactivation...you mean...?"

She nodded. "There is no true body autonomy until one can decide when one has had enough of this life and wishes to pass into the other."

What a sobering, but interesting, thought.

"It is not an easy life, the life of a Mechi-person," Dr. Charlotte admitted and sighed again. "One must be very strong—both mentally and emotionally." Lifting her head, she added, "I would like to go say goodbye to Joshua if that's all right with you."

"Of course."

She got up to see her friend off while Tommy turned in his seat to watch them.

* * *

Edwin waited in the visitor's bay for his Court Guards to bring the prisoner and his Mechi-Enforcer down. Ari, his Captain of the Guard, looked concerned on seeing Old Edwin, hands in cuffs, being escorted their way.

"My Lord..." he said in concern.

"Leave the other Edwin with me," Edwin told Ari. "I want to speak with him alone before he boards his ship."

Ari hesitated as if he might question the command but then decided to follow through, trusting that his Lord knew what he was doing. Edwin only hoped he did.

Alone and face to face with Old Edwin, he leaned forward and deactivated the tight cuffs binding his stick-thin wrists. "I believe you and am taking steps to neutralize the situation. I only hope my trust isn't displaced."

Old Edwin gave him a hard look as he shook his hands out to get the blood flowing again. "Do you think it is, mate?"

"I believe what you've told me..." His voice trailed off but then he added. "But I don't think you're telling me the whole truth and that bothers me."

Old Edwin nodded once, accepting that. "I'm not. But trust I have reasons for doing so. Ones you would greatly approve of."

"It's a big ask."

"It is."

They stood facing each other for several wordless seconds. It was like looking into a damaged mirror. Even after taking action as he was, was he fated to become this half-broken man? He didn't know.

Old Edwin sensed his conflict. "This is perhaps unwise to tell you, but...go to her. Be with her as much as you can. As often as you can. Take her on your mission, no matter how perilous."

The words sank into him dreadfully like some knife, cutting places in his soul he wasn't aware existed. He nodded and stayed silent even though what he really wanted to do was rage and scream and maybe beat the truth out of himself.

"Thank you for letting me go," Old Edwin told him. "My people will appreciate it even more than I do."

Edwin looked his twin in the eye, "No offense, chum, but you look like deep-fried, day-old shite. I sincerely hope I can change things, and that I don't become you—whatever you are."

Old Edwin laughed at that. "Funny...but I wish the same."

Just as he and his unusual Mechi were boarding his ship, Old Edwin turned and waved. "Wanker!"

Edwin smiled at that. But inside, he felt something clench up and die.

xi

"I'm concerned about Oliver," Eliza said to Edwin during the long flight to Earth.

They were seated together in the rear of the nearly empty Phoenix transport. A few seats ahead of them sat Tommy, his Enforcer, engrossed in a book he had taken along for the ride. Edwin had decided on a quick in-and-out mission, no fuss, no muss, and no one to help him but Eliza and Tommy. He almost left Tommy behind, wanting more anonymity than he could attain by dragging around a Colossus with him, but decided his muscle might come in handy, considering how dangerous things were apt to become with Samara.

He secretly hoped things would not come down to the physical. He hoped Samara would respond favorably to Eliza. His wife always had such a positive impact on people. Though, of course, he had ulterior motives for taking Eliza with him. After the conversation with Old Edwin, he wanted to spend as much time with her as he could.

Currently staring out the portal window, she said, "He was tired during our weekly date. And he was fidgety. Do you think he's all right?" Edwin had discussed the mission at length with her the night before, but now her attention had switched to this new concern.

Edwin, sitting with his fists clenched in his lap, shrugged. "I never can tell with Ollie. He doesn't talk to me." He sounded bitter about that, and he soon regretted speaking his thoughts, particularly when he saw Eliza's face fall and spotted the piquing in her cheeks that she got whenever she was upset.

She started thinking about how to respond. He could tell she was trying to be diplomatic. "I wish you had a better relationship with him. I wish you two would spend more time together the way you both did when Ollie was little."

"That was a long time ago, love."

"But he still needs you, Edwin—both as his father and as his Lord."

He steeled himself. He felt certain Eliza would accuse him of not trying hard enough to get on with their son, and if she did, he didn't know how he would respond to that. But she surprised him, as usual.

Nodding, she said, "I know you try. I know it's hard to get on with him. He's stubborn—kind of like someone else I know." She knocked her shoulder softly against his.

Edwin smiled at that. In the past, trying to connect with Oliver had proven difficult, if not impossible. Since going off to college, the distance between them had grown even more.

"I know I should try harder," he admitted, clenching and unclenching his hands. "Maybe after this business is done, I'll see if I can't arrange some kind of activity the way the American dads do."

He paused to think. "Although I'm not sure what they do, exactly. Hunting, fishing, barbecuing?"

"You don't need to take him fishing. Ollie doesn't like those types of activities anyway." She put a hand on his arm. "We'll arrange a family vacation like during the renovations when we went to Earth and revisited Whitby. We were happy then, and Ollie enjoyed exploring his Uncle Baldy's castle. We could go there."

A vacation at Whitby Hall was something all of them would enjoy. Assuming they survived the next few days, of course.

"Sir," came his pilot Rahul's voice over the intercom, "we're approaching Earth. Shall I plot a course for LaGuardia?"

"No, we'll be landing in Munchausen." That was the airstrip that took transports below to an underground hangar adjacent to Poppettown. It was a strip and fueling station popular with certain smaller dirigibles, not all of them strictly legal. Contraband was often transported in and out of Poppettown that way, thanks to the air traffic controllers that could be easily bought off.

While they began the landing procedure, Edwin retrieved his favorite gun Belle and checked his munitions. At the same time, Eliza reached for her carry-on and withdrew a petite boomer hand cannon. She too checked her ammunition—in this case, she made certain it was fully charged. It was much smaller than Belle but could blow a hole through a bloody building. Small but capable—sort of like his wife.

"I didn't know you were bringing the cavalry, love," he said, referring to the gun that perfectly fit the palm of her small hand.

"Poppettown is like the Wild West. You don't go in unarmed." The serious tone of Eliza's voice impressed him. She grinned and slipped it into a holster under her voluminous red tailcoat. "Besides, there's talk of the Red Doors mobilizing. We don't want to get mobbed."

"Really." Edwin knew she kept her ear to the ground where the ongoing Poppet Revolution was concerned. The Red Doors were a Poppet-run militia in the business of freeing enslaved Poppets from their vampire masters. A worthy cause, certainly, but Edwin met a few of the chaps some years prior, and he learned they weren't the jolliest of revolutionaries, more apt to shoot a vamp dead than to talk to one. He was going to have to hide behind

Eliza's skirts metaphorically if he wanted to survive long enough to find Samara.

"This won't be easy," he groaned.

"No, it will not, which is why it pays to have me with you. You don't want to get caught in the middle of a revolution without someone like me having your back, do you?" She smiled.

He grinned back. "Bonnie and Clyde ride again."

After the Phoenix coasted to a stop, Eliza unbuckled and stood up. "Let's go, Bonnie."

He laughed.

* * *

Oliver heard a ping alerting him to a new mind text, but instead of answering it, he pulled the pillows over his head. It might be Jonah, but after last night's disaster of a date, he couldn't handle talking to him.

Eventually, curiosity got the better of him and he saw it was Ariel wanting a chat.

"Took you long enough to answer!" she scolded him when he answered. "I was afraid you were avoiding me!"

"Not you, Ariel," Oliver told her honestly as he leaned against the headboard. "Never you."

"But...you are avoiding someone?"

She asked for details about that, but when he didn't answer, she took over the conversation. She announced she was on a brief leave before being deployed to her first tour in Saudi Arabia on a peacekeeping mission, and she wanted to spend some time with him. "I thought you could cook something yummy and we can watch horror movies all night!"

"Sure," he answered, brightening considerably. "I would like that. What would you like me to make you?"

"Surprise me?"

"Right. See you tonight!" Oliver hung up. It would be nice to spend time with his best friend after what went down last night.

Jonah had invited him to an after-game party, but Oliver had serious misgivings about it. He knew Jonah's teammates would be there, including Reg. A lot of other people would be there, too, as it was being held at one of the more popular frat houses. Jonah said it was going to go all night long and be "lit as fuck." His exact words.

All those people? All that noise? The idea terrified Oliver.

"You just have to be yourself. My friends will love you. That thing with Reg was days ago," Jonah assured him. "No one remembers it."

Oliver agreed to go, but his heart wouldn't stop pounding in anticipation, and he felt sick for hours ahead of time. He had an important biology exam that morning, so he took a little of the Concerta to keep himsel focused. By evening, though, when Jonah was supposed to pick him up, his nerves were jangling again, so he took some more. By then, his eyes were gaining red rims like he'd been crying all day, and his hands had begun to tremble. He couldn't even lift the coffee cups at work without spilling coffee all over the counter.

Jonah, when he arrived at Oliver's apartment, looked incredibly handsome in his suit. "Are you all right, Ollie?" he asked, looking his date over with concern.

Oliver had buttoned his shirt wrong but was having trouble getting the buttons back through the holes. "Sure. I'll be ready in a minute." He returned to the bathroom to fix his clothes. While there, he took one more hit of Concerta.

That did it. When Oliver stepped out, he was feeling Bright. He couldn't stop smiling.

Jonah looked him over uncertainly. "If you want, we can stay in and I can cook for you again," Jonah offered. "I don't mind missing the party."

"No, I want to go," Oliver told him. He couldn't seem to stand still. "I want to meet all of your friends!"

"Okay, okay, calm down, lover," Jonah said, taking his hand and kissing it, which Oliver found incredibly romantic.

The Concerta made the party more enjoyable than Oliver expected. Jonah's friends joked with him, and he found himself laughing and drinking way more than he usually did. A couple of really hot boys came over to flirt openly with him. Suddenly, he couldn't seem to stop talking about anything and everything. Pierce moseyed over, a shit-eating grin on his face, and asked him if he was having a good time.

"I'm great!" Oliver told his friend. "This is a great party!"

He and Jonah were a few of the last to leave the party. He was still smiling as they got into Jonah's car, but Jonah was unnaturally quiet on the ride home.

"What's wrong?" Oliver asked, picking up on the sour vibes in the car. "I know something's wrong."

"I don't know, Ollie. Maybe I'm a little pissed."

"About what?" He thought it was the flirting.

"About you being so wired you're coming out of your skin?"

Oliver's mouth drooped open but he quickly closed it. "What do you mean?" He felt the night had gone incredibly well. Jonah's friends seemed to really like him.

Jonah threw him a look. "Dude, you're high as a fucking kite on a Sunday afternoon. My friends think you're a junkhead. How much of Pierce's shit did you shove up your nose tonight?"

Oliver squirmed in his seat, wanting to defend himself, but that would mean lying. In the end, he stayed silent and let Jonah drive him back to his apartment. Once there, he mumbled, "I'm not a junkhead" as he slid out of the car.

Jonah stuck his head out of the window, "Uh-huh. Go sober up, Ollie. I'll call you tomorrow."

Oliver stood on the curb, feeling like Jonah had kicked him. After Jonah drove off, he trudged up the stairs to his apartment and spent the rest of the night sitting at the kitchen table in the dark, looking at the generous number of pills and packets spread out in front of him. He had spent most of his grocery money this week on Pierce's pills.

Still, the Concerta was better than being hungry all the damned time. Without it, Oliver couldn't concentrate on his work. He could barely think through the hunger pangs constantly gnawing through his belly. More recently, all he could think about was the sweet and nutritious taste of Jonah's blood, the way it coated his tongue and filled the Dimness inside of him with light.

Jonah didn't understand. He couldn't understand. No one could.

Well, that wasn't exactly true. One person could understand. And maybe he could tell Oliver what was happening to him. Maybe he could help.

Oliver started writing a mind text to Lord Edwin. They didn't exactly see eye to eye these days, but he was certain his father would help him if he asked.

He discarded the text. Ask Lord Edwin for help? After how he had lied to Oliver for a good portion of his life? No, he would fix this on his own.

Now, sitting up in bed, Oliver made a decision. He was failing his exams, so it hardly mattered if he went to classes or not. And if Jonah never wanted to see him again, he'd survive that, too. Maybe, Oliver thought, he would take Ariel up on her offer and try the armed forces. Maybe the discipline of the military was exactly what he needed.

It was past noon by the time he dragged himself out of bed. But the promise of seeing his best friend galvanized him when nothing else could. He showered and dressed and drank a gallon of coffee until he was sure he was sober. Then he went out to get some groceries for supper.

The day was incredibly bright, the bustle and noise on the street harder on him than usual, and the sun felt like a burning weight on his shoulders. He felt an immense sense of relief when he arrived at the corner store where he did most of his weekly shopping. It was cool and dark inside, with few customers. He immediately went to the soup aisle to look over the selection. Lately, it was all that agreed with his sensitive stomach. But Ariel deserved something better, so he gathered some produce in a handbasket and then shifted to the meat and eggs counter, looking over the selection. There was a shakshouka recipe he'd read about online that he wanted to try.

While he was gathering eggs, he spotted Jonah turning the corner. Oliver had forgotten that Jonah shopped here, too. His arms were full of different types of vegetables, maybe for his pet rabbit. Oliver felt his heart drop and he immediately turned his back, afraid to move and alert Jonah to his presence.

But after a few seconds, Oliver became acutely aware that he was being watched.

"Are you actually pretending you aren't there?"

Oliver sighed and turned around but kept his eyes on the floor. He felt like a child up for discipline in a principal's office. This was even worse than direct sun.

"I left a bunch of messages," Jonah informed him.

"I know," Oliver admitted. "But I didn't listen to them."

"Why?"

Oliver didn't know how to answer. Finally, he just blurted out, "I didn't want to listen to you yelling at me."

Jonah sighed. "I didn't yell at you in any of them. I was calling to see if you were all right. I was concerned. Are you? All right, I mean?"

Oliver shrugged.

"Obviously sober. We're back to Silent Ollie, I see."

Oliver's cheeks flushed and he looked up. "I'm sorry about last night. I'm not a junkhead."

Jonah waited patiently for him to continue.

"I was nervous. I didn't think your friends would like me…" He hesitated but forced himself to continue in a small, weak voice. "I understand why you want to break up with me."

Jonah let out his breath in exasperation. "I never said I wanted to break up with you, silly! You really should have listened to my messages and not jumped to conclusions! Look…" He glanced around before turning back to Oliver. "Put down that basket and follow me."

Oliver followed Jonah around the bend and through a door with a sign that read Employees Only. "We shouldn't be back here," he said as Jonah dragged him along.

It was a large stockroom full of shelving with dry goods and produce stacked to the ceiling. It seemed to be empty. Jonah turned and pushed Oliver against the wall where an A/C unit rumbled. He gave Oliver a sheepish look and tangled his fingers in Ollie's long braids. "I have a confession to make. I think your bite did something to me. I'm kind of addicted to you." He leaned in and kissed Oliver hard.

Oliver sighed and relaxed against the wall.

It felt so good to be back in Jonah's arms. And the added possibility of being found out by one of the employees made it feel wickedly fun. They made out for several moments, fumbling at each other's clothes as they reached inward, finding one another again. Oliver kissed and licked along Jonah's throat, finally falling upon the little mark he had made.

Jonah angled his head. "Is this what you need?" he asked, putting a hand on the back of Ollie's neck and inviting him to take. "Because if it's blood you need, I don't mind. I'd rather you take from me than do that junk that Piece pawns off on you."

Oliver, entranced by the red rivers running under Jonah's skin, only grunted. When his lips encountered the mark, the sacred mark, it opened up to him automatically, allowing him to drink without needing to bite Jonah a second time. Jonah moaned softly as Oliver gently suckled at the tiny wound.

Jonah's blood filled the empty void inside of him, leaving him warm and calm and, yes, Bright. They kissed and fondled each other for a few minutes before Jonah eased back.

"Are you still breaking up with me?" Oliver asked, hoping it wasn't true.

Jonah smiled and slapped a hand to Oliver's cheek companionably. "I'm still angry with you, if that's what you mean. I don't like you doing that stuff because I care about you, silly. But no...I'm not breaking up with you."

"Right."

Jonah gave him a look.

"That makes me happy."

"Good." Jonah gave him a concerned look. "Look, I'm no Puritan. I like to drink and screw. I'll even toke a joint sometimes. But you could really hurt yourself with that crap you get from Pierce. It's super addictive and cut with god knows what."

"I won't buy any more of it. I promise."

Drawing Oliver close, Jonah slid his hands around his hips. "I know you aren't a liar, Oliver, so I know you won't do it if you say you won't." Jonah kissed him one last time, lightly, and just on the forehead. "I'd like to see you later tonight. Which you would have known about if you had listened to your messages!"

Oliver giggled when he realized Jonah was having a laugh. "My best friend Ariel is visiting and I'm cooking for her. I'm making shakshouka. But I would like to see you tomorrow."

Jonah's smile spread, lighting up his eyes. "Perfect! It's a date! I'll see you tomorrow afternoon for coffee at our café. Don't be high, tiger."

"I won't. I promise."

Our café.

Oliver strolled back to his apartment with his groceries in his arms and a silly smile on his face. He felt buoyed by the turn of events—so much so that he flushed all the rest of the Concerta.

Ariel noticed something was different when she showed up later in the evening. "You look so happy. And you have so much more color in your cheeks! That must be some boyfriend!"

Oliver grinned, perhaps a bit foolishly, while he made popcorn on the stovetop for their all-night horror fest. "I'll tell you all about him!"

***

Poppettown: The grimy underworld city where Worker Poppets ran the great steam machines that kept the city above in proper working order. It was a horrific, crime-filled slum, working was filthy and perilous, and the projects where the Poppets lived rat-infested deathtraps. Drugs and prostitution were rampant. Red collars and minor crime bosses ran the streets.

It reminded Edwin of London during the eighteenth century. As filthy and wild as it was, it was a familiar landscape—almost comforting in a way. Many years prior, he'd even established an otaku-themed nightclub in an attempt to build his own fortune apart from Foxley.

As soon as the lift they had taken settled with a heavy thunk that rattled his bones, Tommy, stationed beside him, rolled up the safety gate. His Enforcer glanced around while simultaneously drawing the sonic rifle on his hip. "Clear, my Lord."

Edwin nodded before noticing Eliza glancing around surreptitiously like an animal on high alert. "Nervous?"

She didn't even make a show of bravado. "Always. Where do we begin?"

"I was hoping you could tell me. Where do folks here go to buy the latest designer drugs?"

"I haven't a club, but we should probably start at the Starlight Casino." She rubbed her holster with the gun. "Everything down here goes back to it in some way."

He and Tommy started out, but Eliza called him back to her.

Edwin waited while she reached into her carry-on case and withdrew a compact. She powdered his pallid face before finger-combing his hair over the tips of his slightly triangular ears. Finally, she handed him a pair of rosy, hippy-inspired glasses for his pale, glowly amber eyes.

"Better?" he asked.

"Less vampiric," she answered. "You're ready for the ball, Cinderella."

He kissed her hand. "What would I do without you, love?"

| xii |

En route to Bamburgh Castle on the Northumberland Coast, 1751

Edwin McGillicuddy decided he'd made a mistake agreeing to Lord Foxley's proposal. Soon after the Vampire Lord took Edwin from the prison where Edwin was to be hanged, they traveled east by coach and four to the estate that Foxley said he owned.

Edwin sat scrunched back on the bench opposite the vampire as they bumped along the well-worn road. He wasn't quite sure if any of this was real and could only finger the crude wooden cross under his shirt.

He couldn't look Lord Foxley in the eyes. He was too afraid of what he would see.

He should have let the hangman have him. One minute on the rope and it would have all been over.

Even though Edwin was only eighteen years old, he felt like he'd already lived several lifetimes. Not pleasant ones. He'd spent his younger years inside a brothel under the constant threat of being sent to a workhouse, at least until he proved he could bring good coin to the owner. Back then, he belonged to the house's procurer.

Now he belonged body and soul to this…thing.

Shifting very slightly, he glanced out the coach window. What a strange adventure. Having never been outside London, the slow change of scenery from grey, smoke-belching factories and decaying brownstones to quiet, bird-song-ladened forests left him faintly terrified.

"We're nearly home, my boy," the vampire said from the opposite bench. The Vampire Lord with the outward appearance of a twelve-year-old boy was watching Edwin again, studying every inch of him in a way that left Edwin feeling horribly naked even though he still wore his tired rags from the prison.

"Oh, aye." It was all Edwin could simper out in response.

"Afraid?" the vampire asked.

"No," Edwin immediately responded, a lie.

But Lord Foxley saw. He knew.

"You're very beautiful," the vampire said in his lilting sweet voice.

Edwin wondered if there was some way out of his predicament. Likely not. Conceivably, he could throw himself out of the moving coach, but he was so weak from a lack of food that there was no way he could hare off into the forest.

The trees finally fell away and Edwin saw the castle for the first time. It was a beautiful dark structure that wended up the moon-silvered hills, one dating back centuries, the location of a Celtic Brittonic fort known as Din Guarie. He sat up straighter to study it. He had never attended school and couldn't read, but he'd had wealthy clients who liked to talk and tell stories—a perk of the business. He knew the castle was famous for the part it had played in the War of the Roses.

Once they had arrived, Foxley was eager to show Edwin around the grounds and estate. The well-groomed staterooms were the grandest that Edwin had ever seen, and the magnificent beach the castle overlooked stole Edwin's breath away. He had never seen the coast or the sea with his own eyes up to that point. It smelled like salt and dreams, and the flashing water made him wonder about the far-off lands he had only ever heard about in travelers' conversations at pubs.

Maybe, he thought, this Heir business he'd agree to wouldn't be so bad after all.

***

Foxley was a perfect gentleman during the first few months of their time together at his estate. He gave Edwin all the food he could eat, a whole wing of the castle to call his own, and a wardrobe full of the finest clothes that Edwin had ever seen.

Edwin even had a personal library—though that depressed him at first. His mums at the brothel and, indeed, all of his friends born under the Bow Bells, couldn't read a lick of English. Books were a fascinating but unfathomable mystery to him. But Foxley soon took care of that as well. He filled Edwin's days with tutors. Reading. Mathematics. Languages. Even astronomy.

Edwin greatly enjoyed learning his letters. He was an apt student. For Edwin, the chance to live like a scholar was the most wonderful dream come true! He looked forward to every lesson, and he didn't even care that Foxley and his vampire friends sometimes made fun of his manners—or lack thereof.

Sometimes, Lord Foxley's vampire friends made unkind advances on Edwin's person. But Edwin shouldered through it like a soldier. The uncomfortable situations were more than worth the price of living a charmed life. Ultimately, Edwin wanted to make the most of his education and improve his circumstances. He owed it to his mums.

Of course, he was aware of the price. As part of their bargain, Edwin was contracted to become Foxley's Heir and Enforcer. But, from the way Foxley spoke of it, he assumed that such obligations were still many years off. Anyway, Edwin wasn't even nineteen yet and still looked very much like a child. Perhaps not around his eyes or the hard set of his mouth, but he still had a deceptively innocent look about him—the full cheeks and barely-there facial hair.

Lord Foxley wanted someone to conduct his business for him; Edwin assumed he would wait a few more years until Edwin looked more mature. And in that time, he was certain (with the rash certainty of youth everywhere) that he would find a way to wriggle out of his contract. Perhaps he would run away across the sea aboard a vessel, never to be seen again. Or perhaps he would negotiate with Foxley for his freedom. He could be extremely persuasive when he wanted to. He had escaped the hangman's noose; he knew he could escape this, too.

Edwin, early on in his life, had been forced to steal, lie, fight, and seduce to remain alive on the London Streets. He thought he'd had Foxley snookered. But things didn't go to plan.

In retrospect, it had been stupid of him to underestimate a Vampire Lord—especially one as old as Foxley. Edwin had been at Bamburgh Castle only a short six months when Foxley took him. He had turned nineteen only the day before. And the whole sordid affair happened in the daytime, which made it even more unexpected.

He had been sitting atop a ladder, exploring a book on world history in the library, the sun shining warmly down on his shoulder through the tall muttoned windows behind him, when Foxley appeared in the doorway. "Edwin, my boy, I would like to speak to you in your private quarters."

It was unusual for Foxley to be up at this hour. He normally rose after sunset and was gone before sunrise. However, as unusual as it might be, it was not entirely unheard of either. Bamburgh Castle's interior was extremely labyrinthine, allowing one to move about with a fair amount of ease without encountering too many windows full of sunshine—probably the reason why Foxley had purchased it. It allowed him to conduct business during the day with his solicitors, a privilege he enjoyed immensely.

So, while Edwin was surprised to see his benefactor roaming about in the early morning hours, he was not unduly alarmed by it at first. Perhaps Foxley had a meeting to attend to before he bedded down for the day in the luxurious and highly detailed box bed that Edwin knew he used as his daytime resting place.

"Aye?" Edwin climbed down to the floor. "What can I do for you, guv?"

"You are nineteen?"

"I think so," Edwin said, and Foxley gave him a questioning look. After a shameful pause, he added, "But I'm not sure."

"I see." Lord Foxley smiled nicely. "Follow me, child."

"Where are we going?" Edwin asked, carrying the book he'd been reading under one arm.

"I did not give you a proper birthday gift yesterday. I plan to rectify that now."

Edwin had his first concerns then. "It's not necessary. Not after all of this."

"But I insist."

When they reached Edwin's bedchambers, Foxley pushed the door open and indicated that Edwin should enter first.

Edwin gave him a pensive look but ducked through the door. His quarter's vestibule looked unchanged. It contained a bowl and pitcher to allow him to wash and a wardrobe containing the fine garments Foxley had purchased for him. Beyond that lay the vast sleeping chamber, and that space had been restructured, he soon realized.

Edwin stopped in the middle of the room with its tall windows and vaulted ceiling and looked at the place where his large, four-poster, cherrywood bed with its many veils had once resided. Foxley had replaced it with a box-bed similar to the one he used. It was beautifully carved out of cherrywood, obviously new, and certainly not inexpensive.

Absolutely terrifying. To Edwin, it looked like an elaborate coffin.

Edwin turned to face his benefactor. "I don't understand."

"After today, sunlight will harm you, and I mean to keep you safe, my boy." Foxley smiled nicely. "You are an important investment to me."

Edwin's mouth fell open but for a few tense moments, nothing escaped. Then: "I thought...thought we were going to wait a few years." He was surprised by how calm he sounded. At the same time, his mind raced, searching for a way out of the room and the castle.

Foxley didn't even have the good grace to look surprised. He boldly approached Edwin, lifting a hand to touch his hair. Edwin shied away and Foxley lowered his arm, not offended. "Yes, well. I've decided."

"Decided...what?" He glanced at the open window, but they were several stories high above the rocks of the shore.

"Why should I wait? The sooner we get you sorted, the sooner you can begin your service to me."

Edwin backed up a step. Foxley followed, keeping apace of him. They repeated the dance until Foxley had backed him into a corner. Edwin's mind bounced around before latching onto a sad, thin excuse. "But...my Lord, I can serve you better when I look a little older."

The vampire smiled at that, showing a hint of teeth. "Truthfully, I don't care. I have solicitors for those purposes." He slid his hands across his middle like someone anticipating a sumptuous feast. His eyes shone greedily in the sunlight that beamed through the portal window set up too high in the wall to be of any aid to Edwin. "You're a beautiful creature and you smell good. I want you now."

Edwin, horrorstruck, tried to counter that with something that made sense, but he came up empty. He realized for all his street smarts, he'd been foolish and very naïve.

Forcing a smile, Edwin said the first thing that came to mind. "Right then. You're the master. My job is to serve—like back in the brothel."

"Correct." Foxley extended. "You belong to me...as we agreed. Now, come to me, little dog."

"Aye, all right...but since we are doing this, I have a small request. Surely, you are willing to grant a dying man a last request?"

Foxley, looking annoyed, lowered his hand. His pale, carnivorous eyes never left Edwin's face. "And that is?"

"Well, erm...I'd like one more walk on the beach. I would like to feel the sun one last time on my face and hair." When Foxley didn't immediately respond, Edwin added, "It's the last time I'll ever know it, aye?"

Foxley seemed to consider that. After a few seconds, he stepped aside to let Edwin pass.

Even though his nerves were jangling and the little hairs on the back of his neck were standing on high alert, Edwin managed to walk casually past the little tyrant without breaking down and running. It was one of the hardest things that Edwin had ever been forced to do up to that point. He even managed to cross the length of the corridor to the wing of the castle that led to the gardens without taking off at a run.

But as soon he was far enough away that he felt Foxley would not become too suspicious, that's exactly what he did. He turned a corner in one of the long, dimly-lit corridors and then another. He soon found himself outside one of several game rooms. One of them led to a bricked pavilion and then to a stretch of lawn reserved for croquet. He even got halfway across the room and within twenty feet of the pavilion doors before he sensed a presence at his back.

By then, his heart was pounding painfully hard in his chest like a fist was pummeling him and his hands were sweaty and shaking, sliding uselessly over door latches. Sensing the threatening presence, he stopped and pivoted, grabbing for the first thing he found—a long cue stick lying across a snooker table—and used it like a blunt weapon on the vampire standing directly behind him.

The stick broke off when it made contact with Foxley's face. The vampire didn't even seem to feel the impact, though the reverberation rang up Edwin's arm and into his shoulder, rendering it numb. Edwin dropped the remaining shard of the stick and stepped back, suddenly appalled at what he had done.

Foxley simply blinked. "How long have you been planning to leave me, Edwin?"

"I...I didn't..." He didn't know how to explain. He didn't know what he could say to keep the monster from ripping him wide open in its fury. He'd been very foolish, he decided. He'd been courting the devil this whole time, and this was the inevitable result.

From the corner of his eye, he noted he was a mere four feet from the door and the gleaming sunshine that could render him vampire-safe. His one escape. He only needed to turn, tear the door open, and run...

But before he could reach it, Foxley was standing there in front of him, inches away. He had moved faster than even Edwin's brain could calculate, and, additionally, he had the broken bit of cue stick in his hand. Edwin glanced at it in the split second before Foxley whipped around, quickly and efficiently, and raised the stick, letting it connect with the bridge of Edwin's nose.

The crack of cartilage echoed throughout his body, followed by nearly unendurable pain. The stick shattered his nose and made his whole world go black for a short time as he slumped slowly to the floor. Unfortunately, he didn't quite pass out, which would have been a blessing. Instead, he was aware of Foxley dragging him back away from the door. He weakly scraped his fingernails across the hardwood floor, leaving marks in the wood.

Sometime after that, he found himself lying on the posh Oriental carpeting on his back with Foxley seated upon him, pinning him down. Edwin's head was twisted to one side at an awkward angle and a terrible, unnatural pain was pulsing its way through his body from a place under his ear. At the same time, something that sounded like a hungry tiger was growling against his neck. It took several seconds of sucking air through the blood and aching, broken bits of his nose for Edwin to realize that Foxley was the creature growling passionately as he gnawed and drank from the massive hole in Edwin's throat.

Edwin choked at the horrible realization that he was being eaten alive. It wasn't like in the penny dreadfuls, the neat and pretty vampire bite. Foxley was tunneling through his body while he gushed red essence over himself and the floor. He tried to move but his body felt electrified with a combination of panic, fear, and pain. Soon, though, he was too leaden to shift even a centimeter. But that didn't stop him from whimpering.

"Quiet, my boy," Foxley growled, coming up for air. He raised his head and Edwin saw the crimson generously staining Foxley's lips and chin and the lacy finery at his throat. It drooled from the corners of Foxley's lips, falling in fat droplets onto Edwin's face. It made Foxley look clownishly demonic even as he casually touched Edwin in unnamable places. The whole affair made him want to beg in a way he hadn't wanted to since he was twelve, when he entertained his first client at the brothel, a presbyter who had done dehumanizing things to him.

The vampire continued to make soothing noises even as he swallowed down each substantial mouthful of Edwin's human life. After some time, darkness pressed in, and, along with it, a kind of lethargy. Edwin no longer cared that he was dying. He even welcomed it.

But even then, Foxley wasn't done tormenting him. Sitting back, the vampire bit his own tongue, black blood pooling generously at the corners of his mouth, and leaned down to kiss Edwin, pushing his burning black essence into him and forcing him to swallow by stroking his throat. Burning pinkish tears filled Edwin's eyes and rolled down the sides of his face, but even those dried up after a few moments as Foxley's blood took hold of him.

Edwin squeezed his eyes closed and silently vowed to hang onto himself—onto the thing that made him human. His back arched when the first spasm hit him. He felt his lank auburn hair curl into voluminous coils around his face and his teeth lengthen in his mouth. Foxley's immortal disease was taking him and having its way with him as Foxley had.

Even through the pain of his transformation, he realized he was lying in a massive, moist stain of blood—his human blood—with his head turned to the French doors that led to the sunny pavilion beyond. He was just beyond the reach of the sunshine in the door, but a narrow beam of sunlight did cut across the carpet.

Edwin reached for it with one spasming hand. It felt hot—too hot—for his fingertips to endure, and soon they began to smoke. He jerked his hand back into the shadows. He really was damned, he realized. Burning sunlight filled his vision in his last mortal moments, as did the sight of an escape that would never be his.

So close, he thought. He'd almost been bloody there...almost free.

The things that came directly after, including being locked inside the bed-box for days and force-fed more of Foxley's blood—were all too terrible for his mind to even recall properly. In the years to come, he would remember only flashes of panic and horror and the terrible, twisting agony as he was transformed into Foxley's puppet.

* * *

Six months later

"Edwin, my boy, please come in."

They were visiting the south of London, staying at the manse of one of Foxley's solicitors. Agew, he name was, or Arness. Edwin wasn't sure. His mind didn't work properly these days. Foxley would give him an order, and sometimes Edwin would need to confirm it or request details before he carried it out because things didn't click as well as they should in ol' grey matter.

He tried. He really did. But it was difficult to think through the hunger.

The constant, twisting, neverending, tooth-lined, demonic hunger.

It consumed him from the inside like a low, simmering fire, always there, always willing to singe him. There were times he feared his blood was, in fact, on fire. In the beginning, as a new Heir, a newly turned vampire, Foxley let him drink all he wanted from a decanter. But as the days and then the weeks came and went, the blood he found in his evening decanter was less and less.

One day, it disappeared altogether. That day, Foxley let him drink from a human—the maid who made his fires—but only a little. Not enough to even take the growling edge off his hunger. If it wasn't for Foxley's queer power to control the blood of other living things, including Edwin's—as miniscule as it was in his body—he might have killed Foxley's servant that night.

These days, though, Foxley kept him hungry and burning like a feral dog a master could only barely control. He fed Edwin scraps—the rime of blood at the bottom of his glasses, or drips of blood from the palm of his hand that he first made Edwin crawl across the drawing room floor on hands and knees to lick up. Sometimes, Foxley held Edwin against the wall (or ceiling) and invited him to bite him so Foxley could experience the unnatural high that came from Edwin's bite. But because there was so little blood in Foxley's vampiric body, it was an excruciatingly frustrating experience that left Edwin whimpering with need and begging for more—or for kindly death.

Lord Foxley enjoyed it when he begged. Sometimes, Foxley assembled his vampire friends into a crush and made Edwin beg on his knees for a shallow platter of blood as part of the evening's entertainment. They fed him as if he were a dog, Foxley and his friends petting him on the head.

And if Edwin tried to steal blood beyond what Foxley provided, Foxley beat him with a rod or used his power to force Edwin to purge the blood. Then Edwin was weak and ill for days. Edwin learned very quickly not to cheat with the rats and other vermin that crawled in the shadow of the castle.

Edwin stood up from the chair he was slumped in. A maid down the hall looked on him in absolute horror, but he barely noticed her expression. He could smell the blood in her. The vampire in him wanted to follow her, but his master was calling to him, and that connection, the connection between Master and Heir, was stronger.

As he made his way inward to where Foxley was, he weaved dangerously and felt the hallway take a half-turn around him, which caused him to clutch the woodwork to keep himself upright. It took him a moment of ragged breathing to turn about-face and let himself past the sliding doors and into the solicitor's library where the man did Foxley's bidding.

And there he stopped.

Foxley stood near the bookshelf. His solicitor was seated in a chair in the center of the room. His desk had been cleared and his papers and ledgers were tossed into a chaotic ring on the floor all around the man. The sight was vaguely reminiscent of an accused witch awaiting judgment at the stake. Foxley glared at the man contemptuously.

The man himself trembled in the chair, his head down. He moaned through his bloodied mouth, his face a mass of shiny fresh bruises. He made no move to try and escape. Edwin was sure Foxley was plying his power against the man to keep him in place. Or perhaps, like himself, the man had simply given up and accepted his fate.

"Arness, may I introduce my new Heir? This is Mr. Edwin McGillicuddy. He's my pretty little pet devil."

Slowly, the man—small, middle-aged, and balding—lifted his head. He looked Edwin straight in the eye. Edwin thought they might have known one another. He felt certain the man had visited the house of prostitution where he had grown up at least once. He trembled.

Edwin smelled the man's fear, the blood in his cuts, and the sudden dampness of his trousers as his bladder let go. "He...he's..."

"Like me?" Foxley inquired. "Not quite. Edwin is a child vampire—one with almost no control over his needs and lusts. He's quite beautiful, isn't he? All citrine eyes and rosy cheeks. Exquisite like some little painted Dresden doll."

"A monster," Arness bit out in fearful anger. "Ugly."

When Edwin turned to glare at him, the man whimpered.

A small sound caught in Edwin's throat—an uncivilized sound. Foxley enjoyed dressing Edwin in the finest tailored suits in the land. He said he looked like a little prince. But whatever Arness was seeing in Edwin's face was so terrifying it seemed to be unhinging his mind.

Edwin, ignoring Foxley's compliment, said, "What did he do?"

Foxley actually smiled. "Arness has served me for many years, but more recently, I noticed certain funds have gone missing. Unlike human lords, I pay special attention to my finances. When I was auditing my books, I learned this man has been able to purchase all manner of finery for himself. Art, cigars, even high-end whores like yourself, my Heir."

Foxley moved in a tight circle around Edwin, touching him lightly with one heavily beringed hand as if to admire his handiwork. "Look at him, Arness. Before I found him, he was like a dog. Naught but a whore. Someone you might have enjoyed once."

Arness moaned low.

Edwin didn't like Foxley speaking of his past so flippantly, but at the same time, he could barely concentrate on even being offended. He was too interested in the panicked sounds the human was making. When Foxley silently indicated that Edwin should approach Arness—on hands and knees—he eagerly crawled across the carpet toward the man, his eyes pinned to the little human's terrified face.

Arness…yes, he remembered him now. He was a frequent visitor to the brothel. He enjoyed using a switch on the women he bedded. He enjoyed their bruises and their screams.

These men. Edwin wanted to kill them all…make them all suffer the way they had made the women—his mums—suffer. He bared his teeth as he stood up, but a quick word from Foxley reminded him to sink to his hunches before the man. He looked into Arness's eyes, which were wide and blue and horrified at the sight of him.

"Do you remember me?" Edwin asked.

Arness slowly shook his head. Of course he did not. Edwin, like the women this man had repeatedly molested, meant nothing to him. They were gutter dogs. Refuse. He'd been poor and uneducated; his kind was nothing but specks of dust to these "noble men."

"Look, I don't know who you are…I'll give you mon—"

Edwin snapped his jaws, making the man whimper before falling silent. Leaning forward, he sniffed along the man's neck and up to his hair. Arness cringed. Beyond the scents of fear sweat and urine, he could smell the blood coming off the man. He always expected blood to smell like a bar fight in a pub, like copper farthings, but it didn't any longer. It smelled like port or wine. Edwin licked his teeth, licked them again, and the man finally let loose a horrific cry like some animal being slowly slaughtered in a meat plant.

Foxley, his small body fitted into the wing chair, cupped his own chin, a wry smile on his lips. "You stole from me, Arness. Examples must be made. I must not tolerate such behavior. It sends a bad message. You understand?"

"M-my Lord, I…I…I…" The man shuddered, then turned back to Edwin. "Please," he begged Edwin. "Please, I'm sorry…whatever I did to you…I'm sorry!"

Perhaps he really was penitent. But if so, it had come too late. Men like Arness were only sorry when they were caught. And Edwin, after all, was the wrong one to beg to. He was no Father Confessor.

Foxley gave the signal.

Arness's eyes widened when Edwin sprang forward with preternatural speed.

All Edwin saw was red. All he experienced was the demand to fill the endless black cavity inside him. He had no memory of the next few moments, only that the hunger drove him, rode him, controlled him as completely as Foxley did. He tasted only life and bitterness and the many panicked, "sorries" this man spoke.

Edwin returned to himself sometime later. The chair lay in fragments around him, the fine Oriental carpet was soaked through with blood, and he was sitting upon Arness's remains, Edwin's teeth and claws raking through the bones and gore, trying in vain to suck up any remaining drops of blood. He had even broken the man's bones to suck out the marrow. Anything to fill the howling emptiness inside of him.

And still he burned. When he could find no more sustenance, Edwin sat back on his heels and screamed his frustration at the ceiling, blood gusting down the sides of his mouth and neck.

Foxley remained near the fire, swirling a glass of fine port. He was watching Edwin and gently masturbating to his panic. "So very beautiful," he mumbled.

Rinse and repeat for the next one hundred and fifty miserable years of Edwin's life.

| xiii |

The manager at the Starlight Casino barely looked at Edwin, but a huge smile spread across his face when he spotted Eliza in the crowded lobby. "Alisa!" he cried, throwing his arms wide open.

Eliza let him clench her. He then looked her over. "Oh, my...you have changed, my little love," the little old man said. He was, in many ways, an important part of how Eliza how gotten where she was today. On escaping from her Vampire Lord, she and Derek Wall, her childhood friend, had taken refuge in the underground, and this little man, a former Pleasure Poppet named Mr. Penny, gave them their first job.

For Eliza, it wasn't a great job. She worked in the laundry for almost two years, saving up the money she needed to improve her life and taking classes in the evening in business management. But if it wasn't for that job, she never would have been able to leave Poppettown and acquire a position with the temp agency that would eventually lead her to Edwin's door.

"Mr. Penny, how are you?" she asked, looking his dear little self over. He was quite old—in his nineties by her estimation—but he was also a Poppet and, as a result, he aged much slower than a regular human being. He looked perhaps sixty.

He indicated himself with a little flourish. "As you can see, little has changed. But you, my pretty, have done amazing things, eh?"

Finally, he glanced up at Edwin. "Found yourself a handsome Vampire Lord and become the Bride of a now legendary Congress!"

She blushed at that, surprised he had kept up with her exploits.

Edwin and Tommy hung back, with Tommy's eyes clocking around the busy casino floor. As usual, he was looking for signs of danger to them both. She knew Edwin was nervous about being identified. Quite a few people, vampires and otherwise, knew the Prince—or, at least, knew of him. Not a few had scores to settle with him.

"You know me," Eliza said when Mr. Penny mentioned her latest predicament. "Always in trouble. I hope we haven't inconvenienced you."

He took her hand and bowed over it before kissing the back of it. "The Red Queen is never an inconvenience."

That made her blush harder than ever. Did they really call her that down here?

People had begun to look their way—probably worried that Tommy might be one of the infamous Red Collars who worked as mercenaries for hire—so she asked Mr. Penny about Samara, hoping that since he was connected to everything happening down here, he might be able to arrange an introduction.

He glanced around before inviting her, Edwin, and Tommy to a private gambling room. Once inside, he closed the door and informed them, "She has been mixed up with the Red Doors for some time now. They are the only ones currently wealthy enough to keep her in her cups."

"Her habit," Edwin guessed.

Mr. Penny nodded.

"But can you contact her?" Eliza asked, a nervous note in her voice that she couldn't squash.

"I can contact Mr. Derek and arrange a meeting, if that is what you wish, my little love."

Derek? Eliza glanced aside at Edwin, who looked pale even through his makeover. Oh lord, things had just gone from bad to worse.

* * *

Mr. Penny agreed to set up the meeting but left the time and place to their discretion. Edwin offered the upstairs money counting room of his club, Tokyo Hoes, which made sense to Eliza. The place was quiet and isolated, and since he owned the place, he could control the environment.

Eliza had high hopes that things would go smoothly, but within minutes of their arrival, Eliza felt her heart sink.

The club, a popular Otaku hangout space complete with virtual reality games, a nostalgia-inspired arcade, a full juice bar, and dancers in Sailor Moon outfits and fursuits, had once been a hotspot for Poppets who wanted to lose themselves in the fantasy that their favorite anime, manga, and video games could provide, but the underground had been besieged by protests, and the club had been caught in several of them. The latest damage was extensive, and the old patronage had wandered away.

These days, the club was a mess of mismatched replacement furniture, some of the walls had fire damage, and all of the entertainment systems like the VR arenas and arcade had fallen into disrepair. The juice bar had been replaced with the cheap rotgut that was all that this underground hellhole imported. It still turned a profit for Edwin, but patrons only came here to drink and moan about the state of their lives.

She could see how it depressed Edwin. Being Lord of a vast Congress took almost all of his attention, and he hadn't been back to visit in years, trusting in his managers to run the place. The backroom was dingy and dark, full of broken debris in cardboard boxes. They had to install new light bulbs just to see.

Eliza braced herself when the Red Doors arrived. She and Edwin stood shoulder to shoulder when her childhood friend Derek Wall led his small cotillion of people in. As soon as Eliza spotted him, she was struck speechless—and Tommy, stationed against one wall, stood at full attention like a soldier bracing for an assault.

Derek, like Mr. Penny, looked virtually unchanged, not aged at all, but he had dropped the fancy cowboy image in favor of a slick urban look. He was still handsome in his black raincoat, a fedora pulled down to the level of his brow, but there was a lean hardness to his face and startling azure eyes that was new to her. His brow was deeply furrowed, and when their eyes met, she spotted a touch of bitterness about his mouth. He no longer looked angry to have lost her to Edwin. He just looked like he didn't care any longer.

It saddened her.

He glanced briefly at Tommy's imposing metallic form, but before he could protest, Eliza stepped up to make introductions.

"We don't ken with the Mechi-people," Derek informed her.

It would take too long to go over Tommy's complex history, so all she said was, "The Mechi-people are loyal to us."

"To you and to Edwin."

"To our Congress."

His posture didn't relax much, but at least he didn't look like he wanted to reach for the firearm under his coat. Turning, he started barking orders to his small retinue. Several stout male and female Poppets moved to the doors to guard them. His right-hand person, a Poppet version of an Enforcer, Eliza assumed, moved sleekly to his side.

She was a teenage girl in a raggedly black leather jacket, torn-up jean shorts, and fishnet stockings. Her long red hair hung like a course bush down her sides and back, and her eyes were blackened by kohl. Her face was full of facial piercings, and there was even a ring in her belly, exposed by her middy shirt. She took one look at Eliza and licked her lips with a pierced tongue.

Eliza cleared her throat and began. "Thank you all for coming," she told the Red Doors. "I know you're busy."

Derek gave her a bored look. "Yeah. Freeing Poppets from the Court system you're still a part of."

She pressed her lips together. He was baiting her into an argument she would not take part in, not now when there were more important things to worry about. "I'm not here to fight philosophical wars with you, Derek. Our mission is far too important."

Derek glanced past her to where Edwin had adopted his typical gangster pose, thumbs hooked in the pockets of his plaid slacks. They locked eyes. And, after lighting a cigarette, Edwin shifted one hand back so the edge of his jacket revealed his pancake holster. Behind him loomed a large, dark, one-way picture window that looked out on the club a full story below.

She saw Derek's unimpressed face reflected in the darkness there. "Hello, Edwin."

Edwin toked his fag. "Mate."

"Still going with that ol' accent...mate?"

Edwin tipped his cigarette at Derek.

Derek indicated his own head. "Need the newsboy cap if you're going for the whole Peaky Blinders look."

Edwin grinned, showing teeth. "Maybe while you're lowering yourself to insults, cowboy, you can get down there on your knees and blow my undead pole."

"Edwin!" Eliza sighed. Every time these two were in a room together it was a battle.

"I don't like her," the teenage girl with Derek muttered, seemingly to herself. She hadn't moved much until now, but she was suddenly animate, her eyes ping-ponging around the room.

Derek turned, looking concerned about her outburst. "Go sit down—" he began, but she interrupted.

"I like him." She pointed at Edwin. "I want him!" With a roar, the girl threw herself at him.

* * *

Oliver flinched when he heard the knocks fall on his apartment door. He was crouched in a corner of his bedroom, frozen in place, unable to get to his feet. When a second set of knocks fell, he finally croaked out, "It's open."

Jonah stepped inside the darkened bedroom and looked around, a scowl of concern on his face. All of the curtains were drawn, with just a sliver of light filtering through the room like the blade of a knife. "Oliver? Ollie?"

"I'm here," he said when he realized Jonah's human eyes probably couldn't pick him out from the shadows.

"I came as soon as I got your mind text," Jonah said, moving toward him. "What happened?"

Oliver shook himself and drew the blanket he'd grabbed off the bed more snugly about himself. "I shouldn't have texted you."

"I'm glad you did." Jonah stopped to look down at him. Thankfully, he didn't ask any stupid questions. What happened? Why are you like this? That sort of thing. He seemed comfortable enough with Oliver's behavior to let him be.

Still, Oliver knew he owed Jonah an explanation for interrupting his day this way. They'd had a pleasant date the evening before. They had ordered at the café and enjoyed each other's company. Then, this morning...

"I haven't been to work or school," Oliver explained. "I'm not high."

Jonah got down on his knees and pushed the blanket back so he could look Oliver in the eyes. "No, I don't think you are." His voice was low, sympathetic. Another reason Oliver loved this boy. He wasn't loud and demanding like so many boys.

Oliver squirmed. The scent of Jonah's blood was almost overwhelming—strong like a jar of pennies. And, if he concentrated hard enough, he realized he could see right through Jonah's skin to the complex branches of red life flowing beneath. He'd been a child, very young, the last time he'd noticed that.

"Something's wrong with me," he admitted haltingly. "Something..."

He turned away as he heaved up the little contents of his stomach all over the floor, mostly just wetness. He'd been dry-heaving for hours.

"Do you want me to call a doctor...or maybe your parents?"

Oliver shook his head. No doctor was going to be able to help him, and his parents were far too busy with important matters to drop everything and run to his side—and he knew that, at least where his mum was concerned, she would.

Jonah guided him to the bathroom, where Oliver was able to wash his mouth out with warm water and even brush his teeth. They returned to his room. "Okay, I can just stay with you, if you like."

For the next hour or so, Jonah huddled under the blanket with him. Oliver loved that he cared enough to sacrifice his afternoon to be with him, but he also wished he had the nerve to tell him to leave. The smell of Jonah's blood was driving him crazy.

Finally, after an indeterminate amount of time, Oliver couldn't control himself any longer. He tangled his hands in Jonah's shirt and drew him close, breathing in the scent of his hair and skin. His teeth ached.

Jonah didn't panic. Instead, he simply reached up and put a hand on the back of Oliver's neck. "I said I was here for you, Ollie. You don't even need to ask."

Oliver didn't. He struck like a serpent, sinking his teeth into the firm meat of Jonah's shoulder so quickly that Jonah barely reacted. He made a small moan but then fell back in Oliver's arms, shuddering in delight. Oliver clutched him tightly and began to drink, Jonah's red life hitting his starving system like a hammer blow. Each swallow was red, sweet heaven and made his heart vibrate like a hummingbird in his chest.

Jonah writhed for him, mumbling out words of love and adoration that Oliver didn't think he was even aware of. High as a kite on a Sunday afternoon, as Jonah himself would say.

Wonderful, Oliver thought bitterly. Of all the abilities he could have inherited from his parents, it was his dad's talent for *El Mal de Amor* that made the cut. A completely useless power!

***

The teenage girl with the piercings moved so quickly that had Tommy not been a machine whose reactions were AI-augmented, surely she would have reached Edwin and ripped him to shreds before he had time to move.

But Tommy, his loyal Enforcer, used his superhuman ability to intercept the oncoming threat. And Tommy wasn't merely large; he was as heavy as a car. Still, the girl hit him with such force that the two of them pinged back against the one-way window.

Even though Edwin had finally moved out of the line of fire, he felt his clockwork heart skip a beat at the bomb-like impact of the two bodies. For one moment in time, nothing happened. Then the glass squeaked and cracked as it protested. It was supposedly shatterproof, but it had never been hit with the force by two Supes. It gave more quickly than he anticipated, and then the two of them were going head over heels down into the club below.

Edwin, much better at flying than when he was younger, instinctively spread his wings, which tore through the back of his custom-designed, double-breasted worsted jacket—one of Eliza's favorite (bloody hell!)—and jumped through the hole in the window after the two of them. But the lift he achieved made no never mind in the end.

Tommy had landed like a warhead, exploding a deep hole in the floor of his club, with the girl landing atop him. The crazy chit had latched onto him, her fingers twisting the tough metal of his shoulders. Tommy was making grunting noises and fumbling with his rifle, but he was incapable of getting back up, and his extra-wide shoulders were stuck in the edges of the collapsed floor. The krsnik—for Edwin had no doubts about what she was now—was striking sparks as she ripped deep grooves in his armor that exposed wires and glinting metal bits.

They lay in the grave-like hole together, destroyed blackjack table surrounding them and half-drunken patrons staggering to stay out of the way. Chips and cards flew everywhere around them in a minor tsunami. Tommy had begun to make weird whirring noises when Edwin glided down atop the two of them.

He had to help Tommy—whatever it took. With a growl, he snatched the girl's head in his hands and twisted it, snapping her neck like it was made of toothpicks. He felt the satisfying crackle of bones, but she didn't react at all. She just glared at him, her head twisted backward.

Edwin had never seen anything like it. He stared openmouthed at her scowling expression.

"Yoooouuuu..." she said and Edwin, stunned, fell back and onto the floor. Head still on wrong, she lifted herself from atop

Tommy's struggling body, turned, and kicked Edwin in the breastbone.

It was like being kicked by a hydraulic machine. He flew the length of the room and crashed into the bar that snaked through the middle of the club, rendering it kindling. The girl smiled. Standing up fully, she gripped her own head and twisted it back the proper way, her bones crackling, then turned her body about-face and started toward him, that maniacal grin still warping her lips.

Edwin scrambled up in the debris and tried to crawl away from the girl, but she followed him with uncanny agility like some human spider, weaving around obstacles as if there were no bones in her body. The crazy chit growled, flashing freakishly long fangs. Her fingers, now armed with saber-long nails, reached for him.

Edwin spread his wings and tried to take off, but she was faster than any vampire—any supe, really—that he had ever seen in action. She tangled those long claws in his slacks, dragging him to the floor and toward her. By then she was drooling, her jaws, full of shark-like teeth, clacking together. Her previously broken neck seemed to have no effect on her at all.

"Bloody...hell!" he said as she drew him close and loomed over him, her body moving almost like warm taffy. He instinctively pop-punched her in the eye, his assault relatively weak in his compromised position, but still powerful enough to knock a man's head off.

She hardly reacted. Just shook her head and eyed him vapidly. Then she leaned back, her rubbery body bowing at an inhuman angle...and something extraordinary happened. A ragged line appeared down her bare midsection. It began at the edge of her middy shirt, which was little better than an elaborate brassier, and stretched down to the level of her hip-hugging trousers. Her pale body cracked wide apart, the wet red lips lining the crevice—her second mouth—separating wide to reveal a giant gaping maw filled to brimming with ragged, crocodilian teeth.

Edwin took one look at the writhing mouth full of primordial teeth and a dozen archaic expletives fell out of his mouth.

The few people staggering around the casino were screaming now. He heard shouting from a story up in the counting room, but he couldn't make out the words. It may have been Eliza. All he could hear was the girl—the krsnik—growling and snapping her jaws—both of them. He tried to reach for Belle under his coat—for all that would do for him—but the girl swiped his arm away, her strength startling. The gun flew off into a corner.

The krsnik lunged at him. Edwin tried to take another swing, but she was too fast, and her second "mouth" (a part of him shuddered internally and hoped it was, in fact, a mouth and not another part of her anatomy) moved swiftly to suck up first his hand and then his wrist. He screamed as the "teeth" clamped down on his forearm, cutting deep like jagged broken glass.

Fark this! He tried to wriggle out from under her, but he could only kick and squirm. "Yes, struggle," she told him with a high-pitched laugh. "I like my meat tenderized."

"Chit, you have some serious issues," he grunted out. Twisting his whole arm harshly, he managed to pry her mouth open an inch, but it cost him some skin—literally.

When she saw what he was doing, she opened her second mouth just long enough for him to pull his arm out—it burned with her saliva—and twist away. Unfortunately, as he turned to retreat at a crawl, he felt his leg go inside next.

With a cry, he clawed at the floor, but his slimy hand made it hard to find purchase in the wood floor and she just sucked his leg farther into her crevice of a mouth, her teeth grating over his flesh. Now, she was laughing and slurping. He felt horribly like some kind of lollipop being sucked on.

"You are so delicious, vampire!" she cooed.

Shite! Eaten alive by a vampire-eating vampire. What a miserable way to die...

He heard a scream then, an inhuman sound of rage that echoed around the interior of the club. Seconds later, a pair of boots landed in front of his face. Not Tommy's boots. He immediately recognized them as Eliza's. Black, shiny, knee-high boots with reasonable heels and embossed red roses and vines twining up them. She always wore them paired with her red tailcoat.

Edwin glanced upward, his heart clunking with worry. Yes, it was Eliza, but not one he recognized at the moment. She seemed larger, darker, and more fearsome standing with her black wings outstretched to either side of her. Her hair seemed to writhe around her shoulders as if stirred by a stiff wind, and her face was twisted into a fierce grin of long teeth and narrow, upslanted black eyes.

"No..." he whispered. Nothing compared to this, not even being eaten...the sudden, unexplainable horror of seeing his wife—his love—in a turned state. It was more painful than whatever the krsnik was doing to him. "No...Eliza...!" He instinctively reached for her, his hand screeking over the toe of her boot.

She ignored him. Her attention was centered squarely on the krsnik. "Let...him...go," she told the creature, her voice a startling basso growl.

The krsnik only hissed at her. "Go away. He's mine!"

"No...I don't think so." Eliza's black eyes flashed, and her mouth stretched inhumanely wide in her pale face before she launched herself at the girl, tearing her off his leg that she was currently chewing on...which hurt a bloody lot!

But he couldn't worry about his injuries. Twisting around, he quickly found his feet and limped forward, but the two creatures were already battling it out at the far end of the club, each dealing the other stunning blows to their faces and bodies. The krsnik slashed at Eliza's midsection, tearing her tunic. Eliza responded by launching a blow to the krsnik's face, her nails ripping right across her smug expression, though the krsnik merely shrugged the blow off. The two grappled and twisted, hair flying and jaws snapping. Edwin dodged left and right, trying to find a way into the fight, but they moved too quickly. Finally, the krsnik turned and threw Eliza into a wall, crushing part of the bricks in.

Were she still human, the blow would have killed her instantly. Instead, Eliza shrugged it off and skipped weightlessly to her feet. With a flick of her wings, she launched herself at her enemy, arms outstretched, clawed hands ready to grapple. The two collided, clutched each other, and together, they spun across the room like a dervish of teeth and malice until they reached the edge of the bar. Finally, they smashed into the tall rack of bottles behind it, ripping most of them down as they twisted to the floor in a growling heap.

Edwin, who had been limping toward them, had to quickly turn and dive in the opposite direction. As he flew at the two women clenched and battling it out, he only narrowly avoided their flailing claws. But by doing so, he plunged into the shelves behind the bar, pulling the remainder down.

By the time he had found his feet once more, the two women were over the bar and on the floor amidst a mountain of pulverized game tables and broken chairs. This time, Eliza was on top, which both impressed and terrified Edwin. He had witnessed her in her vampire form once before when Summersfield forcibly turned her. He was a freakishly powerful Vampire Lord. Eliza, as a result, was an absolute horror of strength and brutality—a baby vampire who was the result of a powerful bloodline and decades of bottled-up rage.

Screaming out her rage, her hair standing on end, Eliza dealt the krsnik a series of stunning blows across the face that left the young girl looking shocked. Then, with a sudden whoosh of her wings, Eliza lifted off, carrying the krsnik with her, her claws twisted in the front of the girl's shirt. The krsnik screamed and her weird second mouth gaped open briefly, but Eliza deftly avoided her teeth, rocketing them both to the cathedral ceiling. The krsnik's eyes opened wide in terror when she realized they might go right through the roof of the club, but Eliza stopped just short of hitting the ceiling and, with a horrendous chuckle, dropped her.

The girl fell a remarkably long time before plunging, screaming, through the floor and into the basement below. Edwin heard all kinds of things crashing down and splitting apart as she continued to fall to the sub-cellar where they kept most of the casks and racks of booze. A whole rack of cheap rotgut toppled over atop her.

Eliza hovered, looking pleased with herself.

Edwin straightened out his borked leg and stood straight. "L...lovey?"

Eliza's attention snapped around to him. Her eyes were still black as sin and her mouth gaped open in a rough "O" of sharpened teeth. She glared blindly as if she did not recognize him.

"L...love..." he repeated, softly now, but that was all he was able to get out before she swooped at him. He was too afraid of hurting her to try and stop her, so she grabbed him up like he was a big rag doll, and the two of them flew back across the room and into the brick wall, which gave at their backs.

Now, the two of them were out in the alleyway behind the club with Edwin down on his back and Eliza on top of him, hissing and spitting. He raised his forearm in defense, which was good, because she swiftly snapped down on it hard, her teeth cutting deep, and began shaking her head like a dog with a bone.

Edwin yelped and raised his other hand, smacking her several times in the shoulder to get her off of him, but she didn't even seem to notice the blows. She was growling and foaming at the mouth, trying to get her teeth into him. Trying to get to his blood.

She wasn't herself, he reminded himself. He needed to get her under control.

He pushed himself up, but she pushed back, almost pinning him. He had no choice but to pick up a brick and hit her in the face—as hard as that was for him to do. That got her attention and she let go of his arm. He hit her again, and while she was shaking her head, working to recover from the blow, he bounded back to his feet. She was strong, aye, but she was no Vampire Lord. He wrapped both hands around her neck and, partly choking her, flew back through the hole in his club.

By then, Derek and his people had arrived at the club floor. Edwin spied them from the corner of his eye as he flew back in.

"What are you doing to Eliza?" Derek shouted.

"Trying...not to...let her...kill me!" He pushed her to the floor, his boot in her neck to hold her down. Quickly glancing around the club, he noted one of the hanging cages on the side of the raised stage where the go-go dancers performed their routine. The inside was empty, the dancer having wisely exited stage left when things began to heat up, and the door hung wide open.

Derek tried to reach for him, to pull him off Eliza, but he shrugged the bloke's hand off. By then, Eliza was keening and her eyes had gone mad with rage. She scraped wildly at the toe of his boot and her wings beat a frantic tattoo against the ruined floor.

"I'm sorry, love," Edwin told her and reached for her, grabbing her under the chin to restrain her snapping jaws. Once he had a good hold of her, Edwin wasted no time diving toward the cage. As soon as he reached it, he cast her inside.

Eliza hit the back of the cage and slumped down, but she didn't stay there for long. After a few seconds, she jumped back to her feet and, with a scream, dove at him, but by then, Edwin had gotten the door closed. Unfortunately, she was strong—stronger than she ought to be—and when she threw herself against the cage door, it rattled and buckled even with his full weight against it.

Edwin, panting, realized he had to think fast. There was no way to lock the actual cage. The cage, though real enough, was only a prop for a dancer and had no lock on it. Still, he turned and put his back to it to hold it closed. Eliza hit it again, jarring him. Edwin gritted his teeth and eyed Derek. "Get some bloody chains, man!"

It took Derek a moment to respond, but when he saw what state his former childhood friend was in, he started to move, directing his people to scour the place for something to secure the cage door. It took a painfully long time for one of Derek's Red Collars to return with a length of garage chain and a padlock.

"Get it on, you gobshites!" Edwin bleated through tight teeth. He grunted at the relentless assault at his back. "I can't hold her much longer!"

Derek joined his man and, together, they got the chain looped around and the padlock on. By then, Edwin was vibrating with each bone-jarring blow, though he was far more worried that Eliza was harming herself with each go at the door.

"Get back!" Derek ordered and Edwin, taking the chance that they had done it correctly, stepped back and turned.

Eliza paced the cage like an enraged lion, growling and spitting, clawed hands clenching and unclenching, eyes flashed blackly at them both. She tested the door, but it held fast, a pretty prison for a pretty if demonic-looking bird.

"Oh my god, Edwin," Derek moaned. "What did you do to Alisa?"

xiv

Whitby Hall, Cornwall

19 years earlier

Eliza plunged both hands into the electrical hotbox atop the castle, creating an explosion that radiated outward with the force of a dirty bomb. Cesar, despite being a vampire and incredibly durable, was blown the length of the rooftop. He hit the flagstone wall of a battlement, the only thing that kept him from flying right off the roof, and then slid to the stones, groaning as he felt several bones crunching loosely underneath him.

He couldn't move. Pain flared up in his body, mostly from what he suspected was his mangled neck and spine. It hadn't killed him; as a vampire, he was hideously durable. But it was all he could do to keep from passing out from the pain.

He lay very still for a while with his back to the wall as the worst of his breaks slowly reknitted themselves. During that period, he watched the stars above flicker and go out like someone was turning off a series of light bulbs somewhere. It took him a moment to realize he was staring into emptiness. Not emptiness as in the lack of light, but emptiness as in the lack of anything, like some great cosmic creature was eating its way cancerously across the sky.

The Darkness, he thought. The Great Empty. Star-eater.

The Nothing.

While he watched it writhe across his field of vision, the creature seemed to slow, to consider him, to recognize him as one of Its own—to look at him. He had become aware of It, and so It had become aware of him. Cesar was afraid.

It was a primal, basic fear—the Nothing, the emptiness, the aloneness, and the primordial things that hunted in it. He heard a whimpering, childlike noise echo up from his own throat. He found he wanted his family badly—his mom, his little sister. Even his dad, whom he had never gotten along with. He didn't care if they loved him or hated him or never spoke to him, just so long as they came for him, protected him. For the first time since his mortality had died inside of him, he was the thing being hunted, he was the thing that could be hurt, could be consumed...

The Nothing moved again, this time away from him.

He blinked and groaned and closed his eyes to the brilliant white light that seemed to be filling and encompassing the whole rooftop. He felt like he was staring into the watery, blinding power of the sun, the whole castle and surrounding area illuminated like noontime by the massive explosion of power hanging over it...

* * *

Cesar woke with a start. He immediately knew he was crying out—crying for help—and quickly gasped and covered his mouth with both hands.

He almost sat straight up, then reminded himself he was locked inside one of the Hydraulic Protection Compartments that the vampire population used for their periods of inactivity. In the past, he'd had the same dream, and, as a result of it, bonked his head on the lid a few times.

He settled back. The HPC was safer than a bed and a good bet if you didn't trust the company you were in. He had been utilizing one for most of the duration of his contract with Foxley—after getting over the initial weirdness of lying in what was, basically, a high-tech coffin. Additionally, his HPC was rigged with all kinds of alerts. If the unit sensed he was panicked in some way, it would double-lock inside and out and wouldn't open unless a special code was inputted. It was engineered to keep a vamp safe at all times.

Something he needed these days. Even though he had his own wing on the administration level of the gyro, life aboard Foxley's ship left him feeling lonely and unsafe, surrounded by people he didn't know or understand.

The unit's AI, sensing his accelerated heartbeat, asked if he required guards or other security measures. "No, Iris, thank you," he told her, having named her after his sister. "Just a lot on my mind these days."

"I'm sorry to hear that, Cesar," Iris told him. "Would you like to listen to some music?"

"Sure, Iris."

The first flutey movement of Igor Stravinsky's "The Rite of Spring" began filtering in a low, murmuring volume through the HPC. Cesar resettled himself in the plush interior of the unit, roomy and cool and full of pillows, and worked on getting his jangling nerves under control.

The loss of his master's proximity weighed heavily on him today. He was still only a baby vampire, and he had come to realize he needed Edwin, both as his master and his friend. There were nights he longed with every inch of his soul to fall asleep in his master's arms—except that Edwin didn't want his company these days. Not that he could blame him. Not after what he had done.

Resting was proving impossible. Cesar keyed in the code and climbed out of the unit, moving to sit on the edge of his vast, four-poster bed in his silk pajamas. Looking at the HPC from this angle, he realized it resembled a space-age coffin.

He sighed. The sight of it just reminded him of...everything. The last undead twenty years of his life.

Being a vampire, at least according to the teenage fantasy romance novels, was supposed to be cool, sexy, exciting. The reality of it was none of those things. You had to work a regular job and navigate messy and stressful interpersonal relationships forever. For added joy (not) you got to watch the most beloved people in your life age into death, and you could do nothing about that because being a baby vampire meant you were unable to make other vampires.

One day that might change, of course. He might one day become a Lord and then be able to make Heirs—companions—but that time was so far in the future that it meant nothing to him now, when he needed it most. An ironic twist in immortality: It was like God, or whoever was running the universe, was having a laugh at the expense of his kind.

Well, may as well get on with it.

He stood, stretched, showered, dressed in a dark navy suit that reminded him of his Air Force cadet uniform from a lifetime ago, and lifted down to the Security Floor to punch in for the day. Halfway to work, he stopped at a bodega to purchase his morning blood. His friends and coworkers waved good mornings as they passed. Several Worker Poppets who were fond of him smiled as they carried on with their various duties.

When he first joined the crew aboard the *Gypsy Queen*—not willingly but duped into it by Foxley himself—he'd been onboarded as Foxley's newest Enforcer. His bully, in other words. He went on tech-finding missions with his boss, intimidating engineers and artificers into surrendering their blueprints to Foxley Enterprises, his master's tech empire. Foxley paid them a pittance.

Cesar wasn't proud of being a part of that. The problem was he didn't have much to say about it. He was contracted to Foxley for 200 years of service. His only respite was the long, comfy periods between missions.

But he tended to get into a lot of trouble during those periods, and he wasn't the best version of himself. Something about the way Foxley used him brought out his most barbaric vampire self, and it carried over into how he was treating everyone else, even the staff and Poppets aboard the ship.

That was a dark time for him. He didn't like to think about the things he had done. The things he was capable of.

Then Foxley disappeared without a trace. No one knew if he was dead or merely MIA. His ship, his Court, and his entire empire were put in legal stasis for five years. When he didn't turn up to claim his holdings, they were turned over to the second most powerful vampire aboard the *Gypsy Queen*, Foxley's older Enforcer, Lady Claire. According to the legalities (as Cesar understood them), Claire was the Sitting Lord for the next 177 years—a very odd number, in his opinion. If Foxley never returned, everything he owned became hers after that.

Edwin, as Foxley's oldest living and most powerful Heir, was given first refusal. Cesar had hoped he would claim his former master's holdings because that would mean Cesar belonged to Edwin again. But Edwin didn't want anything to do with Foxley's empire, so Claire it was.

She wasn't a bad boss, as bosses went. She didn't ask him to do any of the crummy, bloodthirsty shit that Foxley did. Mostly, she ignored him.

"What's my current position aboard the ship?" he asked her the day after she took command.

Lady Claire, lounging on a divan, playing a video game on her tablet while one of her female Poppets gave her head, only frowned. Her cottony white hair was tied up in pigtails and a huge lollipop was jammed into the corner of her lipsticked mouth like a Marlboro. She didn't look up. "What do you mean, Wifey?"

Wifey. She called him Wifey. Edwin's Other Wife.

He ignored the loud slurping going on. "I mean…what's my job? Since I'm not Foxley's Enforcer any longer?"

She shrugged her thin, childish shoulders. "Do whatever the hell you want. You don't have tits, so I don't need you, Wifey."

Even though he hated the idea of working for her Court as an Enforcer, her response still stung. He couldn't even leave the Court and go somewhere he might be happy because he was technically part of Foxley's property in suspension. As a result, he was stuck here until Foxley either returned and released him, his 200 years of service were served, or 177 years passed and Claire officially became Lord of the Court, at which point she would exile him whether he wanted to go or not. His whole life had simultaneously gotten better and worse with Foxley's disappearance.

Well, he thought at the time, it was time he made a decision. "I'd like to put in for a position as Head of Security." It was the same job he'd worked at the casino before Edwin found him.

Another cold shrug. "Whatever, dude. Take care of it."

He waited for dismissal. She finally glanced up, her dark, vulpine eyes flashing under her winged white brows. "Just stay out of my fucking way and it's all cool. Now scat."

Thus, Cesar, once Foxley's Enforcer and Edwin's Heir, became Head of Security aboard the ship—a definite downgrade to be sure, but he didn't mind. Most of his duties were comprised of monitoring the airspace around the ship for incoming craft and making certain they had boarding passes and then seeing to it the visitors didn't get rowdy or rough up the crew or Poppets. Sometimes, he broke up rows between crewmembers, and he occasionally stuck assholes in the drunk tank to dry them out.

When he first joined Foxley's Court, he'd been encouraged to use his downtime to party hard and enjoy the resorts, casinos, and the endless array of different Poppets, but all of that lost its shine after a while. These days, he was more interested in how the Poppets were being handled by crew and visitors, and he had gained a reputation as a real hardass on the matter.

"You know they're just Poppets. Not real people," one of the visiting vamps told him after Cesar locked his sorry, drunken ass in the brig for roughing up a Poppet. "They don't have real feelings or anything."

He thought about Miss Eliza, a former Poppet who not only could think for herself but who was also a genius-level intellect and had strong opinions on the matter of Poppet civil liberties "Do you really believe that?" Cesar asked the vamp. "Because I don't think you do. I think our kind just says things like that to justify what we do to them so we don't feel so guilty."

The vamp, enraged, showed his teeth from behind the vampire-proof bars of his holding cell. "I don't feel guilty!" he howled. "The humans took our one source of food away and gave us them! What did they think was going to happen? They're food...the Poppets, the humans...all of them!"

The vampire's eyes had begun to bleed black with his rage. Cesar looked in at this sad little creature at the complete mercy of its compulsions.

He'd been tempted to think this way once. But were they all so devoid of empathy? Devoid of humanity? So full of...Nothing?

Cesar suddenly appreciated exactly how much work his master Edwin had put into dragging himself out of this hellish pit of anger and hunger to become the respected, established Lord he knew today. Cesar had always assumed that Edwin had always been like that. Now, he realized that probably wasn't true. Edwin had been just as ruthless as the rest of them. The difference was that Edwin put in the work to be a better version of himself.

Maybe he had to do that, too. Maybe this was his chance.

So, yes, over the past few years, he had become more protective of the Poppets and even the humans. He also didn't let anyone push them around. That didn't make him popular, he knew, but he didn't care. By being better than the vamps he knew, he was making up for some of the more egregious behavior he'd displayed over the years.

I will do better. I will be better. And then, maybe one day, Edwin would be proud of him again. Maybe Cesar would be worthy of Edwin's love.

"That vampire has lost her damned mind!" the Warden bellowed when Cesar arrived at the brig for his shift.

"What do you mean?" Cesar, balancing his cardboard cup in the crook of his elbow, slid the security door closed behind him. He looked at the monitors to see if the latest problem vamp was sober enough to put her slimy ass on a transport and get her off the ship, but now he had concerns.

The Warden, stationed behind the viewing monitors, shook his head. "She went completely mad and started tearing up the cell. I don't even know for certain if she's alive. It's a mess in there and no one wants to go in!"

Cesar's mouth dropped open in surprise when he perused the video feed. He'd seen some drunk vamps, but even they didn't compare to this. Hurrying inside the holding cells, he discovered the scene was much more gruesome than even he anticipated.

The female vamp had torn the bench off the wall and even some metal panels down, most of them hanging by wires, though she hadn't made it through the six inches of reinforced space titanium underneath. Unable to escape that way, it looked as if she had turned on herself in frustration. Her long dark hair was mostly torn out at the roots and scattered around, and she had scratched the skin off her forearms and most of her face. She had deep gouges in her neck where she had presumably been ripping holes in her own flesh. She lay in a disheveled, slowly expiring heap on the floor, her blood running out of several deep gouges. Because she had frightened the guards so badly, no one had dared to approach her or feed her. As a result, she had been unable to heal herself.

Cesar quickly unlocked the cell door and ducked inside, kneeling by her side and taking her head onto his knee. He didn't know what rabid madness had infected the vamp, but he could tell she was too far gone for saving. Still, he didn't want her dying alone. No one deserved that.

The vamp groaned and wriggled her almost skinless head from side to side, finally opening her eyes. They were pitch black. Black blood poured from them, a phenomenon he had witnessed rarely and one he knew happened when a vampire was dying the final death. It was as if they could only cry as they were dying, the darkness inside them escaping all at once.

"What happened to you? Are you sick?" he asked, wiping the hair sticking to her face away. "Did you drink something, or…?"

Blood bubbled out of her mouth. He saw she had broken off her teeth in her rage, and her lips, almost flayed from her face, moved silently for a moment.

"I don't understand," he whispered, leaning close so he could hear her words. "Tell me what happened."

The vamp lifted her arm weakly, her fingers trembling and flexing, and laid her hand on his shoulder.

He felt a jolt that made him cry out, and for one painfully long second, he was back at Whitby Hall, looking up at the darkened Nothing unfurling across the night sky and eating its way across the heavens. He once more felt the utter terror of facing that darkness, that all-consuming Nothingness that was eating its way through everything, even their supposedly immortal kind.

Thankfully, it didn't last. Seconds later, he was back in the cell, holding the dying vampire in his arms. The vamp spoke but briefly, but it took him a moment to make out the words.

"He...he was here."

"Who?" He needed to know. Needed to know its name. "Who was here?"

"Mkgor..."

Then she was gone, her body collapsing into a loose, lifeless vessel.

* * *

Joshua Cummins—Joshie to his friends—had never really become a proper vampire. He was sixteen when he was made an Heir in 1992. It happened in rural Iowa, at the height of summer during a Nirvana concert that he'd sneaked out of his house one night to see.

The vamp that chose him was some rich chick who said she wanted to make out with him in the backseat of her vintage Porsche. Joshie knew what she was even before he got in the car, but he did it anyway. He'd never been with a girl—he was too shy—and he had a feeling his virgin status wasn't going to change anytime soon. At least the vamp was willing to pop his cherry for him.

The sex was weird and cramped due to the car, an uncomfortable situation no doubt exasperated by his JNCOS, which were wet from the pavement. But before he could slip out of the car and go cry in the bathroom, the vamp ran her extra-long fingernails through his blond, shaggy hair and said in a sibilant whisper, "You're pretty. Do you want to be mine?"

"Like...your boyfriend?" Joshie didn't know how he felt about a vampire girlfriend. Maybe his friends would think he was cool, yeah, but the two of them couldn't hang out at school or in the park where he liked to read under the trees. He'd heard mixed relationships like theirs never worked out.

"Like my Heir," she clarified.

Whoa...that was something he hadn't signed up for.

"I wouldn't make a good vampire," Joshie confessed. "I just came to this concert so my friends would like me. I'm not cool or anything. I like to read and I want to be a writer someday."

She smiled. "Imagine if you could be a writer...forever."

Joshie considered it, his heart thumping uncomfortably hard in his slightly sunken chest. She made a good point. And since there were kids in school who would probably beat him up on Monday, he agreed to her contract.

Unfortunately, being a vampire wasn't all that. He couldn't go home or see his parents or little brother ever again. He had to go with his master Lily and live with her aboard her gyro for the next couple of decades. It was all right, sometimes fun—mostly boring and lonely. He had to serve her, but she never made love to him like that first time. She treated him like a slave. Then, to add insult to injury, at the end of their twenty-year contract, she kicked him out. She had moved on to someone else.

Joshie had no choice but to return to Earth. By then, he had been away for over twenty years. He had no education to speak of, so he had to take crappy jobs, and he had no money, so he had to drink cheap, synthetic blood. His family had disowned him by that time. Most humans didn't like or trust vampires, and he got a lot of shit from his coworkers. He found and lost a long chain of low-dog jobs. The one he stuck with was a janitorial position in the high school where he used to go. He couldn't write because he was working all the time just to keep a crappy apartment. It was just fucking depressing, and he blamed Kurt Cobain for it all.

He wasn't a cool vampire. He didn't have money or fancy cars or even any groupies. He didn't own a gyro or even a haunted house, and he had no idea how the old vamps gained all of their stuff. Old money accumulated over centuries—or maybe they murdered people and took their stuff. But that wasn't Joshie's style.

He wasn't even old enough or powerful enough to make a companion. His life consisted of working, sleeping, and subsisting on bottom-shelf blood. When he could afford it, he snorted up capsules of dehydrated human blood mixed with bath salts. They had become popular on the street of Cesar Rapids among the undead population. For fun, he went to alternative bands' reunion tours, though all of his favorite artists were old or dead by now.

And then it happened.

During a three-day Memorial Day weekend, he was trying to lose himself in an outdoor rave when he saw the strange boy standing at a distance, waving to him. He climbed out of the mosh pit of aging headbangers and moved to the side of the crowd to see what the boy wanted. He looked like someone Joshie might have known in his teen years: tall, thin blond, very lithe. Except he had wings—well, one wing—and looked to be missing part of his arm.

He didn't know why, but Joshie decided he wanted to go speak to the boy. It wasn't attraction so much as familiarity—like spotting a beloved family member you haven't seen in years. It caused a feeling of warm nostalgia, admiration—even adoration—deep inside of him. He imagined some people felt this when they met their soul mate or discovered the calling of religion.

Yes, that was what it was. He felt like he was standing in a church in the presence of something eternal and holy.

But it's only a boy, he reminded himself. A wounded boy.

Still, he had to speak to him.

So, Joshie followed the boy, who had turned and begun to walk away. He followed the boy to the very back of the crowd in the Winnebago County, Iowa cornfield where the concert was taking place. Soon enough, they ended up standing in the middle of some trampled husks, staring at each other.

"Who are you?" Joshie asked. By now, he was very much in love with the wounded boy that he decided must be a Fae of some sort. Well, he wasn't so much in love with him as he was in worship of him.

"Mkgor," the boy said. And then he added, "The God of Vampires."

Joshie nodded. That made sense to him. "Did you fall from Heaven? Are you going to take me there?"

Mkgor smiled, but his smile was full of velvety darkness. "I am going to make you feel it." Stepping forward, he put his good hand on Joshie's forehead.

Something was dripping down Joshie's face. He touched it and saw it was tar-like tears brimming over the edges of his eyes.

Then: darkness.

Joshie had no idea how it happened, but seemingly seconds later, he was standing in the middle of the cornfield concert, a huge spiral of torn-up, bloodied bodies scattered around him. Body parts were strewn everywhere and steaming in the cool night. A few of his victims were moaning, trying to crawl away.

He was kneeling over a girl, holding her down and chewing through her throat while she screamed through her murder. His belly ached it was so full of blood, but he couldn't seem to stop himself. He continued to chew and chew, her blood and viscera choking up his throat and pouring out of his mouth. Around him came cries of pain and horror, and, above that, the sound of sirens.

Eventually, a forceful—nearly hysterical—male voice shouted, "What did you do? Let her go and get down on your face! Now!"

Joshie let the girl go and turned to look at the large collection of police standing there, many of them armed with high-caliber Supe-killing firearms pointed at him. He counted at least ten, with more emerging from parked vehicles. The cops from at least three counties were here for him.

Joshie slowly climbed to his feet, hands up and the girl's blood pouring down the front of his concert tee. Once more, he glanced confusedly at the frayed humans—hundreds of them. Who had done this? Surely not he...?

"Get down on your face, grottie, arms spread!" another of the cops shouted, though he looked sick at the carnage. "Get down now!"

Joshie looked around for his friend Mkgor, the God of Vampires, but he was nowhere to be seen. He was alone.

"Get down now or we'll fire!"

Joshie turned back to the cops and made a decision. Without saying a word, he rushed the cops, who opened fire. He didn't feel the impacts of the high-caliber rounds even though he knew they were leaving fist-sized holes in his body—holes he would bleed out of to his final death.

Finally.

His dying regret was that he never had a chance to really live the vampire lifestyle. He'd been a loser in life and he was a loser in death. He blamed Kurt Cobain for that too.

XV

"What the hell did you do to Alisa?" Derek demanded as he paced back and forth across the storage room adjacent to the club where they were keeping Eliza. Eliza...who was alternately screaming in rage and crying for mercy now.

Edwin, currently attending to Tommy, whom they'd had to lever up and out of the floor, was doing his best not to listen to the wretched, heart-wrenching sounds she was making. "You all right, mate?" Edwin asked, testing Tommy's arm.

It moved stiffly and some of the circuits were still exposed, but Tommy was able to lift it up and down and turn his wrist. Couldn't hold a rifle, though. "Thank you, sir. I believe I'm operational." He tried to clench his hand, but something made a spirited whirring noise. Tommy groaned.

"Don't worry. I got you." Edwin picked up the sonic rifle and rested it on his shoulder. Giving his Enforcer a friendly jab with his elbow, he added, "I was pretty good with these types of boomsticks back in the day."

They were all waiting for one of Derek's people to retrieve some synthetic blood from the casino. Mr. Penny kept it on tap for their vampire patrons. But it sounded like Eliza was hurting herself, and if they didn't get that synth blood soon, he would need to do something to stop her—maybe even knock her out.

Please, God, no, he thought even though he no longer believed in a God that was merciful or who cared about his kind. *Don't make me hurt her...*

The idea made him ill at heart.

Eliza let out a long wail and Derek cried out in sympathetic response. He whirled on Edwin. "Stop fucking with that robot and do something for her!"

Edwin glared balefully at the man. "What do you suggest, mate? Should I go in there and restrain her? Hurt her? Would you?"

"You did this to her! You made her your Heir even after you knew she didn't want that!"

Up until now, he had let Derek go on and on. He knew Derek still had strong feelings for Eliza and was just reacting to her pain. But this he could not let slide.

With a low, throaty growl, Edwin glared at his nemesis. His look shut the man up immediately. "Do not ever question my loyalty to Eliza!" He took a deep breath and lowered the boomstick before he used it on the man. "Summersfield did this to her!"

"Even so," Derek declared. "You're responsible. If she wasn't with you—if she had stayed with me—Summersfield would never have taken her and done that to her! She would be safe. I would have kept her safe!"

Edwin started toward the man, to do what he didn't know, but Tommy put a hand on his shoulder, and that stopped him from doing something stupid.

Derek eyed him darkly, fingers flexing compulsively like he was thinking about pulling a weapon—which would be very bad for Derek. Even if he was packing some pretty heavy vampire-killing firearms under that long duster of his, Edwin was still faster and could shoot him like a fly off a wall before he ever got his finger on the trigger.

Breathe. Take it easy, ol' boy.

Edwin didn't want to do that to someone Eliza had loved. He knew she wouldn't approve.

Finally, sensing the tension between them and what might happen as a result, Derek's hands relaxed and he dropped his shoulders. Edwin felt a wave of relief, though he felt the smarting weight of Derek's accusation.

"Her life is the one she chose," Edwin explained.

"Chose." Derek snorted. "As if she had any choice with you."

Edwin thought about walking up and punching Derek squarely in the face, but he wasn't wrong. Eliza was in the state she was because she had chosen Edwin. She had put herself in danger just to be with him. Just to have a life with him. It was very much his fault. "I've killed lesser men for talking to me like that."

Derek, a smirk on his smarmy, handsome face, spread his arms. "Then kill me, oh great Vampire Lord. I know you've always wanted to."

Edwin shook his head. "If you believe that, then you don't know me at all."

"I know your kind. Parasites, one and all. You take everything good and make it rot. Tell me if I'm wrong."

Before Edwin could respond, Derek's runner burst in through the door. She looked nearly breathless, having undoubtedly rushed the whole way to and from the casino. "This is all Mr. Penny had." She presented a painfully small metal thermos. "He said the supply line is fubared. He only kept this for an emergency."

"That's not enough," Edwin immediately told her. "I'll feed her myself." How he would do that he wasn't sure. As a vamp, he didn't have enough blood to even begin to satisfy her. Eliza would probably tear him apart.

But Derek held up a hand to stop him from leaving. "Vampire blood has no nutrients in it, Edwin. You know that. It'll just make her hungrier."

Another wail pealed out.

Edwin shuddered. "We have to do something!"

Turning to another of his people, one Edwin suspected was a medic from the big bag he held at his side, Derek said, "Walter, get your works. We'll feed Eliza the old-fashioned way."

Before Edwin could protest, Derek stripped off his coat, which clunked heavily to the floor with all of its hidden hardware, and started rolling up his sleeve. He was going to feed Eliza with his own blood.

The runner grabbed Derek's arm and looked into his eyes pleadingly. Edwin got the impression there was more between them than a cause. "Let me."

"I would never ask one of you to do something like this, Alice."

"I don't mind."

"But I do."

Another of Eliza's wails rose up and up, making the windows of the club vibrate and spurring Derek to hurry. Edwin stayed with Tommy and let the medic work over Derek.

It didn't take long. Within minutes, they had a substantial bag of Derek's blood and Derek was looking pale and ill. It was dark blood, almost purplish in hue: The blood of a Poppet genetically enhanced to be extremely nourishing for a vampire.

Edwin took a step toward Derek, who was weaving on his feet. "Let me feed her? None of you should go anywhere near her in her present state."

Derek thought about that and then nodded.

He snatched the bag of blood from Derek, but he couldn't help but feel a swell of admiration for the man, which irritated him greatly. He much preferred to think of Derek as petty and spiteful, someone undeserving of Eliza's love, not as someone willing to give his own blood for his wife's vampiric needs.

As Edwin turned to leave, Derek grumbled under his breath, "I'm doing it for her. Not you."

***

From the moment the change seized her, everything was different. What was worry for Edwin's safety became rage. What was normal was turned upside down. The pain inside of her—the darkness she had held back for years—became gigantic—all-consuming. It exploded out of her as if she was a dying star.

She couldn't even rightfully say when exactly it happened. She only knew she was looking down at the absolute devastation of Edwin's club and at her husband being brutally savaged by that monster. She was fumbling the little boomer out of its holster when a shiver ripped through her. Not just up her back but all through her body, her blood. For one long moment, she thought she heard Summersfield laugh, her fingers spasmed and she dropped the gun, and then...and then it all went black, and she didn't know what had happened until she opened her eyes and saw she was inside a cage and realized she was different.

Changed.

Turned.

She found it hard to believe. At the same time, it was impossible to ignore. Each time the pain of the hunger swelled, she felt she must burst from it and cried out. She knew it was real, that she was turned. Each time the pain receded, she sobbed in relief but grounded herself for the next wave.

She was lucid—mostly—but she wasn't sure how long that would last. She asked him for more restraints. She was terrified she might turn on herself otherwise or maybe break the cage apart with her bare hands. Lovey, no, he'd said at the time, but when he saw she was inches away from ripping the cage door off its hinges, he asked Derek for handcuffs and any remaining chain he had.

There was a fetish bar nearby. One of his runners brought a few things back, including chainless cuffs she begged him to put on her and a leather dog collar with a large metal ring and a sturdy chain attached to it. It was difficult to get him to bind her the way she needed him to, but after begging and sobbing, he finally did as she'd asked.

Now, Eliza knelt on the floor of the cage, her wrists bound in the small of her back and the collar and short chain binding her far enough away from the bars of the cage that she hoped she wouldn't hurt anyone.

The pain in Edwin's eyes when he stepped back inside the club and looked at her was almost unendurable, almost worse than the agony building inside her once more.

He approached her cautiously. Her interest quickly switched to the medical bag full of blood in his hands. She could smell it even from across the room. But she forced herself to focus on him. "W...what's happening to me?" she managed to hiss out of her scorched throat. "I mean...I know I'm changed. I just d-don't underssstand thisss..."

"You're starving," he said, his voice a low rumble. "Actually, you've been starving for years." When he saw she wasn't following, he added, "You were made a vampire eighteen years ago, lovey. You remember that, right?"

Her body rippled with pain. "Y-yes," she breathed out between her dry, broken lips. That was the night Summersfield forced her to drink his essence and made her his Heir. The night of her supposed "marriage" to him. He wanted her to be his Bride, and when she bolted, he captured her and forced his blood on her in an attempt to make her never leave him again.

He nodded as he came to a halt before her cage. "Even though your vampirism has been in remission all this time, it was never truly gone. You were never really human. You've been a vampire for eighteen years. And you've never fed properly. You're an eighteen-year-old baby vampire who has never eaten anything in her undead life."

The pain flared up again, a crushing agony that sent drips of blood flowing from her eyes and down her face. Eliza screamed, her back bowing with effort. She couldn't help herself. The room echoed with her wails.

He waited until she'd settled into a crumpled pile, sagging with weakness. Then he explained in a small voice, "I've seen this in vamps that have hibernated. Your body is literally eating itself from the inside."

Eliza let out a sob. The wretched pain had left her shaking. Her thoughts were broken and scattered. She had to really think about what he was saying. "H-help me, Edwin...please...help me...or else end me." She hiccupped and made a low keening noise. "I can't continue like this."

Nodding, he let himself into the cage.

Eliza shrank back at his approach, terrified she would lunge at him, maybe even break the chains she was in—they weren't exactly strong, after all—but she found to her immense relief that she was too weak to break anything at the moment. Still, when he undid the collar at her throat and the cuffs at her wrists and sat down on the floor, bravely taking her into his arms, she felt her entire body spasm around her, wanting to run or flee or maybe attack him.

She shook like an epileptic in his embrace.

He pressed the straw-like tube to her lips and she quickly began sucking on the blood in the bag. His grip was incredibly powerful, relentless. She had the feeling he would sooner break her bones than let her slip free, and she was grateful for that.

The blood was gone too soon, but it helped to temporarily ease the roiling agony in her body. Edwin used a handkerchief to wipe her lips. "Better?"

She turned and sobbed against his suit, dirtying it with the blood all over her mouth. "No." She let out a long, trembling sob. "I've never appreciated what you go through. How you live. Is it always this awful for you?"

Edwin tenderly brushed his fingers through her hair. "I don't let myself go that long. Trust me when I say you really wouldn't like me when I'm hungry."

She moaned in response to that. Being with Edwin—her love, her soul mate—curled up safely in his arms, was incredibly soothing. Her body was still so weak from the change, and her hands trembled where she clutched his coat, but soon enough, she fell into an exhausted sleep.

***

It pained him to have to secure Eliza inside the cage, but he did so at her request. She smiled in gratitude as he touched her cheek and then closed and locked the door.

Now, he had to turn his attention to Samara. The whole thing felt oddly inconsequential now that Eliza was suffering from her sudden vampirism, but she had assured him she would be all right and they needed to complete their mission. Otherwise, all of this awfulness would have been for nothing.

"Right." Edwin nodded to her. He stood in front of her cage, gazing in at her longingly, barely able to make himself move. "I just feel so…" He couldn't complete the thought.

"I don't blame you, Edwin," she whispered. "If you're blaming yourself, you need to stop that immediately and focus on the matter at hand."

She looked haggard and tired, but he barely even registered that. Something about the way the curse had smoothed even the smallest blemish from her skin, lightened her eyes to a silvery hue, given her wings so much like a mourning cloak butterfly, and curled her hair perfectly around her face into a fiercely burning black halo had turned her into a heartbreakingly beautiful creature. Perhaps it was the fact that now her vampirism was working in tangent with her already near-perfect Poppet genes. He wasn't sure. But there was something about her that made her exquisitely hypnotic to look upon.

When Derek stepped into the now-silent club to check on them, Edwin felt the palatable waves of shock and rage coming off the man at the sight of his childhood sweetheart. Eliza and Derek exchanged a look before she turned to him. Her face was surprisingly placid.

"Please go, Edwin," she told him from her position kneeling on the floor. "I would like to speak to Derek alone." Even the timbre of her voice had changed, becoming deeper—darker—and as silky as a mouth full of chocolate.

Nodding, Edwin told her, "I will be right back, love. Don't…go anywhere."

She smiled at that.

***

"Goddamnit, Alisa." Derek let out a sharp breath as he came to a halt in front of her.

Eliza lifted her head. "Hello, Derek."

Derek looked her over, taking in her collar and chains and the cuffs binding her wrists. She saw the tears burning in his eyes. He looked at a loss for words.

So she took the initiative. "Thank you. For the blood. I know that must have been uncomfortable for you."

He shook his head and swore under his breath. "I wish you could see yourself, Alisa."

"Derek..."

"Let me finish."

She fell silent and lowered her eyes. Right now, she couldn't meet his gaze.

He spoke softly but with great conviction. "I'm not here to argue with you or judge you," he told her. "I know what Edwin said. That everything was your choice."

She kept her head down, waiting for whatever judgment he intended to pass on her. In another life, she would have been enraged at his audacity to confront her this way and try to shame her, but she was too weak from hunger to even feel anger.

"I just..." Derek choked up. "I just want to ask you something. It's important."

Eliza pressed her lips together. "What is it, Derek?"

It took him a moment to respond. "Do you regret it? Him? Everything that's happened to you?"

She thought about that, ran it through her head before glancing up. She wouldn't say this all bent over and looking penitent. "No, Derek."

"Even after what you've become?" Derek's face twisted. "His Bride. His...creature?"

"This was...inevitable," she concluded. "Vampires were always a part of my life, Derek. Yours, too."

"Maybe. But we were never supposed to become one of them."

She felt a spike of anger but realized how futile it was. She didn't think Derek would ever really understand her. She could scream her reasons from the rooftops, but he would never get it. He was too damaged. Still, she had to try and reason with him. She owed him that much.

"Derek...whatever you think of vampires and Edwin, he and I made a life. We had a son. We have a ship. A Congress. I love him. I don't regret any of those things. They're a part of who I am."

"You mean you're a part of who he is."

Eliza felt pity squeeze her heart. "I can't make you understand what Edwin and I have. But I think that's always been the difference between the two of us. You've always seen yourself as a Poppet—part of the vampires. A cog in their eternal machine. No way out..."

"But you found the way?" he mocked.

She bit back a scathing reply. "I found my own way...for better or for worse. I was free. I am free. But you've never really been free of them, Derek."

He harrumphed—undoubtedly at the sight of her bonds. "If you'll excuse me, I don't think I'll be taking advice from a Poppet who became a vampire who's now chained up to keep from killing everyone."

She realized something finally: He was eyeing her the same way he had always eyed Edwin. She, like Edwin, was now the enemy. It made her flinch inside. "Derek..."

"You're one of them. One of the collective whole. One of the monsters."

She sighed. Everything about Derek tired her endlessly. "I want to sleep now, Derek. I am thankful for your help, but I need you to go away so I can rest."

"Gladly."

He spat on the floor before he left the room, slamming the door behind him.

| xvi |

"Oliver? Oliver, wake up, darling."

Moaning, he tried to turn over and go back to sleep, but a hand kept shaking him until he turned back and cracked his eyes open. His body felt like lead, and his mouth was as dry as ash. "Where...where am I?" he asked Jonah, who was standing over him.

"In bed, silly. You've overslept."

"Huh." Oliver sat up and felt the room tilt around him. His head hurt like it was full of ragged shards of glass. He groaned at the pain and it took him a moment to center his thoughts. According to the bedside clock, it was nearly six in the evening.

Jonah looked concerned. Then Oliver noticed he was dressed in a suit. It made him look sexy as hell, but still...Jonah was not a suit guy.

"Wh-where are you going?" Oliver asked.

"Not me. Us. You promised you'd go with me tonight and meet my dad, remember?"

"No," Oliver answered honestly. "I don't."

"Well, you did." Jonah's face fell. "Would you rather stay home instead?"

Jonah had asked him to meet his family? That was a huge step in their relationship. "No...no..." Oliver waved Jonah back. "I'll go."

He climbed out of bed, weaving a little on his feet. Why did he feel so weak? Jonah had given him his blood. He should have felt invigorated, powerful. But he didn't. He just felt sleepy-tired and...hungry.

As soon as he was safely ensconced in the bathroom, Oliver checked his stash, but the Concerta was almost gone. Just a handful of pills in his pocket; he had flushed the rest. He had promised Jonah he wouldn't take anymore, so to do so would mean he had lied. He threw the remaining pills away.

After showering and dressing, Oliver stepped out of the bedroom and spotted Jonah in his kitchen, scrambling eggs. "I thought I would make you something light to help you get going," Jonah explained, smiling widely. He seemed excited about their dinner date tonight.

But the smell of the cooking eggs turned Oliver's stomach. "Thank you, no. I just can't eat anything right now."

Jonah turned off the stove and joined him in the living room. He went about the task of unbuttoning Oliver's shirt and setting it straight before buttoning it up again. Oliver had done it wrong. As he tucked the tails of his shirt into Oliver's trousers, he said, "You've lost weight. A lot of weight."

"Have I?"

"Are you sure you don't want me calling your parents? You look like the dead, darling."

"Thanks."

Jonah gave him a sympathetic look and leaned in to kiss Oliver.

They retrieved their jackets and went down to the street to catch a steam trolley. Ten minutes later, they were standing on the tarmac of a runway in one of the smaller airstrips adjacent to the college campus. It wasn't until they were aboard a Hummingbird that Oliver realized something was wrong. He couldn't understand why they were on a transport. He tried to communicate that concern, but Jonah distracted him by giving him a glass tumbler full of a thin, blackish liquid that looked like cheap wine but smelled like pennies. "What is this?"

"Taste it."

Oliver drank it down in one fell swoop and licked his teeth. It smelled gross but it filled him with a lovely, drowsy warmth.

"It's blood substitute. Perfect Red, it's called. You've never had it?"

Oliver thought back. Once, when he was small, he'd sneaked a sample of Perfect Red off his dad's wet bar, curious about the taste. He thought it tasted terrible at the time, but now he found it wasn't too bad. Not as good as Jonah's blood, which was heaven on Earth, but it was a decent approximation. He held up the glass and Jonah refilled it from a decanter. Oliver drank that glass, too.

"I lied. Well, not lied, exactly. But I did omit the truth," Jonah explained as he settled in the plush seat beside Oliver as they began take-off procedures.

"What do you mean?" Suddenly, Oliver's heart was fluttering—the drink or Jonah's words, he wasn't sure.

"My dad? He works aboard a gyro. That's where we're headed."

"Your dad is a Floater?"

"He's...well...he's more than that."

"What do you mean?"

"I'll explain everything after you've met him."

Why did that make Oliver suddenly uncomfortable?

After they were in the air, Jonah unbuckled and rose to refill Oliver's glass. "You're really enjoying this stuff. It's like you're a real vampire." Jonah laughed.

Oliver drank the glass in his hand but then put it down in a holder to keep from drinking any more. He didn't like what it was doing to his head.

"You okay, Oliver?" Jonah asked.

Jonah. He was so beautiful, almost ephemeral. He wanted to paint Jonah's whole body with his tongue, a thought that both startled and embarrassed him. But Jonah seemed to understand.

"Yes, Ollie. I feel the same," he whispered, his voice low and husky, seductive. Jonah leaned into him and traced a long coil of Oliver's hair that was stuck to his cheek. "They say you look like Lady Eliza. The Red Queen. But I don't agree with that. I think you look like your dad." Jonah stretched the coil of hair out before letting it go. "All posh and British. Just with all that lovely black hair and those winter blue eyes. A little lost angel."

Jonah's rambling went on, but Oliver was having trouble following it. He felt warm and comfortable. His thoughts were scattered and nothing seemed quite real. When the transport docked, Jonah had to help him up and off the Hummingbird. It was like he was moving through a dream, unfamiliar faces speaking low to him, leading him through a warren of lighted corridors. But with Jonah always at his side, his hand a reassuring pressure on his arm, it felt right. He tried to ask whose gyro this was, but each time he tried, he lost his train of thought.

They came upon a lift and were swiftly transported to parts unknown. More corridors and glaring lights that hurt Oliver's eyes. They eventually came around to a large dining hall set with a long trestle with a white tablecloth, tall white taper candles, and bunches of huge white gladiolas in silver vases. The table was set with fine bone china and crystal goblets for three guests.

Jonah guided him to a chair in the middle of one side of the table before taking the spot beside him. Oliver didn't like this. He tried to get up, but a servant stepped out of the shadows and urged him to sit, then served him more of the delicious Perfect Red. Oliver, losing track of what he'd been trying to do, started to drink.

The servant hovered nearby, filling his glass each time he drained it. He was on his third glass when the Lord of the ship arrived, surrounded by several Poppet servants, two of them holding his arms as if he were frail or weak.

Oliver lifted his eyes and nearly gagged on his drink. He didn't know any of the Lords personally, but Lord Edwin had described many of them in detail. He easily recognized Lord Trasch cutting a path to the table like a tall, humpbacked ship, his red robes brushing the floor. The ancient vampire moved haltingly and with the help of an elaborate and twisty black staff. The embroidery in his white lace ruff glinted in the candlelight, and his red-rimmed, unsmiling eyes took in the full breadth of the room before settling on Oliver.

Choking and coughing, Oliver turned and glared at Jonah, who had stood up. "Thank you for joining us, Reverend," Jonah said formally, moving forward to meet Trasch and take his heavily beringed hand. He even kissed one of his rings, a sign of fealty.

The drink had loosened Oliver's tongue, and the shock had done something more to him. Normally, he would have been too shy and terror-struck to respond, but now he coughed out at Jonah, "Trasch...is your father?"

Jonah turned to him. "Not biologically, of course, but we have a relationship of sorts." Jonah looked to his "father," who nodded that he should continue. "Lord Trasch created me in his laboratory, so, in that way, he is very much my creator. He has also acted as my surrogate father since I was born. I owe Lord Trasch much."

The words coming out of Jonah made no sense. How had Trasch created him?

Oliver tried to stand up again, but Trasch's head swung his way and he said one word—"Stay"—and Oliver sank back down, too stunned and afraid to move. He didn't think Trasch had any powers like Lord Foxley did—at least, he hoped he did not—but it didn't matter. The creature's very presence had left him weak at the knees. It was like looking into the eyes of a demon.

Jonah, looking proud and pleased, linked his arm through Lord Trasch's and walked his father to where Oliver sat. He even reached for Oliver's chair, pulled it out with Oliver still sitting in it, and turned it to face Trasch.

How Oliver trembled. He felt cold and small as he cowered under Lord Trasch's immense shadow. Trasch's eyes, grey with cataracts, roved all over him, making his skin itch as if it were conducting an electrical charge. And the creature wasn't even touching him. The ancient Lord smelled like chemicals and old blood and dust—the world's oldest library.

Finally, Trasch narrowed those rheumy eyes and licked his lips with a sharp grey tongue. "So, this is he. Lord Edwin's son. His biological child."

"Yes, Reverend," Jonah announced, smiling like they were all having a fine time. "This is he. Little Lord Oliver. Quite exquisite, isn't he?"

Lord Trasch seriously considered Oliver. Each time the vampire moved even a little, Oliver expected a plume of dust to rise up around him, but that never happened. The creature did lean in to examine him more closely. Oliver shrank back but stared back. Oliver was no fool. He was fully aware of how much the High Courts, Trasch particularly, hated his dad. But he didn't think even Trasch had the gall to attack him without bringing the wrath of the Sacred Seven down on himself.

Trasch's hand flashed out and Oliver lurched. But the vampire had merely captured a hank of his curling hair. His touch sounded dry and rough as he sifted the black curls through his incredibly long, talon-like fingers. The sound made Oliver's nerves jangle. Trash wetted his lips before speaking. "He is very pretty. But he seems a bit reserved considering his parentage."

"He's not," Jonah insisted. "Don't let his demeanor fool you, Reverend. He's quite the tiger. Quite the krsnik. I've seen him fight. He'll make a fine warrior for the High Courts."

Oliver's eyes moved aside to Jonah even as his lover's words slowly squeezed his heart to pieces. Were they really talking about him like he was...livestock? Something to be purchased at auction?

He sucked in a bit of air and managed to say, "St-top it...I...want..." His voice trailed away.

"What do you want, Oliver?" Jonah asked. "Tell me. Tell us."

"I want my mum," Oliver whispered despite the childishness of it. "I want to go home."

Trasch's eyes clocked around his face. "Really? You want to run home to your mother, little krsnik? I'm disappointed. I thought you were made of sturdier stuff. Still, I completely understand..." Letting go of his hair, Trasch edged back a step. "If you are so very fearful, then run along. Obviously, you are not the tiger that my child thinks you are, and any further discussion on the matter is wasted."

But Oliver stayed in his seat and glanced around, his attention settling on the guards.

"No one here will stop you," Trasch proclaimed. He even made a shooing gesture with one long-fingered hand. "Go now. Be-gone."

Oliver eyed Trasch carefully. Surely, there was some deception to be had here. Someone who would try and stop him. Else, why would Jonah go through with this elaborate ruse of wanting to be his boyfriend? And for what reason? To deliver him like a package to the High Courts? The thought depressed him endlessly.

After a tense moment, Oliver slowly climbed to his feet. A part of him told him to run and do what was necessary to get out of there, but that wasn't exactly reasonable. He was on a gyro, hanging miles above the Earth. And even ignoring that obstacle, there was the situation with Jonah.

Turning to his lover, Oliver said, "You lied to me. You tricked me!"

Jonah sucked in a sharp breath. "No, Oliver! I never told you any lies..."

"You didn't tell me you work for the High Courts!" Oliver clenched his fists. "What are you? Are you a krsnik too?"

Jonah glanced at Lord Trasch and some silent communication passed between them before he turned back to Oliver. "No. I'm something else."

"A vampire?" A sudden horror seized Oliver. "The rabbits...you were eating them—!"

"A vampire hunter," Jonah interrupted, his voice soft but strong. He didn't say it like he was proud of it; it simply was. "I hunt vampires for the High Courts. Lord Trasch made me specifically for the task."

Oliver thought about that and, slowly, it all began to click. Looking up at the monstrous vampire, he said to Jonah, "You're a Poppet?" To Trasch, he added, "You own Biocell, don't you?"

Trasch's smile grew. Biocell was the multi-billion dollar pharmaceutical company that designed Poppets for work down in Poppettown or for pleasure for the Vampire Lords. The same corporation that had created his mum and those like her.

"I founded it," Lord Trasch admitted. "But I don't own it any longer."

"But the Reverend still has the means to make Poppets," Jonah explained. "I was created in Lord Trasch's lab. Well, not the lab per se. I was genetically designed there and implanted into a Poppet, who then gave birth to me."

"So, you really are a Poppet."

"Sort of."

Oliver shook his head. He didn't know what to say to that. A genetically modified vampire hunting Poppet? The High Courts dealt with rogues in some way. But to have mostly fallen in love with one...the thought made him sick to his stomach.

"Is that why we met? Did you set me up?" He glanced up at Lord Trasch. What he was feeling now was so terrible that even his former fear of Trasch couldn't compare. "Did the High Courts order my...execution?"

Jonah broke out in laughter. "Of course not, silly. You've never broken a law in your life! But the Courts do have an interest in you. Like me, you were created under interesting circumstances."

Oliver growled under his breath. "Did you tell everyone that?"

"The High Council already knew. And they have a proposition for you." He glanced at Lord Trasch.

The ancient vampire indicated the table. "Sit and dine with us. Listen to our proposal. It is not anything terrible, Lord Oliver. More of a...job offer, you might say. And if you still want to run home to your mother, you may do so. No one here will stop you. We will even provide the transport."

Oliver's first instinct was to tell Lord Trasch to go to hell. But then he thought about it. What did he have to return to? College course he was failing? Another day stuffed full of cheap synthetic drugs, sleepwalking through his day, just hoping for the night to come when the sun didn't hurt him so much? Maybe a future of hitting dives and hoping someone would share their blood with him the way Jonah had?

The idea of leaving was suddenly fatally depressing.

Jonah eyed the synthetic blood being poured blackly into the tall, thin goblets. "What's in this stuff?" he asked.

Jonah said as he took his seat at the table, "Synthetic blood mixed with Twilight. Bit of a kick, hey?"

Oliver had no serious plans to take them up on their offer, but he was interested in what they had to say.

***

The Phoenix, like all transports, was fitted with a boot that contained a Hydraulic Protection Compartment. They were standard issue, available if a vampire needed one, and built strong enough to withstand most explosions. An HPC could also double as a mobile holding cell, if the need arose.

Once all of them got back to the transport and Edwin saw Eliza on board—she insisted he leave the cuffs on her wrists—he went around to the back. Rahul, his Mechi pilot, helped him roll the HPC out on a coffin trolley.

Edwin turned to Tommy, who had Samara, bound and gagged, over his shoulder. He nodded and Tommy set her down inside the open compartment. Walter, Derek's medic who had accompanied them, immediately went about taking her pulse and checking her vitals. Samara hadn't come around yet, which Edwin was happy about, but he was also a little worried she might have been seriously injured in her battle with Eliza. Perhaps because she was a Poppet-turned-vampire, Eliza was freakishly strong, and he had no idea how durable a krsnik was.

"How is she, Doc?"

Walter straightened up and turned to Edwin. "I'm not a doctor. I'm a CN. But…she'll live. Not that anything can really kill Samara. Maybe a percussion grenade…but then, maybe not even that."

"Huh." Walter's words troubled Edwin. He stood over the HPC, looking down at the girl. Her clothes were frayed from her battle, but she otherwise showed no apparent injuries. Asleep, she looked painfully young—barely more than a child. Crazy chit. He wondered how old she really was.

When her body jerked slightly in sleep, he flinched and Tommy raised his rifle.

"She won't wake up," Walter explained. "I shot her up with enough Ketamine to put an elephant down."

"Do I need to keep her tranqued during transport?"

"It wouldn't hurt."

"Can I remove the ropes?"

"Why would you want to do that?"

Edwin gave the man a funny look. "If she's tranqued, we don't need her bound like some kind of wild animal."

Walter shrugged, which annoyed Edwin. He didn't seem to care one whit that a young girl was tied up in ropes in front of him. Then again, the Red Doors, for all their high-handedness, had turned Samara over to him with remarkably little resistance. He wondered if they even considered her a real person. Probably, they counted even their own disposable in the name of their cause.

"Help me with the ropes."

Together, they got the ropes off Samara.

"What do you plan to do with her?" Walter asked conversationally.

"Once we're airborne...well, we'll see if we can reason with her."

"You can't reason with Samara." Walter snorted. "I've seen her in action. She's a junkie. She only cares about her next fix."

Edwin felt a pang. She looked too bloody young to be a junkie.

Walter showed Edwin how to use the tranq gun he even gave him a good supply of the pink capsules that Samara used. "They're loaded with Twilight, in case you wondered."

Edwin held one of the capsules up to the dim runner lights on the Phoenix. "And these will make her...compliant?"

"If you mean will they keep her from killing and eating you and your wife and ripping your ship apart? Then...maybe."

"She's that strong?" Tommy asked, sounding concerned. The well-being of the ship and its crew was his responsibility.

"She's a krsnik. We've never seen a creature its equal, which is why she makes a good soldier. It's like she was created to just kill and destroy." Walter swallowed, his Adam's apple bobbing. "Why do you think Derek turned her over so easily? She's unstable. More a liability than a weapon these days."

Well, that didn't sound good. Like loading a bomb onto their ship.

Walter saw Edwin's worried expression and elaborated. "The Twilight should keep her in check. The pills don't have any real nutritional value. They just trick the vamp—or, in this case, the krsnik—into feeling like they've consumed an enormous meal of blood. But they waste you over time. Starve you to death without you noticing. And she's been taking them a while. So, word of advice, don't turn your back on her."

Edwin squinted at the pill bottle. "Gotcha, Doc...eh, Nurse."

"Glad to help." Walter reached for his medic satchel and snapped it closed, hanging it around his shoulder. He paused before he left. "What's going to happen to her?"

Edwin programmed the HPC closed. It snapped shut with a hiss of hydraulic air. "Eh?"

"What are you going to do with Samara?"

He looked down at the HPC. "She's important to a mission I've undertaken. She's...well, she has a job to do. Hopefully, if all goes well, she'll fix what's happened to the vampires."

"Ah. That."

Derek's radio had been going off intermittently all day, something to do with random vampire attacks like the lad who ripped apart a whole cornfield's worth of concert-goers. But, so far, no one understood what was happening to them.

"There is no fixing the vamps." Walter glared at Edwin and Tommy before turning to glance at his Red Door friends waiting in the hangar.

"You really don't care about what happens to her at all, do you?"

Walter gave him an odd look. "She's one of your kind, vampire. One of the race that enslaved me since the day I was born. Do you know what your kind does to mine—really know? Why would I care what happens to her? Or you? Or your 'mission?' I'm just doing what Derek asked me to do."

Edwin stared openmouthed after Walter and his friends, who had started to pile into their vehicles. A thought occurred to him. He was doing all of this so the vampire race wasn't turned into rabid monsters. Sleepwalkers. But did they deserve it? Maybe he should let the Nothing take the vamps, transform them, and let the humans have at them with their weapons and their outrage. A mass genocide of the vampire race. It wasn't like they didn't have it coming.

Including Eliza and Oliver?

Therein lay the rub. If the vamps had to be annihilated, nothing was stopping the humans from murdering his wife or child. And as much disdain as he might have for his own race, he couldn't allow his little family to come to harm. Grunting, he slammed the boot in frustration.

"C'mon, mate, we have a job to do," he told Tommy.

"Yes, sir."

He, Tommy, and Rahul boarded the Phoenix. Tommy took a spot up front and immediately opened the book he had brought. Edwin glanced at him, sensing a shift...something...he wasn't quite sure what, only that something had changed with Tommy. He almost asked his Enforcer if something was bothering him, then decided against it. If it was important, Tommy would tell him in time.

Eliza sat in the back on the floor, hands cuffed in front of her. Her head was bowed as if she were praying, which he knew she was not. Eliza was an atheist. In fact, these days, so was he.

"How are you feeling, love?" Edwin asked, kneeling on the floor to check her color.

She lifted her head. Her eyes still looked feverishly bright and dark and largely unfocused. He noticed that she was gripping the little sunflower pin in her bound hands—the same one he and Ollie had given her as a birthday gift over ten years earlier. She was rubbing it like it was a magical talisman capable of protecting her. "I'm hungry again, Edwin." Her voice was small and ashamed.

"We're intercepting my old friend Captain Leo in…" He consulted his pocket watch. "…just under six hours. We'll board his ship for the rest of the journey to the K2. He has substitute blood and Poppets aplenty onboard his ship. Can you wait that long?"

Eliza looked miserable. She had never wanted this. Never wanted to be one of them, with all that entailed. "Edwin, please," she pleaded, "please don't make me drink from a Poppet."

"Lovey, you don't have to drink from a Poppet if you don't want to."

She sniffed and smiled through the obvious pain she was enduring. "Thank you."

He stroked the tangled hair off her face and kissed her forehead. Then used a sharp thumbnail to press a bloody crease down the inside of his wrist and turned it over, inviting her to take from him. "We'll get through this, no worries. And I will be with you every step of the way."

| **xvii** |

"Hello, Alisa. Did you miss me?"

Eliza jerked fully awake. Or rather—alive. She sat up in her bunk, nearly dropping the pin she had clutched in both hands. She quickly realized she had experienced no muzzy transition period. One moment there was nothing—no dreams, no drifty feeling of sleep—and the next she was fully alert, experiencing everything in Technicolor and Surround Sound.

What a vampire experienced coming back to life, she realized. She wasn't used to that. But, she reminded herself, vampires only lived in two states—fully dead or fully alive. And they didn't dream. Or, at least, that's how Edwin explained it. He remembered no dreams because he rarely had them. And when he was "dead," he was quite dead. She knew because she had slept next to him for close to two decades.

Vampires had no dreams. No tears. She no longer had dreams or tears.

It really happened at last.

She kept expecting to revert to her human form, but that wasn't happening. She should have known it wouldn't. If her good (and deceased) friend Dr. Vu were here, she would have been better able to explain it. Something along the lines of her recessive vampire gene having finally caught up to her. But Veronica had been among the many victims of the Ice Pirates when they attacked the *Queen's Gambit* years earlier.

Eliza tried not to let a feeling of despair swamp her, but it was hard. She was going to miss all of the things that had made her human.

A sob caught in her throat like a claw, and she glanced aside to make certain she hadn't disturbed Edwin, lying bravely beside her in the bunk. He was very still now. Dead. After feeding her from his own body, he needed the rest. Besides, he had reached the end of his waking cycle. She knew from experience that he could go as long as forty-eight hours before he was forced to shut down or his clockwork heart would do the job for him—usually against his will.

He was lying perfectly still, face pale and cold, hands clasped over each other at the midpoint of his body. When not in bed or the confines of an HPC, he bound his wrists with a bit of dental floss to prevent them from going slack. In years past, he used his precious old wooden rosary to do so, but, more recently, he had left the antique thing behind for his travels.

Cold and all bound up, he looked like the guest of honor of a wake. Did she look like that too, now?

"Alisa."

Swallowing hard, she got up and stepped into the aisle. She had to be careful since her wrists were still bound by the cuffs, which she had requested he leave on. The cuffs and the pin in her hand helped her to keep from compulsively grabbing at anything with blood in it. Whenever the hunger grew too terrible to bear, she jabbed the sharp point of the pin into her hands. The pain caused the hunger to recede for a time.

"Michael?"

"I'm here." Michael's timbre was low and whispery under the dim hum of the Phoenix in transit. Should couldn't see him clearly but she could feel his presence, which didn't surprise her. He was her creator, after all. He was inside her blood.

"Did you think I would leave you? Especially now, my Heir?"

She shook her head. "I always knew you would return when this day arrived."

"I could never leave you, Alisa," Michael's voice nearly crooned. "I never really have."

She believed that. Even with her darkness-piercing vampire eyes, she could only make out the vaguest of outlines in the aisle between the seats, but what she saw was hauntingly familiar—Summerfield's tall, dark outline, his glinting eyes and teeth. He was still so achingly handsome—and almost mind-numbing horrific. The bogey that haunted her awake or asleep, the phantom that haunted hers and Edwin's ship. She had glimpsed him from the corner of her eyes for years. He had been with her this whole time...waiting for her to transition.

He must be so happy, so proud. The monster.

Eliza took a few halting steps toward him. Up until now, she had hoped he was a figment of her past trauma, but she saw now that he was quite real. Maybe not real in any physical way. It might be alchemical vampire magic or some manifestation of her own psychology, but she knew he was there, as real and malignant as some cancer that had never been cut properly from her body.

Despite Dr. Vu once warning her that if they did not find a way to keep her vampire genes turned off, they might one day swamp her system, Eliza managed to convince herself that such a thing, if it ever happened at all, was in her distant future. Obviously, she'd been wrong. Something had switched them on—and now there was no going back. She was lost.

The closer she got to Summersfield, the more she recognized his mad, holy smile. He opened his arms to her. "Oh, Alisa...my dear, sweet, fierce Alisa!" The runner lights reflected like blue flames in his eyes. "You are such a lovely Heir! A perfect little vampire doll…"

"Stop calling me that! My name is Eliza. And I hope you rot in hell," she told him.

But he ignored her venom. "Truly, God made you for me—my second chance at a family! And once our son joins us—"

Anger flared up in her, making the lights flicker in the ship. She sank the point of the pin deep into the meat of her hand. "You will never have my son! You can take me, you can even break me if that's what it takes to get you off, but Oliver will never be yours!"

Another flicker and the lights went dark.

Eliza stood perfectly still in the almost perfect darkness, the only light coming from the sliver of the moon shining in one of the transport's portal windows. She could feel the blood running down her hand. She could hear her own breathing—raspy and labored. She tasted blood in her mouth from where she had been chewing her tongue.

Seconds later, the emergency lights flared up. Michael wasn't there. But his promise hung in the air like a stinking miasma.

* * *

In the dream, he was fighting a black dragon.

He hoped the creature would never sense the trap until it was too late.

Several of the knights under his command were perched atop the cave entrance, and one of them, giving an imperative shout, led the others in levering a larger boulder over the edge with their swords and staffs. It slammed into the giant dragon's neck, driving him to the earth where his son lay dying not ten feet away. Oliver had acted as the bait, the sacrifice. Now, he lay horrendously wounded on the ground, his body full of grievous wounds from his battle with the dragon while the others sprang the trap.

Edwin hurried to his son's side. A huge part of his soul was dying inside of him. How could he let this happen? How could he ever agree to such a horrible plan?

His knights, perhaps twenty in all, quickly rappelled down off the edge of the cave entrance to end the fallen beast. But their military action was disrupted when the sudden terror of his dire situation sent the dragon into a frenzy, spitting and lashing out.

Still, the knights, all shouting battle anthems, fell upon him, stabbing him with their small weapons. The dragon's scaly skin burned and scorched at the touch of their swords—new weapons forged in iron that cut like fire.

But Edwin didn't care about any of that. He gathered his boy into his arms—his son, shuddering on the ground, gasping, blood upon his lips. "Oliver," he rasped, clutching his precious dying boy in his arms ever tighter.

Oliver's eyes rolled in his head, barely able to focus on him. The pain in his body made him spasm. Edwin, unsure what else to do, gnashed his own tongue and tried to give his son the kiss of life, but Oliver only choked and convulsed. Finally, he fell limp in Edwin's arms. The absolute horror of his son dying so suddenly stunned him into inaction. He couldn't even move as the dragon continued to roll and squeal under the attack of his knights only a few feet away.

Oliver...he lay so still, so strangely unreal in Edwin's arms. Edwin could do nothing but clutch him, hold him close, and wail.

Beside him, the great beast made a bellowing noise of despair when one of his knights plunged his sword into one of its rheumy red eyes.

The black dragon melted into nothing, his soulful death song rising high on the crisp autumnal air. But Edwin hardly noticed. All he could do was weep for his boy.

***

Gasping, Edwin sat straight up in the bunk he was resting in. Eliza stood over him, looking concerned. Her scarab-shaped key was flashing against the lace of her shirt. She had just finished using it to resurrect him—somewhat awkwardly with the way her hands were still bound.

"I woke you early. It looked like you were having some kind of nightmare. Were you?"

"Was I?" He broke the dental floss he'd used to bind his hands and put one to his forehead, trying to remember. The vaguest shadow of a dream, maybe just his imaginings, fluttered by so quickly that he couldn't grasp it fully. He suddenly felt very concerned about Oliver and sent a quick missive to his son over the neural network—not that he expected a reply. Oliver never took his calls anymore.

Looking up at Eliza, he said, "Do you feel odd? Off?"

She nodded, then looked aside as if searching for something. Or someone. He'd known for some years now that something was troubling her, but she'd never really discussed it. "Yes, I've been scrolling for news," she said, "There have been a lot of random vampire attacks. And…they seem to be getting worse."

Giving him a keen look with those bright new eyes of hers, his new Vampire Bride said, "Do you think it's related to the Nothing waking up?"

That was his fear, his suspicion. But before he could respond, Rahul's voice came over the ship's speaker. "Sir, we are being hailed by an unknown vessel—cloaked."

Edwin stood up. *"The Queen Anne's Revenge II?"* he hoped aloud, knowing he could get Eliza some nourishment quick fast if they were rendezvousing. He'd already sent a request on.

"I'm not sure, my Lord. You may want to take a look."

After giving Eliza a reassuring squeeze of the shoulder, he went up front and squeezed into the cockpit. The *QAR2* was an older-model dirigible, one of the first built following World War II, and a kind of prototype for the modern gyro. She had been decommissioned decades ago, but Captain Leo used her as a Black Flag to transport oppressed people across the globe. As a result, Leo was highly connected, and it wouldn't have surprised him if his old friend and former Heir had come into possession of certain technologies to avoid detection.

But Rahul shook his head. "I do not think so, sir. The *QAR2* has a specific energy signal that I and my kind can recognize. This vessel is different, but neither I nor the AI can identify it."

Edwin leaned forward to study the screen. Years earlier, the Japanese had gifted Edwin a thermo-map prototype that could read different heat and cold signatures. Because of the cloaking, they couldn't see the ship, but they could look inside her and see who or what was driving her. The crews' signatures were all cold. Very cold. Colder than even vampires.

Edwin felt his eyebrows crawl to the top of his forehead when he recognized the vessel as a Sky Shark belonging to the Jotnar, the nomadic species of Vampire/Fae crossbreeds that had caused him no end of grief in the not-too-distant past. They traveled in convoy groups, so it was likely that if they were encountering one, others were lurking nearby.

"Any other ships in the vicinity?" he asked.

Rahul checked his instruments. "No, sir. This is the only one. Shall I begin evasive maneuvers?"

Edwin thought about that. The Sky Shark was a thousand times larger than they were, and it likely housed hundreds of Jotnar, but due to the Jotnar's achievements in aerodynamic construction, it could move faster than they could. Running wasn't an option.

"Ask them what they want."

Sending the transmission rendered them a quick response:

LORD EDWIN NOW OR TOTAL ANNIHILATION

***

Edwin stepped out onto the wind-buffeted deck of the Phoenix, which was currently idling a thousand feed aft of the Sky Shark. The Phoenix had been invited to dock inside the modest loading bay of the Sky Shark, but there was no way he was letting Eliza or his crew be swallowed by an enemy ship. So, he'd opted to fly over alone.

Eliza stepped out behind him, accompanied by Tommy, and said, "Are you sure you can manage the flight?"

Edwin turned and clenched her bound hands, looking down at them fretfully. He was wearing goggles and a khaki military-style flight suit fitted to his specific anatomy, the back cut out to accommodate vampire wings, which lay folded to his back at the moment. "I'm about to find out, eh?"

"Don't joke! Edwin, you've never been much of a flyer."

He looked up, offering her a sheepish smile. "Aye, but I did all right during the Jotnar crisis."

She put a small smile on her ashen face, though the worry remained in her sky-blue his fears—any of them. As a result, Edwin had taken flight lessons with an instructor who usually taught new, green vampire Heirs how to fly. He was a good chap and didn't make fun of the fact that Edwin was far too old to not have mastered this skill by now. By the end of the course, he was flying solo and could even land without crashing or destroying anything.

Well, now he planned to put that training to good use.

He kissed Eliza and even tried a spot of humor by patting her rear. "Keep it warm for me, eh?"

She grabbed him by the face and said, "You better not die aboard that ship. We're all counting on you."

"Do not die. Got it."

"I'm serious, Edwin."

His smile dropped away and he bowed his head over her hands. "I promise I will not die. And I promise to keep that promise. After all, Old Edwin is still around."

She considered that, a sadness touching the corners of her eyes. She knew. They both did. A price would need to be paid. And he had no idea how to prevent it. If he sent Eliza home, something might happen to her—the Nothing might take her—but if he kept her with him, she was equally in danger. He was at an impasse.

"I'll be right quick," he informed her. "I want you to stick with Tommy. Trust no one else."

She nodded.

He kissed her one last time. But then he added, "If I'm held up, you'll need to take over the mission."

"Edwin..."

"I'm serious, lovey. I trust no one more than you to get this task done." He thought a moment. "Three hours. That's all we can spare or we won't intercept Leo's ship. If I'm not back by then, you and Tommy go on. That's the most important thing."

Eliza grabbed him by his flight suit. Were she able to cry, he knew there would be tears pouring from her eyes. Instead, she affixed the sunflower pin in her hands to the breast pocket of his flight suit.

"So I'm with you," she told him.

"Lovey, you are always with me."

He turned to Tommy next. He was standing straight as a soldier at his wife's side. "Guard her. With your life, if necessary. And with mine. Understand, mate?"

"I do, sir," Tommy intoned.

"Be right back!" Edwin threw Eliza a wink, turned, and fell backward off the flight deck like a skin-diver slipping into deep waters—not a feeling he relished. After a moment, he righted himself and started gliding toward the enemy ship.

He'd found the secret to flight was simple enough: never look down. He kept his wings fully extended, worked the thermals as his instructor taught him, and didn't bloody look down. The path he took through the wind and clouds was more zigzaggy than it should have been, but he was feeling pretty empowered as he approached the hangar doors, which had been opened fully and set ablaze with blinking lights for his arrival.

He had no idea if he was going to land in a hail of gunfire as he dropped into a run inside the receiving bay and worked to slow himself to a stop, but he didn't suspect it. Much. He saw no reason for the Sky Shark to welcome him aboard only to annihilate him on the spot. It got them nothing.

After sliding to a half, he looked around, marveling at the sight of the spiffy, ergonomic interior of the bay. The Jotnar, for all their ferocity as a species, loved beautiful, gliding interiors, and the receiving bay, with its flying buttress ceilings and softly peaked roof more resembled a medieval church in various shades of antiseptic white than anything that belonged on a flying ship.

But the sight of the Jotnar guard put a damper on his admiration of their architecture. A small cotillion of them in their recognizable silver and blue armor headed toward him. They were enormous creatures, eight feet tall the smallest of them, and built like linemen, both the men and the women. Their skin tone ranged from snowy white to nearly obsidian, but all of them had stark white or pale blond hair, pink scleras, and yellow irises with tiny pinpricks for pupils, giving them an otherworldly appearance.

The brute at their head—their leader, Edwin reckoned—halted and eyed him menacingly. He was on the taller side and at least twice as wide as Edwin at the shoulders, with golden brown skin and stark white hair that fell to his arse in a long, narrow plait. His armor was covered in badges and insignias.

"Lord Edwin," the Jotunn boomed. His eyes were a stormy dark blue, and he regarded Edwin critically.

"Aye." Edwin stood up straighter even though he felt like a Munchkin in the company of this lot. Perhaps they sensed it too because the big palomino's expression changed from menace to an amused smile.

"My name is Vulf, captain of the *Midnight Sun*. You may call me Captain or else Your High Prince. I respond to either."

Edwin started at that. "You're Yrsa's son?"

"I am her firstborn offspring and current Heir."

Edwin knew that, like the Vampire race, the Jotnar produced Heirs, though more traditionally through the act of actual biological procreation. A Jotunn such as Captain Yrsa might have many biological offspring in the course of her long life. All of those offspring were expected to battle for the title of High Prince—essentially Heir to the Kingdom.

Still, it surprised him that the woman he'd been married to so briefly bore a son. Edwin looked Vulf over as a troubling thought crossed his mind.

Vulf smiled. "Relax. You are not my father, little Lord. Were that true, I'd be...rather pathetic in stature."

"Hey, now!" Edwin began and the other guard laughed behind Vulf.

Edwin straightened his flight suit, not appreciating their humor. "I'll remind ye that I may seem small by your lot's standards, but I could take you all in a fight."

Vulf gave him an amused look. "And we could have shot down your silly little transport if we were so inclined."

Edwin held up a finger. "But you didn't. You want something."

Vulf grinned appreciatively at that. "You have guts. Good. You will need them for what is to come. Follow me, vampire. There is someone who wishes to see you."

That...wasn't reassuring. Not that Edwin could afford to look too worried.

As Edwin followed Vulf, the rest of the Jotnar falling in line behind him, he glanced around and said, "So, I take it you're not going to kill me."

"Not yet!" Vulf laughed.

* * *

The Jotnar could only survive in extremely frigid temperatures, a limitation that kept them from colonizing most parts of the Earth and confined them to a nomadic life in the sky. As a result, Vulf's ship was cold. Extremely cold. Minus forty degrees, at least—enough to make his skin itch.

Edwin could endure it well enough without protective gear, but even he was feeling a bit frosty by the time they had finished a lift ride and had traversed several corridors. Eventually, Vulf halted at a checkpoint being manned by a pair of guards. "You'll go on from here. Down two corridors and turn right. First door on the left."

Edwin glanced up at the big wanker in surprise. "Not coming, then?"

Vulf shook his head. "Too warm."

Interesting. He glanced down at the nondescript, antiseptic white corridor, wondering who was waiting for him. He had plenty of enemies, after all.

"Go on, then. The Boss wants to see you. Once that's done, we'll speak about letting your ship go." With a laugh, Vulf marched away.

"The Boss." Hmm...curiousier and curiouser.

Edwin straightened his suit and started down the corridor. Vulf was correct in that this part of the ship was warmer—though not by much. He found the door he'd spoken of and glanced at it for a second before pressing the large, flat button to iris it open.

The interior of the "Boss's" quarters was ergonomically sterile: rounded walls like a gigantic egg, banks of high-tech equipment along the concave walls, and, in the center of the vast, oval room, a comfy if chilly-looking setting set in a conversation pit. It was comprised of two furry white sofas set across from one another, glass end tables, and a large screen hanging over an onyx coffee table dividing the space in half.

Someone was sitting on one of the sofas, his back to Edwin, a tall stem glass in his hand with a nearly black substance swirling in it. On the screen over the coffee table was a feed of the Phoenix in stasis several hundred yards from Vulf's ship. Edwin didn't immediately recognize the tall young man with a fury of blond curls watching the screen. But when he spoke, the sound of his voice—the familiar timber—sent spikes of tension up Edwin's spine like someone dragging a knife.

"My boy, you've arrived."

Edwin stared open-mouthed at the young man as he stood and turned. He was plainly in his early twenties, tall and waspy thin. He moved silkily around the sofa to greet Edwin. He wore a natty off-white suit jacket, a lacy poet's shirt, an icy pink waistcoat, and black trousers with grey pinstripes. The lace of his shirt fluttered around his heavily beringed hands. His golden curls bounced around his ridiculously perfect face with its ceramic pale skin, pale azure eyes, and painted blush at the cheekbones.

"*Foxley?*"

| xviii |

"It's called a Halo ship and it was built around the design for the Sky Sharks," Jonah explained, leading Oliver toward a private part of the loading bays where, he's said earlier, they kept prototype transports. "But better than a Shark."

Oliver hesitated, unsure if he was willing to follow Jonah since learning all about him, but curiosity dragged him onward. The ship they stopped before was long and thin with sleek fins, a needle of a design. Jonah requested the AI iris the hatch open, and Oliver noted it had no seats or aisle. There was barely enough shoulder room to pass down to the cockpit—obviously, the ship had been created for high maneuverability. The cockpit itself was deeply stepped, designed for solo flight, and the dash featured the most expansive and recent upgrades he had ever laid eyes on.

Oliver was still angry with Jonah, but the ship had begun to soften him. "AI?"

"Integrated. But the AI—Kusanagi, her name is—doesn't run on the neural network."

"Why?"

"The *Demeter* was commissioned for private missions," Jonah explained. But before Oliver could inquire as to what that meant, he indicated what he called the "corona"—a thin metal band that fit around the forehead. With it and Kusanagi as co-pilot, a pilot could fly it entirely by thought command. "She's next level, but she's never seen a mission."

"Why?"

"She's too fast and too small to be practical, and so far, all of the pilots who tried to control Kusanagi have failed. Wanna take her for a spin?"

Oliver eyed Jonah. "Is this the part where you tell me she's mine if I join your little murder enclave?"

"Was that a whole sentence from Silent Oliver?" Jonah teased.

Oliver didn't respond to that.

Jonah sighed. "I'm more interested in seeing if you can pilot her. Kusanagi as a mind of her own."

Oliver had learned to pilot when he was still quite young, and he and Ariel had frequently gone for joyrides in his dad's transports while they were growing up aboard the *Queen's Gambit*. There wasn't much else to do on a gyro. When his mum found out, she was horrified he was going to kill himself, so he took formal flying lessons to help assuage her worries even though he knew how to pilot already. His instructors had been, by turns, impressed and terrified by the way he handled a ride.

He liked the idea of the challenge behind the *Demeter*. Slipping the corona on and assuming the pilot's seat, he called up the AI.

"Hello, Master Oliver. I am Kusanagi. Shall I drive?"

"I have experience. I'd like to drive, Kusanagi."

"Very well. If you insist."

Oliver liked her wit. He requested clearance from the tower, then ran the *Demeter* down the chute to the bay doors, flying past them with easy, practiced precision. The ship wasn't overly difficult to handle—just different. He tried her first with manual controls, then switched to thought command, his hands gently resting on the armrests of the cockpit seat. The ship took every hairpin turn he requested almost before he'd fully decided on his direction. Soon, it was responding intuitively. After that, Oliver really gunned the engine, pushing the *Demeter* out to its limit.

There was something immensely satisfying about flying. He felt in total control when he was running a ride out to her resistance. In the *Demeter's* case, he never found out what her limit was because she met him turn for turn and kept pouring on the speed until he felt the whole ship shuddering from the G-force.

"I can tell you're an adrenaline junkie," Kusanagi told him. "I can go much faster than this, but I will need an upgrade first."

"I can do that, he told Kusanagi. Talking to her was easy and comforting. "I could make you the fastest current transport." He rattled off some of his ideas.

"I would like that, Master Oliver."

Back in the bay, Oliver jumped out of the ship feeling energized and almost shaking with excitement. He told Jonah about the upgrades Kusanagi was requesting.

"Can you do that?" Jonah asked all wide-eyed.

"Absolutely. I used to tinker with the ships on my parents' gyro all the time. And I am working on my bachelor's in engineering. I could even make this my school project." He knew if he successfully upgraded the *Demeter*, it would make up for his otherwise crappy grades.

But after a moment he realized what he was saying. He might as well be agreeing to Lord Trasch's terms for joining the High Courts' training program.

Jonah considered. "If you want the *Demeter* as part of the deal, I know the Reverend would be open to that. It's not like anyone else can control that ship."

"I never said I was going to work for him."

"But you haven't left yet."

Oliver eyed his lover seriously. "You lied to me, Jonah. You didn't tell me who your father was or what you are."

Jonah considered that. "It was a dick move on my part. But I was just so afraid you would leave me, and I'd gotten used to you being in my life."

Oliver didn't know if he believed that. If Jonah had withheld parts of his truth in the past, what else was he capable of? But before he could respond, Jonah slid his hands around Oliver's waist, pulling him against his body so their flight suits rubbed. Jonah was hard for him, which was flattering and all, but Oliver didn't know where they stood now as a couple. Oliver wasn't like his dad. He wasn't some mindless slave to sex and desire.

When Jonah kissed him, an incredibly tender kiss, and told him he was sorry, Oliver felt some of his anger loosen up, but most of it was still there, knotted up inside of him.

Oliver tilted his head back. "Let me think about it."

* * *

They had a sumptuous dinner in Jonah's quarters aboard the ship It didn't look much different from his dorm on Earth. He even had several pet rabbits that had the run of the place.

"You don't eat them?" Oliver asked as he sat at the dining room table with one of Jonah's pets in his lap. He trickled his fingers through its multi-colored fur while it shivered slightly.

"No, silly, I told you: They're my pets." Jonah hungrily scooped the meat lasagna into his mouth. "And my rabbit that was missing really was ill, but he was brought up here so my father could make him well. My father always let me have pets like rabbits because he knew other types of animals like cats and dogs frightened me."

Oliver snorted. "You're afraid of cats and dogs?"

Jonah set his fork down. "They bite. I don't like it when animals bite."

"You let me bite you."

A smile broke out on Jonah's face, and he reached up to touch the mark under his right ear. "Yeah. But that was fun. It made me hard as hell—you biting me." Giving Oliver a sultry, come-hither look, Jonah added, "I wouldn't mind you doing it again."

Oliver wasn't sure if that was a good idea. The whole trap was pretty damn obvious: If he stayed, he could upgrade and use the *Demeter*. He could also have Jonah as a lover—and a source of constant nourishment. He could drink his lover's blood and never be hungry again. But he would be beholden to the High Courts. He would be theirs—their krsnik. Their vampire hunter.

He understood the game. He'd watched his dad play similar ones his whole life. The question was: Could Oliver play this to his advantage?

Glancing down at his half-eaten steak—it had left a bloody puddle on his plate—Oliver said, "Can you tell me more about what I am? What a krsnik is?"

"I don't really know," Jonah said, sounding sincere. He took a sip of his wine. "I know you're a hybrid of a vampire and a Poppet, and that gives you abilities that neither has—that, really, nothing out there has. But I don't understand the physiological side of it, if that's what you want to know. I was trained to be a hunter, not a biologist. My father would know more, so you might want to consider picking his brains."

Pick his brains. What a horrible idiom. Rumor was that Lord Trasch didn't drink blood like a normal vampire. He drank the cerebral spinal fluid of his victims. Oliver couldn't even imagine it, and the thought made him feel slightly ill.

Pushing away his plate, he decided it was time to leave and return to Earth. He had a lot to think about.

Jonah jumped up. "Are you going?"

"Will your father punish me if I do?"

"No."

"Will he punish you?"

Jonah's face flushed, which Oliver took as an affirmative. Would Trasch hurt or even kill his son, his creation, if his plan failed and Oliver returned to Earth? He had to consider that. Jonah might have withheld the truth, but Oliver still cared for him. Probably too much.

"Why don't you come with me?" Oliver finally said. "We could fly out to the *Queen's Gambit*. Trasch won't be able to reach you there. It would mean challenging Lord Edwin and his Congress."

But Jonah shook his head. "You don't understand, Ollie. I can ever leave. Things are…complicated between the Reverend and me."

"He'll hurt you if you leave him," Oliver guessed.

"He'll hurt me. He'll hurt my pets." Jonah stared with despair at his rabbits.

Oliver glared at Jonah, appalled.

"You should go," Jonah told him, staring down at his uneaten dinner.

When Jonah stood up to escort him out, Oliver came around the table and wrapped his arms around him protectively. "Not yet."

After a few seconds of squirming around, Oliver kissed him. Hard. Jonah gasped at Oliver's sudden aggression. He wanted Jonah. Wanted to kiss him…taste him. Soon, Oliver was loving on him fiercely and possessively and enjoying the way Jonah melted for him.

"You have your tiger face on," Jonah said.

Oliver lifted him easily into his arms. They moved to Jonah's bed and Oliver set him down. He lay down beside Jonah, touching, caressing, and kissing him everywhere.

"Are you still angry with me?" Jonah asked, a hand fluttering through Oliver's braids.

Oliver moved upward, fitting himself snugly between his lover's legs and nuzzling his throat. "Aye. But give me time."

***

"I'll be down in a moment," Oliver heard Jonah say as he resurfaced from a dream about the two of them living in a cottage in the forest where they grew their own food and made their own clothes. It was an odd dream for Oliver to have, and it made him sit up and focus on the figure of Jonah standing naked in the dark, rummaging through his wardrobe. "Just hold him there—if you can."

It took Oliver a moment to realize Jonah was responding to a mind text. He threw off the blankets. "What's going on?"

Jonah turned. He looked sexy naked, but the look of concern in his eyes made the spit dry up in Oliver's mouth. Suddenly, he was throwing on clothes faster than Oliver had ever seen anyone dress in his life. "It's Lord Adrastas. He boarded the *Asclepius* to conduct High Court business with the Reverend—I don't know the details and they aren't important—but he's apparently gone rogue." When he realized Oliver wasn't following, he stopped, belting his trousers, and explained, "Like the vamps acting out on Earth? He went visiting the Reverend's Poppets and ripped a few up last night. Guards just found the bodies."

Like the vamps on Earth? Oliver had heard about a few incidents, but he'd no idea things had gotten this out of hand. He sprang out of bed and started to dress as well. When Lords visited, they were often given access to the sitting Lord's Poppets as a courtesy, but powerful Vampire Lords knew better than to harm them. It wasn't diplomatic. He wondered what had gotten into Lord Adrastas.

Jonah finished dressing and grabbed a long black leather coat from his closet. Oliver saw the spark of weapons lining the interior of the coat—blades and throwing knives primarily. Some of the blades were even made of a peculiar black metal.

"Can I come?" Oliver suddenly asked.

"These things can get messy."

"I'll be careful."

* * *

"I'm glad you accepted my invitation to visit," Foxley said. He extended a hand to Edwin.

"It wasn't much of an invitation," Edwin answered, staying exactly where he was and eyeing the vampire suspiciously. "I drop in or you annihilate my crew."

Foxley flicked his hand. "I needed to get your attention."

Edwin looked his master up and down. "You've certainly done that."

Foxley had changed. He'd...aged, which should have been impossible, trapped as he was in his twelve-year-old body. But before they got to that, Edwin said, "I wondered where you'd popped off to. Another of your 'little adventures,' eh?"

Foxley smiled.

How did you convince the Jotnar to agree to put their ship at risk for you?"

"This is my ship now," Foxley said.

"Your ship?"

Even beyond whatever it was that Foxley had done to his physical self, Edwin found it difficult to believe his master had total control of a Jotnar ship. They might be space pirates, and unscrupulous ones at that, but the Jotnar had better sense than to commune with the likes of Foxley.

He offered Edwin a glistening smile. "I offered them a deal they couldn't resist."

Edwin gave Foxley a droll look. "You gave them money."

"Oh, it was more than that." Foxley made a quick circuit of the room, running his fingers along the banks of machinery that lined the walls. His long, polished black nails clicked along a random keyboard. "Money…and my know-how." Foxley continued to smile as he returned to Edwin. "I am quite the accomplished engineer, as you know. And the Jotnar love their tech. But as good as they are at it, I'm better still."

Credit where credit was due: Almost every single modern convenience was linked to Foxley in some way. But that didn't mean Edwin liked or trusted his master even now. He grounded himself for an attack, but before Foxley reached him, he suddenly diverted to a wet bar set to the side and poured them both drinks in long-stemmed glasses. From the smell of it, Edwin could tell it was read blood, not substitute. Were the Jotnar feeding him as well?

Foxley returned to offer Edwin a glass. "It's a bit naturally chilled."

"Jotunn blood."

"Amazingly potent stuff." Foxley took a sip. "It'll put hair on your chest."

Edwin shook his head. "That brings us to…" Edwin made an up-and-down gesture.

Foxley smiled. Making a come-hither gesture, he turned and exited a door on the other side of the room. After a moment, Edwin followed. They traversed a long corridor with doors to either side before reaching the end, where a swinging door let them into a cold, vast laboratory. Edwin immediately recognized the Wasp machine set up in the center of the room, the giant 3-D printer that could construct a living body from DNA inputted into the computer's database.

Many years ago, Eliza utilized just such a device to create a copy of him when he fell unexpectedly into a fugue after a damaging fight. His copy was human—not a vampire—but still operated unexpectedly well. He would have happily stuck with it and lived his human life out with Eliza were it not for the Jotnar's assault on his ship.

"That's how you did it." Edwin glanced at Foxley, who looked radiantly proud of himself. "So, where's your real body, then?"

"Someplace no one will ever find it," Foxley grinned. "Though, before I abandoned it, I collected blood samples and then consumed them on awakening." He touched his own heart tentatively. "Clever, yes?"

Edwin didn't think Foxley had the power to surprise him anymore. Obviously, he was wrong. "You...made yourself a vampire with your own blood." It took him a moment to wrap his head around that. "You're your own master."

Foxley sipped from the glass he was still carrying, the red-tinged liquid dying his lips a deeper shade of pink. "I wouldn't have it any other way. Shall we retire to my quarters? We have much to discuss."

| xix |

Lord Adrastas stood amidst what looked to be an abattoir. Oliver knew it was a luxury suite aboard the ship, but the walls and floor were painted with the shining, crimson-black blood of a half dozen Poppets. Blood had soaked into the furry white carpeting. It coated the white furniture and dripped down the lampshades and over the giant TV screen hanging on the wall.

As he and Jonah stepped into the room, Oliver nearly tripped over the body lying in the doorway. It was a female Poppet. She lay on her back, arms akimbo. Oliver crouched down to examine the remains. Most of her face on one side had been shaved away, along with her eye. The skull gleamed beneath. The rest of her body was a ruin of ragged flesh and cloth, like a doll smashed against the walls and left on the floor.

He reached out to touch the unharmed half of her face. The Poppet looked like his mum. She might even have been created using similar genetic materials.

There were others. They were scattered across the room, some on the furniture and some on the floor. One, a male, was laying half on and half off the snowy-white-turned-scarlet sofa. The smell was so strong it staggered Oliver back and he had to catch himself in the doorway while Jonah moved purposely forward to meet the threat.

The room didn't smell good; it smelled like death. Only after casting off the miasma and re-centered his attention on the current situation did Oliver find he could push through the odor and step into the room.

By then, Jonah was already engaging the threat.

Lord Adrastas, naked and crouched upon the giant, blood-soaked bed, was using his claw-like hands to rip the deceased Poppet in his arms apart while he nosed into the body, sucking up any blood he could find that hadn't clotted or spilled to the floor. He was coated from head to foot in the dead Poppets' lifeforce, and even though the body was obviously empty of blood, he continued to rake open the chest and snap the rib bones in his quest for more. But it wasn't enough.

Oliver recognized the madness of the bottomless hunger in the vampire's black eyes. He glared wildly at Jonah. "What's wrong with him?" He had never heard of an old, esteemed Vampire Lord who had lost control like this. This was newbie behavior.

Jonah shook his head. "No one knows, but it's happening more often now. Stay back, lover, I don't want you hurt."

Drawing a long pistol from under his coat and aiming it, Jonah approached the rabid vampire. His voice was eerily calm. "Down on the floor, my Lord. I won't ask again."

But Lord Adrastas only snarled at Jonah and extended his wings defensively. Through the blood, his skin looked blackened and almost burnt so he resembled a blood-slathered gargoyle. Black blood poured from his eyes.

Oliver reached up and touched his own face. It reminded him of what he saw in the mirror in one of his less...human...moments.

"My Lord..." Jonah began as he moved to within range. But the vampire looked up at him, rabid and mindless, and suddenly leaped at Jonah. Jonah fired but the bullet missed and plunked into the wall. Oliver gasped at how fast the vamp moved, but Jonah seemed ready for it and blocked his path. The two clenched.

The vampire and the vampire hunter twisted this way and that as they wrestled. Jonah's fearlessness impressed Oliver. The vampire tried to bite Jonah, but Jonah moved fast, raising his forearm, the thick leather sleeve protecting his neck from the attack. The vamp then lashed out at him, but Jonah, a genetically-modified Poppet, was surprisingly fast and twisted around, throwing the vampire over his shoulder and against the far wall.

The vampire bounced off the wall and flew back at him.

Jonah punched him in response, his blow concentrated to push the maximum amount of power through his target. The vamp, whimpering, dropped to the floor. Jonah tried to bring his gun arm up and around to bear, but the vamp, even stunned, moved faster than any creature Oliver had ever seen and was on him like a red and black shadow. Jonah, with a grunt, turned and threw the vamp onto the bed. But that didn't stop Adrastas, who was on his feet in microseconds, his long, beclawed hands reaching for Jonah's throat.

Jonah never flinched as he blew a fist-sized hole through the center of his target.

The impact knocked the vamp over the side of the bed and to the floor, his blackened insides re-painting one of the walls, but it didn't stop him.

The vamp moved like a blur and was upon Jonah again, driving him down on his back. This time, the vamp was in pain and enraged. It barely looked human as its razor-sharp claws ripped at the front of Jonah's coat, trying to get to the meat beneath. Jonah cried out in pain and surprise and tried to get leverage, but it was impossible with how Adrastas had him pinned. Jonah's legs beat a fearful tattoo against the floor.

Oliver knew he had to help. At first, he thought about grabbing a chair from a corner and hitting the vamp with it, but there wasn't time. Left with no alternative, Oliver jumped on the vamp's back.

He was shocked to discover how fragile the monster felt. He easily grabbed one of Adrastas's wings and bent it back until it broke like kindling so it drooped at an odd angle. Adrastas yelped and reared up, trembling in pain. With a violent twitch, he knocked Oliver off his back. Suddenly, he had no interest in Jonah. He wanted the one who had hurt him, and that was Oliver.

Twisting around, Adrastas eyed Oliver with those hungry black eyes. It—Oliver could no longer call it a he—stretched its mouth wide open, its jaws cracking apart all the way to the ears to show off dagger-like teeth that made Oliver hesitate where he might have otherwise engaged.

He was no vampire hunter. He was stupid to think he could fight a vamp. He slid back a step, but the vampire tracked him. And when Oliver tried to retreat, he found he wasn't fast enough.

Seconds later, Adrastas was on him and slamming him into the floor. His head bounced. Time slowed to clicks. Oliver instinctively raised his arm to defend himself as Jonah had earlier to keep that teethy maw away from his neck, but then noticed he had the time to turn his arm and extend his hand. He reached out and clenched the vampire's bottom jaw, holding it away from him.

The vampire, drooling and foaming at the mouth, snarled at him. Its black eyes rolled crazily in its head and its claws clicked and clacked against the floor. Finally, Adrastas raised a hand to strike Oliver across the face. Oliver knew he had only nanoseconds to react.

* * *

"What is this place?" Edwin asked as Foxley led him into his inner sanctuary. He glanced around, a tick of something like nostalgia but much darker knocking at the back of his brain.

Then it hit him: He'd been in this place before. The proportions were different but the design and furnishings were almost identical to Bamburgh Castle. The flying wooden buttresses and giant fireplaces and polished oak floors had been reproduced in painstaking detail. He even recognized some of the same, books on the shelves of the study.

Foxley turned and spread his arms. "My life's work, Edwin. Don't you recognize it?"

"Aye, I do, except..." He glanced all around at the chandeliers and delicate furnishings and various brick-a-brac, then turned back to Foxley. "...why?"

"What do you mean?"

"Why Bamburgh?" He swallowed thickly when he recognized the French doors leading to some kind of balcony or overlook. They were full of sunshine that would be deadly to his kind except that he was pretty sure there was a UV film on all of the windows.

Foxley looked momentarily confused. "I told you...this is my life's work."

It took a moment, but Edwin burst out in laughter and then stopped when he saw the expression on Foxley's face. "I thought the *Gypsy Queen* was your life's work?"

"It was, but I was wrong to give it importance." Turning, Foxley strolled through his perfect reproduction. He passed a mounted terrestrial globe of the kind that Edwin once used to study geography under Foxley's tutors and started to pour them both drinks from the wet bar. "I loved the *Gypsy Queen*, but it was merely a ship. A mirage. Ultimately, it meant nothing."

Edwin walked over to spin the globe. It worked perfectly, then drifted to the wall of shelves and glanced over the collection of books. All of his novels were here. "You're serious?"

Glancing up with a muted smile, Foxley continued with, "I've made the mistake of attaching significance to a great many things I have done with my long life. I have...been unwise in my achievements."

"I don't follow," Edwin admitted, paging through one of his novels. Parts of it had been highlighted.

Staring at him oddly, Foxley said, "I have overlooked the most important gifts that were ever given to me."

A kernel of concern had started to take root in Edwin and he put the book back. "What...what would that be?"

"My immortality, to start. My education. But also you." Walking back, Foxley handed Edwin a fresh glass. "Blood substitute. I know you don't drink the real stuff."

Edwin took a sip to wet his suddenly parched throat. "I'm...flattered?" He followed through with, "But what does all of that have to do with this?" He indicated the room.

Foxley gave him a devastated look. "Do you remember this place? Similar to the room where I made you my Heir."

It was more than that: It was exactly the room even down to the Oriental carpets and the scratches on the floor.

Edwin looked down at the spot where he had fallen. The place where Foxley drank the life out of his mortal body. But when Foxley touched his cheek, he glanced up quickly.

"I was cruel, yes?" Foxley said, his voice low and intimate. "I made you afraid. I made it horrible for you."

Edwin was at a loss for words. He had no idea where this was going, but he had to make it back to his ship. He had to get Samara to the mountains. His crew and his wife were waiting for him, so even though he didn't feel it, he managed to squeak out, "That's all behind us now, Foxley."

"Is it?" Foxley took his glass and set it and his own on a nearby table before reaching up to brush his thumb across Edwin's cheek again. When Edwin jerked back, Foxley lowered his hand.

"I've decided."

"Decided?"

"I can't possibly move forward in my life without you." Foxley smiled, then laughed, a light, tickling sound that caused Edwin to step back and hit the bookshelf.

Edwin swallowed and his eyes slid around the room, checking for exits. "Look, Foxley, this is bloody deep stuff, granted, but I need to contact my ship and crew, tell them—"

Foxley stepped forward and set his hands on Edwin's shoulder. It felt odd to be looking his master in the eye like this—the two of them the same height. But before he could protest or wiggle away, Foxley kissed him. Foxley's mouth was cold, his teeth incredibly sharp. Edwin tried to jerk away, but Foxley increased his hold on his shoulder, his fingernails digging into his skin with those long, lacquered back black. Edwin had thought it was just some affectation until he felt his skin burn where Foxley was touching him.

Foxley drew back. "My apologies," he said, glancing at his nails. "The lacquer is mixed with cold iron filaments. Deadly to Fae and vampires. Lethal when applied to the Jotnar."

Again, Edwin swallowed, his lips swollen from the kiss. So, whatever arrangement Foxley had with Vulf was precarious at best.

As soon as Foxley loosened his hold, Edwin tried to shift away, but Foxley framed his face, those long, painfully supercharged fingernails clicking against his cheeks. Edwin grew quite still then. He was terrified Foxley would rip his face off with those nails.

"Please stop squirming. I'm trying very hard to be gentle with you, Edwin."

"You...I...you're scaring me, Foxley..."

"That isn't what a want. But you...Edwin! Stop struggling!"

Foxley's nails dug into his temples and Edwin went absolutely still in his grip.

Foxley, smiling once more, reached up, and ran those glassy fingernails down the slip of Edwin's cheek. "That's good. That's better. Now listen closely, my Prince...I need you to hear me out. It's important."

Edwin nodded.

"You have to stay. I don't want to hurt your ship or your crew, but if you run away like you did all those years ago, I will have the Jotnar fire on it. And I promise it will be devastating. You have no idea how I have upgraded their weapons system, though I believe you can imagine."

Edwin swallowed, shuddered, nodded again. There was no way he could fight his master. And angering the lunatic was only going to end in his ship suffering for it. He would need to approach this more carefully.

"Do you understand?"

"Aye," he said, making his voice light and sunny to please Foxley. "I get ya. I'll stay. But you have to let my ship go unharmed. You have to guarantee it. You can do that?""

Foxley eyed him carefully for a long moment before releasing him, those black-tipped nails sliding away. He indicated the divan a few feet away. "Have a seat."

Edwin smiled. "Sure, mate. No issue."

After he'd taken a seat, Foxley joined him, sitting closer than he cared for, but not touching, which he was grateful for. Foxley motioned to the bar and a floating serving try lifted up and carried to them both the bottle of blood substitute and two new glasses.

Foxley poured them both fresh drinks. "Talk to me, my love. Talk with me."

Edwin, sitting very still, a glass in hand and the liquid vibrating slightly, said, "What...what do you want to talk about?"

Foxley smiled charmingly and reached up to touch his chest. "What do you think of this body?"

"I...uh..."

"Be honest."

He had no idea what to say. Best not to upset the sociopath, so he said, "It's...nice."

"Just nice? I made it to be beautiful. To be...what you enjoy." Taking one of Edwin's hands, he forced him to run his palm up and down the silken shirt under his jacket. Blushing slightly, a pinkening barely detectable under his rouge, he detoured to set Edwin's hand on the sizeable package in his trousers. "Feel it? I'm not a child, Edwin. Not anymore. I'm just like you. Nineteen. I chose it to match your physical age. We're like brothers now."

"Um...aye." He tried to remove his hand, but Foxley kept it firmly in place.

"Finally, there is nothing to prevent us from being together. From being an us! No reason for you to turn away from me any longer."

Edwin's thoughts reeled as he sought a way out of his current predicament. But every scenario he ran through his brainpan ended in the same way—with Foxley melting down on him. And if he pissed him off, Foxley would just kill him and then have the Jotnar fire on his ship with whatever space-age weapons he had installed on this ride. He couldn't be so reckless. Not for his crew's sake. Not for Eliza's.

Eliza. She had put up with so much hell over the years. And in the time before, she had endured both the passion and the wrath of the Vampire Lords. Could he shirk now in the face of her bravery?

Edwin tried on a lopsided smile as his mind sought some way of de-escalating the situation. "Aye, it's a lovely body. Not that there was anything wrong with your real one."

"But you never loved that body."

"Foxley..."

"Tell me the truth, Edwin. Did you ever, in all of our years together, have any feelings for me at all?"

He hated that Foxley was asking that. He hated more that there was no way to lie to his master's face. Foxley knew him too well. He would see right through it.

"I tried, mate...but it was difficult. You were...difficult."

Foxley looked strangely contrite and glanced down at his drink. Thankfully, he'd let go of Edwin's hand so Edwin could take it back. "I understand. I was a monster in more ways than one. Life was never easy for me."

Edwin tried not to roll his eyes.

"As a consequence, I didn't make it easy for you. Life...abuse...it's cyclic, you understand?" Looking up, Foxley added, "But I plan to make up for that. I plan to make this second chance beautiful. Everything you have ever hoped for!"

Jumping up, Foxley moved to the wall of books and clicked something into place. The part of the bookshelf slid back like in an old movie to reveal a second attached room. Even from his position on the divan, Edwin could see it was some kind of writing nook set up with more high shelves and a huge desk with a banker's lamp and a typewriter. Edwin took a deep, shuddering breath. He didn't like where this was going.

"Foxley..." he began, but his master interrupted him.

"I had it made for you. So you could write your books."

"Write my books?"

"Yes, here. With me. Aboard our ship."

Our ship. Edwin gawked. "Look, I understand. I do. But I have a life now. I have a fami—"

But Foxley forged on. He returned to Edwin and clapped a hand to his cheek, kissed him again—deeper and longer. Foxley's tongue went into him. Edwin jerked back and stood up.

Foxley released him but there were deep crimson spots on his cheeks and his eyes were huge and incredibly dark. Deep. He looked like he'd taken a hit of Belladonna. "I'm your family. And you're mine. You've always been my family." He clasped Edwin's hands, holding them like some suitor in a Jane Austen novel, and tried to draw Edwin close.

Edwin resisted. He had already decided the French doors were the most viable exit out of here. If he got caught in the sun, he'd just have to pull his coat over his head and hope for the best. But then he hesitated.

If you run, he'll probably kill you. Then he'll kill Eliza. You won't be much good to her dead, mate.

His brain scrambled for a better option. He turned back to Foxley and offered a genuine smile. "All right, mate. I get ya."

Foxley laughed. "All these years…all my tutors…and you still sound so common."

He'd meant it to be humorous, but of course it wasn't. It was cruel because Foxley was cruel. But Edwin's smile never slipped. He even offered Foxley his sauciest smile, the one that had won the hearts and gotten the skirts (and pants) off the aristocracy in the decades they were together. "Got a boudoir?"

Foxley returned that smile. Somehow, he made it both lascivious and terrifyingly full of teeth. "I do, but…" He brushed a glassy thumbnail down Edwin's cheek, diverting to run it over his lips. "But I want to do it here. "

That was problematic because Edwin hoped to get Foxley in a confined space where he could bite Foxley and get him high as hell. Then he could slip away, preferably with the barrier of walls and a locked door between them. The locked door wouldn't help much where Foxley was concerned, but it might give him the seconds he needed to escape.

"Right then." He would just need to adjust his strategy. Grabbing Foxley by the front of the suit, he turned and tossed him down on the divan. It had worked on Emperor Hirohito back in the day. Foxley pushed himself up on one elbow while Edwin jumped on him. He didn't seem unduly upset by the turnabout.

They started out slowly, just kissing and touching. Edwin closed his eyes. There was no way he could keep from shivering when Foxley ran his tongue and then those long primordial teeth up the slope of his neck. Thankfully, Foxley misinterpreted it.

"Yes," he said, his greedy fingers ripping at Edwin's clothes. "Tremble for me, my darling."

The moment Foxley ripped his shirt wide open, Edwin jerked reflexively and they both tumbled to the floor and into almost the same spot where Foxley made him his Heir all those many years earlier. It might have been funny if it weren't so damned horrifying.

Giggling ecstatically as if they were playing a game, Foxley kissed him, his black claws raking up and down Edwin's cheeks and leaving little puffs of smoke. Foxley murmured while he tore savagely at Edwin's clothes, moving just the right things out of his way. Edwin swallowed and squeezed his eyes shut as his body was jerked this way and that.

Foxley wasn't gentle about what he wanted. He left scratches all over Edwin's body as he worked his way down, touching, kissing, and biting. The only thing that helped him through the ordeal was his training from his old days working in the brothel.

When he was twelve years old, one of his seven mums took him by the hand and led him into her boudoir where she usually entertained her clients. She asked him to lie down on her bed fully clothed. Edwin, always eager to please his mums, happily obeyed. She then lay down beside him. Edwin was tall even then, taking up much of the bed. She giggled as she snuggled up against him, putting her arm around his shoulders so she was hugging him against her side.

"My little prince," she said, her smile and flashing green Irish eyes making him feel warm and comfortable beside her. She tickled his hair before pointing upward at the ceiling of her room where she had painted a number of stars with cheap yellow paint she had found in the alley behind the brothel. "See the stars?"

"Aye, Mummy," he said. They weren't painted well but there were many of them.

"I want you to count them."

He thought about that. He couldn't count very high. "That's a lot to count."

"Will you try for your mum?"

"Aye, of course." He wasn't even halfway done counting them when his mum's next client appeared at her door.

"Go back to your room now but keep counting the stars, Edwin."

Edwin sat up and turned to her. "But, Mummy, I don't have stars in my room."

His mum leaned into him and ran her fingers through his hair affectionately. "They're there. The same ones. You just can't see them until you close your eyes."

He gave her a questioning look.

"Close your eyes, my prince."

He did.

"Do you see the stars?"

After a moment, he did. He saw the ceiling and all of the hundreds of stars there.

"Now, Edwin, go to your room and lie down on your bed. Close your eyes and count them."

He smiled for her. "Right then, Mum."

He did as she asked him to, though he didn't finish then, either. There were too many.

The very next day, the procurer of the brothel sent Edwin his very first client. He'd been expecting it. He wasn't an ignorant child. He knew what was expected of him. The only reason Edwin hadn't been sent to a workhouse was because he was as pretty as his mums.

"You'll make me a farthing at least, my scruffy lil' prince!" the procurer said at the time.

Edwin expected a gentlewoman to be his first. She wasn't. The man who cornered him was strong and rough on him. So, Edwin closed his eyes and counted the stars as his mum had instructed.

He counted them now while Foxley went about the business of satisfying himself. Rapists, one and all, he thought, surprised by his bitterness and the heavy, lost feeling inside him. He missed Eliza. Oliver. He missed being free. At least Foxley didn't take long to finish. Greedy and lustful, Foxley's teeth sank deep into the side of his neck. He swiftly began to drink, to satisfy his more vampiric needs.

Edwin, his head turned as he looked toward the French doors, stroked his fingers through the golden curls at the back of Foxley's head. He allowed his touch to remain tender even though he wanted to clench his hand into a fist and drag Foxley off him. He wanted to break him into kindling. Foxley finished quickly that way too and drew back, allowing Edwin to take the initiative.

He never hesitated. He kissed Foxley's blood-slathered mouth before moving to the side of his throat. One bite was all it would take and Foxley would fly away on a tide of *El Mal de Amor*.

But Foxley jerked his head back. "I don't want to slip away just yet. I don't want to miss this time with you." He entwined his fingers with Edwin's. He smiled maniacally.

"Aye, of course," Edwin said, his hopes—and plan—dashed to pieces. Left with no alternatives, Edwin murmured little nothing words of love and applied pressure to the back of Foxley's head. He tilted his head back, inviting him to take more.

"Oh...you are so sweet," Foxley said, licking his lips.

"I've always enjoyed your blood kiss...my master." Edwin pressed Foxley's mouth back against the wound. Foxley's teeth penetrated him a second time and Edwin grimaced at the grinding, ungentle abuse. Foxley drank.

A voracious creature by nature, Foxley took a great deal of Edwin's blood this time. Too soon, Edwin could feel the drag on his body. The more Foxley drank, the more leaden Edwin became. Foxley's whispered words of love between swallows, but his voice was softer now, giddier, as Edwin's blood overloaded his system. Edwin's breath came faster and more erratically. He knew if Foxley took too much, it would put him in a spiral and he could fall into a fugue.

Foxley's mouth finally weakened as he began to suffer the effects of drinking far too much too quickly. His body grew slack and heavy upon him. Taking a chance, Edwin gripped a handful of Foxley's hair and dragged his head back. His eyes were still open but unfocused.

Foxley mumbled in some other language.

"Christ." How much more could Foxley take before he passed out?

Reaching up, Edwin scratched at the quickly mending wound in his neck. As his blood began to seep freely once more—albeit more slowly now—he encouraged Foxley to take him one last time. Foxley latched onto him again—quickly and eagerly. His grip on Edwin was much weaker this time, but the sucking of his mouth was no less enthusiastic. Edwin started to gasp, almost hyperventilating, while Foxley drank and drank, taking him right up to the edge of passing out.

Darkness was finally seeping into the corners of Edwin's eyes, and his body felt like there were cement blocks attached to it. He wondered how he would ever drag himself up off the floor.

Finally, finally, Foxley's mouth relaxed and Edwin felt his body go slack. Edwin waited a tense moment, then pushed his master's body over. Foxley fell like a heavy sack of flour onto the floor beside him. He resembled some bloated tick, his eyes glazed over and his breathing deep and rapid. His cheeks were florid, and blood was smeared over his lips and chin and clothes.

Now, Edwin thought to himself, he just had to get himself up before he died on this floor.

XX

Oliver reacted instinctively. Keeping the vampire's head turned and the jaws away from his face, he brought his knee up into the vampire's groin. Hard. The impact made Adrastas cry out in raw agony. And while the vamp was distracted by its newest pain, Oliver brought his other arm up and stuck his wrist right into the monster's mouth.

Predictably, the monster clamped down on his arm, but Oliver didn't even experience the pain. His body was filling with a rush of power and cold in equal measure, and at the moment, he suspected the ceiling could have caved in and he wouldn't have noticed. The creature tried to shred his hand, but as soon as its teeth sank into the meat of Oliver's hand, Oliver noticed the twining black veins running through his arm rush up to his fingertips.

The vampire choked, but Oliver didn't let go. His other hand, sunk to the fingernail beds in Adrastas's throat, pulsed with those long, snake-like veins. He could see the toxins running into the vamp's body, and, after a few seconds, Adrastas released his hand and jerked backward and off his body.

Oliver lay there a long moment, trying to catch his breath and get his panic under control. He could hear Jonah calling to him, demanding to know if he was all right, but it was difficult to focus on that. He was too entranced by what was happening to the vampire.

Jumping to his feet, his hand bleeding but the pain a distant annoyance, Oliver crept around to face the vamp down on its knees, its head bowed and its features obscured by its scraggly black hair. He almost felt badly at the sight of the vamp; he was shuddering in seemingly terrible pain. And when the monster finally lifted its face, its ghastly white skin was teeming with those black vines. They writhed over its face and down its neck. They had etched themselves into the vampire's chest like primal tattoos. It whined like a suffering dog and raised its claw-like hands, raking at its face in agony until the skin tore into crimson ribbons on its skull.

"What did you do?" Jonah said, approaching them both. He gaped in absolute horror. "Oliver, what did you do to it?"

"I just...touched it." Oliver backed away, looking down at his hand, which he was sure would be badly wounded—a raw, gaping wound. There were teeth marks where the vampire had bitten him, but they weren't bad and quickly healing. He was more concerned about the black vines pulsing under his skin.

His mind flashed back to a childhood memory—a giant Jotnar warrior reaching for him. He had sent those same vines into the great creature the same way, just with his touch, driving it to its knees in screaming agony.

The vampire keened and Oliver's head snapped up at the sound. The vamp had degloved almost its entire face. Blood poured like rain from its terrible wounds, splashing down upon the floor. He thought the vampire's blood should smell dead and rotted, like fly-flecked meat. Instead, it smelled sweet and strong—like the blood substitute he'd had on the transport, only more so.

"Oliver?"

He glanced up and saw Jonah recoil. Jonah said, "Wh-what's wrong with you?" Turning to one of the Court Guards who had just arrived, Jonah said, "What's wrong with his eyes?"

Oliver ignored the expressions on the people gathering in the corridor outside and turned back to the wounded vampire shuddering on the floor. He heard a growl rise up—just not from Adrastas. He was the one making the sound. Before he could even stop himself, he jumped upon the vamp, driving him to the floor on his back. Oliver's teeth ached and the saliva in his mouth was hot and plentiful.

Adrastas tried to fend him off by throwing up his arms, but Oliver's body reacted automatically He grabbed Adrastas's wrists and pulled so hard his arms popped at the shoulders. The skullish creature howled in agony.

Oliver pinned his arms down and lowered his head, his jaws splitting straight across his face in a way similar to the vampire. But instead of teeth, he felt his tongue unfurl, long and black and as sharply barbed as if it was full of teeth. The vamp raised its head in a last attempt to bite him, but Oliver felt a wad of something that felt like pure darkness fill his mouth—bitter, burning. He spat it at the vampire.

The acidic substance blanketed the vamp from head to midsection. The remaining flesh on the vampire's face melted away to reveal yellow bone, and the skin of its sunken chest crackled and broke apart, the charred flesh revealing the rivers of sweet, nourishing blood beneath.

Oliver lashed at it with his tongue, the vamp screaming until he had no voice box left to cry out with. He must have blacked out because he felt that some small bit of time had lapsed. The vampire was silent, its body hacked wide open as if someone had taken an ax to it. Oliver was licking at its bones, but all of the precious juices were gone. Some of the vampire's blood was on the floor, and some was on Oliver's face and down the front of his clothes.

Jonah was carefully dragging him back, but Oliver was growling and swiping at him, trying to crawl back to the dead vampire. "Oliver! Oliver!" Jonah was screeching.

Oliver finally connected with Jonah, easily knocking him into the wall. He knew that his reaction was wrong, and that he didn't really want to hurt Jonah. But he wanted the vampire blood more. He needed it like he had never needed anything in his life.

Jonah recovered and took a step forward, but Oliver backed away, growling and eyeing his lover. He was willing to defend his kill if need be...

"Stop."

Both Oliver and Jonah froze in place at the sound of the commanding voice. Turning, Oliver noted that Lord Trasch had entered the bedchamber. He was leaning his giant, crooked body on the staff he carried, but he was moving as if he was floating. For the first time, Oliver wondered if the old Lord even needed it.

"Stop, Oliver," Lord Trasch said, gliding forward and inserting himself between him and his son. To Jonah, he said, "Step out of the room, my child."

"But...Reverend..."

"I said step out of the room."

Jonah did, but he looked hurt to have been dismissed.

Lord Trasch moved toward Oliver, who was down in a low crouch, ready to spring. Trasch sank low, his red robes spilling all around him like blood. "Oliver...it's over, my good boy. You've done well. No need for fear." The Vampire Lord offered Oliver his upturned hand like a man might offer his hand to a feral dog.

Oliver sniffed it. The juice he was seeking was here, too. But Trasch was much larger and more intimidating than Adrastas had been. He wasn't certain he could take Trasch. At least, not yet.

"Oliver, I want you to turn and look at what you have done."

Grumbling, annoyed, Oliver turned his head and glanced over one shoulder.

Lord Adrastas's body lay in shreds, with his head and part of his spinal cord flung into the far corner. The entire trunk of his body had been plowed open, his organs scattered and some of them minced. He looked like he'd been hit by a train.

It was sort of interesting.

"Now, Oliver...look at me."

Oliver turned back and set his attention on Lord Trasch, who was crouched, unafraid, in front of him. "Do you understand what you have done?"

"Aye." He wasn't stupid or rabid. He understood. Lord Adrastas had attacked the Poppets under Lord Trasch's care. The Poppets were like his Mum. They were Oliver's own people. Thus, he had punished Lord Adrastas. It was messy, yes, but non unwarranted. He thought how other Lords might be less willing to abuse their Poppets upon learning about this incident.

Lord Trasch nodded as if he were picking up on all of Oliver's thoughts. "You understand."

"Are you going to punish me?" Oliver asked. If Trasch planned to do that, then Oliver would need to take care of Trasch next.

But Trasch shook his head. "You did well. There will be no punishment. In fact..."

Lord Trasch extracted a small knife from somewhere in his robes. Oliver stiffened but the old vampire only used it to efficiently slice open a small patch of skin on the palm of his hand. He extended it to Oliver.

"Go on. Drink it."

The black blood that bubbled up smelled sweet like it had in Lord Adrastas.

"Reverend..." Jonah warned, but Trasch held up his other hand to shush Jonah.

"It will be all right, child." Eyeing Oliver keenly, he commanded, "You may drink."

It would be a shame to waste it, so Oliver leaned forward, cupped Trasch's hand, and held it steady as he lowered his mouth to the black blood drooling slowly from the wound and between his fingers.

The moment the blood hit his system, Oliver swore he could see through the walls of the room to the swarms of people beyond. He could smell everything aboard the ship. The gardenias in their vase that had gotten knocked off the highboy...the sweat on Jonah's upper lip and at his hairline, the perfume of the dead Poppets scattered about. The rich, metallic scent—the sweetness of age—in Lord Trasch's blood most of all...

"Easy."

He was careful this time, his long, churning tongue scraping over the wound.

"That's good, Oliver. You are very good at this." Lord Trasch took his hand back.

Oliver thought about jumping on the vampire, maybe spitting on him to incapacitate him, but he'd had enough. His system was settling into a warm, comfortable hum. And, ultimately, he wasn't sure he could take Trasch on just yet.

He eyed the man critically.

"Don't try to attack me," Lord Trasch warned him. "I'm not some mindless vamp like Lord Adrastas. I know how to handle a krsnik. I've dealt with them in the past."

Oliver noted the small knife in the Lord's other hand, half-hidden in the folds of his robe. It was black and probably made of cold iron—deadly to all vamps and their kin. He settled on the floor. If he had jumped on Lord Trasch, the vampire would have sunk that knife into his vitals and ended him.

"Do you understand?" Trasch asked him.

Oliver nodded. He felt warm and sated. The vampire blood was like the high of the Concerto, only a thousand times better.

Trasch smiled. The way he picked up on things was beyond eerie. "That good feeling you're experiencing won't last. But I can help extend it."

"For a price," Oliver said. "If I work for you."

Trasch stood up, tall and Ecclesiastical. "Everything has a price, child. But I can promise you will never go hungry—never lose control. Never harm anyone you care about. If I require something of you in return, that's only fair payment. Don't you agree?"

Oliver glanced around the room at the massacre. Would Trasch betray him even knowing what he was capable of? Further, was Trasch willing to work with him even knowing that Oliver was a danger to him?

Slowly, he stood up. The black vines faded and retreated under his skin. He felt his face return to normal. Glancing aside at Jonah's nervous face, Oliver noted his flitting eyes and jumping pulse. He could conceivably have it all: Jonah, a career, and perhaps be free of his addiction for a while.

But what if Trasch tried to manipulate him?

Well, he was a krsnik. He fed off the blood of vampires. Crossing him was not in the Vampire Lord's best interests.

* * *

"My Lady," Rahul intoned from his seat in the cockpit. "It's been a little over three hours. If we don't launch now, we won't intercept the *Queen Anne's Revenge* in time."

Eliza squirmed in the co-pilot's seat and stared at the gigantic Sky Shark on the monitor. She had stayed close to Rahul, hoping for a transmission. So far, there had been nothing from the Jotnar or Edwin—mostly due to the way the ship was using its cloak to jam all signals to and from it. Blackboxing it, according to Rahul. Even with her techkinetic powers dialed to ten, she couldn't penetrate the neural network the ship used. So, she continued to stare, barely breathing, hoping for a signal.

Finally, Rahul said, "My Lady. I need orders. Soon."

"We can't leave him."

"His orders were a three-hour window and then we must continue the mission. The mission is very important."

"We can't leave yet!" she cried, and everything on the control panel blipped in response. She forced herself to calm down. She was strung out, hungry again, and her nerves felt raw and irritated like everything was exposed. Her teeth hurt and she couldn't stop fidgeting. She wanted to rant and rave and kill something. She knew she could do it, too. Thank goodness everyone aboard the Phoenix was a Mechi.

Stop it, Leeza, she told herself. You don't have the luxury of a breakdown.

Without Edwin, she was their only leader. She had to make the decision.

Shutting her eyes, she took several long breaths to get her bloodlust and her body under control. Please, please…I can't deal with this now, she told herself. She needed her rebel body to work with her, not against her.

Slowly, almost too slowly, she felt the madness recede, leaving her just…empty.

It was strange, but once she'd managed to fight past the crazed need for blood, she found herself oddly calm. Detached. She wondered if it was like this for all of the vampires, a necessary adjustment her mind and body were making to distance herself from potential prey. She was becoming cold—more vampiric by the moment. She feared what she would be in a year. Or a hundred.

If you live that long, she reminded herself.

One last breath and she opened her eyes. She knew without checking that her eyes, which had remained black for most of the journey, had returned to their normal sky-blue color.

She checked the time on the instruments: It was now almost twenty minutes past the hour.

Forgive me, Edwin.

"We go on." It ripped her heart to bloody shreds even as she said it.

"Yes, milady," Rahul said and set the coordinates.

* * *

Foxley had drained him almost to the point of unconsciousness, and getting up off the floor was proving more difficult than Edwin anticipated. He could move his arms minimally, but he didn't have the strength to even lift his head. Leaden with blood loss, levering himself up was proving impossible.

His head was turned and he was glancing into the writing nook Foxley had made for him. What would his character Doctor Blood, Vampire Detective, due in these circumstances? Probably something incredibly complicated and heroic. In the end, he made do by hitting the end table repeatedly with his elbow until the open bottle of blood substitute sitting on it toppled over.

The bottle clunked into the side of his head before rolling to the side, and much of the blood substitute splashed out and onto the floor—that was not how he would have written his hero out of this precarious situation—but the bottle did manage to fall into the crook of his elbow, which he was thankful for. With a little maneuvering, he was able to tilt the bottle toward his mouth.

"Doctor, how did you manage to escape?" Edwin said as he wrote the dialog for his next novel in his head. "You, sir, are certainly too clever to live! You must be destroyed!"

There was only a little fluid at the bottom, but he drank every drop until he was able to get himself sitting up. The drawing room spun around him and he had to clutch a leg of the divan and steady himself before he was able to drag himself up onto the seat.

He was extraordinarily weak. Running on empty, as it were. And the neural network only continued to give him white noise—which made sense. Foxley had done a bang-up job turning this floating prison into his own little black box. There was no rescue coming for him. He would need to save himself.

Edwin sat there a long moment, hanging his head, trying not to be sick and lose the little blood in his stomach. He glanced down at Foxley's unconscious form and thought about ingesting his master's blood. But that would temporarily enhance their link and give Foxley a certain amount of control over him.

He was just giving thought to whether he could surf the updrafts if he went out the French doors when a door shushed open. Then a voice: "My Lord?"

Vulf had arrived to see what had happened.

Edwin pushed himself into a standing position, his hand on the arm of the divan to steady himself. He weaved in place and eyed Vulf, who stood in the doorway of the study.

Vulf took one look at the scene and then Edwin. "What did you do?" Anger crowded his face, which confused Edwin at first. Why should Vulf care a whit about what had happened to Foxley? The Jotnar had no loyalties to the vampire race…

"Ah," Edwin said as it came to him. "He fed you his blood, didn't he?"

Vulf looked confused as if he was trying to piece together what Edwin was saying.

"He's controlling you, Vulf. Pulling your strings," Edwin said, but it did no good. Vulf was Yrsa's child. Like his mum, he was essentially big and handsome and dumb as a stump.

Predictably, he charged forward, a fist raised to cave in Edwin's face. Edwin, struggling with his balance, had no choice but to wait until the Jotunn prince was nearly upon him before unfolding his wings and letting them carry him up and into the air toward the vaulted ceiling. He didn't have the strength to fly, but he could float.

Vulf, puzzled, stopped and looked up at Edwin. He grunted in frustration and even tried jumping a few times to try and snatch at Edwin even though he was too far up.

"Get down here!" Vulf demanded with a grimace of work.

"If you insist, lad." Edwin dropped like a rock, driving Vulf to the floor.

He didn't have to do a thing; his body did it for him. Within microseconds, his hands were clutching Vulf's head and angling it back and his teeth, fully extended, were deeply embedded in Vulf's throat. The Jotnar were strong, but the vampires were stronger still—and a hungry one was simply monstrous in its strength. Edwin pinned the lad's arms and reveled in the freshet of hot, salty blood bursting past his lips and down his parched throat.

Vulf moaned but the time to act had passed. All he could do was shudder as the Lovesickness swept him away on a series of brutal climaxes. Edwin hadn't meant to do that; on the other hand, he didn't care so long as Vulf lay there like a little kitten and he could feel the Jotnar's powerful blood pouring into him.

Much of the blood tasted familiar, tasted of Foxley. It occurred to Edwin that not only was he feeding his beast but he was also relieving Vulf of Foxley's influence. Edwin swallowed one last mouthful of blood and jumped off the man. Perhaps they weren't friends, but neither did he wish to end the life of Yrsa's child. He had no current quarrel with the Jotunn.

Vulf lay on the floor, spasming, his hands clutching at the open air above his face. Leaning down, Edwin slapped Vulf across the face, probably harder than was necessary. "You all right, mate?"

Vulf swallowed hard and his eyes lightened from dark blue to pale, arctic grey. Finally, Vulf sat up, took one moment to orient himself, then glanced at Foxley's prone figure and swore violently in the Jotnar language.

* * *

They nearly missed intercepting the *QAR2*.

Rahul had to do some pretty evasive flying to get them to the rendezvous point on time. Even so, Eliza was fully prepared to find Leo hadn't waited. Instead, they discovered the *Queen Anne's Revenge* cloaked and electronically "tethered" to a range in the Nepalese mountains, about two thousand kilometers south of the base of the K2 where they would need to land, gather gear, and go the final stretch on foot. Although she and Edwin had previously discussed hiring Nepalese Sherpas to guide them into the mountains, they had ultimately chosen to forego the luxury. It would take too long to arrange, and they didn't feel confident it was safe for any human to join their mission.

Thoughts of Edwin made her already bottomed-out mood darker still.

"The *QAR2* should be visible off portside," Rahul informed her.

Eliza glanced out the window and spotted the enormous dirigible wafting into view dead ahead of them. It was an old model used in the World Wars a hundred years previous, and it did not have the sleek, ergonomic design that modern gyros did. It was bulky, fitted with scoops, air bladders, and a complex propeller system.

Rahul expertly piloted them through a designated bay and into a large receiving hangar. It was dimly lit with wooden buttresses high up in the ceiling, a much older design and different from the rounded, blindingly sterile-white style of their own gyro.

"Rahul, I need you to go back for Edwin. Can you do that?" Eliza asked as they settled into a designated slot lit for them. She knew Edwin might be upset that she'd chosen to disobey part of his orders, but she had faith that he would brain his way out of his current situation. He always did. Though he chose to hide it, Edwin was one of the smartest and most resilient men she had ever known, and once he'd neutralized his situation, he would need a ride out of there.

"Yes, my Lady. I will refuel and be off shortly."

Even the runner lights in the bay looked dimmer and more antique as Eliza disembarked the Phoenix. Waiting for her was a tall, blond man dressed in a long, dark blue captain's coat, his hair tied back in a queue. He was painfully young, but his green eyes flashed with age and wisdom. He stood at absolute attention as Eliza approached him.

"Zdravstvuyte, my dear lady." Captain Leo captured one of her hands and pressed his cool lips to it.

Once, she would have been fearful of him as she had been of any vampire she didn't know. But now she smiled, showing a hint of teeth. "Greetings, Captain."

"You look pale," Leo observed. His mouth wriggled into a concerned line. "You are well. Not too hungry?"

"I am, Captain. But Edwin said you would take care of that."

"Da, it would be my pleasure. Anything for Lord Edwin."

As he escorted her to the lifts, he asked after Edwin's whereabouts.

"I'm afraid he's indisposed." She didn't detail the reasons why. Even though Edwin said Leo was someone she could trust, she wasn't about to discuss this latest impediment with anyone. If something happened to Edwin, it would leave his Congress vulnerable and their people at risk. Best to play things close to the vest.

"However," she insisted, "he has sent me on to make arrangements for the final leg of the journey." She wondered if Captain Leo, an esteemed vampire among this crew, would balk at dealing with her in lieu of Edwin.

"I see." Regret flashed in Leo's green eyes, and she had a bad moment when she wondered if he would even be willing to take orders from her. Leo had obviously been looking forward to seeing Edwin again. Then he straightened up and took her hand to lead her from the lift, which had settled. "Ypa! What a loss on Lord Edwin's part that I should have your lovely self all to myself!"

She grinned at his honest, open smile.

"Shall we retire to my personal quarters to enjoy some refreshment? Then we will begin preparations for the journey ahead."

xxi

Full dark had fallen, allowing Edwin to step out onto the private deck attached to Foxley's quarters. It wasn't large, a half-moon pavilion with a safety rail and a small overhang for wind protection.

Edwin moved to the rail and looked down. It was like looking at a sea of thick white fog though he knew they were cumulus clouds. They were so far up, it was impossible to see beyond them, but he heard a distant hum of a huge propeller engine. It was freezing cold at this altitude, but being a vampire, all it did was induce a slight itch.

The Phoenix was nowhere to be found, and for that, he was happy. He needed Eliza to complete their mission, not worry about his sorry arse. It was the main reason he wasn't contacting her now. He didn't need rescue.

The door behind him swung open and Vulf stepped out onto the parapet. Edwin turned and looked the young man over. He was putting on a good show of strength, but Edwin detected a slight tremble in his hands. "You good, mate?"

"I am now." He glanced back at the door. "My crew is still confused by the sudden turn of events."

That was to be expected. After all, one day, their esteemed and level-headed Captain welcomed aboard a wandering vamp and then suddenly turned his ship over to him with no explanation.

None of the other Jotunn were willing to confront him about it at the time, but now that Foxley was safely ensconced in the brig, they had questions that needed immediate answers.

Edwin looked the young man over. He felt an ache. Vulf was the same age as his son. "I know what you went through—what it's like to have that tosser's blood controlling you. Do you want me to explain to them what Foxley did to you?"

Vulf swiped it away. "I will explain. If they can't understand, they can leave my ship—"

The sudden pounding of heavy feet had them both turning. One of Vulf's guards appeared in the doorway. He was panting. He gave them one frightened look and then said, "He's loose! He got loose somehow..."

Almost at the same time, someone grabbed the back of Edwin's coat and yanked him up off his feet. Edwin barely recognized Foxley as the two of them floated up on an updraft. Foxley's face was twisted with bestial with rage. He whispered in Edwin's ear. "Miss me?"

Edwin, crying out, tried to scrabble free, but Foxley shoved his bloodkinetic power into Edwin's body.

His talent was phenomenal, fueled by outrage and twelve thousand years of life. Edwin flew backward and into the French doors, crushing them to shards under his weight as he slid back inside the study and across the floor. He hit a table, pulverizing it. It took him a moment to shake off the impact. Then he was back on his feet.

Foxley stood in the doorway, his clothes awry and covered in the purple blood of the Jotunn, his eyes mad and blackened with rage.

Both Vulf and his guard leaped forward to try and apprehend him—a bad move on their part. With a roar, Foxley flicked his hand at the guard, disintegrating him to blood particles that smashed into Vulf so hard it flung him backward onto the parapet and knocked him out cold. Foxley then stepped primly into the study. "You leave me, Edwin. Every time. You leave me!"

The room positively vibrated from Foxley's rage. Across the room stood two more of Vulf's guards. Both spontaneously exploded as if they had swallowed a bomb, their bloody bits splattering the walls and every stick of furniture.

Stunned, Edwin cowered back away from his master and his awful power. He had never, in all his years, seen Foxley this angry before. At this rate, who knew what he was capable of? Left with no alternative, Edwin raised his hands and held them out in front of him. "Foxley...please...please, mate. I have a family. I have a mission..."

Foxley, covered in the gore of his victim, only licked his lips and glared at him blackly. "Do you think I care?"

This...this was not good. Edwin didn't wait. He knew there would be no mercies from his master this time. So he did the unexpected. Instead of running away from his master as he always had, he spread his wings and flew at him.

The two of them clashed together with force enough to crush the bones of a mortal. Edwin even heard a crunch of bones on impact, but they continued backward, with Foxley hitting the reinforced safety rail and bending it out of shape. Edwin grabbed him by the suit and tried to push him over—he knew the engines were down there somewhere and hopefully Foxley couldn't recover from that level of damage—but Foxley let out a shockingly feral growl and sank his burning black claws into Edwin's shoulder. Edwin yelped at the burning pain and saw wisps of smoke pour from his injuries.

With a grin of dagger-like teeth, Foxley flipped them around and smashed Edwin back against the already distorted safety rail, which gave a worrisome whine. Edwin grunted as he was helplessly rattled against the metal with a force so great he felt something in his spine crackle.

Foxley eyed Edwin hatefully. "I gave you everything. I gave up everything for you!" He raised his hand and swiped at Edwin with those iron-tipped claws of his.

Edwin tried to dodge, but he wasn't fast enough. Foxley caught him near the hairline and unzipped his flesh in a diagonal line to the corner of his mouth. The sudden, searing pain knocked the breath right out of his body and he heard himself whimper. Foxley stood back to admire his handiwork. Edwin dropped to the pavilion, a hand clamped over his right eye. The pain was shockingly intense and he smelled burning flesh. His burning flesh...

Foxley didn't wait. He lashed out again.

This time, Edwin moved faster, rolling out of the way so Foxley struck only the safety rail, leaving deep gouges in the metal. He immediately turned and, with a snarl, floated upward. Foxley didn't fly in the conventional sense. Instead, he turned his bloodkinetic powers on his own body, creating a gravitational shield that allowed him something more controlled than flight.

By then, Edwin was on his feet—unsteady but standing. He trampled all over the broken glass of the shattered French doors as he tried to stay out of reach. Gauging Foxley's exact location with one eye was proving difficult. Edwin shifted back and forth like a boxer.

Foxley, hanging in front of him as if he were suspended on wires, seethed. Edwin could all but see the darkness pouring off him. "You won't betray me again because I'm going to end you, Edwin. And then I am going to end your wife and child. I am going to wipe out your entire bloodline. And then I am going to take your Congress and turn them all into my servants."

Maybe because he was getting old in the way of men and vampires, but Edwin understood what Foxley was doing almost immediately. He was doing what he had always done when he wasn't getting his way.

"Why?" Edwin protested. He squinted with his good eye through the pain. "Why hurt me? It won't make you happy."

Foxley seemed confused by the question.

"Fark, you are such a child," Edwin cried. "It doesn't matter what you do with your physical form, Foxley, you will never grow up!"

"I was never a child!" Foxley screamed.

"Really? You don't get what you want so you throw a temper tantrum." Probably that would only make Foxley angrier, but he needed to stall for time. Maybe more guards would come. Or maybe Foxley would do something stupid. "That tells me you're a child. Nothing better than that."

Foxley's eyes burned full of wild black fire. "A child who gave you everything! I made you my Heir! I made you! I loved you!"

"Don't act noble," Edwin spat out. "You bought me like one of your devices—one of your many toys. You never loved me. You only cared about how I could make you happy."

With a roar, Foxley lunged at Edwin.

Edwin dodged but miscalculated. Foxley grabbed him by the front of his flight suit as if he weighed nothing, turned, and slammed him back into the safety rail. But this time, it could take no more abuse and snapped. Then both vampires were in freefall.

**

June, 1940, Paris

"What do the French drink in the morning?" Edwin asked Foxley while he dragged the young SS soldier across the café floor to the bar by his brown shirt.

"Café au lait," Foxley said offhandedly. He was seated on the bar, legs crossed, hand raised in the air. Across the room, the young soldier's commanding officer was pinned to the wall like an entomology experiment, Foxley controlling the older man's blood and holding him up by will alone. "Though I much prefer a Café Americana."

"White coffee?"

"Yes, that's the white coffee."

Edwin dragged the young Brownshirt through some broken glass from an overturned table, making him shriek. The whole café had been wrecked by the soldiers who'd shown up to throw tables over and threaten the patronage. The older SS officers, dressed in their summery white tunics, favored these nothing back-alley cafes. They often catered to the poofers who wanted to meet up in secret.

Edwin liked these places. They were generally quiet, they offered good music, and the drag was amusing. He and Foxley were taking their evening tea here when the jackboots arrived, and when the officers got rough with the patronage as they were wont to do, he and Foxley got rougher still. German soldiers might be savages, but they couldn't compare to annoyed vampires just minding their own business.

On reaching the bar where Foxley was perched, Edwin easily threw the young man atop the counter as if he were a bundle of dirty laundry. He oofed on landing and his eyes bounced around like billiards balls before landing on Edwin, who crouched over him.

The boy was blond and blue-eyed, surely a prize among his supposed Aryan kind. He was maybe nineteen or twenty years old—the same age Edwin had been when he was made an Heir, not that he was sympathetic. Edwin had witnessed the German squad using homeless Parisians for target practice, including a few prostitutes just going about their nightly business. He didn't care how young the boy was; he was going the way of all murdering rats.

Edwin grinned upside down at the child. "You enjoy it, don'tcha, mate? The blood. The pain. We have that in common."

The boy made gasping sounds and his eyes widened at the sight of Edwin's black eyes and dagger teeth. "Bitte nicht!" the boy said, begging for his life. He'd begun to blubber, which pleased Edwin immensely. As the Devil who worked for Foxley, he enjoyed watching his victims break down in tears on thinking it would save them. He enjoyed watching grown men weep before he ended them.

Edwin went about the task of pouring himself a coffee from the French press on the counter. But instead of adding the cream from the pitcher left available, he used his pinky to slash a deep wound in the boy's cheek.

The boy screamed and trembled even though it was hardly a killing blow. Edwin put a hand on his chest to stop him from rolling off the bar. "Relax, mate. I ain't gonna kill ya."

Slowly, the boy's trembling slowed. Edwin lowered the cup on its saucer to a spot just beneath the young soldier's head so his blood could drip into the coffee. Still smiling, Edwin raised the cup and used a spoon to mix the concoction. Edwin sipped the coffee and made a face. "As a lad, I used to trap and eat rats. They taste like shit, by the by..."

"Nein...nein...bitte tu mir nicht weh!"

"You taste like shit, too, mate," he told the boy, who had started to whimper. Edwin drew his lips back over his teeth and detected the faint odor of urine in the boy's neat brown jodhpurs. Grinning, Edwin reached up and adjusted the boy's black tie, which had come loose.

"Stop playing with your food, my Heir," Foxley insisted. He rolled his eyes before turning his attention back to the officer. He too smiled. The older officer said something in German that Edwin didn't catch, but Foxley cut him off with a "Halts Maul, mein Freund." His grin spread to both ears. Then he added, "You know, I invented the German language. It was I who put all of that saliva into it."

"I didn't know that," Edwin said. He glared down at the boy while slowly unbuttoning his shirt. The boy started whimpering again but Edwin shushed him with a finger to the lips. He was trying to decide where to begin.

"It's a greasy language. Rolls off the tongue well." Foxley moved his hand back and forth, then side to side, causing the officer to shift all over the wall at high speeds. The officer screamed like a little girl.

"Hush," Foxley commanded. "You must be punished for interrupting my romantic supper with my beloved Heir." Foxley squeezed his fist.

The officer gave a little, almost polite, squeak before his head popped like the cork on a champagne bottle. Blood hissed forth like a geyser, and the still-flailing body slid to the floor in a sitting position, the head, still blinking in confusion, sitting in the officer's lap.

"Well, that was anticlimactic," Edwin said. "And a bloody stupid waste of food."

"I disagree." Foxley admired the mess he had made like it was a painting in the Louvre, perhaps one the Nazis had stolen from him. "It amused me. Very little does these days." After the body stopped kicking and all of the blood had poured out onto the floor, he turned to Edwin. "Are you going to eat that?"

Edwin considered the boy. He had left his black tie on but had opened his shirt all the way to the top of his trousers. "Don't know. Not my vintage."

"How can you tell? You haven't let the bottle breathe yet."

"You're right, of course, my master," Edwin said. Reaching over the boy's prone body, Edwin hooked his sharp fingernails into the soft flesh near his groin, right in the area that created the "V" in the boy's lower abdomen and ripped upward quickly and efficiently.

The boy never had a chance to cry out. His body fell open in two fleshy flaps that resembled the wings of a butterfly, exposing his organs all the way to the bloody ribcage like a cadaver that had been autopsied.

Blood gushed up and onto Edwin's face. Some hit Foxley, seated inches away. Edwin groaned, his teeth aching with hunger. This too was a bloody waste of good food, aye, but it was also a great deal of fun. Edwin grinned through the blood at his master and Foxley grinned back.

Foxley reached out and stroked a finger down his Heir's cheek, cutting a white path through the mask of blood there. "I love you so," he said with a lustful grin. "With you, I forget all of the pain of my past. With you, there is only the future."

* * *

Cloud cover had obscured it, but Edwin learned there was a deck below the one they had been battling on. Well, he didn't learn about it so much as just crash into it on his back, with Foxley on top of him, pinning him. With the breath knocked out of him temporarily, he found he couldn't move.

He didn't recognize his master. Foxley, always chilly and smooth and remote, the Vampire Lord always in absolute control of everything and everyone around him, was lost to a black-eyed frenzy. Gibbering incoherently in a foreign language, Foxley grabbed him by the collar, lifted his head, and smashed it against the pavilion tiles.

"Uhh!" Edwin said as stars and birds flew across his vision.

Switching to English, Foxley started to smash Edwin's head against the tiles in a rhythm with every word spoken. "You make me remember all of the pain of my past!"

With the last, he drove Edwin's head so hard against the tiles that they shattered under him and pieces flecked upward, scratching tiny wounds in Foxley's face. He didn't even feel it. He just grabbed Edwin by the hair, yanked his head to the side, and ground his face against the broken tile until Edwin had had enough.

Edwin grunted and begged, but Foxley ignored him.

Foxley was going to kill him. No mercy this time. His master was going to end him for good.

Edwin spread his wings to both sides and clapped them together over Foxley's ears. The vacuum it created caused Foxley to howl in pain and let him go. Edwin followed through with a right hook that knocked Foxley to one side, allowing Edwin to climb unsteadily to his feet.

His vision was spinning, there was blood in his one working eye, and he was finding it difficult to stand, but he managed to grab onto a nearby patio table. He realized this balcony was larger than the one above, more of a pavilion. There were tables scattered about—large, tall tables with large, tall chairs like those one might find in a pub. The Jotnar, themselves unusually large, sat at many of them and were enjoying a meal. He realized they were battling it out in some kind of outside café. The altitude and the lateness of the hour made the atmosphere cold enough to allow the temperature-sensitive race of hybrids to enjoy a meal outside.

Beyond the door at the far end, Edwin detected the sounds of a restaurant at work, and he could see more Jotnar sitting at other tables inside a large dining space, drinking from tall glasses, making chitchat, and, most of all, looking their way in horror. The ones on the pavilion were already getting to their feet in alarm.

"I...uhh..." Edwin began. He was still feeling delirious after having had his head bashed in, and there was blood on the back of his head. But before he could regain his balance, Foxley seized his shoulders and spun him around. Edwin tried to assume a boxer's stance, but his coordination was off and he couldn't see well. Foxley easily grabbed him by the throat and lifted him off his feet.

Edwin pedaled uselessly against the air.

"If you won't be mine, then you'll be no one." Foxley grinned horribly. Releasing his hold, he used the raw power of his bloodkinetics to blow Edwin back through the collection of tables, knocking them and their occupants aside, huge bodies rebounding off the stones as Edwin cut a cannonball-like path through them.

Edwin scrambled up, but Foxley was moving too quickly for him to follow. Foxley grabbed Edwin by the throat. Choking, Edwin grabbed at Foxley's claw-like hands and fought to get him to let go of his throat, but his strength was enormous and his rage unstoppable like a locomotive. Several of the patrons barked at them, but Foxley ignored them. He just shoved Edwin backward until they reached the inside dining area. Then Foxley threw Edwin down on the floor and lunged at him with his claws and open mouth.

Edwin slid across the well-waxed floor and hit the huge grand piano in the center of the dining room. He immediately scrunched back against it and turned his head. Foxley's teeth clicked closed on the skin on his neck, just missing his most vulnerable spots. Edwin, now boiling with rage, slammed a hand into Foxley's breastbone. He'd had centuries of hand-to-hand fighting experience. But

Foxley absorbed the blow without moving. Christ, it was like fighting a concrete wall. Edwin twisted and scrapped on the floor. Meanwhile, Foxley worked to restrain his wrists and pin them to the floor. He growled through the blood foaming up past Edwin's wound, but he couldn't get more than a shallow bite in with Edwin's fighting as hard as he was.

He had to get out of here. He had to get back to Eliza and Oliver. Foxley might be a Vampire Lord, but so was he. With a roar, he kicked out, surprisingly himself by knocking Foxley off him and sending him reeling backward. He collided with a large trestle table, flattening it. Bloody impressive that was. But within seconds, Foxley was back on his feet and ready for more.

"Shite!" Edwin quickly scuttled to his feet and backed up, hitting the grand piano and easily knocking it out of his way. Tables and chairs followed, some flying across the room. But Foxley wouldn't let up. He followed Edwin as he dodged left and right and started closing in fast. Finally, Edwin reached the far wall. They clenched and clawed at each other, Edwin barely avoiding Foxley's snapping teeth and lashing claws.

They had reached a large stone fountain with a statue of one of the Jotnar gods in the middle of it, pouring out a conch shell of water. Foxley struck the edge of the fountain, kicking up sparks with those deadly nails of his.

Edwin tried to dart away, but Foxley grabbed Edwin under the chin, poison nails piercing his face, and lifted him high with no trouble at all. Roaring incomprehensibly, Foxley plunged Edwin down into the near-freezing water. Edwin choked and thrashed, but Foxley held him under, Edwin's world turning into a sputtering, bubbling nightmare. The impromptu dunk couldn't actually kill him, but if he passed out, Foxley would have free reign to do whatever he wanted to his body.

Kicking out, Edwin connected with Foxley's chin. The impact knocked his master back an impressive few feet and Foxley released his hold, black nails leaving burning grooves in his cheek.

The pain was shockingly potent. Edwin surfaced fully and shot out of the fountain like some wet, unlikely phoenix, wings spread wide as he took to the air. Foxley didn't hesitate. His let his wings rip through the back of his pricey suit and intercepted Edwin in mid-air, the two clashing together under the multiple chandeliers. For several moments, the two vampires lashed out at each other, their claws striking blows, their wings knocking down the various lighting fixtures across the length of the dining room. Thankfully, by then, most of the patrons had decided to retreat in the face of the airborne battle.

"Some Devil," Foxley said. "Pathetic." Foxley kicked Edwin in the bread basket, the impact so powerful it drove him across the length of the room and into the wall, knocking down a huge portrait of the Jotnar royal family. The frame hit a mantel below and cracked in half. Almost before Edwin could recover, Foxley was upon him, slamming him back against the wall and bouncing him off it like he was a ball.

Edwin's head hit three times before he ducked, swishing below Foxley and coming up behind him. As Foxley turned in mid-air, Edwin, now more vampire than man, instinctively lashed out and ripped Foxley's shirt down the middle, along with a hearty layer of his skin, creating a glistening diagonal red gash that ran from Foxley's shoulder to his hip. Foxley looked down at his grievous wound, his expression surprised at what Edwin had done.

Looking back up, Foxley said, "You always were a vulgar lumpen. What did I ever see in you? Wretch. Harlot."

Edwin laughed. "Aye, I was that. Perhaps I still am. But at least I was never a monster until you made me one. You, though...you were born this thing."

Producing a sound so raw it might as well be the scream of an angel, Foxley slammed full force into Edwin. They rebounded off the wall, flew across the room, and then hit that wall. They bounced on impact and proceeded to arrow toward the ceiling, ricocheting off it before hitting the floor and then repeating the whole sordid series of impacts once more. The room rumbled from the impacts and the flying buttresses in the ceiling cracked and plaster fell all around them. The few remaining diners screamed and ran for cover. By then, they were going to fast they were ripping giant holes in the dining hall walls and the buttresses were falling like timber.

Finally, Foxley got on top and drove Edwin down into the floor, cracking the fine tile and sending splintered cracks out in a huge, web-like pattern. Snarling through the blood on his mouth, he reached down and clenched those long, black-tipped fingers around his Heir's neck and squeezed, but not quite enough to break Edwin's neck. He leaned over Edwin, blood drooling from the corners of his mouth. "Do you know what I'm going to do to you, my boy?"

"K...kill me?" Edwin choked out. How original.

"No. I'm going to wrench out every drop of blood and pleasure from your wretched body on this floor."

Edwin choked and struggled, but he couldn't move. And anyway, it wouldn't have mattered much if he could. An Heir couldn't kill his master. Eliza had been the exception to that universally accepted rule, but he was pretty sure he wasn't as strong a vampire as she was.

Foxley grinned bloodily, all teeth and madness. "And after I am done with you, I am going to put you broken and bloody in a cage. Then I'm going to go find your wife and I am going to violate her in ways you never dreamed possible. And after I kill her..."

Edwin snarled but the darkness was pressing into the corners of his eyes.

"...I am going to do the same to your son right in front of you."

Edwin's eyes flew wide open. Somehow, Eliza had found the strength to turn on her master. He never understood how she had done it. But he thought he might have an idea now. His own death was something he always anticipated would happen at some point in time. But the idea of Eliza and Ollie dying—dying at the merciless hands of his master—was more than he could bear.

Screaming with indignation, Edwin spat blood in a literal sense in Foxley's eye. But he did it with his weak bloodkinetic powers—powers he had inherited from Foxley himself. The single drop of blood blasted like a gunshot through his skull, blasting a hole through it and out the back of his head. Foxley roared and reared back. Edwin then raised both hands and clamped them down over the sides of Foxley's exquisite head.

"Farking die already, you wanker!" he cried and applied pressure, ripping Foxley's head straight off and throwing it halfway across the room, where it smashed against the wall.

Edwin fell back on the floor like a dead thing, panting and moaning. For several minutes he could do nothing but lay there, trembling with adrenaline and horror. Foxley...was he gone? Before he could even contemplate it, his entire body bowed violently and he felt the physical force of Foxley's blood—his lifeforce—leaving his body in a fountain of blood that shot ten feet into the air and splattered down all around him. At the same time, every inch of his body jerked and his cells seemed to want to tear themselves apart. Had it been like this for Eliza? he wondered.

Was he dying now that his master was dead? But after a moment, the seizures slowed and his body shuddered still, leaving Edwin sweating with exhaustion on the wrecked floor of the dining room. When he was finally able to lift his hand, he found red tears on his face.

He was so surprised by what had happened that he didn't even realize Vulf and several of his guards had piled into the room and surrounded him until he heard the Jotnar speaking to him.

"You killed him. You killed Lord Foxley."

Rocking his head back and force, Edwin was finally able to center his attention on the leader of the Jotnar. He looked haggard and older than his year. "Uh...aye. I guess I did." It was all he could manage.

Vulf commanded his guard to get Edwin up and taken down to the medical ward for treatment. But before they carried him off, Vulf took a step forward and gave Edwin a nod. "And for that, we are grateful, Lord Edwin." A smile formed on the young man's lips. "Because of you, we are free at last."

| **xxii** |

"**M**y Lady? My Lady!"
Eliza snapped awake and glanced around at her unfamiliar surroundings. After a moment, she realized she was sitting in the cockpit of Hummingbird. But how she had gotten there—and why—were a mystery to her. Her last memory was of being led to Leo's quarters, but somehow, she had evaded the guards and ended up here.

Someone was shaking her, his hand on her shoulders. For a moment, she started, then turned to glance up at him. It was Tommy, and though he had no real face to speak of, he still managed to look worried.

"My Lady," he said, hand now clamped over her shoulder. "Were you going somewhere?"

"I..." She glanced around the cockpit. Her hands were on the controls and the engine was humming. She didn't know how to fly a Hummingbird. Correction: because of her techkinetic powers, she could fly the Hummingbird if she asked it how it worked. But she wasn't knowledgeable about flying itself. She wasn't a pilot.

"I don't know..." she said sadly.

Tommy, ever her husband's loyal Enforcer, turned off the engine and escorted her out of the cockpit seat. He led her out of the transport and into the loading bay of Leo's ship.

Leo was here, too, looking worried. "If my Lady needs to fly out somewhere immediately, I would happily lend her a pilot." Leo nodded toward his Second, a seasoned pilot named Hugo. A huge werewolf, Leo mentioned he was also a talented engineer. The werewolf, currently working on a transport in the next slot over, mimed tipping his hat to her.

"No...I don't think so," she said, sounding uncertain. Earlier, Leo said they were already ascending the Himalayas on their way to Alpha Station where they would need to pick up a smaller transport to take them along the last leg of the journey. She remembered that clearly, and then Leo offering to take her up to his quarters for nourishment. After that...she couldn't remember anything.

She had blacked out. Lost time.

A shadow scuttled in the corner of her eye, causing Eliza to flinch and turn to follow it. Vampire eyes were particularly astute at picking up motion, a trait most predators had, but when she tried to follow the darkness, she saw only Leo's people working on various parts of the ship or the other transports. No deep shadows.

Hello, Alisa. Have you missed me?

She gasped aloud at the voice seemingly whispered right into the cup of her ear. Summersfield.

"My Lady?" Leo asked, looking concerned.

Eliza shook herself and turned to link her arm through Leo's. Hopefully, that would get her where she wanted to go.

"How long was I gone?" she asked, dreading the answer.

"Only about ten minutes. It was not difficult to locate you. Hugo found it odd you would return to your ship and summoned me over the network." Still looking worried, Leo led her into a lift and up to his personal quarters. "Does this happen...often?"

"No." She thought for a long moment.

"Were you trying to get back to Lord Edwin?"

That was the worst part. "Not Edwin. I think I was trying to reach Oliver."

A horrible chill scraped up her back. Leo seemed to sense this and once the lift settled and the doors opened, he led her into a vast ballroom-type space offering a scattered medley of all furnishings. A male Poppet was here, waiting for Leo. He immediately went to a small wet bar to pour two tall stem glasses of blood substitute.

As the Poppet—Leo introduced him as Marcus, his special one—handed her a glass, he said, "And why must you see your son?" Seemingly thinking about what he just said, Leo amended, "Ah, you must miss him."

"I do miss him but that's not why I was trying to see him."

She was still feeling an intense need to call Oliver, to check on him, but it wasn't normal concern. She realized that now. In fact, it was taking every bit of her willpower not to run to him.

Oliver is fine. Oliver is at university. Summersfield can't reach him. Summersfield is dead!

He was. But he also wasn't.

"Captain, this may sound very odd, but would you cuff me to that chair?" She indicated the captain's chair at his long trestle table.

To her surprise, Leo didn't question her. He just requested what she needed through the network, and when one of his crew appeared at his door with the cuffs—surprising heavy, old-fashioned things—Leo thanked him and did as she requested.

Having the cuffs back on helped her to relax. Watching Captain Leo sitting so still and attentive across the table from her, she finally blurted out, "Can vampires transcend their own deaths through their Heirs?"

A thought line appeared between Captain Leo's deep green eyes. "I do not know. Perhaps. I know that even when Lord Edwin and I washed each other of our blood and parted company, I could still feel vibrations from him from afar." He tapped the side of his head. "Not like a Lord and Heir should—not as intense as that, not as intimately—but enough that if I concentrated, I could feel what he was feeling, and he could experience my stronger emotions. He has admitted he experienced this phenomenon as well."

She had drunk down her drink too fast and held her glass out for more. Marcus fetched her the whole decanter. Would she never be filled? She didn't know. "So you never were really rid of one another?"

Leo's eyes tracked the chains jingling on her cuffs. "What is this about, exactly?"

She didn't know if she should explain it. It wasn't that she distrusted Captain Leo exactly. But if she talked about it, it would become more real. More...apparent a problem.

Finally, after playing out a miniature war in her brain, Eliza swallowed hard and went ahead with her fears, explaining her unusual relationship with Summersfield now that he was dead. She said aloud all of the things that made her feel ill, and she drank down two more glasses before Leo was ready to respond.

"I have never heard of a dead Lord living through one of his Heirs," he admitted, which gave her hope. But then he crushed it by saying, "But I also have had remarkably little experience in the world of vampires. My whole life has been aboard this ship and among my crew—and we seldom entertain vampires."

Gaining a remote expression, he added, "Truthfully, I do not really understand my species."

"So it's possible. Summersfield could be trying to claw his way back to life."

"Through you?" Leo tilted his head.

"Maybe." It was so hard to say the next. "And maybe he is trying to get to Oliver? To...live through him somehow?"

"I really do not know, my Lady. But in my time, I have seen great wonders and terrible tragedies, and I do not dismiss any possibilities."

* * *

Vulf said, "I really cannot thank you enough for freeing us from Foxley's control. Because of what you have done, we are in your debt."

Edwin was sitting on a gurney in the medical bay while one of Vulf's paramedics attended to his injuries. "Did you really end Lord Foxley's life?" the doctor, an older female Jotunn asked. She towered over him by at least two feet as she went about flashing a small light into his blind eye—not that he could tell.

"Aye...well, maybe. I ended the copy of the body he was using. As for his real body, the one he abandoned, I have no bloody clue where it is or if he's still alive."

Foxley had likely secreted away his real body somewhere that no one, not even Edwin, would ever think to look. As to whether the trauma of ending the Foxley copy was enough to end his real one? He didn't know enough about the tech. It was a working theory he'd heard about some years earlier while he was going through something similar. A brilliant scientist on the leading edge of the technology warned him that any copy was tethered to the original and could impact its life, possibly even ending it.

Edwin hoped it was true. If he never saw that blood wanker Foxley again in all of his existence, he would die a happy vampire.

"Do you feel any discomfort?" the Jotunn, Dr. Helina, asked.

"No...nothing."

Dr. Helina frowned and mumbled, "Well, that is not good."

He gave her a worried look.

"You were injured by cold iron, my Lord, and that is never a good thing for one of your species. Or one of ours." She sighed. "If you were experiencing any sort of pain, it would mean the nerves were intact and could theoretically heal in time."

Edwin considered that. "So, what you're saying, Doctor, is that I'm thoroughly farked in that one eye. Blind."

Her face crumpled. "I'm afraid so. However, a prosthetic is not beyond the pale. You have had one in the past?"

Edwin reached for an especially shiny canister on the counter beside the gurney. The damage was...profound. Pinkish scars on one side of his face where Foxley scratched him, a blind eye as white as a boiled egg on the other, a long puckered scar bisecting it. He felt a pang. Maybe it was shallow of him, but he'd always enjoyed being pretty. Handsome Prince no longer.

"The ole ticker? Aye," Edwin said, setting the canister down and pushing it away. He tapped his heart to indicate where it lay—the Cronus Clock, as it was called. The device that kept him alive and would theoretically allow him to live for eternity—though now that he was such an ugly wanker, he didn't necessarily see it as an advantage.

Shite. It occurred to him that he'd been living a hard life to need so many replacement parts...

Dr. Helina ran her practiced fingers over his scars. "I could arrange a surgery. We have the best prosthetic parts here."

Edwin shook his head. "We'll have to put a pin in that. Have a train to catch...er, rather, a Darkness to meet." He glanced over at Vulf, turning his head at a more extreme angle to focus. His vision, no longer binocular, meant everything was flat-looking like a painting. No depth perception. He would need to keep that in mind whenever he needed to target something with a weapon. "You have transport for me, mate?"

Vulf nodded. "I can arrange it, my Lord. It's the least I can do to repay you for releasing us from Foxley's tyranny."

"Arrange it and we'll call things square." Turning back to Dr. Helina, he popped to his feet. She still towered over him. "Thanks, Doc. I appreciate the diagnosis."

"I only wish I could do more. I wish I had better news, Lord Edwin."

"Borked eye. Got it. Moving on to more important matters." Turning to Vulf, he gestured. "Lead the way, lad."

Right now, the most important thing was to meet up with the *QAR2* and complete the mission before the world went to rack and ruin. He would deal with his disability at a later time.

As Edwin stepped aboard a transport down in the loading bay, Vulf saluted him. "I left you a surprise!" he said just as the door to the ship slipped shut.

* * *

She thought someone was talking to her.

Eliza jerked awake, and, for several heart-pounding seconds, she had no idea where she was. Everything was dark and close, and the air tasted artificial—filtered. Lifting her arms, she spread the fingers of both hands across the roof a few inches above her face. She panicked for a moment, a deeply primitive fear of being buried alive eating through her sizzling nerves.

She almost cried out. Then she remembered that Leo had lent her an HPC when her time for death sleep came. Slowly—too slowly—she calmed down and took several long breaths. Eventually, her fingers found the touch-sensitive button that lit up the compartment. She let out her breath in a relieved sigh and settled down inside the HPC that vampires regularly used to sleep securely and without being disturbed.

She couldn't stop thinking about the night before.

Wracked with fear for her son, Eliza asked Captain Leo if he had a virtual room so she could spend some time talking to her son. He didn't. The ship wasn't outfitted that way. But he did have a two-way viewer of a design abandoned decades earlier. It gave her a grainy picture of her son to see while she talked to him, but she was still grateful for it. Until she saw how drawn and pale Oliver looked. He looked as if he'd been dragged.

"You're not sick?" she asked even though she hated the panic in her voice. "If you're sick, tell me."

Oliver, who did not lie, didn't answer, but he did say, "I'm taking care of myself, Mum."

"Do you want me—?"

"No, Mum."

"Baby, look—"

"Is Lord Edwin available?" Ollie asked suddenly, interrupting her.

"Edwin?" she said, surprised. Her son never seemed interested in talking to his father. "No, but whatever it is…"

"Where is he?" Ollie demanded. He was gently scratching at his skin, his eyes sunk into deep shadows. "I'd like to talk to him."

"Your father isn't available," she explained. "He's taking care of important High Court business." She didn't want to detail his ordeal.

A darkness passed behind Ollie's eyes. It went by so fast she almost thought she'd imagined it. Then he said, "He never is."

"Your dad loves you, Ollie!"

"You always have to say that," Oliver's voice sounded painfully young and broken.

"Ollie!"

"Bye, Mum," he said and cut her off.

Now, she shuddered as she lay there, replaying the conversation over and over. Oliver was asking for Edwin. He didn't look well. And she wanted—needed—to go to him. But she couldn't.

My Lady, are you awake?

The voice—the one that had awakened her, she now realized—was coming over the ship's neural network and streaming directly into her head.

Yes, Captain. I read you.

"Good evening, my Lady. The network informed me that you were rising from sleep."

Oh. I didn't know the network could do that.

You informed me that you wished to know when were arriving. An uncertain pause. *We are beginning approach. We will be reaching Alpha Station in fifteen minutes.*

I understand. I'll be with you shortly.

Now that it wasn't so dark, she was finding the compartment strangely comforting. It was nicely padded with soft latex that conformed to the body in it. In higher-end models, scents such as essential oils were filtered in, and even entertainment like music, video, and internet could be piped in. Leo's HPCs didn't offer those services, but they were still very nice. Eliza could understand why vamps enjoyed spending time in them.

Commanding the lock to disengage—something that could only be done by a code from the vampire inside—she slid the roof back and climbed from the compartment. Soon, she stood beside it in just her chemise and sleep bonnet. Unlike when she rose in the morning, she didn't feel the least groggy, and there was no sand in her eyes. She was as alert a she was when she first went into the coffin.

Coffin. As nice as it was, it was still, essentially, a coffin.

Turning to the adjacent walk-in closet/dressing room, she dressed quickly in her day suit: A frilly white blouse and high-low jacket, black trousers, and knee-high boots, all freshly laundered by Captain Leo's crew. She would have to thank him. With her bonnet off, her curls bounced freely around her face.

All of this, of course, was a distraction. She was worried about Edwin. She missed her son. She missed her whole ship. She stood a long moment in the dimness of the guest cabin, just trying not to break down in a panic.

It didn't take long to break you down.

Eliza lifted her head and glared into the shadows. This time, the voice speaking to her was not Leo's. And it was not coming over the neural network.

Summersfield was here, lurking in a corner of her cabin. She could make out his outline quite clearly: The arrogant tilt of his head, his burning pale eyes.

She could feel the hunger radiating off him. His need to...to....

"You can't have me. And you will never have my son."

He didn't argue. He just laughed at her before vanishing into the walls.

Eliza went down on her knees and clutched her head. It took her a long moment, but eventually, she pulled herself together and exited the cabin for the lift that would take her to the captain's bridge. But once inside the narrow lift, she felt his presence return. It hung over her like a dark cloud.

Shaking her head as if that might throw him off, she started writing to Ollie with the hopes that he would answer her quickly. She needed to hear his voice—even if it was an artificially created mind text.

Summersfield leered over her left shoulder. Yes...call him, Alisa...call him to you...

She stopped and turned her head. She couldn't quite see him except from the corner of her eye.

Call him...to us.

With a cry, she shut down the message and clutched her aching skull, shaking her head until the doors of the lift opened. Tommy stood there at attention, looking at her curiously. Eliza quickly straightened up and sucked in a deep breath. "I have to see Captain Leo immediately."

"Yes, of course, my Lady." He even offered her his arm and walked her down the narrow corridors to the bridge.

Captain Leo was standing at the monitors when she and Tommy stepped inside. There were two officers stationed near the door—Leo's henchies, Edwin once called them. But the vampire himself turned when he heard her approach and waved his soldiers away. "I would like to speak to the lady alone, please."

The two henchies didn't move for a moment, so Leo added, "I assure you, she means me no harm. We must discuss docking procedure and our plans to travel." He nodded at his concerned officers, who tilted their heads in acknowledgment and finally left her and Leo alone on the bridge.

Leo, ever the gentleman, took her hand and kissed it as he had the first time they met. "You had a pleasant sleep?"

"It was fine. Something to get used to, but I'm managing."

Leo smiled.

Eliza turned her attention on the screen. Through the steamy cloud cover, she had only just begun to recognize the outline of an unfamiliar landscape far below covered in various patches of green and white. She assumed the white was ice. "How long until we dock?"

"We have begun docking measures already. Please..." He indicated that she should move forward and examine the panel.

Eliza watched the horizon glide toward them on the screens. The land was barren and remote, with only some greenery and an occasion, lonely-looking station cutting through the rocky terrain. There seemed to be no villages or civilization of any kind.

As if to read her mind, Leo slid up behind her and whispered rather closely to her ear, "The altitude makes it uncomfortable for human settlements, though I have heard that some of the heartier Fae make Xinjiang their home."

"We're in China."

"We are."

She had never been to China before.

"Do you see that station about thirty-five kilometers on?" Leo asked, indicating some crosshairs at the top of the screen.

With her new vampire vision, she could see it with remarkable clarity, a small dark dot on the screen.

"We should be meeting our Fae Sherpa there within the hour so they may guide us over the moun—"

Leo's voice was cut off by an explosion so loud it immediately deafened Eliza. She didn't have even a moment to wonder about it as the *Queen Anne's Revenge II* was torn in half by a sword of fire and force. Much later, Eliza would learn the ship's demise was due to a dirty bomb secreted away in the engine room of the ship, set there by an agent of Trasch's and meant to obliterate Edwin and the important members of his Congress.

But at the moment, everything became black smoke and fire. As the ship crumbled, the creatures inside of it were ripped out of the massive holes punched through the hull, most torn to shreds before their battered bodies ever reached Earth.

But Eliza was one of the lucky ones. Tommy, standing nearby, folded his incredibly durable body around her as they were, together, torn from the ship. It saved her from being torn in half during the impromptu exit from the ship.

Soon, both of them were in freefall.

| xxiii |

Dagger-like peaks rose up into the distant, icy darkness.

In his mind, he was panting, his imaginary breath pluming as he marched through the unrelenting veil of white. He wasn't actually breathing, of course. His respiration was entirely controlled by the armor he wore over the remnants of his body—his tree-like nervous system, spinal cord, and brain, which was all that was left of his biological form. But he liked to imagine himself breathing. It made this nightmarish existence more tolerable.

Every fifteen minutes, he took a reading on himself. He had minimum damage—a bad joint in one arm and some fire damage to his side. But otherwise, his vitals were good, though his communication circuits were crushed. That or there simply wasn't a signal this far up in the mountains.

When he and Lady Eliza were forcibly evicted from the ship, the fall had been long, almost tedious, really. Perhaps she, as the newly undead, would survive the impact, but he couldn't be sure, and there was no way he was facing Lord Edwin without her safe, so he'd taken the time to wrap himself around her body. The two things that had saved them were the fact that they hadn't encountered any debris on the way down and some trees and a deep drift on the side of the mountain had cushioned their fall. The snow and cold also cooled Tommy's body, which had begun to overheat from friction.

Tommy had taken the impact remarkably well. Lady Eliza suffered some minor burns and a few scrapes and bruises that quickly healed themselves even as he cradled her unconscious body in his arms. Unfortunately, they had landed at midday, and so, Lady Eliza's vampire skin had quickly begun to blister in the sun.

To save her, Tommy quickly buried her under the snow, then went picking over the detritus of the ship for something he could use as a compartment. He eventually came across the HPC, now empty, that they had been transporting the krsnik. It was durable enough to have survived the fall and fire. He set Lady Eliza inside the HPC, closed and locked it, and took a reading of his location.

Their destination wasn't far. Just ten miles east that they would have covered with their Sherpa guides, had this not happened. The plan had changed. Tommy was now the guide, and he had to get himself and Lady Eliza to the rendezvous point. There he hoped to meet up with Edwin (assuming he had survived his own trails) and, together, the three of them would decide how to proceed now that the krsnik was dead or missing.

Edwin had entrusted his wife to him. Getting Lady Eliza to safety was his priority. A reason for Tommy to go on. The only reason, really.

He started trekking through the deep snow, dragging the HPC with a fragment of an electrical cord he had found, the ridiculously heavy compartment leaving a deep rut behind him. But the weight was feather-light to Tommy. He could have dragged a boulder.

Assuming the rest of this ill-fated mission went off without a hitch, he wondered what they would all do, especially since it seemed the world was coming to an end.

***

As the sun dipped low behind the mountains and cast a deep reddish hue through the warren of office hallways, Lieutenant Sherman Stroud of the US Army Supe division strode into the office of his superior, General Charlee Greer. His expression was a mix of urgency and determination.

"General, we have an update on the situation." He was trying to keep his voice steady and strong despite the weight of their forthcoming conversation.

General Greer was perched behind her desk, a phone in her ear. She held a finger up to halt him. "Yes, that's correct, Madam President. Mobilization is available on all fronts. Yes, ma'am. I shall keep you informed."

After General Greer hung up, she gave Sherman a pointed look. "Talk to me, Lieutenant."

He nodded as he briefed her on the latest series of incidents, his voice flat, even robotic despite the grim news. The whole country was in turmoil with the bizarre wave of murders. Everyone, human and Supe, was on edge and law enforcement was scrambling to clean up the various messes left behind by the suddenly bloodthirsty vampires. All the major terrorist groups were taking credit for mobilizing the vamps, but Michael knew none of them were responsible.

It made no sense that the vamps, having attained citizenship status only twenty years prior, should choose to act like this. It was more likely they were being controlled remotely, though by what entity was anyone's guess. Probably the High Courts, he thought to himself. Whenever something unexpected happened, the Courts and that decaying collection of fucking grotties were usually behind it. But it wasn't diplomatic to accuse the United State's newest minorities, and, anyway, the General seemed to actually like the vamps, so he had to approach this situation more delicately than he would have liked.

He tried to emphasize the way they were using the tech offered by CoreCivic to gauge when attacks would occur, but it was obvious from her expression that the General was feeling the pressure from the Oval Office to do better.

"Lieutenant, what are our options? All of them?" The general furrowed her brow with concern and leaned back in her seat. Her hands were shaking. A seasoned leader with years of experienced etched into her once beautiful face, she looked haggard and her eyes kept returning to the small collection of pictures on her desk, her grandchildren. These attacks were unprecedented; lives were at stake. The last time they had faced a threat this all-encompassing was the Middle Ages, before the accord that had allowed humans and Supes to co-exist. Neither of them wanted a war that the humans would not be able to fight or win.

The lieutenant held up a hand as he counted off the measures they were discussing down in the war room. "Increased surveillance, collaboration with federal agencies, and more troops deployed to key locations ..." He left it at that. It was a short list, encumbered by too much diplomacy. "But, General, it feels like we're just scratching the surface."

The general nodded and her eyes darkened. "We need to take more drastic action," she agreed. "Madam President isn't pleased with our progress and..." Her eyes went to the pictures again.

"I could summon our best soldiers. Charlee, I can dust off the werewolf army—"

The general grunted. After a moment of deep contemplation, she sat up. "Werewolves won't cut it. We need to escalate our response. I'm implementing Plan X."

The lieutenant raised an eyebrow; he knew Charlee well enough, had been involved in enough campaigns with her, to know even mentioning Plan X wasn't easy for her—it meant going all out. Once, not so very long ago, they'd briefed on what strategies they might need to implement if things ever went south with the vamps, and everyone in the war room looked sick to their stomachs by the end of it. The president herself had attended, and during that time, Charlee outlined how they would proceed in the worst case scenario.

"Will CoreCivic comply?" Sherman said. "You're asking a lot."

CoreCivic, who controlled the Mechi-people—possibly the most powerful creatures who had ever existed—were fundamentally loyal to the Vampire Lord Edwin McGillicuddy. And Sherman knew what they were capable of. They guarded The Vault, the world's largest gulag, which held some of the more dangerous criminals—Supes so deadly that only Mechi-guards could handle them. He had seen the machine people do absurdly violent things. They could tear the head off a werewolf. They could turn a vamp inside out.

"This is...pretty off-script." Sherman found he had to take a seat on the chesterfield against the wall. "Those things have some pretty precarious programming, and ever since Lord Edwin took them over..." He shook his head. "I'm not sure they can be trusted."

Lord Edwin McGillicuddy, quite possibly the most troublesome Vampire Lord who ever lived, had granted the Mechi-people full autonomy after the battle aboard the Vault some years prior. The problem was that Sherman didn't trust Lord Edwin any more than he did his walking piles of scrap metal. Grotties, all of them.

The General nodded her appreciation at Sherman's concerns. They'd been in the trenches plenty together. They knew what grotties could do. "I hear you, Sher. But..."

"Charlee, come on...!" Sherman's outburst surprised even him. "How are we even going to initiate that kind of takeover? We don't even know where the good Lord is to talk to him about recruiting his tinpots..."

Charlee pressed her lips together. "We don't need him." Her voice was quiet and heavy. "We can initiate remotely through the CoreCivic neural network."

Sherman frowned at her. "Remote control? I thought CoreCivic is run by the tinpots—the ones who take their orders directly from that clockwork disaster?"

"They do, but Lord Edwin was never really in charge. Do you think a vampire would be allowed full control of the Mechi-people? Do you think the President would allow that?"

Sherman sat up straighter. This was a revelation.

General Greer glanced one last time at her collection of grandchildren before turning her full attention on Sherman. Her eyes were narrow and dark. She'd routed the Russians from Ukraine. Sherman knew she could do well-nigh anything. "War room. Now. We have much to discuss."

**

Somewhere over the Karakoram Range, a few hours later

Rahul, ensconced in the cockpit of the Phoenix, had been unusually quiet throughout the ride to the mountains, and that was not like him at all. Among the Mechis, Rahul was one of the most boisterous. He enjoyed having free will and had an opinion on everything. During long flights, he enjoyed piping music into the cabin or talking your ear off.

"Rahul?" Edwin glanced over, turbulence making it difficult for him to suck down the sub-blood from the MRE tube without getting it on his face. Since getting back aboard his ship, he had been too anxious to sit, too worried about what was happening with Eliza, so he stood instead, hanging onto a strap in the ceiling while he leveled up on vampire MREs. They were less than sixteen kilometers from their rendezvous point, Rahul and the Phoenix having picked him up from Vulf's ship a few hours earlier on Eliza's orders.

But now something seemed to be amiss with his pilot.

He seemed to be ignoring Edwin, attention soldered to the control panel in front of him but his head turned slightly like he was listening to a transmission that Edwin couldn't hear. Finally, after too long a silence, Rahul said to someone else, "Understood, Controller. Returning now" and initiated a hard u-turn that sent Edwin sliding into a wall of the transport.

The MRE, what Eliza sometimes jokingly called a juice box, went tumbling down the aisle of the Phoenix. "Rahul!" Edwin said, a bad feeling gathering somewhere under his clockwork heart. "Mate!"

Rahul, ignoring him, reached across his dashboard and hit several buttons. Edwin thought he might be putting the Phoenix on autopilot. Edwin, suddenly concerned, slid back a step and centered his weight.

Rahul got up from the cockpit and turned to face him. He, like all his fellows, was a large Mechi-person (they did not like gendered names like Mechi-man or -woman and Edwin had dutifully granted them that preference along with their autonomy). His white plastic outer armor reflected the dim lights of the ship in dull flashes. There were scars in his armor, and Edwin recalled that Rahul, along with being an excellent pilot, was also a seasoned soldier. He was one of the Mechis who used to work The Vault, and one of the first to follow Edwin when his people became part of Edwin's Congress.

"I will need you to hold very still, sir," Rahul said, sounding eerily calm.

"Aye?" Edwin said, his voice not quite trembling.

"I do not want to damage the ship when I dispose of you."

The statement ripped up and down Edwin's nerve ending. "Oh? Aye?"

"Yes, sir." The pilot powered a step toward him, going slow because of the tightness of the vessel and the width of his shoulders.

Edwin didn't move just then. They were thousands of feet in the air, and though Edwin could fly, getting out of the transport was going to prove problematic. "And…why must you…dispose of me?"

Rahul never hesitated to explain. "You are a vampire, sir. And all vampires must be disposed of by any means necessary." He hesitated before adding, "It is orders, sir, from the Controller of home office."

"I see," Edwin said, still afraid to move. "And if I told you to override those orders and listen to my instructions instead?"

Rahul looked almost sad. "I'm sorry, sir. I have to follow home office's orders."

"We've been through a lot, you and I. Nothing I can say can dissuade you?"

"No, sir." Rahul reached for him. "If it helps, it has been an honor serving under your command."

"And it was a pleasure to have you as an officer, Rahul." Edwin saluted the soldier.

Rahul paused and saluted his senior officer back. Edwin used the distraction to reach up and, in one smooth, flawless gesture, twist the Mechi's head right off his shoulders, neck bones and all. There was a gush of golden hydraulic fluid in lieu of blood and a crunch of neck bones as the head popped off. The hands continued to work, the armored fingers sinking deep into Edwin's shoulder bones, but they didn't stay there. They flexed open after a second and the body shuddered as the shock of Rahul's sudden death tunneled through his body.

Then the body crumpled forward onto its knees like some penitent man. Edwin danced back a step, watching as his pilot crashed to the floor of the ship. He looked at the head in his hands, the lighted eyes still seemingly alive before they finally went dim. Out of respect, Edwin set the head on the floor next to the body, then straightened up.

This pained him. The Mechis weren't machines. They were people. They were his people, part of his Congress. He had no idea who had messed with his people, but when he found out, they were going to answer for this. They were going to pay the price.

"One of these days you sods will stop underestimating me," he told whatever powers were in play. He felt a deep pang of rage and held it deep inside. "But today is not that day."

Seconds later, he heard an alarm going off in the cockpit, along with a warning that they were on a collision course with the side of the nearest mountain. "Fark," said Edwin, who did not know how to pilot.

So he spread his wings and rocketed through the roof of the ship and took off into the night sky.

* * *

Tommy watched through the whiteout as the small Phoenix craft smashed into the side of the mountain half a mile due east of him. There was a brief flash of fire and a subtle sonic boom as the craft burned up and fell to the earth in glittering pieces like metal confetti. He shuddered internally at the destruction of the ship and then started in that direction. He wondered who was aboard her, and he fretted it might be Edwin.

* * *

The day would go down in history and be remembered as the "Tinpot Revolt," the day the Mechi-people were mass compelled to attack and kill any vampire in their vicinity, and in any way possible—even if it meant going through regular human citizens to do so.

Centuries later, when the event would appear in history books, it would sound almost comical, like robots that had lost all control. Children in classrooms would giggle over the name. Teachers and historians would cringe to have to teach it in class. It sounded ridiculous. Fictional.

The films that would come out of it would highlight the many acts of heroism and cowardice in the first days: The mother who selflessly saved her children from a burning car after a Mechi-person tossed it off the road to get at a vamp, the soldiers on gyros who tried to prevent a Mechi from tearing up a group of Poppets to get to his former Vampire Lord. But soon enough, the incident would begin to mock itself. The various stories, both real and fictional, would become humorous anecdotes on modern life and the humans' dependence on machines. The more observant would see it as the beginning of the end of the Supernatural races. Pundits would comment on the use of what they called "weapons of mass destruction among us."

That, in turn, would lead to the humans trying to shut down the Mechi-people to prevent them from turning on their creators as they had the vampires. But the Mechis—the "tinpots"—were already aware of this threat. After all, they had been human once, too. They understood the human mind all too well.

They would soon take action to prevent the humans from shutting them down, which would lead to a whole new conflict, a darker chapter of human existence, a story needing telling in the future...

***

Someone knocked on the lid of Cesar's HPC.

He opened first one eye and then the other. He started to breathe again. "Claire?"

She thought she was funny and sometimes did knock-knocks on his coffin. "Awake, Wifey?" she would giggle before slipping away on those inline skates she favored.

But Claire didn't answer this time. Instead...a familiar voice said, "Cesar? Lad? Open up."

Edwin?

Cesar scrambled to input the code to open the HPC. He had to do it twice with his clumsy, shaking hands. But once the lid slid back, he virtually flew out of it. "Edwin? Edwin!" He could hardly believe his eyes when he landed on the floor and saw his master standing there, looking dapper and delicious as always.

He immediately took a step toward him. "What...what are you doing here?"

Edwin smiled. "Visiting."

Cesar, ready to jump into his arms, hesitated and really looked at Edwin. Something was off. It was probably a small thing, something subtle pinging in his brain, maybe his posture or his smile. But this was not Edwin. "What the hell are you?"

"Clever little vampire baby," the creature said even as it began to change. It shimmered like a mirage, all of its cells shifting size and shape...but it was shifting into what? It took a few seconds for the creature to reorient itself, but when it did, Cesar felt like someone kicked him in the heart.

Tommy stood before him—the human Tommy, not the Mechi-Tommy—looking all...Tommy-ish: tall and foxy, with silvery hair and sky-blue eyes. He was even smiling and holding his arm wide open.

Cesar glared at the creature. The Chimera. "What do you want with me?"

Chimera tilted his Tommy head, his expression concerned. "Don't you hear it?"

By no means did Cesar trust the creature that had repeatedly threatened and tried to murder his master, but when he took a moment to listen, his sensitive hearing picked up on some ruckus going on in the hallways just beyond his virtually soundproofed personal quarters. "What is that?"

Shaking his head sadly, the non-Tommy said, "The gyro is currently under siege by a Class-S ship deployed from The Vault." After a dramatic pause, it added, "That means that Mechis are boarding this ship."

"Why would they want to board Foxley's ship?"

"They're here to eliminate all of the vampires on board. Orders from above."

Cesar took a moment to digest that. His first instinct was to ask why the Mechi-army, which belonged to Edwin, should be hunting vampires. But then his former instincts as a soldier kicked in and he decided that immediate escape was more important than the whys and wherefores.

"But I have a way out," the Chimera informed him. It nodded toward the extended balcony attached to Cesar's quarters. It lay just outside the huge floor-to-ceiling windows.

Glancing that way, Cesar recognized a small Hummingbird transport. A two-seater of the type of most often used as a taxi on and off the gyro. The Chimera apparently had piloting experience enough to land it on a dime. It was kind of impressive.

Shifting his attention back to the Chimera, Cesar said, "And...?"

"And what?"

"Why are you telling me this?" He flinched at the sound of a violent bang outside his door. "And why are the Mechis after the vamps?"

"Ah." The Chimera's thin smile flattened into a grim line. "That's an interesting story. Rather complicated. But come with me and I'll tell you all about it."

Cesar held his ground. "I'm not going with you! Are you crazy? You tried to kill Edwin...!"

"That wasn't me. That was my master. My other."

"I don't care who it was. I don't trust you...whatever you are."

The Chimera snorted and took a step forward. It reached out to Cesar, who backed up a step—but not in time. The moment the Chimera touched him, Cesar felt his cells shift. It was an unusual feeling similar to an all-over Charley horse. He didn't shift often because it was so painful that it usually dropped him to his knees.

It doubled him over now, but he was gradually getting used to the pain. When he stood up straight again, he saw from the long, narrowness of his arms and hands that he resembled Tommy. Meanwhile, the Chimera had changed into him—which was weird as hell. Like a mirror, except the shit-eating grin it wore wasn't very like him.

"What I am is the same thing as what you are," the Chimera insisted. "Do you trust yourself?"

"That doesn't make any sense."

"If I wanted to kill you, Chimera, I would have done so already."

"I'm not..." Cesar stopped himself. It was impossible to lie and say he wasn't like the Chimera when it was so obvious he was. He shifted uncomfortably and glanced back toward the transport. "Is that why you've come for me?"

"Maybe. Does it matter...?"

A heavy body slammed against Cesar's door. He could hear the screaming quite plainly now. It sounded like a wholesale slaughter out there.

The Chimera extended his Cesar hand. "I can change shape. I can be anything you desire, my darling." He shifted once more into various people, his transformations smooth and quick. Cesar knew none of the people. Perhaps they were people the Chimera had worked for—or his victims. Finally, he settled back into Edwin's form. "But I strongly suggest you come with me before the Mechis find you."

More screaming. Pounding on his door. It sounded like people being ripped apart in the hallway outside his quarters. With a shudder, he reached for the Chimera's hand and felt the bones of his fingers close around his wrist like a cuff.

* * *

At first, Edwin caught an updraft, but the chilling, sub-arctic winds off the Karakoram Range were too strong and threw him off his course, sending him into a downward corkscrew. Snow and pine needles crumbled around him. A branch snapped under his weight, and suddenly he fell through the tree limbs that had caught him and landed in a snowdrift at the foot of a copse of pines. Lucky for him, it was full dark out, or he would never have survived the fall. He would have burned up like the Phoenix.

Sitting up, he swore and shook snow off himself before climbing to his feet. The vertigo still had him, so he staggered in a circle until he was able to find his equilibrium. Snow crunched under his feet, and sheets of white hit him full in the face, but he hardly felt the cold. He was just happy to be alive.

When a Mechi-man came trudging up over a hillock of snow unexpectedly, Edwin was so wired he nearly jumped on him to rip his head off. Then he recognized the creature who was dragging a leaden HPC on a cord, and fell back in the snow with exhaustion.

Tommy's eyes glinted with relief. "Lord Edwin! You survived!"

"If anyone can, it's me," Edwin muttered, though he didn't sound especially happy about it.

| xxiv |

Captain Violet stood at the main control deck of the *Queen's Gambit*, one hand on the gyro's controls, the other pressing an old-fashioned communications headset to the side of her metallic head. Her Second, Haruki, stood nearby, waiting for a report. Though he was absolutely still, she felt his nervous energy. Ari stood at the door to the bridge, his arms crossed over his well-muscled chest.

Haruki finally stuttered, "D-did they get through yet?"

"Not yet. Patience, my friend," Violet intoned, and Haruki grunted at that.

Approximately three hours earlier, they had lost all outside communication due to a sudden burst of Hawking radiation. Lord Edwin's gyro was stationed too close to the black hole and that was becoming an issue now, especially when they discovered the event horizon's gravitational pull had increased. The collapsed star was gradually dragging debris into its maw. As a result, Captain Violet had made the decision to move the ship, no small feat as the vampires' massive, gyroscoptically-controlled ships were not designed for easy travel. It cost a lot in fuel costs and it was going to take a toll on the ship.

Now this.

They had lost all communication with Earth, including The Vault, which should have been impossible since the Mechi-people were built to be linked to each other and to home office. It felt odd to be cut off for the first time since their creation, and Haruki, who was a nervous sort, was profoundly disturbed by it. Captain Violet and her crew could still communicate with each other through the ship's neural network, but outside of it was just white noise.

She listened closely while a scratchy sound finally came over the transom she had rigged. She recognized the voice as belonging to Henry, the Controller. She had served with him on the Vault. "Vi...vi..." it said over and over again.

"Henry? Henry, please speak to me."

Haruki shifted nervously.

More static. Then, after a few moments, she heard Henry again. "Violet...Kill...them. Kill them..."

"Henry? Who are talking about? Kill whom?"

He repeated the order, but Violet was no longer his junior officer. She was the Captain and sometimes pilot of the *Queen's Gambit*. She was the highest-ranking officer aboard Lord Edwin's ship and she did not have to follow any order but her Lord's.

"Henry, what are you saying?"

The static cleared as the gyro, which was on the move, shifted away from the radiation. His voice came over the transmission much clearer now. "Kill the vampires, Violet. Kill them all."

In her head, Violet knitted her (now non-existent) brows together. "Henry, I don't understand. Why should we kill the vampires?"

Haruki spoke up. "Should we open a line to JAXA? Maybe they can tell us what's happening down on Earth..."

Violet held up her finger. "No open lines. No transmissions. I do not understand what is happening on Earth, but if this is some sort of virus, it may infiltrate the ship."

Haruki fell silent a moment and then said, "You are very wise, Violet."

Violet ignored the compliment and tried to summon Henry back on the line. She managed to get him back briefly, but all he had for her was gibberish. Word soup. He kept inexplicably telling her to kill all of the vampires on board the *Queen's Gambit*. She kept asking him why, but he wouldn't give her a direct answer. It seemed to be a directive coming from home office. And though Violet still respected and often missed her friends from the Vault, she was a Captain now. She made her own decisions.

And, ultimately, she liked Lord Edwin. He had given her and all of her people free will. Upon her synthetic shoulders he had placed a great deal of responsibility. His faith in her humbled her.

She decided to shut down communications with Earth. Looking at Haruki, she said, "No transmission on or off the ship until we discover what is happening. I want total Black Box status, my friend."

Haruki nodded. "I understand, Violet. It shall be done."

Turning to Ari, she said, "Officer, can we put together a small recon to find and collect Lord Edwin? He should have reached the K2 by now and I need his attention on this matter."

Ari nodded. "Yes, Captain Violet. It will be done."

* * *

"What happened to the ship, mate?" Edwin said while he and his Enforcer marched side by side through the deepening snow. Their goal was finally within sight, a barely visible grey smear on the horizon.

"Destroyed. The debris made me think of some kind of homemade bomb."

Edwin swallowed hard. He trusted Tommy to know what the evidence looked like. He'd once been an officer with the FBI and been involved in terrorist counter-intelligence. He undoubtedly knew what a dirty bomb looked like—likely up close and personal.

It took him a long moment to ask the next question. "And Leo? Hugo? Have you seen them?"

"No. But I also did not find their bodies in the debris."

Edwin felt a sharp pang. Someone had blown Leo's ship to shreds and destroyed his crew, his cause. Maybe because they thought Edwin was aboard her. The destroyed ship. The dead crew. All of that was his fault.

He stumbled and dropped to his knees in the snow. Tommy stopped but out of respect for his master, he did not look. Under normal circumstances, this would have put Edwin down in the snow. It might even have sent him into a fugue, the vampire equivalent of a coma. But he couldn't afford the luxury of a breakdown. He had to finish the mission they had all started.

After a moment, Edwin got back to his feet and they proceeded on.

"Yours?" Tommy asked.

"Destroyed. Rahul lost his bleedin' mind and tried to murder me. I had to put him down."

Tommy nearly stumbled at the news. "Are the Mechi-people supposed to do that? I thought they were part of our Congress and under your control."

"Not anymore." Edwin slowed and watched Tommy drag the HPC, which held the unconscious body of his wife. It was sinking ever deeper into the snow. He could tell Tommy was really working at dragging it along. And he was doing it entirely for Edwin's sake—because it was what his master wanted.

"Stop."

Tommy did as he requested.

Edwin stepped up to the compartment and put his hand on it. He could feel her in there, not dreaming but resting. Her mind was mostly silent in the way of vampires, but occasionally he got snatches of images—beautiful estate gardens and swaying yellow grasses like those on the moors. He knew how much she enjoyed the English moors. "I appreciate what you did for Eliza. More than you can ever know. But we can't go any farther with her."

Tommy waited for orders.

"Let's bury her here. We'll come back for her later."

While the two of them set about digging a hole in the snow by hand, Tommy said, "We could try to wake her up."

Edwin thought back to the fantasy world he'd fallen into during his own fugue some years earlier. "She's happy where she is. And we are all safer for it—trust me." Tommy nodded as he used his powerful mechanized hands to move snow aside at a rate even faster than Edwin. But he did not look up.

"What don't you tell me what it is you've been wanting to say?"

His Enforcer stopped digging and just peered into the hole they had created together. "Are you commanding me, my Lord?"

Edwin, kneeling in the snow on the opposite of the hole, nodded. "I am."

Tommy thought about it a long moment before saying, "While I was speaking to Dr. Charlotte, she told me about deactivation. She said it is an option you offer all of the Mechi-people who live under their own will."

Edwin didn't like where this was going. "I do."

"Do you extend that courtesy to...all?"

Edwin was surprised by the severity of the pain of this. "Do you want to put in for it?"

Glancing up, Tommy's mechanical eyes centered on the ebony sky and white-sickle moon. He exhaled a long moment, blowing a light veil of snow away from his respirator. "I miss Maggie. My wife. I still dream of her when I am resting."

He shuddered a moment before continuing. "After the incident with Foxley, when I was...dying...I even visited with her. I saw her and understood that she was waiting for me in the next world. But I could not reach her because..." His voice trailed away.

Edwin filled in. "Cesar stopped you."

"He...this..." He briefly touched his armor. "This holds me back. Without this...I could move on. I could go to her and be with her again." Tommy's voice sounded weak as he added, "Surely, you more than any other understand."

Edwin eyed the HPC. "Aye."

"Perhaps it is not the same—"

"My wife is dead too, Tommy," Edwin said, surprised by the pain in his voice. "She's dead. Summerfield killed her years ago. The only difference is she isn't lying still. Neither of us is..."

It took him a moment to wind up his courage, but he knew he had to say it. "Eliza's childhood friend Derek told me something recently. He said it was my fault she was like this. At the time, I thought he was just being a prick, but he was right."

He liked that Tommy didn't challenge him. He just listened. They understood each other on a deeply primal level.

"Eliza wouldn't have chosen this. She never wanted to be a vampire. But I dragged her into this life. I selfishly did it to her anyway. Without me...she would have been happy."

He knew she loved him, that she had done everything for him and Ollie. She was painfully—disgustingly—selfless in that regard. And look at what it had cost her? Dead in a box. But not even dead enough to rest.

He lowered the HPC into the ground himself. Eliza. Cesar. Narissa. Leo. Tommy by extension of Cesar. Foxley. If he hadn't felt utterly cursed before, he did now.

Once snugged into the deep hole they had dug, Edwin fought the increased gales to climb down and lay down on top of the compartment. He pressed his hands and face to the lid even as the storm shoveled ice and snow down into the hole.

Eliza was quiet, lost in some distant, manufactured paradise.

"My lord?" said Tommy from above. "My lord, the storm is getting worse. We have to go now."

"Aye."

They resumed their climb. The storm was fiercer now, blowing heavy swaths of snow into their faces. Even Tommy seemed to struggle against the wall of freezing sub-arctic temperatures that could end a human in less than fifteen minutes.

They were close now. Almost there.

Along the way, Edwin said, "You have my permission for deactiva—"

He never got the rest out as the whole glacier they were hiking collapsed and swallowed them up with a grumble and a white grin of icy teeth.

* * *

Cesar woke from a deep sleep full of shifting shadows and vague, shapeless memories.

On opening his eyes, he sat up but quickly realized he didn't recognize the room he was in. He was lying on a huge bed with veils and a furry comforter in a room full of tall, arching windows. Old-fashioned furnishings were scattered about, and, directly opposite, reared a tall wall of books with a rolling ladder.

The bank of windows to his left allowed a flood of yellow, early-morning sunlight in. At first, Cesar recoiled at the sight, terrified the light would burn his sensitive vampire skin, but then he realized he'd by lying in the path of the light for some time, his bare feet warmed by it.

"Must be UV protection," he told himself, moving slowly to the foot of the bed. Through the windows, he spied a vast, sandy valley with trees growing sparingly along the edge of a winding, snake-like river. The isolation and remote beauty of the place touched him.

The click of the chamber door made him turn.

An unfamiliar man stood near the wall. He was carrying a flask and two tumblers on a serving tray. Cesar looked him up and down. He was tall with brown skin, curling dark hair, and black, shiny eyes. He wore what Cesar knew from his time in the Air Force was called a jibbah with pants—modern Egyptian clothes. But he didn't think the man was Egyptian. Or, rather, he didn't think he was human.

"You," he said only.

"Yes?"

"Is it you? The...Chimera?"

It looked at him curiously, its head tilted slightly like a lizard's. "What do you think?"

Cesar rubbed the space between his eyes. His last memory was of talking to the creature in his quarters. Then it touched him and...that was it. He couldn't recall anything else.

"You took me away," Cesar said. "Are you...going to kill me?" He realized if that was its intention that he probably had very little chance of escaping from it. He wasn't nearly as strong as the ancient shapeshifter. Certainly, he couldn't fight it.

"If I was going to kill you, I would not have saved you from the ship and brought you here." It held very still, waiting for his reaction.

"All right..." Cesar said uncomfortably. "If...if you're not going to kill me...why bring me here?" He glanced around. "Whatever here is."

"The Siwa Oasis," the Chimera provided. "In the Great Western Desert. We are extremely isolated. There are no Mechi-people here—no one to harm us. And very few people. But I have a home here, among the Siwi. That is why I brought you here."

"That doesn't answer my question," Cesar said, slowly getting to his feet. He moved slowly to the window and peered out. On the distant, hazy horizon, he saw some crude structures made of sandstone. They looked ancient. A greenish salt pool lay beyond, some palm trees—not much else. The wind soughed loudly, unbroken by modern structures or the burble of people. The place looked desolate.

"There are UV shields," the Chimera explained. "You may leave if you like, but I don't suggest you walk far."

"So, I'm your prisoner."

"This is my home," the Chimera said as if he didn't understand what it was saying. "This is where I live when I am not on work duty."

"And you've brought me here—to where you live."

"You are Chimera. The last one—aside from me." After a moment, it added, "We are one. We are a we."

Like that made sense.

Cesar scowled at it. The Chimera looked reprimanded. But, after a moment, it seemed to recover. "Will you come and drink with me?"

"I don't trust you."

"That is fair. Perhaps if I become something else? Something more familiar?"

"Don't do that," Cesar snapped. "I don't like it when you become people I know."

"All right. I won't do that." The Chimera set the tray down on the bed and sat on the edge to pour itself a glass. Real blood, Cesar thought. It looked and smelled as such.

The smell of the blood did more to draw Cesar back to the bed than anything else. His need for it even overcame his fear of the Chimera.

It handed him a glass. Cesar stood, drinking it, but eyed the creature sitting there with its vague expression. It looked so…innocent.

"Do you steal the blood?"

"The Siwi people offer me their blood in exchange for my protection. They have prospered greatly in the last few centuries."

The blood was good and nourishing. He held out his glass for seconds.

The Chimera refilled his glass. "You are hungry."

"I'm always hungry."

It laughed at that, a strange noise. It sounded so human, so harmless. And yet Cesar knew it was one of the greatest assassins in history. "It is nice to converse with a we again."

"A we?"

"It is what we call each other. We are the same—you and I. We are the we. We are an us."

Cesar's head swam and he sat down, looking over the creature with less fear and more interest. "So…it's finally happened. The vampires have snapped and the humans have begun eradicating them."

"I'm afraid so. But not us. We are safe from the Darkness."

"I wonder why."

"It is perhaps something with what we are. Chimera. Or it may be our bloodline. Those of the Chrysanthos bloodline appear unaffected. Foxley. Lord Edwin. All of their Heirs. You."

"You're one of Chrysanthos's children?"

The Chimera smiled. "I told you we are a we." That harmless smile widened. Not monstrous—almost childlike in its wonder.

"Come. Sit with me, Chimera, and I will tell you everything I know about our kind."

XXV

The fall took longer than Edwin expected. He tried to spread his wings and catch an updraft, but a slab of ice hit him on the way down, causing him and Tommy to crash into the walls before hitting the floor of an ice cave. After that, thousands of pounds of snow and ice smashed into them, burying them alive. Luckily, they were both durable and strong enough to dig themselves out, with Edwin emerging first and dragging Tommy out of the icy grave he was stuck in.

Tommy staggered on his feet and Edwin said, "You all right, mate?"

It took his Enforcer a moment to respond. "I...am alive," he finally answered but it almost sounded like a question.

"You sound disappointed," Edwin pointed out. He reached out and grabbed Tommy's right arm, which had been jimmied into a weird angle in the fall. He clicked it back into place.

"Thank you." Tommy's voice echoed in the dim, icy cave. "Not disappointed, I—"

It happened in the blink of an eye. The creature, little more than a twisted shadow, fell on top of Tommy, driving his huge, armored self to the icy floor under its weight. Edwin spotted the cracks rolling out from the impact point. He didn't think; he jumped on the creature holding his Enforcer down.

It wasted no time whipping around and hissing at him. For one long, breathless moment, he came face to face with Samara, or the thing that Samara had become. Considering she hadn't had a fix in hours, the creature barely looked human. It was blackened like it had been in a fire, with rags clinging to its spider-like body.

With an animalistic roar, she smashed the flat of her palms against his chest, propelling him back into an icy wall. Edwin wheezed with the impact, then slid with cartoon precision to the floor. Samara straightened up, climbed off Tommy, and turned to face him.

Samara's limbs looked like they were on wrong somehow, twisted this way and that at unnatural angles. The only thing that clued him in that it was the krsnik was the long, toothy slit down the center of its mostly naked body—that weird alien mouth full of shark-like teeth. It warbled ominously.

For a moment, they eyed one another uncertainly. Ice crystals shimmered all around, reflecting the little moonlight pouring in through the hole in the roof. It glinted in her eyes. At the same time, the rattle of Samara's loose bones clicked like wooden wind chimes in the chilly air as she took a step toward him.

Edwin forced himself to take a step forward. It was obvious she was hungry—starved. Bestial with need and blackened with that particular toxin that the krsnik's seemed to harbor. Even so, he saw a flicker of something sentient in her stone-black eyes. Maybe he could reason with her?

"You survived the crash of Leo's ship," he said, his voice hitched higher than usual through his constricted chest. "Were you the only one?"

She ignored the second question and said, "He said track you. Stay with you."

Edwin tilted his head. "Who, love?"

"Daddy."

"Lord Trasch?"

"Daddy said stay with you. Kill you."

Edwin eyed her coolly. For the first time, he wondered if Lord Trasch hadn't set him up. Leave it to the old lizard to hand him over to Samara. "Did you blow Leo's ship up? Were you even truly asleep in that coffin?"

"You should have been on that ship. You should have died with all of them."

"Sorry to disappoint, love."

He watched her fearsome second mouth crack apart and expand. He reacted automatically. Unlipping his fangs and expanding his wings, he took to the air, letting a cold draft lift him high, then dropped low, bulleting toward her.

She moved too, and just as fast, dodging his attack. He scented the fetid breath of the creature as he twisted in mid-air to face her. She was right there, and he got a flurry of icy breath from his bony adversary as she reached for him, now moving even faster than he could.

Snatching him by the throat, Samara tossed him back against the same frozen wall, the impact so brutal he heard the primordial ice crack at his back and a spider web of cracks reached out, going in every direction. His head swam.

Before him stood the rag-covered skeleton, arms up and claws clacking together. The fearsome mouth rumbled and something like a tongue licked the makeshift lips and jagged teeth.

Edwin shook his head to clear the bells from it. He glared at the krsnik. "Is it even here? The Darkness?"

"Daddy said not to underestimate you. He said you are smarter than you look."

As he climbed uncertainly to his feet, wings alone holding him up so he didn't topple over, Edwin wondered if that was meant to be a compliment or an insult. Maybe a bit of both.

He was surprised by Samara's willingness to explain. "He exhumed the Darkness long ago." She glanced around the cavern. "From this very place in fact."

No wonder the glacier had collapsed. Trasch had probably had his people drill into it to free the creature. "So...you really are still working for him, and all of this was a ruse to get me here alone with you."

"Daddy said I was the only one who could defeat you."

Edwin stood taller and puffed out his chest. He ignored the blood dripping down into his eyes from his injuries. "You sure about that, love? I defeated Foxley. I defeated the great Lord Summersfield."

Samara snortled at that. "That was Lady Eliza, little vampire."

Edwin shrugged. "Fine. But I helped." He didn't wait but lunged forward once more.

They snapped together in a bear hug, clicked and clattered as they clawed at one another, Samara's second mouth growling away an inch from his chest. "You won't be flying out of here tonight!" Samara screamed as she raked her claws down his back, trying to tear gouges in his clothes.

But Edwin remembered what had happened to Ollie. He knew the krsnik's touch, while in this state, was poisonous to his kind. He wasn't going to let that happen. Letting an updraft take him a few inches off the ground, he kicked her backward. At the same time, he pulled Belle from her holster at his side and shot directly into the center of Samara's body three times.

The gun blasts drove her all the way to the other side of the cavern. As she smashed to the floor, he saw the bullet holes smoke and watched her go from that black shadow state to her human state. He must have really hurt her for that to have happened! He looked at the gun, even popped her open to glance at the munitions. The bullets were clear with a viscous black liquid inside of them. Liquidized iron? He recalled Vulf's final words. I left you a little surprise.

Who knew that under all those layers of frost and ice lurked the mind of a chemist?

"Thanks, mate," Edwin said and slammed the cylinder home.

Samara wobbled to her feet. That didn't surprise Edwin. Like Oliver, she was part vampire and part Poppet. Incredibly resilient, even as compared to the average vampire. A liquid iron bullet that should have ended a vamp was going to be merely an annoyance to her.

While she recovered from the blast, Edwin wasted no time following up his attack. He spread his wings and took off, darting like a shadow round and round her while trying to sink his teeth into some exposed bit of flesh. Meanwhile, Samara countered by going all black again and unleashing long, inky blasts of vines from her very flesh with every swing of her arms.

The vines, more like writhing tentacles, tried to ensnare him as he dodged this way and that, but he never went too far from her. He needed to grapple her. He needed her wounded, not at full strength, and she seemed to be recovering at an alarming rate.

As he swung around her, he blasted two more bullets at her, one going through her shoulder and another missing completely and plunking into a wall of the ice cavern, sending a shockwave of cracks up toward the ceiling. The whole cavern groaned ominously.

Snarling, Samara lashed out at him with her vines, those writhing black ropes striking the walls and floors as she tried desperately to track him. One finally managed to wrap itself around his forearm, jerking him close enough for her to reach him. They clashed amid towering ice formations that threatened to shatter at any moment. The fight wasn't just about survival; it was about pride in their peculiar way of life. He would be damned if he let her drag him down into death now.

Finally, entwined in her vines, Edwin rocketed toward the slowly crumbling ceiling with her in his arms, twisting at the last moment to propel her into it on her back. They both struck the icy roof, making it shudder and knocking down a freshet of snow and ice. Samara, screaming, dropped to the floor. Edwin took a bead from high up. Samara, sensing what he was doing, lashed out at him, her tentacle entrapping one leg. She jerked him down to the floor and his final shot went wild, hitting the ceiling and bringing down more ice on them both.

Edwin pushed himself up on his elbows on the cracked floor. He was tiring, almost out of moves, and the entire glacial cave was rumbling and crumbling apart, telling him it could take no more abuse. Lying a few feet away, Samara was trying to find purchase on the slippery floor and dancing over the ever-widening cracks.

Edwin staggered up while the cave rocked side to side. Out of bullets. He hung his head a moment. "Be the Devil," he told himself. "Be the Prince of Hell."

He felt his eyes go all black. Standing up, he bit his wrist and let his blood flow into his trusty manriki. With a ferocious cry, he unfurled it. The blood manriki snaked around the krsnik's neck and jerked her to the floor.

"I'm not dying in this farking cave!" he roared while they eyed each other venomously. He snapped back on the manriki. That shortened the distance between them, Samara's hungry second mouth cackling at him voraciously. Behind them, the plates of ice that made up the floor began to separate and slide down into a quickly widening hole. For a moment, the two of them, separated by only a few feet, danced on the edge, but then Edwin felt the floor tilt upward and send him tipping back.

Fine. If he was going down into the new crevasse and an unknown fate, he was taking Samara with him. He jerked her skeletal body close and, releasing the manriki, which melted away, hugged her against him, her vicious mouth sealed between them. "Hang on, love," he said with a velvety smile and shiny black eyes. "We're going for a ride."

Samara screamed out of both of her mouths as they began to fall backward.

Second later, something smashed into them both, separating them. Edwin caught a glint of light off shiny armor and recognized it as Tommy. Edwin adjusted his fall and spread his wings, the updrafts from the incredibly deep crevasse catching beneath them and lifting him up and up so he hovered above and was able to look down.

Tommy looked up at him, Samara wrapped in his tight, synthetic embrace. He almost seemed to be smiling as the two of them began the long fall into darkness. He heard them both smash against the sides of the abyss several times. What followed were the teeth-jarring noises of Tommy's armor being torn to shreds and Samara roaring with rage and pain. Their echoes seemed to go on for a long time, but soon enough, even his sensitive hearing could detect no further sounds.

All was silence.

* * *

Too tired to fly, Edwin scaled the icy walls of the cave until he reached the top and was able to jerk himself over and onto his stomach. He lay there a long moment—numb, but not from the cold that he barely felt. He rested his brow against the ice and breathed out, "Tommy."

A short time later, a Phoenix descended into the clearing ahead of him and Edwin watched Ari step out of the ship and hail him.

* * *

As soon as they were alone in the sumptuous suite that Lord Trasch had given Oliver, he turned and pushed Jonah down on the huge, four-poster bed and climbed atop him, kissing him hungrily. Jonah moaned in response and reached up to hook an arm around Oliver's neck, which only made Oliver want him more. There was much to be said about not being hungry, about feeling full and happy and victorious. It made him feel especially amorous tonight. He settled down beside Jonah, ran a hand affectionately over his cheek, and then reached up to snag him by the hair and yank his head up harshly.

"Who are you really?" he asked. He didn't let up.

Jonah, lying there helplessly, looked up at him with luminous eyes. "What do you mean?"

Oliver licked at the taste of Jonah on his lips with his long, snaky tongue. His blood would be sweet—the sweetest thing that Oliver had ever tasted. But that told him something about Jonah.

"I'm a krsnik. And krsniks aren't like other vampires," Oliver said. "They have to feed on vampires. They can only feed on vampires." Oliver pinned Jonah with a sharp look. "So what does that make you?"

Jonah lay there a long moment, breathing heavily. Finally, he said, "If you let go, I'll show you."

Oliver unwound his fingers from Jonah's hair. "You wouldn't hurt me, would you?"

"Depends on what your answer is."

"Christ, you're cold, Ollie."

Oliver didn't respond to that. If he was cold, it was because the world made you that way. "Show me, Jonah. I'm starting to lose patience with your 'family.'"

Eyeing him carefully, Jonah got out of bed. "Follow me."

Jonah led him through the warrens of the ship. They passed through two security checkpoints. Like most Poppets, Jonah had a barcode on his wrist that allowed him to pass both points. They were deep in the bowels of the ship now, somewhere in the archives section of the science labs. Clerks in white coats passed them or shifted purposely around sterile rooms full of racks of containers. This part of the ship was dimmer and colder, less populated. The smell of age, old documents, and musty artifacts filled the air, reminding Oliver of a museum.

They stopped at the end of a dark hallway with almost no lights. Jonah keyed in a code and a door irised open. It was completely dark inside and the air smelled stale. Oliver considered the dangers of it, but when Jonah commanded the runner lights on, he saw it was, if not empty, at least unoccupied. The lights here were dimmer than in the tubes, but Oliver could see well enough in the dark.

"Your eyes glow dimly, do you know that?" Jonah laughed, trying to lighten the mood.

Oliver grunted and followed him inside.

The room was octagonal, with a raised dais in the center. It was otherwise empty except for what lay there. It looked like a huge husk of some kind, grey and amber, and at least twelve feet long and seven feet around. Jonah went up to the husk and touched it. It pulsed a dim, yellowish glow as if responding to him. After a moment, Oliver recognized it as petrified wood.

"This is my...well, I guess you could call it my cradle. My incubator."

"I don't understand."

Jonah turned to glance at him. His eyes glowed too—the same amber as the petrified tree. "My name isn't Jonah. It's Ainslee. Jonah is the name the Reverend gave me—after his son who died when he was only a baby." He went on to tell a bizarre story that began millions of years earlier when giant creatures hunted across the plains of the earth. He spoke of the Fae, and he told Oliver about the tree he became entrapped in—or, more specifically, his shadow form became entrapped in.

"The Reverend owned several ancient Sumerian stone slabs that told of my story, which is how he knew where to look for the tree amid the K2 Mountains." Jonah—or, rather, Ainslee—patted the tree, his eyes dark with pain and time. "He exhumed it and used gene splicing to separate my shadow self from this prison. The Reverend is an accomplished biologist, in case you didn't know. But once he freed me, we discovered I was too old, too…damaged…to survive on my own. I needed some kind of corporeal form to hold my shadow. So, he created this body for me."

Jonah turned and put a hand on his chest as if he still could not believe such a thing as his body truly belonged to him. "It's been a long time since I've had a corporeal form. So long…you can't even imagine, Ollie."

"You're a shadow," Oliver said doubtfully. "Not real."

"On the contrary, I'm quite real." With a sad smile, Ainslee admitted, "They call me the Darkness. The Nothing. Some call me the god of vampires."

Oliver, standing near the door, glanced over the frail blond boy he'd been so intimate with in the recent past. It seemed ironic that he should be a god. And yet, he knew what Ainslee was saying was true. He felt it. He also knew Ainslee was likely so old that there was no way he could fight him.

The idea kept his thoughts oddly placid. "So, the reason I'm able to feed on you—"

"I'm a vampire—of a sort." Ainslee tilted his head. "The first one." Ainslee spread his arms and Oliver gained a new impression of him. He had one long, thin, dragonfly-like wing and only one arm. He glowed faintly. Darkly. "Part Fae. Part star creature. My blood has the power to create vampires. Ultimately, I created you."

Without really thinking about it, Oliver withdrew a small, very sharp knife from the inside of his coat. He had found it among Jonah's vampire-hunting effects. It was completely black. Cold iron with an ancient bone handle. Vampires and Fae were fatally allergic to cold iron. He knew it would hurt the hybrid in front of him.

"I'm not going to hurt you, Ollie. You're the first soul I've ever found that I can really talk to. In fact, I have blessed your whole bloodline so that no one in your family need fear my influence over them."

When Oliver didn't react to that, Ainslee added, "We're much the same, the two of us. Hybrids."

"I'm nothing like you."

Ainslee took a step toward him.

"I'm not trying to bring about the end of the world," Oliver said.

Ainslee made a strangled noise in his throat. "I'm not doing that to hurt them—or the humans!"

"Then why?"

"I'm trying to get the vampires to feel something! To feel what I feel! No one has felt the way I felt since...Lara. But you...Oliver, know what I feel..."

He took another step, his face twisting with pain. "If they could just feel how lonely I am...how painful it is to be apart...alone...hungry..." Dropping his hands to his sides, Ainslee looked up, eyes glowing with a maniacal fire as the darkness poured down over his face. "I'm so hungry, Ollie! I'm so alone!"

Oliver swallowed hard, the iron knife falling from his hand. He knew what that felt like.

Ainslee nodded. "You understand."

Oliver didn't answer. So Ainslee took another step and put his hand companionably on Oliver's shoulders. "I know you understand me."

"I do," Oliver told him.

With a sob, Ainslee fell against Oliver. Ainslee clung to Oliver. And that was when Oliver moved with efficient speed and snagged Ainslee by the hair and twisted his head to one side. His jaws split apart.

Ainslee cried out in surprise, but already Oliver's teeth were in his throat, Ainslee's red, hot life pulsing into his hungry mouth. Oliver swallowed his life down so rapidly that Ainslee could do nothing but jerk in response like a marionette on strings, but that only dragged the hole in his throat open wider, plashing Oliver with his blood.

The taste...the Darkness... it sent Oliver into a frenzy of need. Soon, he was swallowing down huge gulps of sweet dark blood. He even let it spray over his face and hair. He swallowed and swallowed until Ainslee was too weak to move. Then Oliver threw him to the floor and dropped atop him. He grabbed Ainslee by the hair and jerked his head to one side, making the giant wound gape even bigger and even more grievously. Ainslee, his body not quite dead yet, made a hiccupping noise. His eyes rolled in his head. "Oll..." he began, but it was much too late for Ainslee to defend himself.

Oliver, crying tears of black, snaked his tongue through the wound, sucking up every drop until the physical embodiment of the Nothing lay empty and lifeless in his arms. By the time several Court guards had arrived, perhaps alerted to the fact that Ainslee had activated this part of the archives, Oliver was gently lowering Ainslee's body to the floor.

Even the Reverend was here. The guards parted, allowing their Lord to step into the dim room where Oliver lay holding the empty vessel that was Ainslee. His eyes were wide open, but the darkness in them was gone. Oliver had swallowed it. And yet, he did not feel Dim now. He felt Bright.

The ancient vampire looked dumbstruck, as if he could not believe that Oliver had just done this thing. "Why...why did you kill my son?"

"He wasn't your son," Oliver explained. "Your son died centuries ago, Reverend."

"Still, you—"

"You said you wanted me to work for you. You gave me a choice. I've chosen to do so."

The giant vampire hovered over him uncertainly. "But...why...?"

"Jonah was a liability. He would have brought about the end of the world. Now, that's no longer a threat."

"But you loved him."

Oliver stared down at the red ruin of the dead boy in his arms. "Yes."

"Why would you kill what you love?"

It took Oliver a moment to reason it out—a moment for his logic to catch up with his reaction. Jonah lied to him. He'd kept the truth. Like Lord Edwin, who never told the truth. When Oliver, desperate, finally asked to speak to his father, he wasn't there...because Lord Edwin was never there. *I will always be here for you, mate.* Another lie. He never loved his family the way he loved his Congress. And he never loved his son the way he loved his Bride. He never would.

Liars, all of them. Lord Edwin. Jonah. Trasch.

"Jonah lied. I don't like it when people lie to me." And Oliver rolled his eyes up to meet the Reverend's.

* * *

As soon as Mkgor fell silent, the vampires lost all of their programming. Most were not aware of where they were or what they had done. But the Mechi-people sent to hunt them neither knew nor cared about such details. They continued to hunt. And when the world militaries tried to intervene, the Mechis decided they did not need to take orders from the humans who had used and manipulated them in so many unspeakable ways.

In the home office aboard the Vault, Henry, the Commander and leader of the Mechi army, sent out a new initiative to his people: The vamps were no longer their primary target. Now, the humans were.

| xxvi |

Aboard the Midnight Sun, one week later

"Are you sure you're all right, sweet pea?" Eliza asked her son. Her heart was hurting for him again.

They had met once more in virtual space, but things were different now. For one thing, the virtual café she was using was aboard the Jotnar's flagship, the *Midnight Sun*. And Oliver himself was changed.

He no longer wore his stiff suit. It had been replaced with the black combat uniform of the TCT, the Tactical Combat Team, sometimes called Tack, a subdivision the High Courts used to keep Supes in line. They flew combat missions into and around areas of high-concentration conflict, sometimes parachuting down to lend support. Eliza wasn't pleased with the direction that Oliver's life was taking. She never wanted a life in the military for him, but in light of how problematic the Mechi-people had become, Oliver had decided this should be his path. She'd wanted him to find his own way. Thus, she knew she had to respect his decision.

The entire world had changed overnight. A large swath of the vampire population had been eradicated, and every place the now-dead vamp held power now belonged to the Mechi-army. They had captured several Vampire Lords' holdings, and they weren't big on giving it back. Additionally, they seemed especially bitter about how their creators had treated them. Many people down on Earth found it ironic that the "disease" of vampirism was being wiped out by a cure that was, in many cases, even more deadly.

Oliver, like many young men and women who had swiftly joined the military following the Tinpot Revolt, decided his place was on the front lines. Eliza was beside herself at the news of his enlistment, but she managed to put on a brave face. It was, after all, Oliver's decision. And, anyway, this was the last time she was ever going to see her son.

"You know I love you and I worry about you. I can't help it," she told him, her voice even and without revealing even a hint of dread. As a vampire, she was able to modulate her emotions in horrifying ways.

"I know, Mum. But I'll be all right," Oliver assured her. "I'm stronger than I look." He even smiled. His face was thinner and his teeth looked sharper. He looked more like Edwin than ever before. There was a coldness in him, a darkness, she didn't recognize.

Someone called to him off-screen, and he glanced over, his face lighting up. "I have to go, but we'll see each other in a week. I promise, Mum! Bye!"

"Yes," Eliza said softly. "Goodbye, sweet p—" she began but Ollie had shut down the connection.

For a long time, Eliza sat in the empty virtual room, head down, not weeping—for she could no longer do that—but shaking with misery. Finally, perhaps concerned about how long she was taking, a door opened and the lights came up.

"Lovey?"

Eliza raised her head. "Yes, Edwin. I'm ready."

He helped her up. Her hands were bound in her lap with painful, iron-lined manacles, impossible for her to break, but she'd kept them under the table where Oliver couldn't see them.

On the ride down to the labs, which seemed to both take forever and go much too quickly, Edwin held her close against him and said, "You don't have to do this, you know. We can look for another way."

"There is no other way, Edwin," she murmured low into his shoulder. "I can't be allowed to go on like this. If it was just a case of dealing with my vampirism, that would be simple. I could have you teach me. But I want...I want so badly...to see Ollie. To touch Ollie. It's like a mania inside of me. And I know it isn't a mother's love, that's for sure."

She shivered in his arms. His arms...the only thing keeping her from racing down to the cargo bay and stealing a transport so she could go to Oliver. She had been telling Edwin for days, trying to make him understand. When she began to sleepwalk in earnest, he finally seemed to grasp how bad it had become.

How badly Summersfield wanted their son. And Eliza knew in her heart of hearts that if she were able to get him alone, she'd have no control over herself at all. Summersfield would crawl inside of Oliver and take him in some arcane way that neither she nor Edwin fully understood.

They arrived at the lab. Two of the Jotnar guards escorted them through the facility to the inner lab where a nervous Dr. Helina stood waiting for them both. Beside her, resting on a dais, lay a long capsule. It was somewhat like the HPCs that Eliza was now familiar was, but this one was of a newer and more advanced design. It was made entirely of space titanium, with locks on the outside and a special key code that once inputted could not be undone.

Eliza looked at it, her final resting place, and felt her heart sink inside of her.

***

Walking his Bride into that cold, antiseptic room was the hardest thing that Edwin had ever done. It was even more difficult than killing Foxley.

A part of him, a huge part, yearned to snatch her up and race from the room, take a lift down to the ship's loading bay, and load her into a Phoenix. He imagined programming it to fly on autopilot and escaping back to the *Queen's Gambit*. He could see the whole adventure unfurling before him. But one look from Eliza told him that no, that wasn't what she wanted.

He swallowed against the horror in his throat. "I don't know if I can do this, Eliza."

She smiled and reached out to touch his cheek. "You know, you almost never call me that."

He took her hand and held it against his cheek for seemingly forever before turning to Dr. Helina. "You said this device was experimental."

Dr. Helina nodded once. "A prototype that Lord Foxley helped me develop." She looked between them, the Vampire Lord and his Bride. "It freezes the subject instantly. Totally. I've tested it on rats and other lab animals..." She struggled to finish. "There is no way to wake them. They aren't quite dead but they may as well be."

Eliza nodded. "I understand."

Dr. Helina gestured to the compartment. "Foxley's mind was a dark labyrinth. Perhaps one day someone will be born who can truly understand how he thought and designed and find a way to bring you back using his technology. But, I assure you, my Lady, that person isn't me. That person has yet to be born."

Again, Eliza nodded. Bravely, she offered her hand to Edwin. He walked her up the steps of the dais and helped her into the empty compartment of the casket.

He stood at the top of the dais, looking down at his wife. She looked like Snow White in her glass coffin. An undead Snow

White about to be put to rest forever—no kiss from a prince to awaken her.

"Do you want some time alone?" Dr. Helina asked.

"No, I'm ready," Eliza said. "We talked last night."

Last night, they said all they had to each other. Last night, Eliza made Edwin promise not to tell Oliver that they were doing this. "Please...please don't tell him. Tell him anything but that I chose this. If he knows what I did, that I did it for him, he'll blame himself. He's more fragile than he seems. If he knows I did this to protect him, it will kill him, Edwin. For the love of our son, never tell him."

Eliza nodded up at him now. Pleadingly.

Edwin nodded back. "I promise."

"Once the capsule is sealed, we will take it with us into deep space," Dr. Helina told Edwin. To Eliza, she said, "We will take you to a place so remote that no one will ever find you. And then...we have devices to make us forget even what they place is. No one will ever discover you again."

"Thank you," Elisa said.

"It is not a good thing I do," Helina reminded her.

"But it is a merciful thing," Eliza insisted.

Edwin leaned down to remove Eliza's cuffs. She immediately reached up and grabbed at him as she tried to bolt from the coffin, but with a single glance, he held her down. Or, rather, her blood. Of late, something had begun happening to him. He no longer needed blood whips or swords. He could manipulate the blood in living creatures the way Foxley had.

Tears in her eyes. Real tears. "Thank you...thank you for doing this, my Lord."

"My saucy little Bride," he said and leaned down to kiss her for the last time.

Seconds later, he drew back and the lid of the capsule slid into place, freezing Eliza instantly. Forever.

He'd kept his face placid and serene all through the process. It was only after it was done that Edwin collapsed to his knees and roared for want of her and the whole ship shuddered in response.

* * *

Rising from her little nap, Eliza dressed in an elegant, Greek-inspired peplos dress. It enwrapped her body like a white lily and was pinned with a burnished antique brooch at her shoulder. She let my hair down in long, blue-black electric waves and painted her eyes carefully with catlike, Egyptian-inspired strokes. She then blinked her large azure eyes in the mirror and practiced looking shy and demure, which always made Edwin a happy little vampire. She wanted to look as sensual as possible for their special occasion. The white stripe in her black hair seemed to glow.

She took a deep breath and forced her heart to slow down as she let herself out the French doors of their little manse on the moors and onto the terrace. It was a warm day, but not unpleasantly so. The weather of Cornwall could be erratic—overly warm days followed by incredibly cold, stormy nights and vice versa. It was wild coastal country, beautiful and unpredictable—a bit like their marriage, she thought.

The bounty of the garden raised its colorful heads up to the searing brightness of the bluest of skies. Smiling at the glory of the sun on her skin, she followed the meandering flagstone garden path until she reached the part of the estate they had dubbed the Meadow. It was a large clearing full of apple and pear trees. She ran her fingers over the fury of long, untamed yellow grasses and sapphire cornflowers that looked like stalks with little blue flames atop them. They let the garden run riot, preferring to let the Cornish countryside do as it liked. The summery trees were full of bright jade leaves, but no fruit had yet to leaden the branches.

Edwin had spread a blanket on the ground under one ancient Cornish oak with zigzagging branches. He was reading an H.G. Wells novel, When the Sleeper Wakes, but when he saw her approaching, he set it aside. "Wife!"

"Husband!" she cried, hurrying to join him. He was dressed casually in dark tweed slacks and a white dress shirt open at the throat. The sight of him smiling so devilishly, even after all these years, still made her breath catch in her throat. Every time seemed like the first time with him.

"Did you enjoy your sleep, lovey?" he said, indicating she should join him.

She snuggled down under his arm, nearly purring with pleasure. "It was lovely! Too long, though. Good book?"

He grinned at the discarded book. "Too turgid. I could do better."

"I know you could!" she laughed and leaned in to kiss his cheek. "You're my favorite paperback writer, you know!"

"Aww..." he said and kissed her back. "Hungry?"

"Yes!"

He leaned forward to retrieve their tea from the picnic basket and to set out an assortment of delicate pastries. Everything looked so lovely, and the day was just perfect. Just like him.

"This is so beautiful!" Eliza remarked.

After they had decimated the treats inside the picnic basket, they lay side by side on the blanket and stared up through the twisty branches of the old oak, staring in wide wonder at the bluest of skies. Edwin talked about his current writing project, and Eliza pointed out different images in the puffy white clouds, their fingers entwined the whole while.

"I can't believe it's all real!" Eliza sighed. "That we made it—you and I!"

Epilogue

The Queen's Gambit, 439 years later

The Phoenix twisted as it entered the *Gambit's* gravitational orbit, a warning bing ringing through the interior of the ship. Nova had been warned ahead of time that the approach would be rough, but she wasn't prepared for the stomach-dropping torque as they swiveled erratically toward the gyro's open bay door.

"Christ, that thing's ugly," she'd said of the rig only seconds before the orbit started messing with their instruments. "Like a deep-space spider."

Her catgirl Amber informed her, "I counted twelve support stations. Too many for a spider."

Nova rolled her eyes.

For the past hundred years, JAXA had relentlessly added the parts of decommissioned gyros to the *Gambit*, now the last of its kind. The last gyro. Where once it was almost perfectly spherical, it had morphed into more of an oblong spider's body. Support stations stretched like long legs in eight different directions, some out, some up, and some down. Gravitational rings had been Frankensteined in at various levels, and now the deep space rig crouched like a Lovecraftian nightmare about a hundred million kilometers from Earth, or roughly halfway between it and Mars. Nova thought it resembled some ugly Christmas ornament.

That last thought made Nova giggle as their small transport slid into a docking bay.

"Laughing?" Amber intoned. Her ears twitched. "You laugh when you're nervous."

"I'm worried he won't listen. That he'll ignore me," Nova admitted as they disembarked the transport. "They say he never leaves this place, that he eats the people who bother him."

"They say a lot of things," Amber reminded her.

Even though the *Gambit* saw meticulous upkeep by the Japanese, the interior of the docking bays still managed to look dim and aged. A century in deep space had done the rig no favors.

Nova spotted a collection of spindly black Sentinels powering toward them. Some walked on two legs and some used their many arms and legs in an eerie, spider-like combo to transport themselves along. They gave her a shiver.

"Welcome aboard the *Queen's Gambit*, princess," the head guard said. "My name is Guy, and I will be your guide." He was remarkably well-spoken and even gestured like a human. "We have been expecting you and have prepared your rooms in advance."

"Thank you." She knew from the histories that Lord Edwin had fostered a strong connection with almost every Supe species on Earth: vamps, werewolves, Fae, and even Jotnar were fiercely loyal to him—the Jotnar who had invented the Sentinel race.

Many had worked as willing servants in his Congress for centuries. But as the Great Wars rolled across the world, changing its landscape in remarkable ways, many of those species became endangered or even extinct, and his Congress—and the *Gambit*—had been forced to employ the Sentinels for maintenance, security, and other positions. It wasn't that she wasn't prepared for the sight of them, but they were intimidating creations to behold.

It made her even more nervous as she extended her hand and shook Guy's hand. His grip was firm, but not at all painful. His expression, which she was surprised to find he had, was set to welcoming lines and angles.

"I'm honored to be here and grateful to his Lordship for granting me an audience," she announced formally.

"Lord Edwin is quite accommodating, Princess. Now, if you follow me, I can escort you to his Lordship's quarters."

"So soon?" Nova glanced nervously at Amber, whose ears had flattened out as she sniffed the air for possible signs of danger. Nova had hoped they might settle in first and refresh themselves before meeting with such an old and powerful Lord.

"Lord Edwin has begun working on a new History. It's best to get him before he becomes too enwrapped in it!" Guy said, sounding surprisingly chipper.

He and a few of his fellows walked the two of them through a warren of tunnels until they reached the collection of EV floaters, then it was off into traffic, which she was surprised to learn the rig had—huge commuter tunnels that could take you anywhere in the ship, including a bazaar level so huge it was the size of a modern-day city. They passed over buildings, inner cities, and several attached suburbs. Then it was back into the tunnels. They took many turns and, soon enough, the traffic thinned out until there were only a few scant patrols of Sentinels going this way or that.

It was quieter—emptier—in this part of the rig. And it looked a little older, more rundown.

Guy, sensing her tension, said, "This is the private sector, where Lord Edwin and his private enclave live. He enjoys his privacy."

"Enclave?" Nova asked.

"He and his guards and Poppets, mostly." Guy pointed out some of the older architecture. "Remnants of the old *Queen's Gambit* before she was added onto."

Many turns later—too many, Nova's mind insisted (it was obvious to her that the Sentinels were doing maneuvers to guard the location of the Lord's inner sanctum)—and then they were back in the tunnels again, though these were different from the previous ones, with dreary yellow runner lights along the walls.

After some time, they settled into a different bay area, and the small party exited the vehicle and walked toward a group of old-fashioned Mechis standing near a far wall.

Nova eyed them carefully.

"Lord Edwin's Court Guard," Guy explained. "But they are not loyal to the Mechi-army. Only to him." Guy inclined his head to the lead Mechi. "Violet."

Nova knew there were some Mechi loyal to the humans and the Supes, some who had escaped the historical Tinpot Revolt, and, so, as a result, they had no programmed hostility toward humans or supernatural creatures. But she was still surprised to see them here.

"I promise they're safe," Guy assured her. "Lord Edwin has had them with him for...well, more centuries than most of us have been alive."

"Greetings, Princess Nova," Violet said. "I will take you on from here."

"All right," Nova said, throwing a quick glance at her pet. Amber's ears were still flat. "Lead the way."

"Thank you for your confidence in me." Violet walked them through a number of security checkpoints until they reached what Violet called "the Inner Sanctum," the place where the good Lord lived and made all of his decisions.

This part of the ship looked older, archaic, with dim lighting and shifting shadows. "N-Nova, can I stay here?" Amber inquired. Her paw-hands were pressed together prayerfully and her yellow eyes were darting everywhere. "I don't want to go in there."

Nova got down on one knee for her pet. She made her voice light and airy for Amber's sake. "Of course. You stay and be good and I'll be right back!"

"Thank you, Nova!"

As she and Violet moved down the darkened warrens of the older part of the ship, Violet warned, "He's rather...tired looking. And his mind wanders something. You'll need to keep him on track. Also, try to be brief."

"I will," Nova assured her, more nervous than ever now. She wondered if it was true, if Lord Edwin, sometimes called the Scribe in the Stars, ate the people who displeased him. She thought it sounded silly, but looking at the dim, cobwebby wreck of this place, she wasn't so sure anymore.

They reached a pair of double doors and, using a sensor, Violet let her into Lord Edwin's private quarters. It was dark inside, and the architecture was built on several levels that drifted gently in the sea of near-complete blackness. No stairs or ladders. A place built to perfection for a being with night vision and wings.

The walls themselves emanated a jaundiced light that picked out only occasional details, visible when the level drifted past. A library full of dusty books. A lounger with uncomfortable-looking chairs and a divan. A grand piano on a music room level that looked never used. The main hall that they traversed between the levels was huge and arching like a cathedral with dimly lit amber windows at the very top. A long trestle table ran down the center of it—where Lord Edwin did his summit meetings with various groups and races, something that had not happened in a long time. Not in Nova's lifetime, at least.

Violet led her to a room at the very end of the hall. Along the way, Nova stopped and studied a huge portrait on the wall. It was twenty feet tall at least and featured a much different Lord Edwin. He looked young and vibrant in the picture, red-haired and smiling. He stood behind a divan upon which sat a beautiful, brown-skinned woman with endless coils of black hair and azure eyes that seemed to hold a light all their own. On the woman's lap sat a solemn boy with eyes like she had. Behind them, the artist had painted open French doors leading to a stone veranda and a sunny meadow beyond. The picture was full of light and color and completely at odds with the decaying husk of this place.

"The Scribe in his younger years," Violet explained. "And his wife, Lady Eliza. They called her the Red Queen."

Nova sucked in a quick breath. Red Queen, Black King. She knew something of Lady Eliza from reading the Histories. Some great tragedy occurred to take her from Lord Edwin centuries earlier, but no one knew the details. The one story the Scribe in the Stars would not write.

In the picture, Lord Edwin looked so alive, so happy to be with his little family. She didn't even recognize him.

Nova shivered in the icy darkness and took a deep breath to try and steady her jackhammering heart. She was a low-level empath, a gift from the Striga side of her family, and the vibes she was getting from this place were not good. She tasted bitterness and heard the creaking echoes of great, wrenching loss.

"Come along, Princess." Violet indicated that she should follow and she moved on to the room at the end.

Nova was surprised to discover his inner sanctum lit by candles. Like the rest of his quarters—indeed, the whole rig—the room had a feeling of age and decay about it, a dusty sweetness that made her want to sneeze, though she never did.

Edwin sat near a lit hearth in a large, Victorian throne chair. She had heard countless stories about him growing up, but nothing prepared her for seeing him in the flesh for the first time. They said he was handsome and princely once, that he cut a dashing figure as the commanding Lord of his Congress in a time so long ago that Nova couldn't conceive of it.

Some of that remained, but not much. He was very tall but positively emaciated, with a carven, skull-like face and hands like talons, his yellowish nails clicking against the armrests of the general." Her voice squeaked like she was a frightened little girl. "Someone to lead the new army we have been designing."

Lord Edwin muttered to himself is a disconcerting way.

"It has to be someone who has experience with the Tinpots, and so few have these days. We have high hopes that you…"

Her voice trailed away as he glanced up sharply. Refocusing his attention on her, he closed the distance between them faster than she expected. He looked ancient and threatening like some monstrous thing she once dreamed about lurking under her bed. Nightmarish, really. How had they said he'd been beautiful once? He raised his hand, palm out, and Nova felt the floor fall away as he lifted her up, manipulating her blood with his strange talent.

She hung there in midair, trying not to panic.

"Go on." Lord Edwin grinned at her, his teeth ruthlessly sharp in his mouth.

She swallowed hard. "We had hope…you might be the one to lead us to victory."

Lord Edwin considered her request. She saw the shadows flit across his face and behind his eyes. "Aye. Perhaps. But only for a price."

"A…price?"

"You," he said and that black-velvet smile deepened across his monstrous face. "You, Princess. After all, one must pay the Devil his due."

About the Author

K.H. Koehler is the bestselling author of various novels and novellas in the genres of horror, SF, dark fantasy, steampunk, and young and new adult. She is the owner of KH Koehler Books and KH Koehler Design, which specializes in graphic design and professional copyediting. Her books are widely available at all major online distributors and her covers have appeared on numerous books in many different genres. Her short work has appeared in various anthologies, and her novel series include *The Kaiju Hunter*, *A Clockwork Vampire*, *Planet of Dinosaurs*, *The Nick Englebrecht Mysteries*, and *The Archaeologists*. She is the author of multiple Amazon bestsellers and was one of the founders and chief editors of KHP Publishers, which published genre fiction from 2001 to 2015. She has over fifteen years of experience in the publishing industry as a writer, ghostwriter, copyeditor, commercial book cover designer, formatter, and marketer. Visit her website at https://khkoehler.net.

www.ingramcontent.com/pod-product-compliance
Lightning Source LLC
LaVergne TN
LVHW031609060526
838201LV00065B/4784